THE
SECOND
SON
OF HEAVEN

Books by C. Y. Lee

Flower Drum Song
Lover's Point
The Sawbwa and His Secretary
Madame Goldenflower
Cripple Mah and the New Order
The Virgin Market
The Land of the Golden Mountain
The Days of the Tong Wars
China Saga
The Second Son of Heaven

THE
SECOND
SON
OF HEAVEN

A Novel of
Nineteenth-Century
China

C. Y. LEE

William Morrow and Company, Inc.
New York

Recognizing the importance of preserving what has been written, it is the policy of William Morrow and Company, Inc., and its imprints and affiliates to have the books it publishes printed on acid-free paper, and we exert our best efforts to that end.

Library of Congress Cataloging-in-Publication Data

Lee, C. Y., 1917–
    The second son of heaven : a novel of nineteenth-century China. / C. Y. Lee
      p.   cm.
    ISBN 0-688-05140-5
    1. China—History—Taiping Rebellion, 1850–1864—Fiction.
    2. Hung, Hsiu-ch' üan, 1814–1864—Fiction.   I. Title.
    PS3523.E3158S4   1990
    813'.54—dc20
                                                                89-48315
                                                                CIP

Printed in the United States of America

First Edition

1 2 3 4 5 6 7 8 9 10

BOOK DESIGN BY WILLIAM McCARTHY

To the memory of Hung Shiu-ch'uan (Hung Hsiu-ch'uan), whose Taiping rebellion laid the foundation for the Chinese revolution and all the later uprisings against tyranny; and of Charles George Gordon, whose troubled conscience raised a small but first voice against the foreign invasions of China.

PART ONE

GOD'S
SECOND
SON

1

When Hung Shiu-ch'uan was letting out his first cry in a midwife's hands on a summer night in 1812, a comet flashed across the evening sky. Those who saw it claimed it was a golden dragon leaping across the heavens from south to north. Happy Valley immediately became the subject of speculation. Many awed villagers believed that an emperor had been born. Some even secretly kowtowed to heaven and earth, praying that the little one born into the Hung family would indeed one day leap from the famine-devastated south to the rich north and land on the dragon throne of the Forbidden City in Peking. He would single-handedly return the empire to the Hans, the majority race that had been enslaved by the Manchu barbarians for more than three hundred years. Overthrowing the Manchu Dynasty was every Han's wish.

Hung Tai, the excited father, however, tried to hush such gossip in the streets, for anyone harboring such a dangerous thought, if dis-covered, would meet instant death and his severed head would be hung over the city gate to feed the vultures. "Kill a monkey to warn the chickens," the Manchu government often declared publicly, as many peasant uprisings had been reported in the southern provinces.

The Hungs were poor. In Flower County a plot of land was measured by a stone's throw. Hung Tai owned a plot that was less than a stone's throw. Most of the rich absentee landlords lived in the county seat ten miles to the north.

Happy Valley, tucked away in the foothills of Flower County in Kwangtung Province, was dull and not very happy. The three-hundred-odd villagers had only three surnames: Woo, Feng, and Hung, all of Hakka descent, a branch of the majority Han race. There were a few other families with different surnames in Happy Valley, but they were poor tenant farmers and outcasts. The three major family clans had been intermarrying since the Hakkas were driven to the south by the Manchus. As a result, every Hakka was somebody's uncle or cousin. None of them had much money. The poor bartered with their better-off relatives, exchanging labor for merchandise and food. New Year or birthday gifts were usually half a dozen eggs or a few heads of cabbage. The biggest gift, which would set people's tongues wagging, would be a Japanese clock.

Once or twice a year there was some big news; the biggest in recent years was that one woman had allowed a jealous woman's husband to pinch her bottom, and the jealous one had clubbed her with a bundle of wet laundry. The Hakka women were usually shy and docile, but when provoked they could outshout and outscream any other Han. That was why the bottom-pinching incident had been the biggest news in Happy Valley until Hung Shiu-ch'uan was born.

Flower County was beautiful, dotted with little villages nestled in bamboo groves. The hills were lush with pines and bougainvillea, the meadows covered with wild poppies, snapdragons, and blue grass. While water buffalo and goats grazed, birds landed on their backs and sang; rabbits and chipmunks raced around seeking food and watching the other animals swat flies with their busy tails. At sunset, young women's trilling voices sang Hakka love songs that echoed in the hills and were answered by young men who were in the market for wives.

Hung Tai was a proud man, sturdy and hardworking. He had selected a wife who could carry a heavy load on her head while carrying a baby on her back. She could dig and rake in the mud longer than any man and ate not as much. But she bore him only two sons then died. Like all other fathers, he wanted "Five sons to glorify the family." To achieve that, he took a second wife, who became pregnant at a rather late age. Hung Tai was very happy when the baby was born—a big and strong boy with a powerful voice, a "dragon seed" who might one day be the Emperor of China.

Although over fifty and poor, Hung Tai was treated as a respected elder and the unofficial village head. He enjoyed his duties, greeting officials and tax collectors and acting as an arbiter of family squabbles. More serious matters were settled by the family association in the county seat, without his meddling. He was proud of Happy Valley's criminal record. During the past twenty years only one villager had been subjected to fifty strokes of buttock-beating for stealing chickens.

The family lived in a small three-room house with a thatched roof. In the back was a bamboo grove on which the family depended for extra income, selling bamboo as material for tables and chairs, and bamboo shoots as a food delicacy. A bubbling brook supplied fresh, cool mountain water that ran into a small lake nearby. The lake was shallow but rich with carp and catfish. In good years, if the government did not increase taxes, the Hungs could live comfortably on the two crops of rice their land yielded annually. But good years were rare. Famine was a constant threat. Luckily, according to a local fortune-teller, the lake provided good *feng-shui*, the "wind and water" that warded off evil spirits. And nobody in the Hung family smoked opium, which had become a curse in Kwangtung Province since the foreigners had started pushing it in their China trade.

Hung Shiu-ch'uan, the "dragon seed," became a famous child as he grew up in Happy Valley. The Hung clan regarded him as their communal son, hoping to claim "royal blood" when the boy mounted the dragon throne. They lived harmoniously with neighbors and relatives, and helped each other during hard times. When Hung Tai had a bad year, he could always depend on distant cousins and nephews for a helping hand, or a loan of a few strings of brass coins. In worst times, neighbors would leave some eggs or a head of cabbage at his door to keep the family from eating grass roots like animals. Eating tree bark and grass roots was nothing new in Kwangtung Province during the frequent droughts.

In silence, Happy Valley watched their "communal son" grow, studying him and examining his features, watching every sign that might indicate his ascending to the dragon throne. In 1821, at seven, Hung Shiu-ch'uan began to wonder why so many elders in the village behaved so strangely toward him. Some dared not look him straight in the eye, others sank to their knees in his presence, pretending to scratch an itch on a foot or to pick up a lost coin.

He had the largest room in the family hut while the other members of his family shared two cramped smaller rooms. His father always told him bedtime stories going back to the Ming Dynasty days. The older Hung hinted that the Hungs had noble ancestors who had held offices at the Ming court. A few had even been blood relatives of the Ming emperors. At the end of a story, his father never failed to say, "My son, one day a little boy from a humble family will glorify the Hans with world-shaking deeds. Remember that!"

While listening to such stories, Shiu-ch'uan had a hard time fighting off sleep until one day one of his two older brothers told him that their father was talking about him, predicting that he would be the one to drive the Manchu barbarians out past the Great Wall. They told him that if he wanted to become an emperor it was about time for him to stop wetting his pants.

After his brothers had enlightened him, Hung Shiu-ch'uan became obsessed with the thought that one day he would recapture the throne in Peking. From Cantonese operas, he studied a Ming emperor's walk. As he grew tall and handsome, he began to enjoy more privileges at home. At the dinner table, his mother would pick the choicest morsels of pork fat and heap them on his rice bowl while the rest of the family had only skin parts to eat. His father ordered his two older sons to shoulder the heaviest chores on their meager farm—carrying manure to the field and bringing water from the lake. As a result, Hung had little to do except take the dozen skinny goats to the hills every morning. Sitting under a pine, he would watch the goats grazing and daydream of an emperor's life in the Forbidden City. Occasionally he would get up from a rock and waddle to the goats in an imperial manner, as though holding an audience. Gesturing majestically, he would issue edicts, blowing imaginary whiskers in anger and ordering the beheading of traitors. He had perfected the mannerisms of the Ming emperors as depicted in the Cantonese operas. Oftentimes the scenery was beautiful, the birds chirped happily, the cool, fresh air soothed his lungs and occasionally a rabbit leapt out to watch him with pricked ears, like a minister paying obeisance. The only thing that marred such serene royal scenes was the billy goat trying to climb onto a female.

Growing up, Hung saw his two brothers' big muscles develop through hard work. He decided to help out by chopping wood and carrying water. Since his classics studies were progressing nicely, he could now compose poetry with ease and write essays in the eight-leg style with flair. He made all his essays stand on eight legs, or strict rules, including an opening, a statement, several examples and a certain number of comparisons, followed by a grand conclusion. He had studied many eight-legged essays and had learned that the frame was more important than the content, which seemed to him just a lot of loud groaning without real pain.

During festivals, he wrote most of the lucky sayings on red paper for the villagers, who posted them on doors to ward off evil spirits. At sixteen he was full grown, tall, and broad-shouldered, with fully developed muscles. But since he was also a scholar, he adopted a scholarly stoop, a sign of nobility.

It was not until after his twenty-second birthday that he began to feel a mysterious yearning that often made him restless. One day, after he had returned from the village school where he taught the classics for an annual stipend of a pig and a goat, he had a sudden attack of such unbearable restlessness. While at his desk, looking at himself in a mirror, he dreamed of the day he could cut his hated pigtail, the symbol of slavery and sign of submission imposed by the Manchu conquerors. He dreamed about the young women in the village. He felt a strong attraction to them, especially to a fifteen-year-old girl named Su San-mei. He fantasized about all the women's nude bodies, long and short, fat and thin, and wondered if a man could enjoy them as much as his family billy goat enjoyed its harem.

He imagined that he cut off his pigtail, led his army on a tall horse, cut off heads right and left, and galloped straight into the Imperial Palace in Peking. As he was fantasizing, he heard his bedroom door squeak and his father's cough. He rose quickly and bowed.

Hung Tai took the tallest chair in the room, which was reserved for the elders. Only the other day he had been visiting a teahouse and a fortune-teller had told his audience, "There is an emperor with short ears on the throne. Short ears indicate short years; so an emperor with short legs will sit on it and wet his pants."

Everybody knew what the story meant: The emperor would soon die and a child would mount the throne. A bad prediction. The next morning the fortune-teller's head was seen hanging over the city gate. Since Hung Tai had seen so many bloody heads dangling over the city gates in Kwangtung, he had long since given up the dream of overthrowing the Manchu emperor. Along with the pragmatic elders in the village, he wanted his son to bring glory to the village by becoming a high government official. The only entry to officialdom was through the Imperial examinations. The only subject to be judged in such examinations was the classics and the ability to write perfect eight-legged essays.

"Shiu-ch'uan," he said to his son, deliberately emphasising every word, "you can recite the classics while shaking your head in the correct rhythm. It has been decided by the entire village that you should take the Imperial examination at the provincial level, since you already passed the county level at fifteen. We predict that you will eventually pass Han Ling, the highest degree in Peking, and return home as the Governor of Kwangtung. Two families in the village have each agreed to send a son to be your study companions and take the examinations with you. We elders have all agreed that it is much better to become a high government official with a red-buttoned cap than a daydreamer whose head dangles over a city gate." He finished the speech with a shudder.

Hung looked stunned, his lips quivering. He was too upset to say anything. His father had raised him as a patriotic Han; now he wanted him to become a traitor.

The older Hung sensed his son's feelings. He took a deep breath and tried to rationalize his change of heart. "Son, I remember an old saying, 'If you cannot fight an enemy, join him and change him.' Do you know who said that? Lao-tzu, the wisest of all our sages."

As a filial son, Hung decided not to argue. He had other matters to worry about. He brought up a subject that he knew would please his parents. "Father," he said calmly, "I have met a girl that I like. I want to marry her."

Hung Tai's face lit up immediately. "You have?" he asked, controlling his excitement. "Who is she?"

"She is Su San-mei, the daughter of Old Su, who leases two acres of rice field from Old Master Woo in Flower County."

"Ah, a tenant farmer," Hung Tai said, somewhat disappointed. "How did you meet her?"

"We fell in love by singing love songs to each other."

"That is not the correct way to meet a young woman. How old is she?"

"Fifteen."

"Hm," Hung Tai said with a nod. "Young enough to bear many

children, if she is plump. But the Su family is so poor that I have never seen them wear clothes without patches."

"Su San-mei is always neat and clean," Hung said, trying not to sound too anxious. "She is hardworking, gathering firewood all day without complaining. She has the best voice, singing mountain songs in her trilling tones that echo in the hills . . ."

"Shiu-ch'uan," Hang Tai interrupted, "to meet a woman through singing mountain songs is only for the peasants. We are from a family with a high door, related to the Ming Emperors. There is no great hurry in this. Think about the Imperial examination. We elders have already started to raise funds for you to travel to Canton." He quickly withdrew from the room as he saw his son opening his mouth to argue.

After his father had left, Hung Shiu-ch'uan stared blankly for a moment, feeling depressed for the first time in his life. He should have told his father more of Su San-mei's good points, such as her white skin without blemishes, her delicate hands and feet, which were not big and hamlike, like most of the other Hakka women, a sure sign of inherited nobility. She had many other features he liked. Although she worked in the hills every day, she never had scratches or scars, and she was full of energy and bounce, walking with quick little steps as if she were always running. She had an upright gait, with her well-developed breasts moving seductively in her tight blouse. He often imagined that he cupped them in both his hands and squeezed them gently, feeling the warmth of her smooth skin.

She was a few years younger than his sister, Little Treasure, but a lot more lively and interesting. Little Treasure sang mountain songs, too, but had never attracted any suitors. He smiled as he remembered when his mother was carrying her. His father had measured her every day with a tape, expecting a boy. When the measurements grew to enormous size, the excited Hung Tai was sure it was twins—two more boys to make the blessed number of five. "Five sons to glorify a family" was his most cherished wish. When the baby was born it was only a big fat girl. His father threw up his hands with a moan, but quickly recovered, laughed, and named the baby Little Treasure.

"It's Heaven's will," he said philosophically. "All my food offerings and incense burning at Kwan Yin's altar are wasted. I hope it all helped another woman."

When his relatives realized that his wife had reached an age when "the silkworm can no longer spin silk," they suggested that he take a young concubine. But Hung Tai rejected the suggestion, saying that at his age conjugal duties had become more of a chore than a pleasure.

Hung Shiu-ch'uan liked his sister, big-boned and quiet, not very good-looking but dependable and hardworking, brighter than his two half brothers, Run-ta and Run-mo. He was sure that Su San-mei would get along with her very nicely.

The sun was setting. He hurried to the brook where he met Su San-mei each day and they washed their feet together. She was already there, sitting on a rock, singing and splashing water with her feet. He sneaked behind her, listening. Her shapely body, slim and straight, was so tempting that he controlled a strong desire to grab her and squeeze her. He had no idea if she would marry him, but today he would find out without asking. A girl's opinion never counted in such matters, anyway. It was the father's consent that was required, and he was sure that Old Su would be more than happy to climb the social ladder, marrying a daughter into a family with a "high door," even though the Hung family door was actually so low that he often bumped his head.

He listened to her singing for a moment, savoring every word:

> Little cabbage, little cabbage,
> Always tender, always fresh.
> But treat it tenderly,
> For it can laugh, it can cry.
> Little cabbage, little cabbage . . .

Her crisp voice was so clear that he could hear it echo in the hills across the brook. A girl's song should be answered, he thought. He could not help answering it in his deep, sonorous voice:

> Little cabbage, little cabbage,
> I'll pick it tender, I'll pick it fresh.
> It can laugh, it can cry.
> Little cabbage, little cabbage,

Don't be shy.
I'll treat it tenderly. You are mine.

She sat staring into the water without response. He sat beside her quietly, disappointed. He had expected her to turn excitedly and look at him anxiously, or sing another stanza to express her feelings. "Look at the fish," she said.

He looked. A school of small fish was swimming in the clear water, seeking food.

"Papa fish, mama fish," she went on in a longing voice, "sister fish and brother fish. See how happy and free they are!"

The fish indeed seemed happy and free. He could let his feelings fly and compose a poem or an essay about them without the restrictions of the eight-legged style, which he had perfected but hated. In school the pupils' chanting of the Four Books and Five Classics and "Confucius says . . ." droned in his ears all day like a thousand flies humming. It almost drove him mad by the end of each day. How he longed for freedom. He said softly, "It would be wonderful to be able to swim like that—papa fish and mama fish, happy and free! Su San-mei, I have something to ask you."

He waited for her to look at him anxiously, but she did not. She kicked the water, frightening the fish away. "See what you've done!" he chided.

She sprinkled a little water on his face and laughed. He laughed, too. She was so playful, like a child. He was sure that she was still a virgin. "What do you want to say?" she asked.

"Will you marry me?" he blurted out.

Without answering his question, she started to sing again:

Avoid the hills, take a detour.
Watch the goats, wait for her man;
Follow the winding road, take a turn,
Cut the wood, meet his woman.
Use two fingers, blow a whistle;
Sit on a rock, wait all day.
Cover her face, say "Guess who?"

When she finished, she playfully covered his face with her hands and said, "Boo!" She was so close that he could smell her sweet breath and feel the warmth of her body. Still, he was a little disappointed that she had acted so childishly. It almost dampened his desire to discuss marriage and the future with her. But then he remembered that Confucius had said, "Ignorance is a woman's virtue." According to the sage, perhaps a man should feel superior. He turned, grabbed her and kissed her deeply.

After dinner, when Hung and his father were alone, he mentioned marriage again.

"Shiu-ch'uan," his father said, sipping a cup of tea noisily, "don't think that I have not pondered on your matrimony for many years. Every summer we butcher a pig to celebrate your birthday, a luxury that we cannot afford even during the New Year celebration. Every time we ate your pig I felt the quick passing of time. Your single state always weighs heavily on my mind. Last year I told myself that in another year you would be too old to marry and that no decent family would waste a daughter on a twenty-one-year-old man. But times are changing, son. Today, even twenty-two is still a proper age for a man to take a wife. Before you go to Canton to take the Imperial examination, we will find you a bride whose front door will be as high as ours and your horoscopes will match."

"But father," Hung Shiu-ch'uan protested, "I have already found the girl."

"You have?" Hung Tai asked, raising his eyebrows inquisitively. "Who is she?"

"The only daughter of Old Su. She is well bred, hardworking, and honest. She has already consented to marry me."

"Oh, I remember," the senior Hung said with a frown. "That poor peasant's daughter whom you met by singing mountain songs. Teach your sister to sing some good ones. For you, the entire village has other plans."

"But I don't belong to the entire village . . ."

"Shiu-ch'uan," his father cut him short, his voice firm, "the Sus are tenant farmers. Our doors do not match. Besides, it is highly irregular for a man of your status, an Imperial examination candidate, to pick someone secretly and discuss marriage directly. Marriage is made in Heaven, arranged through a proper go-between; horoscopes are studied and matched. No, son. You will not marry a woman whose family wears patched clothes."

With a nod of finality, Hung Tai left the room hurriedly to avoid further argument. Hung stared after his father, tears filling his eyes.

2

On January 28, 1833, a boy was born in an English village near London, some five thousand miles away from Flower County in Kwangtung Province. His father was a British Army lieutenant general, a descendant of a warring Highland clan, his mother a daughter of a rich, shrewd London merchant. At birth, the baby was so full of energy that it howled and kicked violently, as though it were already protesting the injustice of the rotten world it had been born into.

"My God!" General Gordon remarked with a groan and grimace. "Now we have a powder keg in the family."

His prediction was not too far off the mark. Charles George Gordon, dragged from one army camp to another while growing up, proved to be a boy of unpredictable temper and full of mischief.

When he was nine, the family settled at Woolwich where they lived in a dilapidated official mansion that was overrun with mice. Used to discomfort, the young Gordon treated the mice as entertaining playmates; he often let loose a dozen or so in his younger sister's room, then watched the little girl stand on a chair and scream with fright. With his equally naughty older brother, he broke many neighborhood windows using discarded nails and screws fired from slingshots.

During those years, General Gordon indeed felt that he was sitting on a powder barrel, but he was an easygoing man who talked about discipline and Victorian ethics more often than he practiced them. Mrs. Gordon, raising a total of eleven uproarious children, was already tired and haggard although not yet forty, but she remained cheerful and often delegated her authority to her eldest daughter, Augusta, who was a deeply religious young lady twelve years older than young George.

Through the tumultuous years, General Gordon saw his son gradually change into a serious young man. The young Gordon, still rebellious, began to have good manners when occasions called for them. He developed a strong character, showed uncanny courage and boundless energy. He was impatient and intolerant with injustice and stupidity; his peers predicted that he would one day wind up as one of those British eccentrics, stubborn, intolerable, and childless.

In 1848, when Gordon was fifteen, he was accepted as an officer-cadet at Woolwich Royal Military Academy. "I don't know what you did to George," the proud General Gordon said to Augusta, "but the change in your brother is a miracle. It looks as though he's going to grow up to be a gentleman after all."

No sooner had the senior Gordon made the remark than something happened that made him blush with embarrassment. He learned that while young Gordon and the rest of the cadets had been left waiting in line for the dining hall doors to open, George had grown impatient. He had demanded to know why they were waiting. The corporal who was blocking the door only shrugged indifferently. After repeated requests for an explanation, Gordon was still ignored. In a fit of temper, he rammed his head into the corporal's stomach, sending him tumbling through a glass-paneled door.

The incident immediately brought an instructor to the scene. After a long-winded reprimand, he said sarcastically, "You want to become an officer? I wouldn't bet two pence on your success!"

Gordon's face reddened as he fought a strong desire to ram his head into the instructor's stomach, too. After they had glared at each other for a moment, Gordon tore the epaulets off his own shoulders, flung them at the instructor and retorted, "I'll bet you're quite right. You can have these!"

He was promptly brought to the commandant's office. General Parker, the Royal Academy commandant, an army veteran who had lost a leg at Waterloo, was a friend of General Gordon. He gave young Gordon a tongue-lashing instead of more severe punishment. But George was still defiant. After he had aired his resentment against injustice, he saluted smartly and walked out.

Back home, General Gordon confronted his son and demanded an explanation for such abominable behavior. George did not try to justify himself nor show any regret; instead he said, "General Parker is unfit to be the commandant. Never employ a man minus a limb to have authority over boys. A one-legged man is apt to be irritable and unjust."

It was Augusta who soothed the flabbergasted father. "George is a descendant of a restless Highland warrior clan, Father," she said. "Naturally he's a bit rowdy and wild. It's in his blood. But he's endowed with a strong sense of justice and will have a great military future. You don't want him to be docile, do you?"

George Gordon had always been fascinated by the mysterious Orient. When he was a boy he had read strange stories about China, where people talked like birds and their women walked on "lily feet" the size of lotus buds. Once he had read in the *London Times* that a New York circus sideshow featured "two creatures from a faraway land who ate with bamboo sticks and spoke singsong gibberish." These strange creatures were drawing big crowds to the circus, like visitors from another planet. He was sure they were Chinese. Such information increased his curiosity. He often wondered what chance he'd have at life in China if he decided to go there.

As he read everything about China avidly, he found fairy tales and contradictions in many books and articles. Some sounded as ridiculous as the stories told by Chinese about the "Western Barbarians" who were covered with yellow hair like apes, smelled like foxes, and ate raw meat with knives and prongs. One story even described foreign missionaries eating fried children's eyeballs to make them see better.

Those stories amused him as well as irritated him. He would like to go to China to set the record straight. He would like to show the Chinese his white body with only a little hair on his chest, and he would demonstrate his perfect table manners while eating well-cooked meat. When he returned to England, he would do the same for the Chinese, spreading their correct image and introducing their five-thousand-year-old culture to the British.

He wrote a letter to Father Theodore Flanagan in Hong Kong, a friend of his father's, inquiring about the possibility of his going to China as a missionary. After six months he received a reply:

Dear George:

I am happy to receive your letter of inquiry; your noble desire is commendable. But no pampered Britisher can come to the Orient to preach Christianity to the ignorant peasants, eat dog meat and monkey brains with the pagans. It takes a young man with an iron will as well as an iron stomach to fulfill such desires as yours. He must be devoted to God and loyal to his country, regardless of what he is ordered to do. Remain where you are, my boy, and enjoy your mother's kidney pudding, which is the best in all England.

George Gordon read the letter again and wondered why Father Flanagan had underlined the word *regardless* twice with his heavy pen. He reread this line, "... loyal to his country, *regardless* of what he is ordered to do." It sounded as though a missionary had a double mission, one religious and one political. As he analyzed the recent reports from China in newspapers and magazines, he was convinced that some Western missionaries in China indeed had other responsibilities besides preaching the gospels of God. A few members in Parliament had even openly objected to the use of religion as a front for espionage work in the Orient; others criticized the government policy of exporting opium to China. Meanwhile, the British military establishment had been rattling its sabers, clamoring to send men to war in China to protect the missionaries, "who had been mistreated by both the Manchu government and its slanty-eyed citizens."

He wrote to Father Flanagan again, saying that he had both an iron will and an iron stomach, that he was loyal to both God and government. He would like to volunteer his services as Father Flanagan's assistant without salary . . . only passage money from London to Hong Kong.

In six months a reply arrived, blunt and direct: "In Hong Kong I can easily find a Britisher or an American who will work for adventure or for the love of God. But I have absolutely no use for anyone who does not speak the native tongue . . . of which China has five hundred different kinds. Learn a few words before you write to me again."

Where was he going to learn the singsong language in a small English country town? The letter stopped Charles George Gordon from pleading for a job in China again.

3

Hung Shiu-ch'uan got up early. This morning he was the guest of honor at his family's going-away ceremony. Tomorrow he and his two study companions would start the trip to Canton to take the Imperial examination at the provincial level. August 5, 1836, only four more days away, would be one of the most important days of his life.

His study companions, Feng Yung-shan and Hung Run-kan, were already in the family middle room, waiting. They were all dressed in new gowns and had the front part of their heads clean-shaven. In front of the elders, the young men observed their proper manners, greeting each other with bows and speaking educated language. Feng and Run-kan were his cousins and childhood friends. Together they had caught rats and snakes for Longevity Tan, the open-air-restaurant owner who paid good money for snakes for his famous snake-armadillo stew. As armadillo was hard to come by, Longevity Tan had been substituting rat meat. Hung and his friends knew the secret and never patronized the open-air restaurant. Since they also supplied rats to Longevity, they still publicized the stew as an aphrodisiac that was better than "deer's horn" or "seal's whip," which was dried male seal sex organs that reputedly enabled even an octogenarian to become a father. In Longevity Tan's open-air restaurant, it was not unusual to see decrepit senior citizens arriving in sedan chairs. They all had young concubines; the old men sat on rickety benches and picked at snake-rat stew while peasants and coolies devoured the famous dish with gusto.

This morning Hung's father had also changed into a new gown. Smiling broadly, he seated himself in the master's chair that faced the entrance. He watched the three young men take their seats politely. His wife had prepared a special breakfast for this occasion—rice porridge with meat dumplings and a large steamed fish, which symbolized wealth.

"Shiu-ch'uan," he said to his son, "the entire village is of one heart.

26

Everybody is behind you. They have contributed money for your traveling expenses and I have pawned my Japanese clock to buy food for this good-luck breakfast."

Hung was tired of hearing, "The entire village is of one heart." The support of the villagers made him uneasy. What if he failed the examination? He felt that it was a burden and a responsibility. But the trip to Canton, the provincial capital, with two of his closest friends would be a pleasure. They would be out of the sight of their elders for a few days. They could act and talk as they pleased, and visit the big city full of excitement—tea houses, theatres, gambling and opium dens, shops selling expensive foreign goods, factories, monkey players, street acrobats, and city girls.

As Hung Tai kept talking about the importance of the examination to their future, the three young men enjoyed the breakfast quietly. It was a rare treat and they were glad that they did not have to talk much. Feng was the eldest of the three; a cousin, he was from the only well-to-do family in Happy Valley. He was tall but not as good-looking as Hung, with a head too large for his frail frame. Run-kan was also Hung's first cousin, tall and handsome. At eighteen, he was a serious young man with a perpetual frown, as though he were always trying to solve a difficult problem. Like Hung, both of them adopted a scholarly stoop. They could quote the classics fairly well without saying much. It was on the strength of that ability that they had been selected as Hung's study companions.

"The glory of Happy Valley depends on you three," the elder Hung was saying. "When you return triumphantly from the provincial capital, you will be ready to go to Peking in two years. Again all the expenses will be paid by the entire village, as everyone in Happy Valley is of one heart . . ."

The elder Hung's speech was interrupted by the explosion of a long string of firecrackers. Trooping into the middle hall were Hung's two older brothers, Run-ta and Run-mo, and his sister, Little Treasure. Run-ta was holding the exploding firecrackers, Run-mo was carrying a plate of cash—five strings of brass coins and twenty taels of silver. Little Treasure brought in a new gown, which she had made for her brother. As prearranged, the cash was placed in front of Run-kan, who had been appointed as the group's treasurer because of his serious look. When the firecrackers stopped exploding, Hung's two brothers and sister bowed to Hung, congratulated him, and wished him good luck. Beaming at this prearranged send-off ceremony, the elder Hung coughed, pulled at his whiskers and said, "Heaven has eyes, my son. Even your sister has made a gown for you . . . a woman who had never learned to sew, and yet the clothes she made are fit for a king. It is destiny. Every sign points in the correct direction. Set your sights high, my son. Glorify your ancestors. Always remember, the entire village is of one heart to support you!"

Hung cringed as he heard his father repeat the last line, but nobody noticed it as they all plunged into the food.

As soon as the breakfast was over, Hung excused himself. He wanted to say good-bye to Su San-mei and did not want to be late.

The hot sun was rising from the Eastern Hill as he started for the brook where Su San-mei had promised to meet him. He felt energetic and lighthearted, breathing deeply the fresh morning air. The birds chirped happily in the roadside elms as though they, too, wished him good luck.

Su San-mei was late. When she arrived, she was out of breath from running. She said that she had almost been unable to get away because the landlord's rent-collection agent was visiting, and she had been obliged to serve him tea and light his opium pipe.

"He's visiting your family so early?" Hung asked, surprised.

"Yes, he wanted to make sure that we were in."

"He visits you a lot. Do you still owe him rent?"

"Yes."

Su San-mei lowered her head. She seemed reluctant to discuss it. She also lost her cheerfulness and playfulness. Hung had already learned about her family's difficulties. Her mother had consumption, coughing all day in her bed. Su San-mei and her father were obliged to do everything—cooking, washing, and laboring in the rice field and in the hills. The rent agent, who lived nearby, seemed to have an eye for Su San-mei. Hung suspected that collecting rent was only an excuse, for the landlord, Master Woo, who lived in a palatial mansion in the county seat, certainly would not care for the few taels of silver that a poor tenant owed him.

"Don't worry," he said, trying to comfort her. "When I return from Canton I shall give the turtle's egg a warning."

Su San-mei looked up hopefully, but she cast her eyes down again almost immediately. "He is the 'teeth and claws' of Master Woo," she said. "He is not afraid of anybody."

"When I come back from Canton, I might not be just anybody. Did he make a threat?"

"No. My father says he is a smiling dog. But you can't trust any opium smoker. This morning I heard him asking my father if I would be willing to work as Master Woo's personal maid."

"Are you willing?"

Su San-mei spat, her eyes glaring. "Who is going to gather firewood? Who is going to wash and sew? Who is going to take care of my sick mother?" For a brief moment she had transformed herself from a lovely girl into an angry little tigress, ready to claw somebody's eyes out.

Hung watched her, amused. "All right," he said. "You don't have to shout here. Nobody will force you to do anything. The way you spit will frighten away any opium addict. You almost frightened me. Thank Heaven you are a cat, not a kitten. I hate helpless little kittens."

He kissed her. She clutched him tightly, refusing to let him go.

Early the next morning, Hung changed into traveling clothes and packed. He selected two changes of underwear, some cloth socks, and his new gown made by his sister. He rolled them into a bundle and tied it on his back. Then he put his toilet articles and writing supplies in a rattan basket, which he carried on his shoulder balanced with a stick. The stick would come in handy when dogs attacked. In the countryside, dogs were ferocious—barking, snarling, and chasing passersby like wild animals. Hung still bore a few teeth marks on his behind.

The three travelers were to meet at Feng Yung-shan's home. Since it would take a whole day to reach Canton, they had decided to start early. Hung told himself that if he hurried, he still had time to visit Su San-mei briefly in the hills where she gathered firewood every morning.

She was not there. He called out but there was no response. When he looked around, all he saw were running rabbits and a few birds, which flew away from him screaming.

He hurried to her house. Working in the little vegetable garden in front of the shabby hut was Old Su. He wiped his brow with a rag as Hung approached him. After a quick bow, Hung inquired about Su San-mei.

"She went to the seat of Flower County yesterday," Old Su said with a long sigh. He looked old and haggard, his bloodshot eyes sad and watery. "She went to work for Master Woo."

"She said she would not go," Hung said, his voice tinged with disappointment. "Was she forced?"

"No, she went willingly," Old Su said, choking with emotion. He kept wiping his face with the rag, his bony hands trembling.

Hung stared at the old man, his heart sinking. He could not believe that Su San-mei would change her mind so easily. Only yesterday she had spat so vehemently, as though she would rather die than work for Master Woo.

Old Su stepped closer and touched Hung on the arm, his eyes pleading. "Go see how she is, Mr. Hung. Stop at Flower County seat on your way to the capital. Tell her I will find the money to pay my arrears so that she can come home."

"What!" Hung said, his face reddened with anger. "Was she taken away as a pawn for the rent you owe?"

"No," Old Su sighed. "She went of her own accord. If she hadn't, they would have taken the land away. How are we going to live without the two acres?"

Tears started welling out of his eyes. He wiped them quickly with the rag and turned away, as if ashamed to be caught weeping.

Hung left hurriedly, burning with anger. He had never felt so helpless. It made him all the more determined to pass the Imperial examination.

4

It would take a half day to reach the Flower County seat, less than half way to Canton. Hung Shiu-ch'uan wished he did not have to carry his inkstand, which weighed heavily in the basket; but presentable stationery and writing equipment were the main tools he needed in this examination. The inkstand was made of smooth rock with a dragon carved at its head for good luck. He had also brought several writing brushes and a long ink stick. All had lucky sayings carved on them. His father had insisted that he make fresh ink at each examination by scraping the ink stick against the inkstand, an elaborate process that required time and skill because the ink must have the correct consistency and color. His father had been more anxious than he was about this examination, having prayed to both Buddha and Kwan Yin several times. Now, waiting for the result would probably make the old man a nervous wreck.

Hung remembered the county examination for the Qualified Student degree, which he had taken seven years ago and passed easily. It had been a good year; his father had saved some money and prepared an elaborate welcome party for his triumphant return. In front of the house a little stage had been built for the performance of *Ascending to Officialdom*, a Cantonese opera which depicted a scholar's rise from poverty to Viceroy of Kwangtung and Kwangsi. It had been quite an occasion, with firecrackers and lion dancing, almost like a lunar New Year celebration. His father had even given a speech. With traditional modesty he had described his "dog son" as a stupid, slow learner, and credited all his son's success to Heaven's will and the ancestors' virtues. The fifty-odd invited guests had properly disputed such a humble description of the son and had predicted a glorious future for the new Qualified Student. To thank the guests, his father had ordered him to give them three kowtows.

He had had a good time in the county seat after the examination; he had listened to storytellers in a teahouse and witnessed a buttocks-beating at his family association.

In the distance, the township of Flower County could be seen vaguely through the haze. He and his two study companions had been walking on the dusty winding road all morning. Now that the town was in sight, he remembered Su San-mei and his heart sank.

"Shiu-ch'uan," Feng Yung-shan asked, "why are you so quiet?"

"I am thinking of the Imperial examination," Hung said. "I have an errand in town. Do you mind waiting?"

"What errand?" Feng asked.

"He wants to visit Su San-mei," Run-kan said with a knowing smile.

"It may take all day," Feng commented. "But we will wait."

Run-kan, Hung's confidant, had analyzed Hung's situation. He suggested that Hung should visit Su San-mei after the examination. With a Talent degree, he could tell Master Woo to dig his own grave. "If you go now," he said, "they may not allow you to pass the first gate. The turtle's egg has many 'teeth and claws' guarding his doors."

Feng thought differently. "With a Talent degree he can demand Su San-mei's release. If Master Woo refuses, he can ask the county magistrate to intervene. The Talent degree can open many doors. Visit her now and tell her to wait for the good news. We will tell the 'teeth and claws' to let you in."

They arrived at the county seat around noon. The town was the same as it had been the last time they saw it, except that the wooden buildings looked a little older and shabbier. The wet cobblestone narrow streets were slippery and the smell of animal manure was strong. Hung walked briskly, glancing to right and left, watching for housewives who had a habit of throwing dirty water onto the street from doorways. Hung had been splashed a few times before.

Everybody knew where Master Woo lived. He was the richest landlord in Flower County, indulging in every luxury. He had a palatial mansion in the center of the town. They had already sighted the yellow roofs of his house, surrounded by red walls and greenery.

The massive vermilion door was closed. There were no "teeth and claws" guarding it, except two stone lions, one on each side, sitting on pedestals and snarling at visitors. Hung wanted to see Su San-mei alone and asked his friends to wait for him in a teahouse. He gave them the name and the address.

"We will wait for you half an hour," Feng said. "Then we will come and rescue you." Laughing, they left.

Hung knocked on the double door a few times. A servant answered. Seeing that the visitor was wearing a long gown, he bowed and inquired politely the purpose of the visit. When Hung told him that he was Su San-mei's brother and wanted to see her, the servant took him to the courtyard and told him to wait. Su San-mei came out sooner than Hung expected. She was dressed in pantaloons with a plain dress over them that reached to her knees. The servant took them to a corner and gave them ten minutes to talk, then stood nearby and watched.

Hung and Su San-mei looked at each other for a moment, unable to find the right thing to say. Hung broke the silence.

"You look well, Su San-mei," he said, remembering to act like a brother. "Father tells you not to worry. He will raise the money to redeem you."

"How is Father?" she asked, her voice so low that it was barely audible.

"Fine."

"Mother?"

"I did not see her."

Su San-mei nodded and tears welled out of her eyes. She looked away, blowing her nose into a handkerchief. With a little bit of rouge on her cheeks and her queue well braided and oiled, she looked like one of the maids he had seen in storybook illustrations of the Imperial Palace.

He went on, "I will tell your . . . uh, Father that you look well and happy." He paused, then asked, "Are you?"

"Tell him that Master Woo wants me to become his ninth concubine," she said, "unless Father can come up with a thousand taels of silver to redeem me."

"A thousand!" Hung asked, shocked. "He owes Master Woo only a year's rent, one hundred taels."

"But Master Woo wanted a ten-year lease on me, at one hundred taels a year. That way, my family can work the land free of charge for ten years. If they want me back, they must pay a thousand taels."

Hung, burning with anger, stole a glance at the servant, who was standing a few yards away glaring at him. He changed the subject, knowing it was impossible for anyone in Happy Valley to raise that much money.

"I am going to Canton for the Imperial examination," he said. "After I obtain the Talent degree, I will come to see you." He took another quick glance at the servant, then whispered, "Are you willing to become a concubine?"

"I would rather die!" she said. Realizing that her voice was too loud, she lowered it quickly and added, "The old turtle's egg is over seventy. I cannot bear even to go near him. My heart is always in Happy Valley. I will die there!"

Hung thought that Happy Valley was certainly not a happy place to live, especially for the family of a poor tenant farmer. "Why?" he asked.

"So I can be near you!" she said, looking at him tenderly, her voice serious. He had never heard her say anything seriously before. She had always been playful, sometimes even a bit naughty. Now she talked like a mature woman. The change surprised him and he was touched by what she had just said. He attempted to kiss her but withdrew his hands quickly.

"I love you," he whispered.

"Soon you will be a Talent, then a high government official," she said, her eyes full of tears. "If you must marry, I will split my heart in two . . . half for you and half for your wife. If I must marry, I want you to find a man for me. If you find me a chicken, I will follow the chicken. If you find me a dog, I will follow the dog . . ."

"Time is up!" the servant shouted, coming over to stop their conversation. Hung touched her hand lightly and hurried away.

5

They arrived in Canton at dusk. Hung was not impressed by the city at first. What he saw was somewhat like the Flower County seat— small restaurants, grocery stores, ironwork stalls, and teahouses. But as he continued, he discovered that they were only in the outskirts of the city. After they entered the massive city gate, the scene changed. There were long and wide boulevards with two- or three-story buildings lining both sides. Gold-and-red signboards were hung out in every direction bearing lucky names of stores. The pedestrians walked leisurely amid carriages, wheelbarrows, sedan chairs, and pushcarts, many wearing long gowns and black satin caps to show that they were from families with high doors. The street noise was deafening, with peddlers ringing bells or crying out their wares in loud cracked voices. Among the milling crowd, giggling peasant girls mingled with well-dressed ladies in silk and brocade gowns. Some were followed by maids or servants carrying parcels and boxes.

Hung and his friends had never seen such busy streets before. Tired, hungry, and dusty, they kept going, shifting the weight of their luggage on their backs, craning their necks to see better. They soaked in the sounds and sights, and breathed deeply the aroma of spicy food and herb medicine. They were dazzled by their city, the provincial capital of Kwangtung.

They avoided the fancy hotels. In a little lane they found a small hotel with a white lantern hanging over its door. A small red sign over the door bore its name in golden characters: Five Blessings Inn. The lane was narrow but tidy and clean, and the squat buildings were all whitewashed and had vermilion front doors, elegant in their modesty, inexpensive but tasteful. Hung suggested that they stay in this inn for the night.

The moment they stepped inside, an old man with white whiskers

35

met them with a bow. He wore a clean old silk gown, his eyes deep and bright, a kind smile on his thin but smooth face. "Ah," he said with repeated little bows, "you three gentlemen are here for the Imperial examination, I can tell."

"How do you know?" Hung asked.

"From your dress and your physiognomy," the old man said. "Your high foreheads mean intelligence and your walks show scholarly status. It is written on your looks. My humble name is Wong Pu. Just call me Old Man Wong. I am the owner of this little place. It is cheap but quiet, and only an arrow's distance from the examination compound. Welcome!"

He asked them if they wanted separate rooms or one room, and quoted a modest rent. All rooms came with two meals—breakfast and dinner. They decided to take one room which cost only a string of brass coins per day.

The inn had a courtyard with the lobby-dining room in the main building facing the entrance. They took a room in the west wing, at the owner's suggestion. It faced east, with excellent *feng-shui*, or wind and water. Most of the Imperial examination candidates who followed the owner's advice had passed the examination, he told them.

"Dinner is at seven," Old Man Wong said after he had pocketed the rent. "Five dishes and a soup. You will meet some interesting people."

Their room was spacious and airy, with the back window facing a garden. Insects were singing outside. Run-kan pushed the latticed window open. A full moon hung among the branches of an old pine, and a faint scent of magnolia drifted in, carried by a gentle breeze. There were four narrow beds in the room. The bamboo pillows looked hard but the bedding was clean. They unpacked and selected their beds. A servant boy came in with a bucket of hot water. They washed their faces and feet in a brass basin.

The dining room was full. Sitting around the large round table in the middle of the room were eight men and a young woman. Hung took one of the three empty high-backed chairs and introduced himself and his companions. The others did the same. There were two young men from a distant county who had come for the Imperial examination; three merchants who were passing through; Mr. Hu, a fortune-teller from Hunan Province; Master Li, a martial arts teacher and his teenage daughter, Mei Mei; and a mysterious Mr. Fei, who wore an expensive blue brocade gown and a foreign felt hat. A short, plump man, Mr. Fei looked well fed and well educated, speaking many dialects in a deep voice. He carried on a long conversation with the eloquent Feng Yung-shan, who was sitting beside him. They touched on a wide range of subjects, from food to herbs. Hung found out that Fei was a writer-traveler who dealt in herbs on the side. There was a late arrival, a seaman from Anhui Province, a big muscular man with a large, weather-beaten face. He wore a faded blue cotton blouse and loose trousers. His large braided queue was wrapped in a blue cotton turban. Laughing easily, he called himself Golden Rooster.

During the meal, Run-kan kept his eyes on Master Li's daughter, Mei Mei, who ate quietly. Her eyes downcast, she spoke only when she was spoken to. Rosy-cheeked and pretty with large sparkling eyes, she looked lean and strong, obviously a martial artist.

The examination compound, behind the governor's yamen, was lit by several large lanterns. Three-hundred-odd candidates arrived before dawn, carrying thin meager luggage in bundles and bags, looking nervous and tense. Hung and his friends mingled with them, chatting and laughing, exuding confidence, especially Feng, who offered free advice to others and made guesses as to what topics they were to write about on the first day. A few candidates prayed that the subjects would be easy. To fortify themselves, many started munching dried fruit and biscuits they had brought.

Hung learned that such examinations took place every three years in Canton, for a duration of four days. The candidates lived in assigned cubicles in the compound, cooking their own meals. During the four-day confinement, they could not communicate with the outside world. They would write two eight-legged essays and four poems in their cubicles; subjects would be provided by the provincial governor, who had passed such examinations himself all the way to the national level.

With connections, a man with a Talent degree could find a good position in a yamen, such as an assistant to the provincial governor. Without connections, he could become a private tutor, earning hard silver instead of hogs and goats.

Hung noticed that some of the candidates were already middle-aged, their hair dyed and their faces clean-shaven. Despite their efforts to look younger, they reminded him of haggard ladies with rouged cheeks and painted lips. They gave him a chill, making him wonder if he would suffer a similar fate, taking the examination every three years but never making it. The burden of his family's expectations, the doomed future of Su San-mei . . . all weighed heavily on his mind. He envied Run-kan and Feng, who were only study companions; though they would take the exams too, there was no pressure on them to succeed. No wonder Feng was so gregarious, talking freely and full of confidence.

Feng's mother had even said, "Take care of yourself. Don't study too hard. Enjoy the sights and bring back a souvenir or two."

Presently a loud roll of drums was heard and the massive gate of the examination building opened. While passing through, the candidates were searched then assigned their individual cubicles and told the rules. For four days they were to remain in their cubicles, eating, sleeping, and writing the essays. While visiting an outhouse nearby, the candidates were not allowed to communicate with each other. If a candidate was caught cheating, he would be subjected to a buttock-beating of twenty strokes. A second violation would result in lifetime banishment from Imperial examinations.

After another roll of drums, the subject of the examination was announced, and the candidates were allowed to enter their assigned cubicles, which were lined up in several rows like army barracks. Hung's cubicle was two rows away from his friends'. It had a small bed, a stove, a water basin, a crude table, an oil lamp, and a bench. In a corner was a pile of charcoal and a bucket of water. Meat, vegetables, and rice would be distributed every day; candidates could cook and eat at any time. They shared half a dozen outhouses a short distance away. Everything seemed clean and tidy, and the kitchen utensils, bowls, and cups were of good quality, neatly placed on a shelf over the stove.

Hung unpacked, laid out his supplies and the stack of paper he had just received. He made some fresh ink and settled down to write the first eight-legged essay immediately. The subject, "Essence of the Four Books," was easy enough. As he hummed and shook his head in a scholarly manner, words poured out onto his examination paper.

During the next four days, he composed two long essays and four poems, according to subjects that were assigned to him. He wrote carefully, making sure that his calligraphy had strength and fluid strokes. By the time he had finished rereading what he had written, the cubicle was full of cooking smells. He was grateful, for it overwhelmed the outhouse smell that had started drifting into the cubicles.

At the end of the fourth day the gate opened, and the candidates, carrying their luggage, met in the compound. Some looked pale and haggard. A few even had tears in their eyes. Many walked around in a daze, looking for friends and relatives. Hung found Run-kan and Feng. They looked fresh and spirited.

"How was it?" Hung asked.

"I need the blessing of the Goddess of Mercy," Feng said modestly, faking a grimace, but his cheerful voice told his friends that he had done well.

Run-kan said with a laugh, "According to the silly subjects they dished out, they ought to take the examinations themselves. You and I should grade them. Heavens! Those turtle's eggs . . ."

Hung hushed him and left the compound quickly. On their way back to the inn, he said, "Run-kan, you were twisting the tiger's tail in the tiger's den. You could get twenty strokes on your bottom for saying things like that in the examination compound!"

They all shuddered but returned to Five Blessings Inn in a good mood, full of confidence.

Three days later, an hour before the names of the lucky ones were posted on the red wall of the examination building, three hundred heads were bobbing in front of the wall, waiting anxiously for the results. When Hung, Feng and Run-kan arrived, twenty names were being fastened in place. Everybody pushed and craned his neck to read the list. Some candidates cried unashamedly; several fainted. Most shrugged philosophically, swearing that they would try again in three years. Hung stared at the poster, feeling blood drain from his face. He hid his trembling hands in his sleeves, trying to fight the onslaught of depression. All his hopes and ambitions were dashed.

He wondered what he had done wrong. Had there been a mistake on the part of the examiner who had graded his paper? Was the turtle's egg a moron or was he a vindictive man who was taking out his vengeance on someone's examination paper?

He felt a sympathetic hand on his shoulder. "This is the Year of the Snake," Run-kan said, giving him a gentle pat. "The Year of the Monkey will be better."

Feng's ego was crushed. He was too overwhelmed by disappointment, which he expressed by mumbling sarcastic remarks and curses. Hung felt anger building in him. He fought off his despair and vowed to become a Han Ling in six years. He would move into the yamen of the Mayor of Canton, if not the yamen of the Governor of Kwangtung. He announced this in such a loud voice that a few candidates who had also failed were startled. They turned to him, awed by his audacity at first, then looked at him admiringly and gave him an encouraging thumbs-up sign.

"See you in three years," one of them said.

In the evening, the dinner table was loaded with additional dishes. Old Man Wong, the owner of the inn, had ordered extra food to soothe those who had failed the examination. He personally poured wine and drank a toast to their future success.

"Be patient," he advised. "Wiseman Kiang Tse-ya did not meet his emperor until he was eighty. Great men always achieve their goals late."

All the guests agreed and proposed a toast to the five failed scholars. The wine and good food changed the evening's mood. Everybody talked and laughed. Master Li and his daughter entertained the guests with a Flower Drum Song, singing and dancing together to the beat of a little flower drum which Mei Mei beat with a hand. Run-kan could not take his eyes off the girl. As he watched the performance, he kept swallowing. Feng, somewhat tipsy, shook his shoulders in time to the music and beat his rice bowl with a chopstick. Everyone had such a good time that they exchanged calling cards. Mr. Fei, the traveling gentleman who wore the foreign hat, produced several copies of a thick book. He presented a copy to each of the five scholars.

Hung, having downed half a dozen cups of mao-tai, felt as if he were walking on clouds. All his frustrations and worries had been washed away by the excellent 130-proof drink.

Later, he did not remember when or how he had gone to bed. He was awakened by his companions' loud snores. The sun had risen high and birds were chirping outside the window. He rose languidly, feeling a slight headache. In the distance were faint street noises. Somewhere in Kwangtung Province twenty happy new Talents were celebrating. How he envied them! He caught sight of the thick book that Mr. Fei had given him. Somebody had put it beside his bamboo pillow. He picked it up and opened it. The first line read:

"Heaven and earth were created in six days by a universal God named Jehovah . . ."

6

Life became harder. Hung Shiu-ch'uan had heard that there was something called an industrial revolution going on in Western countries, where they were now manufacturing fabrics with machines. One machine equaled the work force of one hundred men, and their product was better and stronger. This revolution resulted in unemployment in England.

Run-kan had started studying English, saying that many British priests had arrived in China to preach a foreign religion and had a hard time convincing people that God was a skinny bearded man nailed to a cross. If he were a God, the people said, how would he have fallen into such a miserable situation, nailed to a cross and bleeding all over? God should not have flesh and blood, even though he might partake of human food at an altar.

Run-kan said he had met a foreign priest called the Reverend Pike, who had offered to teach him English in exchange for some housework. He asked Hung if he was interested in learning some of the foreigners' wormlike writing.

Hung was obsessed by only one desire—to pass the next Imperial examination. He was determined to save all his energy for study of the Chinese classics and to improve his writing of the eight-legged essays. He was also curious about what was going on in the West, and he wanted Run-kan to inform him of whatever he learned from the foreign priest.

For three years Hung had studied day and night and practiced martial arts under the tutorship of Master Loo, a distant uncle who had served as the bodyguard of a rich merchant in Flower County. Master Loo specialized in The Monkey Fist, Twelve Ways of Kicking, and Swordplay, learned from a Buddhist monk from the famous O Mei Mountain of Szechwan.

The family had become even more indulgent of Hung. His brothers had taken over all his chores and his parents pampered him with additional nourishing food—snake soup and armadillo stew cooked in herbs. His sister washed and sewed all his clothes. They selected a wife for him without his consent. He liked his wife, Lotus, a quiet amiable young woman with a moon face and stout legs, not very pretty but kind, never losing her temper or saying a bad word about anyone. There was not much love in the bedroom, but every time Hung touched Lotus, she became pregnant. After two babies, Hung stopped touching her altogether. When he discussed his domestic life with Run-kan and Feng he always sighed, a bit sadly, quoting an old saying, "Same bed, different dreams."

Feng said Hung was still in love with Su San-mei, the woman beyond his reach. Feng's theory about women was, "A wife is not as desirable as a mistress; a mistress is not as desirable as someone beyond one's reach. That's life."

Hung often wondered if there was a point to Feng's philosophy. He liked Feng and enjoyed his eloquence. His idle talk was often interesting, containing weird ideas and philosophy, like gems in sand.

The three friends met every other day in Feng's spacious home, discussing the classics, world affairs, and the deteriorating conditions in Kwangtung. Run-kan supplied all the information about the foreigners, and the natives' resentment of the foreign religion. He said that recently a foreign priest had been chased out of Canton by an angry mob because the priest had insulted Confucius in his preaching.

Feng had a theory: "If you sell dog meat and hang out a lamb's head, it is all right. If you hang out a lamb's head and forbid people to eat dog meat, it is not all right and you are asking for trouble." So the lesson was, he concluded, that if the foreigners want the Chinese to believe in the foreign God, they should also allow them to believe in Confucius.

Hung retained his teaching job at the village school. His annual salary had increased to fifty catties of rice delivered in a wheelbarrow, in addition to a hog and a goat. He also received, on his birthday, extra gifts from his pupils—a chicken or two, a bottle of lamp oil, a package of salt, or a can of tea. On important occasions such as New Year's Day and the Moon Festival, he often found gifts at his door—a dozen eggs, several heads of cabbage, sometimes a salted catfish.

He had many new pupils, who started their schooling with the Three Character Classics. The boys chanted loudly in unison in a separate room every morning. In other schools, most of the seven-year-olds could chant it rapidly without the slightest idea of what the classics meant. But Hung insisted that his pupils understand every word.

"Men at birth are pure," he explained the meaning of the opening six characters, and since the boys understood the words, they chanted with more animation and enthusiasm. He was regarded as the best teacher in Flower County. The consensus was, "The other teachers only teach the children how to shake their heads and wag their tails while they chant."

Being a Talent degree candidate, Hung found his prestige increased, even though he had failed the last examination. People started consulting him about personal affairs, asking for his advice on how to raise children, even how to deal with rebellious seven-year-olds. Hung only knew one such boy well—himself when he was seven. It had been in 1821 when Emperor Tao-kuang had succeeded to the throne. The villagers were ordered to offer food and wine to the Jade Emperor in Heaven, and to pray for the new emperor's good health. Hung's family had obeyed, kowtowed, and prayed; Hung had followed suit, but in his prayer he had mumbled, "Oh, Jade Emperor in Heaven, kill the Manchu devil and make me emperor." He had behaved well, but in secret he had been the most rebellious seven-year-old he had ever known.

He found today's children lazy and docile, and the rebellious ones very rare. Once he had found a pupil urinating in his classroom, but later he was disappointed to find that the boy had not done it to rebel but to answer nature's call.

The people of Happy Valley had also become more superstitious. Mr. Ting, the fortune-teller, was getting more popular all the time. Quite often Hung found him arriving at his house in a sedan chair. His father entertained Ting in the middle room with tea and tidbits, and the skinny old man in his Taoist loose gown told fortunes in a turtle's shell and analyzed horoscopes. He explained to Hung's father the meaning of the eight Taoist diagrams, the significance of yin and yang and the importance of their balance. The last time Hung had heard Mr. Ting talking to his father, he was discussing Little Treasure's fortune. Obviously his father had been worrying about Little Treasure's single status.

In Happy Valley children married early; sometimes a family arranged their children's marriages when they were ten or eleven. A neighbor had married his twelve-year-old daughter to a nine-year-old boy. Hung had watched them doing family chores together. They played, teased, and quarreled like children, but they were husband and wife.

He wished that his father would find a husband for Little Treasure soon, so that Mr. Ting would stop coming to discuss the harmony of yin and yang, the balance of positive and negative, and the importance of wind and water. Mr. Ting's Taoist gown with the Eight Diagrams sewn on his back, his long goat-beard, and his long fingernails had become eyesores to Hung. He saw the man everywhere—telling fortunes, conducting funeral rites, selecting burial places, giving general advice on geomancy, and discussing good and evil in building positions. He was sure that Mr. Ting had had a hand in selecting his wife.

The loveless match saddened him and made him feel sorry for Lotus. Because of his guilty feelings, he often found himself being extra kind to her, and yet the feeling of "same bed, different dreams" persisted.

But Mr. Ting was a welcome guest to the other members of the Hung family, who trusted him. Hung's two half brothers even swore that they had seen Mr. Ting perform miracles, such as treading fire, swallowing knives, and spinning on his bare stomach on the point of a spear.

"He has such magic power that nobody can hurt him," Run-ta said. "Slash him with a sword . . . see if you can draw blood."

Hung regretted hearing such talk. Superstition was rampant in Happy Valley, a sure sign of a disastrous future.

One evening, when he returned from the village school, he heard his father's voice speaking to Mr. Ting in the middle room.

"What is wrong with her horoscope?" his father asked.

"She was born in the Year of the Dragon," Mr. Ting said. "The boy was born in the Year of the Chicken, which represents the Phoenix. Dragon is yang, Phoenix is yin. In this case yang and yin are reversed, resulting in the female dominating the male. Such a match is bad for the parents."

Hung did not believe such rubbish. Mr. Ting was again destroying somebody's romance, probably Little Treasure's. He felt a strong desire to go into the middle room, grab Mr. Ting's pigtail and throw him out, but he controlled himself. Mr. Ting had said that the match was bad for the parents; to a filial son like Hung, the parents' benefit must come first.

The Imperial examination was approaching fast. The three friends met more often as they counted the days. Run-kan's English improved rapidly, but he neglected his classics studies, knowing that if Hung passed the Imperial examinations and climbed the ladder of officialdom, he would take his friends up with him. He believed that the high government officials were all ignorant of world affairs. He had heard that the viceroy of an inner province had even made a remark that nobody in that province disputed. "Don't be threatened by the foreigners," the viceroy had said. "Besides England and America, all the other foreign countries do not exist. They are pure inventions created by England to frighten us."

Feng and Run-kan talked about England more as Hung became more interested in this aggressive foreign country. At each meeting, Feng served the best tea, sweetmeats, candy, and five-flavored watermelon seeds. Hung noticed that everyone in Feng's family had started wearing clothes made with machine-manufactured fabrics imported from England. They also discussed Emperor Tao-kuang.

The new emperor was not doing too well. The rich were becoming richer and the poor poorer. The landlords began to own most of the cultivated fields, buying out the poor farmers during bad years. A famine would drive the poor to begging. Sometimes landlords would seize their plots and pay them enough to stave off starvation for a few months. After a famine, beggars roamed the countryside, marauding bandits attacked villages and little towns. Secret societies staged rebellions, sacking government officials' residences and yamens.

The biggest secret society was Heaven and Earth Society, or The Triads, which recruited peasants, handcraft workers, laborers, and vagrants in the southern provinces. In Canton, posters were often found pasted on the city walls saying:

OFFICIALS ARE WORSE THAN BANDITS; CORRUPT MANDARINS ARE
NO BETTER THAN WOLVES AND TIGERS. CRIMES COMMITTED BY THE

RICH ARE NOT PUNISHED AND WRONGS TO THE POOR NEVER RE-
DRESSED. TODAY THE COMMON PEOPLE HAVE PLUNGED INTO THE
DARKEST DEPTHS OF SUFFERING. ARISE, BRETHREN. TOGETHER WE
WILL OVERTHROW THE ROTTEN MANCHU DYNASTY!

One day, Hung witnessed a public execution in the county seat.
Half a dozen rebels were made to kneel on the street and their heads
were chopped off one by one by a husky executioner with a wide heavy
sword. With each stroke, a head rolled, blood spurting a few feet high
from the severed neck. A few moments later the heads were hoisted on
poles over the city gate for public viewing. Posted on the city wall was a
large notice written in eight-legged style, punctuated with red ink. It
warned people that anyone suspected of treason would follow the fate of
the six men. "Kill the chickens to warn the monkeys," people said.

But the killing of the chickens failed to warn the monkeys. Uprisings
were reported in every province; heads were seen hanging on every city
gate, their bulging eyes glaring angrily. They would be left there for
days, rotting and stinking while vultures pecked them clean and maggots
grew fat.

The day before his trip to Canton, Hung finished his class with a
sigh of relief. He was anxious to visit Canton again, even though the
forthcoming examination was a burden and a responsibility. But he felt
more confident this time and decided to relax.

He was putting some brushes in a box when a dirty boy in rags
ran into the room and breathlessly muttered something that Hung barely
understood. The boy said that he was a neighbor of Old Su, who wanted
to see Mr. Hung before he left for Canton.

Hung wondered if Su San-mei had come back? The possibility of
seeing her again excited him. He had written to Master Woo, requesting
her release. A rich landlord's ears were always open to pleas from a
man who had taken the Imperial examination, even if he had failed.

Old Su's shack with its mud walls and thatched roof looked more
unlivable than ever as Hung approached it. A skinny yellow dog was
sleeping in front of the open door; a few chickens pecked in a pile of
trash nearby, cackling contentedly. As Hung drew near, the dog struggled
to its feet and growled, baring its yellow fangs. Hung ignored it and

marched toward the door. The dog fled with its tail between its hind legs.

As he entered the shack, Hung was hit by a strong smell of opium. In the semidark room, Old Su was lying on a wooden *kang*, or daybed, puffing away on his opium pipe. At fifty, he looked sixty, his skin leathery, sun-scorched, and lined with wrinkles, but he was still muscular. His hands, thick, scarred, and powerful, gripped the bamboo pipe tightly as he puffed and sucked, the opium sizzling in the pipe over the small lamp beside Su's wooden pillow. He did not acknowledge his visitor until he had finished the pipe. Then he looked up with glazed eyes.

"Mr. Hung," he said, struggling to a sitting position. "I am happy that you can come to my humble home."

He tried to rise but Hung stopped him. He took hold of a low rattan chair, pulled it toward the kang and sat down beside Old Su. "How is your wife?" he asked.

"Skin and bones," Old Su said, shaking his head sadly. "Coughing, coughing, and coughing."

Hung looked around. The messy condition of the shack told him that Su San-mei had not returned. Then he heard a woman's violent coughing in the next room. When the sound subsided he heard her groan. "Is she taking medicine?" he asked.

"It is no use," Old Su said. "Whenever a doctor visits her, she always waves him away and says, 'Let me go in peace.' She wants to go."

"Why have you sent for me?" Hung asked.

"Su San-mei has gone to Canton," Old Su said, his voice starting to choke. "Please pay her a visit. Find out how she is."

"Gone to Canton?" Hung asked, frowning. "Why?"

"Master Woo thought she was not cooperative. He sold her to a flower boat on the Pearl River."

Hung felt his anger rising quickly. He clutched his hands together to control it. "He has no right to sell her. She is your daughter."

Old Su turned away, too ashamed to look at Hung.

"Old Su," Hung said angrily, "are you selling your daughter?"

Old Su blinked tears out of his eyes and wiped them with trembling hands. "Mr. Hung, where am I going to find a thousand taels of silver to redeem her? I am getting deeper into debt every year."

"But you have money to smoke opium."

"The rent agent supplies it free," Old Su said. "It soothes my pain and makes me forget."

"It ruins you! It's a trick, can't you see? Those turtle's eggs want you to be weak and lazy so you will never be able to raise the money. You will never see your daughter again!"

Old Su nodded and banged the kang with a fist. "What can I do? What can I do?" He broke down and sobbed.

7

Hung Tai could not put his son's second try at the Imperial examination out of his mind. He met the village elders often to discuss it. All of them felt the excitement as the date approached; the anticipation of Hung's "ascending officialdom" caused them many sleepless nights. Since they had claimed relationship with a Talent candidate, people greeted them with lower bows. The connection also brought polite smiles to the faces of snobs. More girls flirted with their grandsons. At market fairs some girls even looked at them from the corners of their eyes and giggled coquettishly. Hung Tai was sure that the entire Flower County was discussing his son. A few families with marriageable daughters had even inquired about his son's horoscope, hoping to marry their girls into the Hung family as concubines. Hung Tai knew that Run-kan's parents had also received marriage proposals from families with high doors outside Happy Valley. One matchmaker had presented a young woman's detailed horoscope and an analysis of her physiognomy, which indicated that fertility was guaranteed, with the possibility of even producing "Five sons to bless the family."

Hung Tai was disappointed, even hurt, when he discovered that outside Happy Valley not everyone gave him equal respect and attention. When he felt resentful, his wife had to soothe him with the old saying, "Some people have eyes but not all of them can recognize Mountain Tai."

Hung Tai was named after Mountain Tai, the most famous mountain in China, which symbolized wealth and nobility. His wife's quoting of this saying indeed soothed him. He said philosophically, "To a Talent degree candidate, many doors are still closed; but just wait until after our son passes the examination of the Han Ling degree in Peking. Those same rich people and snobs will come visit us with gifts and greet us with kowtows. Relax, my son's mother. All this will come to pass. Mr. Ting has seen it clearly in his turtle's-shell divination."

Carrying their own luggage bundles on their backs, the three young scholars made an early start. Walking part way with them were their family members. At the end of one mile, the relatives stopped and bid them good-bye. Hung Tai, his eyes moist and a proud smile on his face, took the hands of his son and said, "Shiu-ch'uan, I wish you ten thousand blessings. The Hung family is historically kind—for hundreds of years we have treated people with fairness and respect. It is Heaven's reward that you were born to this family and we all have our ancestors to thank."

His mother stepped forward and took his hands. She said with a worried smile, "Shiu-ch'uan, watch the temperature. Always wear enough clothes and eat more. I have put a jar of thousand-cure pills in your basket. Don't forget to take a pill when you feel unwell."

It was his older brother's turn to speak. Lumbering forward, Run-ta grabbed Hung's hands and said, "Younger brother, it is good to pass the Imperial examination, but if you fail, it is good for you, too. You can always come back to help me carry water and night soil . . ."

"Enough!" Hung Tai cut in quickly. He was afraid that his rough-hewn eldest son might say more unlucky words. "The sun is rising. It is time to be on your way."

Before parting, Lotus took Hung aside and whispered, "A man is a dragon in a cloud. A woman is only a chicken in a coop. Don't worry about me. Pursue your success, my husband. Bring glory to our ancestors. One day you will feed the poor and scatter blessings everywhere. I shall burn incense and pray to the Buddha day and night for you." With tears in her eyes, she pressed a tael of silver into his hand. "Spend it on food, my husband. You must eat well in Canton."

After Hung left his family, he suddenly felt lonely . . . lonely for Lotus's gentleness, lonely for his mother's care and concern, and his sister's constant attention. He loved the women in his family much more than he did his father and brothers.

He caught up with Feng and Run-kan and the three were on their way.

* * *

Feng made a list of what to do and where to visit in Canton. He had heard that there were things in the capital now that had not been there three years ago, such as public gambling and opium dens, large pawn shops, and a black market.

"Silver is in big demand in the black market," he said. "A tael of silver is worth a thousand coppers now. We have twenty taels of silver. We can make some money by playing the black market."

"How?" Run-kan asked.

"Sell the silver in Canton, buy it back in Flower County for half the price."

"We need the silver to spend," Run-kan, the treasurer, said. "Who has money to play the black market?"

"Brother Feng," Hung said, "your family is contributing to the silver shortage. The British are draining it. They demand silver for everything they sell in China, especially opium and machine-made goods. Your family is spending a fortune buying their machine-made fabrics."

For the first time, Feng became quiet. They walked at a brisk pace, anxious to arrive in Canton as early as possible.

The provincial capital seemed more crowded now. Like the people in Flower County, the people in the city were also a bit shabbier. Many had sunken cheeks and hollow eyes; some walked in a daze, their steps slow and laborious. Run-kan pointed them out as opium addicts. Some were lying in doorways, puffing on their opium pipes, oblivious to what was going on around them.

Hung avoided looking at them. He visualized a country full of skeletons who had nothing to eat but still puffed on their opium pipes. They reminded him of Old Su, and his heart ached.

The Five Blessings Inn also looked older. Old Man Wong welcomed them with happy smiles and repeated little bows. He gave them the same room, the largest in the inn, and ordered the servant-boy to fetch tea and hot water. "Dinner at seven," he said. "Red-cooked pigs' feet and fried frogs' legs. Lucky dishes." He smiled.

The three gentlemen had arrived on "teeth-worshipping day." Once in a while the inn celebrated such a day to show gratitude to the guests' hardworking teeth, which often chewed nothing but cheap food.

Hung and his companions quickly washed their faces and feet, changed into clean clothes, and repaired to the dining room, hungry for the delicacies. Sitting at the round table were some new people. Run-kan glanced around. He did not see Master Li and his daughter. He tried to hide his disappointment but failed to conceal it from the clever owner of the inn.

Old Man Wong pulled his white whiskers and laughed. "Master Li and his pretty little daughter did not come this year. But last year they both inquired about you. When I see them again, I shall be happy to convey your greetings to them." He looked at Run-kan for a response. Run-kan only blushed.

Hung asked what had happened to the big man with the big laugh. "Golden Rooster?" Wong asked. "He moved to Lin Ting. He is a sailor. All sailors retire to Lin Ting. You remember Mr. Ha, the fortune teller who sells silk on the side? He went back to Hunan and became a rice merchant. He said it was in his destiny, selling rice. It might as well be. Silk is only a luxury but rice is a necessity. He said that filling people's stomachs is better than dressing rich men."

Hung inquired about the other two Talent degree candidates. "One of them committed suicide," Old Man Wong said sadly, shaking his head. "The other became a professional letter writer, working in tea-houses and wine shops. They have come to my humble inn for many years, but officialdom was not in their destiny."

Hung remembered the two candidates well. He had talked to them in the examination compound and watched their heartbroken reaction when the "Golden List" appeared on the wall. The suicide news hit him hard and he lost his appetite. He felt revulsion for the examination. But it was the only door for a man of ambition. He was glad that he was well prepared for it this time. He made an excuse and left the table early.

"A headache," Old Man Wong said with a laugh. "The premonition of a great future. What high government official does not have headaches? I never have headaches, therefore I am still a small innkeeper. *Kan pei, kan pei*, drink up!" He raised his wine cup and drank a toast to everybody.

Hung and his study companions spent the next day sightseeing. They first went to the marketplace to see what they could buy for their families. Hung was surprised that the examination did not worry him at all. He only regretted that he had wasted the best part of his life studying the classics, which only gave praise to feudalism and preached loyalty to authority. There were memorable poems and essays by famous poets depicting man's sorrow, woman's love, and nature's beauty, but those were not required studies. How wonderful it would be if the Imperial examination were to cover those subjects instead of only the works of Confucius and Mencius. If he were to write about the plight of the poor and the oppressed, he was sure that words would pour out smoothly under his brush and with feeling. He could compose poems with relish on subjects of beauty and love, or sadness, happiness, and anger. But about the Four Books and the Five Classics, he could recite them backward and rehash them in perfect eight-legged essays, yet they always left him with a hollow feeling of total emptiness. That was what the Imperial examination was all about—a perfect essay that said nothing.

The marketplace was as noisy and crowded as ever. Peddlers carrying baskets or pushing squeaky carts called out their wares with a hand over an ear or by ringing a bell. People haggled over prices at food and clothes stalls. The aroma of herb stews and frying food was overpowering; dogs sat nearby waiting for leftovers or snarling at each other over the bones which customers had sucked clean. Run-kan shouldered in and out of the crowds, craning his neck, looking around anxiously. Hung knew that he was looking for Master Li and his daughter.

There was a large crowd that attracted their attention. They pushed their way to the center and found a big bearded foreigner speaking animatedly in unintelligible Chinese, one hand carrying a thick book and the other hand waving up and down. His voice was deep and loud but nobody understood him. They only watched him curiously, as though he were a strange creature from another planet. Standing beside him was a short, plump man who looked familiar. He was busily passing out copies of a Chinese book that he took from a large pile on a little desk behind him. Hung recognized him after a moment or two. He was Mr. Fei, the mysterious man who wore the foreign felt hat. Mr. Fei caught sight of the three friends; his face brightened and he waved.

As soon as the foreigner had finished speaking, Mr. Fei introduced him as Rev. Issachar Roberts, an American preacher who was spreading the gospel of the universal God, Jehovah. The Reverend Mr. Roberts greeted the three men warmly in Chinese and shook their hands with a strong grip, then repeated the names of his new friends twice to make sure that he pronounced them correctly. He spoke Chinese as though his mouth were full of marbles, but nobody corrected him. He went on talking, inviting them to visit his church, which was being built in the foreign concession in Canton. Mr. Fei asked them if they had read the bibles he had given them at the Five Blessings Inn three years before.

Run-kan and Feng looked blank. Hung, who had only glanced at the first page, still had it at home. His wife had often put it under the oil lamp to raise it while she sewed.

"Yes, I have read it," he lied, trying to be polite. "A wonderful book. Very interesting!"

"Only interesting?" the Reverend Mr. Roberts asked anxiously. He wanted to hear more.

"Please take the second volume," Mr. Fei said, offering each of them a new copy. "This is the New Testament." Taking this opportunity to popularize the Bible, he clapped his hands for attention and told the crowd, "Brothers and sisters, here is a friend who has read the first volume. Let us hear what inspiration he has received from God through the Holy Bible, volume one, the creation of Heaven and earth, and the wisdom of Moses who led the Israelites to the Land of Hope. Mr. Hung, would you be kind enough to tell everybody your glorious experience in reading the Holy Bible? Through the Bible, have you visited God in Heaven and witnessed all his glory? Or has God descended upon you, enlightened you, and inspired you? Has he pointed you in the direction that will eventually lead you to the Kingdom of Heaven and all its glory? Brothers and sisters, let's wash our ears and listen to his words, then follow his steps in embracing the Holy Bible and the gospel of Jehovah!"

Everyone looked at Hung, waiting for him to speak. Hung searched his mind frantically for something to say. He regretted that he had not read a few pages of that thick book that had become his wife's lamp stand. Staring at the anxious faces around him, he took a deep breath. He decided to take the opportunity to speak out, not about the Bible but about something that disturbed him like a chicken bone lodged in his throat.

He cleared his voice slowly, then said in a loud clear voice, "Sisters and brothers, we have constant flood and drought. Our people have died everywhere. We have studied Confucius and Mencius and other sages, but the Kingdom of Heaven is always beyond our reach."

The Reverend Mr. Roberts clutched his bible to his chest and listened, his head nodding, his face gleaming expectantly. He liked what he had heard so far.

Hung went on, "Sisters and brothers, the Kingdom of Heaven will always be beyond our reach if we are always blind to a great threat that is about to ruin our lives. It is worse than war and famine. It is like an invisible monster marauding through the land, destroying everything in its path. Yet some of us are so blind that we don't see the harm and the destruction."

"That is the demon," the Reverend Mr. Roberts commented with a smile. "It is written in the Bible, Book of Genesis, chapter three, verse one."

But the reverend's smile waned as Hung talked on, his hands slashing the air for emphasis. "Do you know what that demon is? Opium! The foreign tobacco. The poison that is draining our silver, weakening our nation, reducing our people to skeletons! Brothers and sisters, wake up! I know of a father who is addicted to opium. Now he is pleading for mercy. He is crying out for help. This is not one man's fight! The crying for help could be the voice of your own neighbors, your own friends. Your own loved ones! The drain of silver is horrendous! One hundred million taels of silver a year ago. This year the amount reached two hundred million taels, a staggering cost, a terrible burden to every one of you! Remember, wool always comes off a lamb. Soon the lamb will be shorn clean. What is left will be only skin and bone. My friends, this is the time for all of us to stand up and shout, 'No opium! No opium! Damn those who bring this foreign tobacco to our shores! This demon, this poison must be stopped! We will fight this war together. Shoulder to shoulder, we will charge!'

"Let us say this to all opium traders: 'No more opium! Death to opium peddlers!' Say it, brothers and sisters. Say it loudly and clearly!"

The crowd, stirred by now, all shouted, "No more opium! Death to all opium peddlers!"

8

As the candidates milled around in the examination compound, Hung studied their faces. There was not a single smile. The general gloominess was depressing, making him wonder if the candidates this year were a different breed. But he spotted a few familiar faces. Most of them returned his polite bow but looked away as though they were ashamed to be seen and recognized. He wanted to cheer them up and tell them how lucky they were to be trying again—not like those who had ended their efforts in despair or even in death. But they walked away quickly, ignoring his attempts to talk.

Feng remained light-hearted. Run-kan was dead serious, looking as though a deep frown had been carved on his brow. While waiting for the gate to open, Run-kan stood in a corner and read, murmuring passages from a book that he had tried to memorize. Hung looked at him and his heart warmed to this little cousin, intelligent, conscientious, a man to trust. He thought that it would be the government's blessing if Run-kan could pass the examination and ascend to the top in his own right.

Hung also thought of Su San-mei. He could hardly wait to see her on the Pearl River, and yet he dreaded finding her working on a flower boat, sitting in a fat man's lap, feeding him with ivory chopsticks and drinking from his goblet. He wondered if she was haggard, her face covered with rouge and her feet hidden by long pantaloons to cover her faked small bound feet. Her clear trilling voice still rang in his ears singing, "Little cabbage, little cabbage . . ." She had never been timid or demure like the traditional Chinese woman. She was capable of exploding like a little firecracker. Perhaps it was that which had attracted him in the first place. With her, he would never say, "Same bed, different dreams."

This time he was assigned a larger cubicle with room for him to exercise. But there were cobwebs hanging in the corners near the ceiling and he saw a mouse scurry away under his desk. Cobwebs and mice did not bother him because they represented luck. Some traditional medicines were even named after them. When he was little, he had taken a pill called "Droppings of the Golden Mouse."

As expected, the subjects of the examination were quotes from the Four Books and the Five Classics. He composed quickly, shaking his head rhythmically as he reread what he had written, punctuating it with red ink dots. Beautiful calligraphy, perfect eight-legged stanzas, meticulous rhyming, and no original ideas that might upset the examiner. When he had finished, he stretched on his narrow bed and thought about his trip to Peking for the examination on the national level. It was too premature to dream of himself as a Han Ling waiting for an appointment from the emperor, but the thought was exciting. He wished to achieve that before his father died. His success seemed to be his father's only goal in life.

The four days passed quickly. Again he composed two lengthy essays and four poems, his examination papers clean and tidy, without one single correction. He handed them in, ate a simple meal of rice and vegetables, and packed his belongings. Then he lay on his bed and waited for the gate to open. When the final gong sounded, the candidates came out of their cubicles with their luggage and lumbered toward the gate, looking pale and tired with reddened eyes. Hung saw a few smiling faces. Smiling himself, he wished them luck and they bowed politely, exuding confidence.

As he went out through the gate, looking for Run-kan and Feng, he wondered who among those happy ones would become a Han Ling, return to his village triumphantly in a sedan chair accompanied by attendants, gong beaters and lantern carriers. He pictured such a glorious return and could not help shivering with excitement.

Back at the hotel, Old Man Wong, having sensed Hung's happy mood, once again ordered extra food for dinner. While proposing a toast to the three scholars, he said the proper lucky words, wishing them each a red-buttoned official cap. The three friends accepted the good wishes with traditional modesty. After a few cups of mao-tai, Hung felt that the whole world was smiling at him. The road to Peking seemed wide open; everything seemed within his grasp—love, ambition, wealth, and glory.

The day that the successful candidates were announced, Hung stayed in his room at the hotel; Feng and Run-kan would report the results to him. He lay on his bed, planning his immediate future and savoring the comfortable feeling of good luck. Now his life looked like a bowl of eight-treasure rice with all kinds of delicious fruits imbedded in it like jewels.

Run-kan and Feng returned before noon. Hung was stunned by their gloomy faces. He stared at them and waited for them to speak.

Run-kan threw himself onto his bed without a word. Feng stamped his feet, hitting his bed with his fist repeatedly and cursing. "Damnation! It is all a waste! Six years of preparation for nothing!" He kept moaning and hitting the bed, agonized by his failure.

Hung felt as if a bucket of cold water had been splashed on him, but he was surprised that his friends took their failure so seriously. He clutched his hands together tightly and mumbled an old saying to calm himself and them. "To achieve scholastic success takes ten years of sitting in front of a chilly window," he said. "We have four more years."

Feng turned to him and shouted, "Yes, we have four more years, but where are we going to raise three thousand taels of silver to buy a name on that golden poster?"

"What do you mean?" Hung asked.

"A candidate threatened to commit suicide this morning if he was not told why he had failed. The yamen clerk told him that nobody would see his name on the golden poster until he had donated three thousand taels of silver. They are selling Talented degrees. For a Han Ling degree it will cost five thousand taels!"

The floating brothels were gay with flowers, lanterns, and music. Hundreds of the flower boats were docked along the Pearl River. From their verandas the heavily powdered courtesans waved and smiled, swaying like willows on their small lily feet. Some luxurious boats, leased by rich customers, sailed back and forth on the river, sculled by sturdy coolies. A few were large enough for a ten-table banquet plus a stage for opera performances. Each carried over a hundred guests who celebrated birthdays or the promotion of a government official. Hired sing-song girls entertained the guests with songs and dances. The first-class singsong girls even composed poems and played moon guitars and flutes. Those who had no literary or musical skills sat on guests' laps, feeding them delicacies with ivory chopsticks and playing finger-guessing games. The least skilled urged the guests to drink up as they refilled their empty cups. All the singsong girls performed their duties with studied happy giggles. Hung had never attended such a party but he had read about them. It was no secret that hiring a flower boat to celebrate an important occasion was a must in high society, a status symbol of the rich and the powerful.

Feeling depressed, he watched the merrymaking on these boats with envy and disgust. The music and the aroma of food, the laughter and clacking of mahjong tiles all contributed to a gaiety that seemed strange in this distressing world. Hung walked along the river bank, reading the names of the flower boats, ignoring the festivities and inviting smiles from the girls.

He found Su San-mei in one of the permanently docked boats, a medium-size gaudy vessel with its name, Half Moon Pavilion, painted on its side. It had the standard reception room in the front and living quarters in the back. The owner, a beefy man who owned three girls, wore a weapon under his loose gown. He sat in a chair in the reception room, picking his teeth and studying his customers' shoes to decide who could afford the best. His "turtle woman" or mama-san, was equally stout. She wore a dark brocade Manchu gown, an easy smile on her heavily painted moon face. Two large gold teeth gleamed between her thick lips.

Hung inquired about Su San-mei. The woman acknowledged a nod from the owner and told Hung that Su San-mei was busy. Hung knew that his shoes did not qualify him for first-class treatment. But he had no time for bargaining. He took out all his silver and asked for only a brief visit. The silver brought a smile to the owner's face and he nodded twice. "Twenty minutes," the turtle woman said, pocketing the money. "Come with me."

Su San-mei was plucking her eyebrows in front of her dresser when the turtle woman led Hung into her small room. Dressed in a red silk blouse and matching pantaloons, her hair decorated with little velvet flowers, she did not look at Hung. After the turtle woman had made her standard speech about how skillful and how beautiful her girls were, she withdrew.

"It is me," Hung said, happy to see her and yet feeling sad.

With heavy paint on her face, Su San-mei looked like one of the paper maidens burned at funerals as companions for the deceased. She recognized the voice and turned sharply. As they stared at each other, tears began to well out of her eyes. Her lips trembled. He took her hands. It was an emotional moment, neither knowing what to say at first. Finally, they called each other's names. She moved to the bed and invited him to sit beside her. Then smiling a little, she dried her eyes and asked about her father and mother.

He decided not to tell her everything. They talked about their families—the goats, the water buffalo they had ridden when they were children, and the brook in which they had washed their feet together and watched the happy schools of fish. She asked about her father again. Knowing that her father would never be able to redeem her, he said, "Don't worry. I will come to redeem you. It is a promise!"

"Oh," she said, looking disappointed. She had hoped that he had come to rescue her. "Why did you come?" she asked. "To take the examination again?"

"Let the examination be damned!" he mumbled angrily. "One day I will abolish it and banish all those eight-legged essay-humming turtle eggs!"

She knew that he had failed it again. "No matter," she said quietly. "I was sold again. In five more years I will be sold again as somebody's maid. I will scrub and wash for the rest of my life . . ."

"Never!" Hung interrupted her. "I will come to rescue you . . . through fire and high water, no matter what, even if I fail to destroy this rotten Manchu Dynasty!"

Su San-mei quickly put a hand over his mouth. "Never say that!" she whispered. "Have you become suicidal?"

"I don't care," he said. "All I care about is how to rescue you."

"You have only twenty minutes," she said, touched. "Do you want me? You have paid for me."

"No, I am not a customer."

She looked at him tenderly, new tears welling out of her eyes.

"I am ready to be rescued now," she whispered. "Both of us can swim well. Why don't we slip into the water and disappear? I will follow you wherever you go."

A knock was heard. The turtle woman shouted outside the door, "Twenty minutes are up."

"He is coming out," Su San-mei called back. Then she lowered her voice and said, "I have saved a few ounces of silver. Many girls have saved a little money and escaped this way. Only a few corpses have been found floating on the river . . ."

Before she finished, the turtle woman pushed the door open and stepped in, a hand outstretched and a broad smile on her round face. "All right, another six ounces of silver and you can stay twenty more minutes."

"I have no more money," Hung said. "Allow me to say good-bye to her. It will not take more than a minute or two."

"That is what you all say," the turtle woman grinned. "Time costs money. To Su San-mei a minute or two are worth an ounce of silver. Do you have brass coins? We will give you two minutes for a string of brass coins."

"No, my pockets are empty."

"Then get out!"

"Leave us alone!" Su San-mei said heatedly.

"Ah Kung!" the turtle woman yelled. Ah Kung, the owner, stepped in, a hatchet in his hand. He glared at Hung and jerked his head toward the door. "Out!" he said ominously.

Hung tried to argue but the turtle woman quickly pushed him through the door. "We don't want trouble. Come back when you have more money. She will wait."

9

Hung coughed and trembled in bed with a high fever. Old Man Wong wanted him to stay a few more days and have an herb doctor examine him, but Hung insisted on going home. The next morning, he was carried in a sedan chair that Run-kan and Feng had hired in Canton. Run-kan and Feng followed the chair, giving Hung food and drink, and seeing that he was comfortable. The all-day journey was slow and torturous, for the sedan chair carriers had to stop every now and then to smoke a pipe of opium. It was not until after dark that they finally reached Happy Valley, welcomed only by some barking dogs.

Back in his room, Hung was still sweating with high fever. His family hovered over him, asking questions and trying to feed him, but he lay on his bed hardly breathing.

"Send for the Taoist priest," Hung Tai said to his eldest son.

By the time Mr. Ting arrived, Hung was delirious, moaning and mumbling things that nobody understood. Mr. Ting believed that he was possessed by an evil spirit. He ordered incense, ghost money, and food offerings. He also drew an incantation on a piece of yellow paper, with a few ancient characters written under it. He burned the incantation to frighten away the evil ghost, burned incense, and offered food to Chung Kwei, the ghost chaser, who protected homes from wronged ghosts who were seeking revenge. For an hour, the priest exorcised evil spirits by striking a bell, sprinkling magic water, and murmuring prayers. Hung twisted and moaned until he finally fell asleep. It was midnight before Mr. Ting left, declaring that Hung had been cured.

Hung had not really recovered. He lay in bed every day staring at the ceiling, speaking little and hardly eating. His parents had been planning his sister's wedding to a silk merchant from Kwangsi Province, Yang Shiu-ching, who visited Kwangtung Province frequently. Since silk had become rare and was almost monopolized by large firms that did business with the foreigners, Yang had given up his trade, stayed in Kwangtung and become a porter, working on the West River. Hung Tai anxiously waited for his son to get well, hoping that the family would not have to postpone Little Treasure's wedding. But Hung's strange illness lingered. Having consulted with Mr. Ting every day, Hung Tai decided to proceed with the happy occasion, a lucky date that had long since been selected from the lunar calendar.

The wedding ceremony was simple, attended by only a few close relatives. A small banquet followed the usual kowtows to Heaven and earth and the ancestral tablets, then three more kowtows to the elders. Times were bad and such minimal ceremonies were excusable, said Mr. Ting.

Hung stayed in bed through it all. But his mother managed to feed him a few morsels of meat from the wedding banquet. At night he was visited by his new brother-in-law, Yang, who sat in a rattan chair beside his bed and chatted with him.

Yang was a square-jawed man, short and muscular, his face pockmarked. But he had saved some money, he was eloquent and knowledgeable, and had charisma. Hung liked him. He seemed to come alive when Yang talked about his plans for his future and Little Treasure's. He was sympathetic about Hung's failure in the examination; he believed it was Heaven's will because the Manchu Dynasty was dying; it had eyes but did not recognize Mountain Tai.

"Heaven is angry with the emperor," Yang said. "Disaster is Heaven's way of punishing a bad ruler. That is why we have constant plagues and famines. The people in my province, Kwangsi, have rebelled many times against bad emperors, weak ministers, and corrupt leaders. It is the will of Heaven that we will eventually put a Ming emperor back on the throne."

Yang also listed many recent events that would help foment rebellion everywhere: the earthquake in Chekiang Province, the drought in Honan and Hopeh, the draining of China's silver reserves by the Western Barbarians, the increased land taxes to be collected in silver, and the sale of scholastic degrees and officialdoms were all signs that signified the demise of the Manchu Dynasty.

"What are your plans?" Hung asked.

"I am going back to Kwangsi with your sister. She is a capable woman. We will do what we can to establish a good business and raise a large family." Then in a lowered voice, he added, "And help put a Ming emperor on the throne."

Hung was impressed. He had seldom met such a vociferous and volatile man. With his scanty bristling moustache, Yang looked older than his age, but Hung secretly congratulated his sister for having married such a capable man whose good qualities more than made up for his lack of education.

Still feeling weak and depressed, Hung stayed in bed. Run-kan and Feng visited him often, telling him what was happening in Kwangtung and some good local news to cheer him up—mainly about births of babies and the release from jail of relatives. Feng, formerly a gregarious man, had changed after the failures in the examination. He had become quiet, serious, a bit retiring, and pedagogical. He began to wear plainer clothes of local material; he was always clean-shaven, his queue well braided and oiled, a contrast to the somewhat sloppy Yang, Hung's new brother-in-law.

Hung was glad. He liked friends who were different. He had always dreamed of being surrounded by men of different talents and character, who offered different opinions and philosophies. Recently he had been reading the two volumes of the foreign Bible which Mr. Fei had given him. One morning while he was reading the Old Testament, Run-kan paid him a visit. His young cousin looked thin and tanned, and there was a tinge of excitement in his voice.

"I just returned from Canton," he said. "Do you know who I saw? Mr. Hu, Master Li, and his daughter, and that big fellow, Golden Rooster. I learned that the Five Blessings Inn is really a gathering place for members of secret societies. Most of the guests are the heads of secret organizations that plan to overthrow the Manchu Dynasty. Master Li and his daughter, Mei Mei, are members of the Heaven and Earth Society in Hunan. Golden Rooster was a pirate and is now training fighters. Old Man Wong wants to know if we are interested in joining an organization. Since we failed our examinations, he thought we would. I told him we will let him know."

Hung asked him why he had visited Canton again.

"I went to see my foreign friend, Mr. Lindley. He wrote to me saying that he was going back to England soon. I decided to pay him

a visit and practice some English, which I have neglected for too long."
He said that he had stayed at the Five Blessings Inn for two nights. He
would have stayed longer if Mei Mei and her father had not been obliged
to return to Hunan so soon. "I am thinking of joining the Heaven and
Earth Society. Do you want to join?"

Hung was noncommittal. The Bible had given him an idea and he
had been thinking of organizing his own society. He had had quite a
few strange dreams in which he had seen himself as the leader of a
national organization engaged in open rebellion.

"Run-kan," he said, "I have had strange dreams recently. When
the time comes, I will tell you about them."

Run-kan shook his head. "No wonder you don't look so good. Avoid
spicy food and you will stop having nightmares."

"Who is Mr. Lindley?" Hung asked.

"A British merchant who sells machine-made fabrics. But he is
sympathetic to China's plight. He is thinking of giving up the fabric
trade and going home. He is a good foreigner. But he likes the stuff in
the cup a little too much . . ."

Hung closed his eyes. He looked weak and tired. Run-kan covered
him with his comforter and left quietly.

Two weeks later, he visited Hung again. He had attended a meeting
of the Heaven and Earth Society; he had seen Mr. Fei again. Mr. Fei
was one of the men who had helped translate the Bible. Recently he
had been arrested for distributing unorthodox learning materials outside
the governor's yamen. Rev. Issachar Roberts, using diplomatic means,
had rescued him. Run-kan had also visited the reverend's new church
in the foreigners' concession in Canton and had received baptism from
the foreign priest. He had also met Rev. Robert Morrison from the
London Missionary Society, who had translated the Bible into Chinese
originally; but he had often used wrong characters, translating "Jehovah"
into "Love to torture China."

"What is Golden Rooster doing?" Hung asked. He was always
curious about the big man with the big laugh.

"He commands a fleet of pirate ships in Ting Lin. Old Man Wong
said that he transports merchandise for the foreigners and robs them
on the side, especially the opium smugglers. He robs them to subsidize

the Triad Society, the parent of the Heaven and Earth Society. As a sideline, he trains fighters and sailors for future uprisings. He is an excellent sailor—knows all the pirates up the coast and is familiar with all the waterways in Southern China."

Hung was fascinated. He was sick and lonely, grateful that Run-kan had become his eyes and ears. All such information was like water to a man dying of thirst. He told Run-kan that he had dreamed about Yen Lo, the king of ghosts in hell. During another recent dream, he had had a horrifying encounter with a tiger. Not all his dreams were bad, however. On one occasion he was carried to Heaven in a sedan chair. While passing through beautiful and luminous palaces, he had been joyfully saluted by multitudes of men and women. In a great palace, he had recognized many sages and kings. Then he had been taken to the golden throne room, a luminous hall of wonderful beauty and splendor. There was soft music and a marvelous scent in the air. Enjoying a floating and soothing sensation, he had found himself standing at the feet of God, a gentle bearded man in a flowing white robe. His face was not clear to Hung's blinking eyes because it was the source of the brilliant light that illuminated the great Heavenly hall. The God's eyes, gazing upon Hung, shone like two bright stars, yet they were kind and compassionate. When God began to speak, Hung immediately sank to his knees and knocked his head repeatedly on the ground, his heart full of love and devotion. While kowtowing, he heard God's words:

I am your God. All human beings are created and sustained by me. They eat my food and wear my clothes, but they do not venerate me; they only worship demons. Hung Shiu-ch'uan, I choose you to correct this wrong. I bestow upon you wings of power and a heavenly sword. I command you to exterminate the demons!

Suddenly Hung closed his eyes. He lay pale and thin, hardly breathing. Alarmed, Run-kan tried to wake him by shaking him and slapping his face, but Hung did not respond. Lotus and Old Mrs. Hung rushed in, calling his name and trying to feed him a spoonful of ginger-root soup.

Hung Tai, hearing the hullabaloo, came in breathlessly. He had been building an extra room in the back of the house, since both of his older daughters-in-law were pregnant.

"Leave him alone, leave him alone!" he said, not worried. "He is having another dream. He has gone through this before."

The women became quiet. Lotus wiped Hung's mouth of the ginger soup, which he had refused to swallow. Old Mrs. Hung, her hands clasped together, murmured a prayer to the Buddha. Run-kan watched quietly, wondering if Hung was dead or having another dream. He grabbed Hung's hand and felt his pulse. Everybody watched Run-kan tensely, fearfully waiting for his response. When a smile broke over Run-kan's face, Hung Tai sighed with relief. "As I said, he is having another dream."

Suddenly Hung's mouth started twitching. "Behold!" he said, his voice clear and strong. "Behold the people on earth. They are crying for help because the demons are torturing them."

He opened his red and tearful eyes, blinked several times, then opened them wide, staring into space. "Behold," he said, getting up from the bed.

"Leave him alone," Hung Tai said as the women tried to help Hung back to bed.

Hung walked a few steps unsteadily. "Behold!" he cried, "the people are rising. The demons are hacking them down! The Emperor of Heaven commands that all men must turn to me for salvation."

While he talked, he staggered out of the room. His family followed him, wringing their hands. Outside the house, Hung steadied himself, breathing hard, his eyes staring. "Behold! The golden figure of God has spoken. I am his Second Son! He has commanded me to exterminate all the demons on earth!" With a battle cry he leapt and kicked like a warrior in a Cantonese opera. "*Sha, sha!*" he yelled in a terrifying voice, wielding an invisible sword, chopping and slashing violently. "Kill! Kill all the demons! No one can withstand a single blow of my sword!"

Hung's two brothers had dropped their chores and rushed over to see what was going on.

"Go call the Taoist priest!" Hung Tai told them, his face whitened by fear. "He is going mad."

| 10 |

Emperor Tao-kuang made a decision: He appointed an antiopium official, Lin Tse-shu, as viceroy to suppress the opium trade in Kwangtung Province. When Viceroy Lin arrived in Canton, he immediately instructed the foreign traders to furnish an inventory of their opium stocks and to pile them on the docks for inspection. He also demanded that they never again bring opium into China. This was exciting news for the Chinese. Hung Shiu-ch'uan, fully recovered, went to Canton to give more antiopium speeches. His last one had been so well received that many newspapers had reported it.

Staying in Run-kan's room, he wrote a series of speeches, injecting some antigovernment sentiment into them, subtle yet clear. He instructed Run-kan to learn the foreigners' reaction to Viceroy Lin's antiopium campaign and their attitudes toward the antigovernment uprisings.

Run-kan went to work with pricked ears but failed to find anything satisfactory to report, except that Viceroy Lin's arrival and his public announcement had caused some grumbling among the foreign dealers. But to everybody's surprise, the big traders meekly submitted their inventories to Lin and had thousands of cases of the "black gold" piled high on the docks without protest. Run-kan heard people say on the street, "You see? The foreigners are all paper tigers."

During the week following the viceroy's arrival, the British and the American traders surrendered over twenty thousand cases of opium. The docks were full of soldiers and curious onlookers. Dozens of inspectors poked and opened boxes and bales that were piled up like mountains.

The morning was hot in mid-May, 1840. Everybody was waiting for Viceroy Lin's decision. It was the day the viceroy would announce what he intended to do with all the "black gold." Speculation was rampant. Some people guessed that the opium would be confiscated and sold to raise money to build China's navy. Others said it would be dumped into the sea. Still others were sure that the opium would be returned to the foreigners if their envoys would kowtow to the emperor in Peking and their missionaries would stop eating children's fried eye-balls.

Hung and Run-kan arrived at the docks early, where a large crowd had gathered. Hung stood on a stool he had brought, and gave an antiopium speech—the same speech he had delivered in the central marketplace sometime ago. He kept only the most subtle antigovernment messages in his speech so that the slow-thinking soldiers and government officials would not react negatively. He did not want to risk arrest while he had this golden opportunity to address a large crowd.

Again the people listened to him with grunts and nods of approval. At the end, they all joined him in some slogan-shouting. Suddenly, Viceroy Lin's orders arrived, a long-winded document written in eight-legged style. Hung summed it up in one word: "Burn!"

Some soldiers lighted torches. Others piled dry straw over the opium. In half an hour the mountains of opium were ablaze. With flames licking the sky and people cheering, it burned all morning. Thousands of people watched it, some taking deep breaths to fill their lungs with the choking smoke and opium smell, which spread over several square miles. Many people winced, groaning at such a loss and declaring it a horrible waste. It could be sold back to the foreigners for enough money to feed the hungry. Most people looked proud, their heads high and chests out, applauding. Quite a few held their thumbs up and shouted, "*Ting hao, ting hao!* This will show the foreign devils!"

Hung mounted his stool and started his second speech. This time he did not delete any anti-Manchu messages. He talked about his dreams and visions, his Heavenly mandate to slay the demons and clean out corruption. As he spoke, his voice rose, forceful and exciting. His audience listened intently, fascinated. He attacked opium openly and the government subtly; his messages went over the heads of a few who watched him with wide-open mouths and puzzled looks. But the majority applauded him at the appropriate moments, smiling and nodding to each other. At the end, they all enthusiastically joined him in shouting slogans. "Slay the demons! Down with the oppressors! Arise! Unite! Charge!"

Before they had finished, Run-kan tugged at Hung's sleeve. Hung looked in the direction that Run-kan had secretly gestured. He saw a government official and several army officers moving toward the crowd. Leaping down from the stool, Hung picked it up and shouldered his way into the crowd. Run-kan followed him closely. Soon they disappeared.

11

A half moon gleamed in the dark sky, playing hide-and-seek with some fast-flying clouds. It reflected on the wide Pearl River. It looked like a lost toy, floating on undulating water that was broken occasionally by riffles from a passing boat.

Suddenly, a dark bundle appeared beside it, rocking slowly back and forth. When a large ship approached, somebody yelled, "There is a body! There is a body!"

The Sea Hawk was a large sailing junk, fifty feet long, sitting tall in the water. The three tattered sails, patched in many places, hung loosely on their ribs. There was almost no wind except for an occasional gentle breeze that sent whiffs of night soil from the shore. In the distance, a rooster crowed. It was an hour before dawn.

Golden Rooster climbed out of his cabin, smacking his lips sleepily. He slept lightly, for a pirate was always on the alert. "Where is it?" he asked as he stepped on deck.

"Over there." The sailor pointed at the bundle that was drifting closer. "Beside the moon. It looks like a woman."

"Fish her out," Golden Rooster ordered, and withdrew to his cabin, grunting and smacking his lips. Inside, he yawned and poured himself a cup of Black Dragon tea from an ancient tea warmer. He rinsed his mouth with the tea and swallowed it, his large Adam's apple going up and down.

Two sturdy sailors came into the cabin carrying a woman. Her wet clothes were taut on her shapely body. They laid her on the floor. Golden Rooster examined her eyes and declared that she was still alive. They flipped her over. Golden Rooster stepped on her back and massaged her with his bare feet until all the water had been drained from her stomach and lungs. She roused. As soon as she realized that she was on a boat, she scolded her rescuers for having saved her. She had wanted to die.

"You are not ready for the other world yet," Golden Rooster said, his voice cracked and stern. "Otherwise Heaven would not have sent you to me." He tossed some clean clothes onto the bunk and ordered, "Change your clothes. I don't want to hear anymore about death. After some hot food, you will be all right. What is your name?"

"Su San-mei," she said, staring at the giant of a man. She studied his clean-shaven head and weather-beaten rugged face. "A pirate," she thought. "Or a smuggler." She was so hungry that she decided to wait until after a hot meal to die.

She was surprised that nobody touched her. After the men had withdrawn from the cabin, she changed into the man's clothes, which were several sizes too large. Soon a sailor delivered a tray of hot food —stir-fried cabbage with some pork in it, hot and spicy, and a heaping bowl of steaming rice. She ate ravenously. The more she ate, the less she desired to die.

She thought about what had happened. The turtle woman had slapped her and she had slapped her back. Later, they had tied her to a chair and the boat owner had started burning the soles of her feet with sticks of incense. The pain was excruciating but she did not cry, knowing that they would stuff some dirty cloth in her mouth if she did. She had seen them torture another girl this way.

They burned her feet until she fainted from the pain. When she woke up, she heard the turtle woman say, "You will not be able to walk for a few days, so forget about escaping. If you behave and do what we tell you, you will eat well and be treated well. You are a good 'money tree.' We want you to be happy and enjoy a comfortable life on this flower boat. No more escape attempts."

She admitted that entertaining impotent elderly men was not much of a chore . . . probably better than washing and scrubbing and slaving in the rice fields. But she had been unhappy. She had missed her freedom; and she was angry with Hung. For three years she had waited for him to rescue her. She had heard about his activities in Kwangtung. He had organized thousands of aborigines who worshipped him like a mountain god. In fact, he had announced to the world that he was the son of a foreign God, all-powerful, with a heavenly mandate to save the oppressed. Su San-mei had often thought about him. If he was that powerful, why had he not come to rescue her as he had promised? Was she not one of the oppressed? The more she had thought of him, the more angry she had become. During her attempt to escape, she had swum almost a mile down the river. As a strong swimmer, she could easily have reached shore, but she had kept swimming toward the Pearl River estuary, her heart shattered and her mind torn between freedom and death. She had lost faith in love and loyalty. As she glanced at the buildings on one side of the river and the trees, vegetables, and rice fields on the other, she had felt no strong desire to land, knowing that the world was dirty, rotten, and cruel. She had wondered if the other world was better. She had kept swimming until she felt cold, exhausted and sinking. While struggling, choking, and swallowing water, she had blacked out.

The burning sensation in her feet had disappeared. By going barefooted all her childhood, she had toughened her feet. She was glad. After finishing her meal, she curled up on the bunk and slept. It was a long, comfortable, deep sleep. When she woke up again, she felt relaxed and refreshed. But then she realized where she was. A pirate boat was no flower boat; now she was facing a fate that might be even worse than before.

She was surprised that nobody disturbed her until the moving sun had shone into the tidy little cabin. It must have been midafternoon. The ship was rocking. From the round window, she could see nothing but a vast expanse of water rising and falling with waves of white foam rolling in the distance. She knew it was not too far from land, for a few sea gulls were following the ship, gliding and dipping outside the window.

There was a knock. A familiar voice called, "Are you awake?"

She got off the bed quickly and straightened her oversized men's clothes. "Yes, I am out of bed."

The door opened and Golden Rooster came in, ducking under the lintel. Su San-mei had never seen anyone so tall and wide. With some black whiskers he could have been mistaken for Chang Hwei, the legendary dark-colored warrior in the opera, *Three Warring Kingdoms*. He looked at her with distaste.

"We'll have to get you some woman's clothes," he said, sitting down on the only chair in the cabin. "Your name is Su San-mei?"

"Yes," she said. She stared at his eyes. It was a lesson she had learned on the flower boat. The turtle woman had taught the girls a few techniques. If they wanted to please, they should cast their heads down, since men liked shy girls. Looking directly into a man's eyes was bold, unwomanlike. Men hated it. "I worked on a flower boat," she added.

Golden Rooster nodded. "I know."

"How did you know?" She looked up, afraid that he might return her to the flower boat owners for a reward.

"From your clothes. I had them thrown overboard. Nobody wears such clothes where we are going."

"Where are you taking me?"

"We are going to Ting Lin. But you don't have to go there."

She thought about going back to Happy Valley. Immediately she changed her mind. Master Woo's collection agent lived not far away. He might sell her to another flower boat. Going to the magistrate's yamen would be worse. For a bribe of a few taels of silver the agent could keep her case from reaching the magistrate. She might even wind up being punished for escaping from a legitimate owner and suffer a bottom-beating. She had seen girls go through that on the Pearl River.

"Where do you wish to go?" Golden Rooster asked.

"Ting Lin," she said without hesitation.

"Do you know who I am?" he asked.

She shook her head.

"I know," he said, looking at her sympathetically. "You don't care one way or the other, do you? But whatever you decide, it will be better than going to Yen Lo's ghost world." He laughed. It was a big loud belly laugh that startled her.

"Who are you, old master?" she asked, having already guessed what he was.

"Don't call me *old master*," he said, scowling. "I am not a yamen official or a landlord. Call me Golden Rooster. I'll call you Su San-mei. Who am I? I am a sailor. I work for the foreign devils."

Su San-mei looked at the kind but ugly face and felt somewhat reassured.

"I transport goods for them," he went on, lighting his long bamboo pipe. "They are maggots growing on rotten meat. One day we'll get rid of the rotten meat. You'll understand soon enough."

Su San-mei already understood. She remembered that Hung had

once referred to the Manchu Dynasty as rotten meat. But she hesitated to reveal how much she knew.

"Come, it's mealtime," he said, rising to his feet. "You'll eat with us."

As he straightened up, his head bumped against the ceiling. With a curse, he rubbed his head then laughed. "Don't worry, the foreign devils have promised me a bigger ship."

|12|

Run-kan knocked on the door of the little white cottage in The Factory, the foreigners' concession outside Canton. There were many foreign companies in The Factory, with mostly foreigners working in small cottages and in tall three-story buildings that were structured like those in Western countries. Since Hung and Feng had left for Kwangsi Province, Run-kan had become a frequent visitor to The Factory. Soon he would join his friends in Kwangsi, where many natives, especially the mountain aborigines, had been actively engaged in subversive activities against the local yamen officials. The famine, the high taxes, and corruption in that province were even worse than in Kwangtung, and the aborigines were easier to recruit, for they had not studied Confucius or Mencius and they were not loyal to an emperor who was thousands of miles away. Above all, they were good fighters; they were in superb physical condition, running up and down steep mountains in their bare feet and eating wild-animal meat, which was good for a man's courage. Snake and wildcat meat were the most popular on their dinner tables. Wildcat made a man limber and snake gave a man patience, always advancing, slowly but steadily. Nobody had ever seen a snake going backward.

Run-kan knew exactly why Hung had chosen Kwangsi as his next destination. But Run-kan had to stay behind to meet with his old foreign friend, Mr. Lindley, who had postponed his trip back to London and had a proposition to make.

He knocked on the door once more. The door opened and a large bearded foreigner smiled at him. "I am David Brown," he said, giving Run-kan's hand a strong brief pump. "Mr. Lindley is waiting for you."

Brown took him to a cluttered room in the back of the cottage. Lindley quickly rose from behind his desk and shook Run-kan's hand warmly. Lindley liked to speak Chinese. Like all foreigners, he spoke

Chinese with marbles in his mouth. He inquired about the health of every member of Run-kan's family. He was a foreigner who had learned all the Chinese customs and courtesy, and he could outdrink any Chinese, downing jars of mao-tai without getting drunk and gallons of tea without going to the outhouse.

"You know why I postponed my trip, don't you, Mr. Run-kan?" he asked.

"Yes, you told me in your letter," Run-kan said. "But I don't see the possibility of a war."

"That's exactly what the Manchu government is thinking. No war. Both the East and the West believe they are only paper tigers. They snarl but they never bite. But the truth is, the West is a bunch of hungry tigers, all capable of biting."

"What is your proposition, Mr. Lindley?" Run-kan asked.

"After I abandoned my textile trade, I thought of retirement. Since the British have started rattling the saber, I won't be able to retire if I want to. So I've decided to remain in the Orient and go into another line of trade—arms and ammunition. Today you can't fight wars with swords and spears. You need guns and cannons. I have already developed several sources of weapons. Mr. Brown here has contact with the secret societies that are in need of weapons. Mr. Brown has opened some markets. I want you to help sell them to the government. That's my proposition. I'm always sympathetic with the Chinese, you know that."

"But I don't know anybody in the government."

Lindley looked at him wide-eyed in surprise. "Didn't you take the Imperial examination? Anyone who passed the Imperial examination is a high government official, a minister of some sort in the Imperial Court. Is that true?"

"Yes, but I failed. I can't even sell the government a straw sandal."

Lindley threw his head back and laughed. "Well, well, in that case you still can work for me. In this business I need a good interpreter and a good consultant who knows how to deal with the Chinese. The Chinese mentality is still a mystery to us. Some people believe that when a Chinese says *yes* he means *yes* or *no*. In other words, all answers are a polite *yes*. It is up to me to find out if it means *yes* or *no*. Is that true?"

"Yes."

Lindley laughed again. "What does that mean, *yes* or *no*?"

"Yes," Run-kan said, laughing with him.

Run-kan wrote to Hung about Lindley's job offer. Hung, by return mail, strongly advised him to take the job for many reasons. "Take the opportunity to learn their policies, to gather information about their activities in China, to study their customs and languages." Run-kan accepted the job and moved to Canton. He rented a small room near the foreign concession and walked to work at Lindley's cottage every day, seven days a week.

In Lindley's office, both foreigners and Chinese merchants trooped in and out. Run-kan heard rumors of increased arms trade and opium smuggling. England was unhappy about the Chinese uprisings, which disrupted trade and violated the Treaty of Nanking. Riots against opium alarmed many large foreign companies at The Factory. There was a rumor that Emperor Tao-Kuang might lift the ban on opium in China. Run-kan saw the excitement spreading in the concessions. Opium smuggling increased and warehouses expanded.

From Chinese sources he also learned that several viceroys in China had petitioned the emperor to change his mind. They even suggested the death penalty for opium traders and smokers. This in turn prompted England to warn China against such extreme penalties. Meanwhile, opium smuggling continued.

Run-kan was writing some Chinese letters for Mr. Lindley, when suddenly gunshots rang out and people were heard shouting and running in the street. He rushed out to investigate. He saw a large crowd trying to hang a man in front of Nelson and Nelson, the largest opium trading company in the concession. A few company guards were firing into the air, trying to disperse the crowd and rescue the Chinese opium trader, while members of the angry mob were trying to nail him to a large wooden cross.

The rioters, more than a thousand strong, beat gongs and drums, brandished swords and spears, and shouted antiopium slogans. They did not disperse until the guards started shooting into their midst. Several of them fell. For a moment there was utter chaos with people running in all directions. Some rushed the guards, others tried to kill the opium trader before he was rescued. Many withdrew to a safe distance, shouting insults. "Kill the opium devil! Damn his mother!"

Now all the guards from the other companies joined the fight. They fired indiscriminately, killing and wounding rioters as well as bystanders. When the turmoil was over, more than a hundred people were dead. The wounded were dragged away. The concession was washed in blood.

Lindley paced in his office, flailing his arms and angrily denouncing the killing of innocent people. Suddenly he plunked down in his chair and gave his desk a triumphant blow.

"Mr. Brown," he said excitedly to the American soldier of fortune, "what did I tell you? Western firearms are the key to victory in any conflict! This riot set an excellent example of what foreign arms can do against inferior bird guns, swords, and spears. How many were in the crowd? A thousand? Two thousand? How many foreign guards? Fifty? A hundred? No matter. All the dead are Chinamen. Only a few guards are bloodied. And I'll bet you a hundred quid that you'll find them dancing and drinking themselves into a stupor at Polly's saloon tonight."

David Brown grunted. He had been bargaining with Lindley about his commission, which was all he was interested in.

"Run-kan," Lindley called. "I want you to write some letters. How many provinces are there in China?"

"Twenty-four," Run-kan said.

"I want you to send a letter to each governor of the twenty-four provinces, telling them how effective Western arms are. Describe this riot scene the best you can. You are a clever writer. I am sure you'll do a good job in selling Western arms to these provinces. I'll tell you what, I'll give you as much commission as I pay Mr. Brown here."

David Brown turned to Run-kan with a grin. "Enough to buy yourself a box of toothpicks," he said sarcastically.

"Now, come, come," Lindley said, giving Brown a friendly slap on his shoulder. "You and I are partners. You have a cut of the profits. Now, let's sit down and count how many secret societies you represent."

With a shrug, Brown resumed his discussion. Lindley poured himself another drink.

In the following two days, demonstrators streamed into the concession. They pelted the large companies with rocks along Thirteen Factory Street and shouted, "Down with the foreign devils! Burn their opium!"

Run-kan started a diary, recording everything he saw and heard. He had promised Hung a regular report.

13

Hung fled to Kwangsi with Feng after several narrow escapes. He promised to keep in touch with Run-kan. Along the way he preached the gospels of God to the aborigines who lived along the Kwangtung-Kwangsi border and planted many seeds for future uprisings.

Run-kan worked in Lindley's office, secretly gathering information, which he kept in a diary. He wrote in sesame-size characters to save space so that the diary would not be bulky and could be carried in a small hidden pocket in his clothes.

A foreigner's office was different from a Chinese office in a yamen, where people sipped tea and chatted about nothing. In Lindley's office, people came and went, looking tense and worried, filling the air with tobacco smoke. Lindley seemed to work long hours, a cigar box on his left and a bottle of whiskey on his right. On hot days he worked in shirtsleeves, his shirt open, showing a mat of black curly hair on his chest. Run-kan kept a distance from him in his office to avoid his liquor-breath. He discovered that the foreign whiskey tasted and smelled better than mao-tai, but both became equally objectionable when turned into breath.

He enjoyed working at his small desk outside Lindley's office. His English was improving, for Lindley spoke English when he was busy and Chinese when he was not, and lately he had been extremely busy most of the time. David Brown was a frequent visitor. He and Lindley often talked alone. Run-kan had been wondering what kind of secret deals they were making. Lindley had not only abandoned his textile business, he had also persuaded a few small opium traders to work for him selling arms. Run-kan had overheard him tell his visitors, "Mark my words, there will be wars. Selling arms is the only business a bloke worth his two pence should get into."

Lindley also talked about his conscience a lot. "Besides," he often said in a loud voice, "you're poisoning a whole race by selling opium. Doesn't it bother your conscience?" When he talked to a Chinese trader, Run-kan could hardly understand him, for his accent was so thick.

The secret societies' uprisings in Kwangtung had been switched from antigovernment to antiopium. Run-kan attended a meeting called by Rabbit Kao, a professional gardener who headed the Triad Society in Canton. It was an initiation meeting. The new members, following an old ritual, took an oath in front of Kwan Kung, the god of war, and drank their own blood in a wine goblet. Waving a three-star flag, they pledged to fight with no fear of death. Rabbit Kao was a popular leader who joked that he could outrun anybody in victory or in defeat. He was also a fast talker, very persuasive. With his self-deprecating jokes he was able to recruit everybody—peasants, coolies, textile handicraftsmen, masons, and vagrants from the Canton slums.

The day after the initiation, the Triads assembled on a small hill outside the city, drilled and discussed strategy. The following day, they marched, unfurling flags that read: QUELL THE FOREIGN IMPERIALISTS!

They beat drums and gongs, wielded homemade weapons—spears, tridents, long-handled swords, and rattan shields. Many carried bird guns and matchlocks. A few were armed with Western weapons; Run-kan was sure that they were supplied by Lindley through David Brown. They attacked a British encampment nearby.

The British were having breakfast. Suddenly they heard thunderous battle cries and saw people sweeping toward them under brightly colored banners. The British land force commander, Sir Hugh Gough, hurriedly ordered the bugler to sound the signal for assembly. He divided his forces into three groups for counterattack. Two thousand men, armed with muskets and artillery, charged. The Chinese lured them back into their own territory. When Sir Hugh sensed the danger, he ordered a retreat, but it was too late. Five thousand armed villagers, beating gongs and drums, roared out of hiding and attacked. Suffering heavy losses, the British broke through the lines at two points and beat a hasty retreat. Pursued by the Chinese, some British hid under cucumber trellises. Other fell into muddy rice fields. Quite a few laid down their arms in surrender. It was the first victory in their war with foreign forces.

Following the victory, Run-kan discovered that the secret societies' uprisings increased sharply against both the foreigners and the government. Many panicky viceroys petitioned the emperor to legalize opium to appease the foreigners. They believed that it would be better to yield to the foreign powers than to lose the throne to the bandits. One viceroy even suggested that in case of a foreign invasion, the defending armies, instead of fighting, should present the invaders with cattle, sheep, wine, and other food. "Preferably no pigs," he added knowledgeably. "A lot of cows, because foreigners love cows' milk."

But the uprisings infuriated the opium smugglers. They asked Charles Elliot for help. Elliot, the chief British trade superintendent, notified all the foreigners in the foreign concession to prepare for battle.

"So you see?" Lindley told Run-kan after a swig from his bottle. "The peasant uprisings are an excellent pretext for a British invasion."

"Pretext?" Run-kan was puzzled.

"Britain has been frustrated in dealing with China," Lindley said. "Traders and missionaries suffer all kinds of travel restrictions, many important seaports are still closed to foreigners, foreign envoys are still requested to kowtow to your emperor. British and American opium was burned. A British encampment was attacked. Prick up your ears and open your eyes, Mr. Run-kan. A war will be declared . . . a war that will open China up. Vultures and scavengers from all over the world will swoop down to share the carcass. This war will open all kinds of opportunities for profiteers. It's a shame but what can you do? You can't change a country's policies. You might as well become a scavenger and pick up a few crumbs."

Lindley held meetings with weapon traders every day and kept his telegraph machine busy. David Brown was seen in his office night and day. Run-kan discovered that the big foreign traders had surrendered their opium on that fateful day in mid-May for a good reason: They had hoped that Viceroy Lin would burn it so that the British could send more troops to China. The people's attack on the British encampment was another welcome event, making the pretext of invasion even stronger. So far all the events had proved Lindley's theory true and accurate.

He offered more predictions: "Elliot has assured me that nobody is going to lose a penny. After the war we'll get all the money back. China will pay war indemnities, penalties, and compensations for trade losses. I understand you are a government hater, are you not?"

Run-kan nodded hesitantly. He wondered how Lindley knew.

"You don't have to hide your inner secrets from me," Lindley said. "I am sympathetic to all you rebels. I do think your government is rotten. So be a maggot, my dear boy, and feast on it as much as you can."

From Lindley's office Run-kan learned what was going on in the foreign concession. Superintendent George Elliot was made full pleni-potentiary to China. His strategy was, "Keep cool. Surprise the enemy." His strongest support was from Jardine Matheson and Company and Nelson and Nelson, the most powerful opium trader, second only to the East India and China Association. Together they planned the war.

Run-kan found Lindley's predictions of war plausible; they were worth reporting to Hung. He wrote: "A lion will kill a sick giant; carcass rots and maggots grow. There is money to be made."

14

Charles George Gordon liked the army but hated the officers' full-dress uniform with its gold braid and scarlet waistcoat. When he was ordered to buy one, he immediately studied the possibility of altering it to a civilian tunic he might use when he retired from the service. He was frugal, a trait he traced to his Highland ancestry, and he was not ashamed of it. At home he enjoyed eating leftovers and believed that clothes should be worn by the oldest and then handed down to the youngest, as long as the knees and the elbows held up.

However, he mellowed after he graduated from the military academy, and he was determined to carve a career in military or missionary work. Faraway lands still held him spellbound and he had not stopped writing to his father's influential friends, trying to wangle a position overseas, especially in the mysterious Orient. If he could never be a successful officer, as that rat at the academy had prophesied, he would then tramp the Malasian jungles or the Shanghai slums spreading God's gospels with the Bible in one hand and a sword in the other. If he could not correct injustices and wrongs in the deprived areas of the world with messages from the Holy Bible, he would try to do it with his sword. The British saber was still the most powerful. Great Britain had rattled it all over the world and various kingdoms had crumbled. Burma, India, and Malasia had hoisted the British flag and their peoples now scurried around doing their Western masters' bidding.

Gordon had been studying everything about the Orient that he could lay his hands on. He had been especially interested in the Opium War in China. He read the war's history as he did the Bible, taking sides as members of Parliament argued the pros and cons of the war's wisdom. He was not ashamed to say loudly, even today after so many years, that his sympathy was with the enemy, China. He abhorred the motive of that war—to force China to buy opium so that Britain could earn silver to buy China's tea and silk. To Gordon it was highly immoral; it was like robbing a man, buying poison with the money, then killing him with the poison.

He had seen a picture of a Chinese opium addict lying in the slums, puffing away on his bamboo pipe, oblivious to rats that were gnawing on his dead child nearby while skinny dogs snarled at each other over his wife's bones. He swore that if such an immoral war were waged again, he would rather go into another line of work to ease his conscience. Fighting the world's evils as a missionary was his first choice.

Britain fought the Opium War twice in China and won both times, resulting in the signing of the Nanking Treaty and the Tientsin Treaty. China ceded Hong Kong island and other territory in the first Opium War and was forced to lease the New Territories in the second. China paid heavy war indemnity and compensation for opium loss and other losses of the Western merchants. China also opened five important seaports—Amoy, Foochow, Ningpo, Shanghai, and Canton—in which foreigners could reside and trade freely. China surrendered its own tariff rights and judicial rights. When a British subject committed a crime in China, China had no power to punish him; the matter had to be handled by the British consulate, which, in many instances dismissed such cases with a reprimand and a fine of ten quid. Gordon had written many letters to newspaper editors condemning such unequal treaties, accusing Britain of violating China's sovereignty and turning the country into a semicolony. But none of his letters ever saw print.

He wrote to the Reverend Mr. Issachar Roberts, the American missionary who had published many articles recounting the Opium War in scrupulous detail. Gordon sent a letter similar to the one he had written to Father Theodore Flanagan many years earlier asking the Presbyterian missionary if he could use a British young man as his assistant in China. From Roberts's articles he knew that the American missionary was not a spy, nor was he an adventurer hiding under God's cloak. He had written many dull, lengthy articles about China in religious magazines, which Gordon had read in the public libraries. The Reverend Mr. Roberts had gone through the Opium War as an observer and had reported it in detail with comments and footnotes. Gordon, keenly interested in the subject, had read the dissertations like a hungry man eating a tasteless meal. It was Roberts's comments in footnotes that sometimes lightened his ponderous prose. All his footnotes were numbered and printed at the bottom of each page. Gordon sometimes glanced through the texts but read every word of the footnotes, such as:

Comment 1: Britain's China policy is simple: a bloody beating first and explanation later.

Comment 2: Britain's first invasion force includes 16 men-of-war with 540 cannons, 20 transports, 4 armed steamers, 4000 men, and Admiral George Elliot, whose only experience on the high seas has been to sit in a deck chair and watch the seagulls. He bravely let the cannons do the talking and won easily without getting out of his chair.

Comment 3: The Union Jack, unfurled so near Peking, alarmed many ministers in the Imperial Court. One of them, who had never seen a ship except Chinese junks, reported to Emperor Tao-Kuang, "In view of the enemy's sturdy warships spitting fire and cannons roaring like thunder, the war will be hard to win." He is as ignorant of Britain as George Elliot is ignorant of China.

Comment 4: Emperor Tao-Kuang was so frightened of Britain's fire-spitting ships that he removed Viceroy Lin, the opium burner, and appointed Ki Shen, the Imperial Uncle, to negotiate peace. Ki Shen tried to humor Admiral Elliot with delicacies and wine, which the admiral tossed into the sea to see if fishes would belly-up.

Comment 5: Admiral Elliot was finally humored when Ki Shen dismantled defense installations, cut down marine forces, and disbanded the "water braves," who had done most of the fighting. Ki Shen even invited the British Admiral to send his skiffs to reconnoiter China's inland waterways. This was like inviting a wolf into a chicken coop. That is why China ceded Hong Kong. But Emperor Tao-Kuang regarded the loss of Hong Kong as a loss of his Imperial face. He ordered that Ki Shen be hauled back to Peking in chains. Ki Shen should have dismantled more defense installations instead of giving up that rocky little isle called Hong Kong.

Comment 6: The British, annoyed by China's unpredictable

policies, started rattling their sabers again. The emergency saved Ki Shen from being sent back to Peking in chains. The Emperor ordered him to fight or negotiate. Choosing fighting at first, Ki Shen lost all his ships. When he hoisted the white flag, the British Admiral promptly occupied Canton and demanded a ransom for the city—nine million taels of silver. He should have negotiated first. A welcome banquet for the British conquering hero would have saved nine million taels, a sum to be paid by the Chinese people. "All wool comes off the lamb," as the Chinese used to say in tears.

Comment 7: All the Imperial forces were defeated. Many brave generals and admirals were killed because of poor strategy and uncertain policy. In Hsin-hsiang peasants organized 500 "water braves" to fight their own war; in Pao An people built flotillas of "fire rafts" to make night raids on the British warships. It was like a school of shrimps attacking a shark.

Comment 8: Mass discontent and anger mounted rapidly; secret societies joined hands with peasants and laborers and launched united attacks against the invaders. Alarmed again, Ki Shen decided to humor his old enemy and friend, Admiral George Elliot. He declared martial law and posted notices in Canton prohibiting resistance. This further angered the masses, and fierce fighting flared up in San Yuan Li Village near Canton. The British armchair Admiral enjoyed nothing better than counting enemy dead. Waves and waves of brave Chinese have become cannon fodder. China's policy of, "talk talk, fight fight," finally did her in.

Gordon discovered something else in the library that attracted his attention. A British journalist reported that a crazy man had started a holy war in China. He called himself the Younger Brother of Jesus Christ and declared that he had a mandate to slay demons on earth.

Gordon searched for more information about this man but nobody had written about his background or sanity. Most journalists thought he was a religious fanatic who was trying to overthrow the Manchu Dynasty. But numerous such fanatics had staged uprisings in China for the same purpose. Most of them had wound up with their heads chopped off. As a Christian, this man aroused Gordon's curiosity more than the others had. He wondered what the man was like.

Gordon wrote to Roberts again. By now he had developed an insatiable desire to go to China. Britain's war with China had not concluded. The military were still rattling their sabers, warning China to honor the treaties she had signed with the Western powers. One violation of the terms would immediately bring more men-of-war to her coast. According to Western analysts, the emperor did not know what to do. His Majesty was torn between two factions in the Imperial Court, one advocating peace, the other supporting resistance.

"Fight to the death," was the latter's slogan.

Gordon wished he knew the answer. The whole China affair was such a bloody mess and he had a yearning to go there to pick up the pieces.

The Reverend Mr. Roberts's reply finally arrived: He wanted Gordon to submit a brief biography, stating his experience, philosophy, and ambitions. "No lengthy description of your family tree or detailed list of your work," Roberts said. "I am more interested in your personality and character. In addition, end the biography with some physical description of yourself."

Gordon spent a whole night writing and rewriting his biography. He was so anxious to give Roberts the right impression that he found the task like pulling his own teeth. He started by writing a first-person narrative, but it sounded overly egotistic. Changed into the third person, he began to feel more comfortable. Finally, at dawn, he finished the torturous composition:

Although Gordon is proficient in engineering, the dull nature of the work has no appeal for him. He is adventurous, always wondering what chance he has to work in the Orient as a missionary. He likes to mingle with primitive natives, wearing their clothes and eating their food with bamboo sticks.

He was moved from one army camp to another while growing up; therefore he proved to be a man of uncanny courage, with boundless energy. Besides having a wry sense of humor, he is impatient with anything dull and intolerant of stupidity. Rather than waiting for the ferry, he prefers to wade across the river in his clothes.

He dreams of becoming a trusted friend of the primitive people and a commander of irregular troops if he cannot become a missionary. His faith in God and country never falters; he is capable of humility and love, hoping to be a soldier saint, a bit eccentric perhaps and not at all interested in money or women.

His father is a Lieutenant General from a Scottish Highland clan, tight with money; his mother is a puritanical lady from a rich London family, even tighter with money but generous with love. Inherited traits: indifference to fear, boisterous, and high-spirited but religious, suspicious of one-legged army commanders, resentful of injustice.

He lives within his income; he always knows that he is in the hands of God.

He has vivid blue eyes; he always searches the inner soul, with a curious mind. He is serious and precise, always pays his bills, is indifferent to discomfort. He dislikes all aristocrats. Sometimes he hates shaking hands with them, especially the shabby ones, for their hands are always sticky. He is rarely sick and is incapable of fatigue.

At twenty-two years of age, he is slight and wiry, five feet nine inches tall, full of nervous energy. His hair is red and curly, he wears a small mustache and whiskers from ear to jaw; his voice is sweet and gentle, his bearing modest and kind. All in all, he is considered fairly attractive without obvious blemishes, mentally or physically.

He ended the biography with a sigh. When he read it, he winced. But he was no writer, only a military man. "It will do," he told himself, and signed it with a flourish.

15

Ting Lin, lush with pines and tall brush, sat among other isles off the Kwangtung coast like a hidden jewel, beautiful but hard to find. The harbor was surrounded by layers of mountains on the mainland and some large islands off the coast. It was deep and spacious enough for ocean-going junks and steamships to anchor and trade illegal merchandise. Pirates and smugglers, if not living on their vessels, made Ting Lin their temporary home.

Golden Rooster had settled in a hut behind a mud wall that was thick enough to ward off a small cannonball. In the back he had built two escape routes. One led to sea and the other to the hills. In the harbor, a cove was tucked away close to his camp. It was the best hideaway for pirate ships. Through years of pirating and robbing rich merchant ships, Golden Rooster had acquired sixteen large junks and dozens of sampans, which also served as living quarters for some of his men and their families. The single men lived in huts which dotted the hills, increasing in number every year, for Golden Rooster also trained fighters for secret societies.

Su San-mei found life on Ting Lin fascinating. Golden Rooster treated her well. At first she was afraid that he might take her as a concubine, but to her surprise he adopted her as a daughter. He even chopped a man's head off for attempting to rape her. After that, his glare was sufficient to stop any man from even stealing a glance at her.

She shared the main hut in the all-male camp. Her room faced Golden Rooster's, her window looking out to a sheer cliff. Wearing men's clothes and barefooted, she resembled a good-looking young man more than a woman. But she decorated her room with many feminine touches. There were always fresh flowers in earthen vases and handpainted colorful fans nailed to the matted walls. And her room was the neatest, with her bed carefully made and dresser spotless. Incense was burning constantly, filling the room with a pleasant camphor scent.

For almost a year she lived a busy life, surrounded by smugglers and pirates, all ruthless men who were famished for a woman's flesh. Besides cooking and washing for Golden Rooster as a filial daughter, she joined the secret societies' training program. Golden Rooster personally taught her the popular martial arts—Shao Ling Fist and Twelve Ways of Kicking. In training sessions she had defeated most of the men. She also trained in modern weapons—guns and artillery supplied by a big-hearted American named David Brown who was known on the isle as The Foreign Devil.

David Brown was well liked. He lived in a hut close to the main hut. He and Golden Rooster met often to discuss business and drink mao-tai together. Both men had an ocean capacity for Chinese liquor. At each meeting they would consume half a dozen jars without getting drunk.

Brown did not mind being addressed as The Foreign Devil, which had become his permanent nickname, as it was always spoken with fondness and a smile. He spoke good understandable Chinese and laughed frequently. His appetite for spicy Chinese food was enormous and he ate like a Chinese coolie, smacking his lips and belching to show his appreciation of good food. He never asked what he ate. When told what he had swallowed, he would shrug or laugh and help himself to more. He liked snake and armadillo stew the best and wildcat meat next. Whenever he was offered those special dishes he would rub his hands eagerly with a happy sigh and reach for soy sauce. He would pour soy sauce over his rice and go to work, hitting his rice bowl with his chopsticks once in a while to show his appreciation.

Su San-mei loved to cook for him because he ate with such appetite. Whenever Golden Rooster entertained The Foreign Devil, he always ate more, too. She often wondered how Brown looked without his big beard, which covered almost half his face. He had very strong even white teeth; he cracked lobster shells and walnuts with equal ease, making her wince. He not only enjoyed her cooking but also openly praised her beauty, which no other man dared, for praising a woman's beauty in front of her was deemed indecent, indicative of having a dirty mind. Nobody took offense when The Foreign Devil did it, however, because they all understood that foreign devils had different standards and customs.

While praising Su San-mei's food, Brown would sometimes laugh and say, "When are you going to marry me?" Su San-mei never answered that question, wondering if he was serious or joking. Besides, no woman would discuss matrimony so openly. She found him interesting, but she certainly would not marry a man with such a bushy beard. Sometimes such a question made Golden Rooster glance between them with widened eyes. When Su San-mei cast her eyes down without response, Golden Rooster would laugh and say, "Not until I've robbed a few more foreign devils' ships. Dowries cost money." Both he and Brown would laugh uproariously, as though the whole thing were only a joke. No matter how often they joked, Su San-mei felt safe with Brown; The Foreign Devil had never attempted to touch her, nor even look at her with hungry eyes, which she could easily recognize after years of dealing with men.

Brown and Golden Rooster held meetings more often after the Opium War, discussing smuggling, pirating, and uprisings. By eavesdropping on their conversations, Su San-mei learned that they not only trained fighters, they also supplied smuggled weapons to the White Lotus Sect, the Heaven and Earth Society, the Big Sword Brotherhood, and The Triads all over Kwangtung and Kwangsi Provinces. Occasionally Hung's name was mentioned. Whenever she heard it, her heart ached. Since arriving in Ting Lin, she had tried to forget Hung, telling herself that Hung was a heartless man who had never intended to rescue her. By now he had probably forgotten about her altogether. But somehow Hung still kept popping up in her mind. She could still hear his voice saying that he would rescue her from fire and high water no matter what. Now that she had escaped without his help, she harbored a secret desire to show him that she was not helpless and that she was happy. She was also anxious to do something daring that he would hear about.

While washing rice bowls in the kitchen one evening, she heard Brown and Golden Rooster planning a large delivery of arms to the Triad Society in Canton. Obviously it was an important trip, for they were to use the Sea Hawk, the largest and best-armed junk in Golden Rooster's fleet. It had eight sails and four cannons and could carry two hundred tons of cargo. After she had put the bowls away, she went to the middle room where the two men were discussing the trip. She blurted out, "I want to go, too."

Both men stared at her. "Go where?" Golden Rooster asked.

"To Canton with you," she said.

Golden Rooster looked flabbergasted. "What? Do you think this is a pleasure trip?"

"I've learned how to handle Western weapons, including firing a cannon."

"Why not?" Brown said quickly. "If she's a good shot."

"I'm good. Besides, I can fight with bare hands or swords like any of your sailors."

"That'll be most helpful," Brown said enthusiastically.

While Golden Rooster was grimacing, Su San-mei pointed a finger at him and said, "Father, once you told me that I'm equal to two good men. Didn't you say that?"

"I'm a turtle's egg to have said that," Golden Rooster replied, shaking his head in disgust. "The answer is *no*. We have never taken a woman on a smuggling trip."

"Why do you object to taking a woman, Father? I can cook and wash and sew, which is more than a sailor can do."

"Hey, Golden Rooster," Brown said, "why not? Her cooking will make us happy."

"What about the danger?" Golden Rooster said. "What about the inconvenience? What about luck?"

"What has luck got to do with it?" Brown asked.

"A woman is bad luck on a warship. The men won't like it."

"Who's going to treat her like a woman if she wears men's clothes and has a bit of dirt on her face? Tell your men she's a mascot."

"No! No! No!" Golden Rooster said, shaking his head.

While the two men argued, Su San-mei looked between them anxiously, busily thinking of something that would help change Golden Rooster's mind. Golden Rooster was indulgent, but if he said three *nos* in one breath, the nail was hammered down. She wondered if she should resort to using a woman's powerful weapon—tears. She had almost never cried in all her life, except when saying good-bye to Hung at Master Woo's house in Flower County many years ago. Those had been real tears. Now she would have to smear a bit of hot pepper into her eyes to cry, and she was ready to do it. She would do anything to change Golden Rooster's mind.

"Hey, Golden Rooster," Brown said, "you are a stubborn fellow and it's no use arguing with you. Let's flip a coin. The Chinese character side comes up, you win. The Manchu character, I win. Fair enough?"

"No, no." Golden Rooster shook his head resolutely.

Su San-mei waited. The scales seemed to tip slightly. Golden Rooster had reduced three *nos* to two.

"Listen, Rooster," Brown went on, "this shipment is mine. It's my merchandise and your ship. We stand toe to toe and face to face. We're equal. I want your daughter on the ship. Let the coin say *yes* or *no*."

With that he fished out a coin and flipped it. He let it drop onto the dinner table. The coin rolled a short distance and fell flat in front of Golden Rooster's darkened teacup.

"Manchu characters," Brown said with a smile.

The Sea Hawk sailed before dawn loaded with British muskets and ammunition which were covered with bales of cotton from the Sunshine Cotton Company. The small arms had been purchased from Lindley through David Brown, whose fictitious Sunshine Cotton Company had smuggled opium and arms before, but most of the time he had used only sampans. This was his biggest haul.

Su San-mei did her best to prepare the meals for the twenty-four-man crew in the small, hot galley, hating it. But the adventure excited her. She was sorry that Golden Rooster was not too happy, although he grumbled less at every meal and finally admitted that he had never eaten so well during a smuggling trip.

The crew, all superstitious desperadoes, did not protest her presence. Most of them believed that she was The Foreign Devil's mascot; any bad luck that she brought onboard would be The Foreign Devil's. Besides, the food was good.

The sea was calm and the traffic heavy. Sailing junks and ocean-going vessels dotted the clear blue water, with sampans floating around them like little water bugs. After the Opium War, five Chinese ports had been opened to foreign trade without restriction. Machine-manu-factured merchandise flowed in, tea and silk poured out, and opium was smuggled into the country in large quantities. China customs boats still patrolled the sea and the inland waterways, examining suspected ships unless they flew the British flag. Pirates were as active as ever robbing everything except warships. Their favorite targets were the East India Company's opium boats. The Opium War had almost legalized opium in China and a great many more Chinese had become addicted. They puffed and inhaled it for extra energy, resulting in soaring silver value and more sunken cheeks and hollowed eyes among the populace.

When the Sea Hawk sailed through the Tiger Gate toward Canton, a customs boat was sighted. The crew hoisted the Union Jack on the Sea Hawk's main mast and David Brown donned his American Revolutionary War uniform, which he had bought from a New York theatrical company during his acting days. He had always wanted to revisit China, where he had been born during his parents' sojourn as Presbyterian missionaries. While the large British flag flapped in the wind, he planted himself at the bow in his uniform and triangular hat, his legs apart and his arms akimbo, striking a figure as the ship's captain.

But the customs boat did not speed by. It approached the Sea Hawk gingerly, with the chief inspector looking at it through a pair of field glasses. The inspector, who had familiarized himself with all kinds of British uniforms during the Opium War, had some doubts about Brown's attire. To him, all white men looked alike, but this foreigner's uniform looked nothing like that of a British sea captain. He ordered the Sea Hawk to stop.

Golden Rooster, after a quick conference with his men, decided to obey. They had more important missions than just smuggling weapons and deemed it unwise to fight. David Brown also calculated the risk of fighting. A cannonball might explode his ammunition and set the ship on fire. It was foolish to lose it all when a hundred taels of silver stuffed into the inspector's pocket might easily solve the problem.

But the bribery failed to work, to Brown's surprise. When the inspector and his five deputies, all armed with the latest British muskets, discovered the ship's real cargo, they seized it. Golden Rooster surrendered meekly, already planning his escape. He knew that the Triad Society, with members planted everywhere, would be waiting for the shipment and they might already have prepared for such an emergency. It was the largest secret society in China, with branches in every major city. The members communicated in secret code, and information flowed quickly among them. The seizure of the Sea Hawk would alert their Canton headquarters and they would undoubtedly take immediate measures to save the shipment and rescue the crew, who had all joined the society and drunk their own blood from silver goblets.

The jail was almost empty because the only crime the government prosecuted vigorously was rebellion. Rebels were usually beheaded on the streets without even going to jail.

Having discovered Su San-mei's real sex, they put her in a separate cell while Golden Rooster, David Brown, and the crew were thrown into one large cell. Golden Rooster remained calm until after he recognized one of the jailers as a Triad. They communicated with several finger signals. To avoid suspicion, Golden Rooster became boisterous, cursing and singing and banging on the iron bars with his head. He demanded to be executed immediately so he could join his ancestors in Yen Lo's ghost world.

When Su San-mei heard his demand, she began to panic. She was not ready to die yet. And if she must, she would not accept such a fate without a struggle. Life was more precious now, and her desire to perform a great deed was getting stronger . . . a deed that would impress everybody, especially Hung. She must break out of jail at any cost.

"Eh, older brothers," she heard Golden Rooster's cracked voice yelling in the larger cell, "feed us something good before we die. How about a shark's fin dinner? You jailers would not begrudge us a last good meal, would you, eh, older brothers?" She heard him laugh, a laugh that sounded like a rooster's crow. It was cheerful and full of hope. She wondered if Golden Rooster was waiting for a chance to break out, too. She knew him well by now. He was a man who would never accept adversity without a fight. But the Jade Emperor from Heaven would not just come down and open the jail door for them. They had to open it themselves, and they had to do everything they could to help each other.

Frantically she searched her mind for a way to help, hoping that Golden Rooster was doing the same. Locked in a thick-walled cell, she knew that her martial-arts skills were no help; nor were her tears. Suddenly she remembered a woman's best weapon. Its power had been proven in history and in famous stories. Many brave kings and generals had succumbed under a woman's "pomegranate skirt," as the old saying went. Why not use it to conquer a few jailers?

She started to sing, wriggling her body seductively. When the dozen jailers were attracted to her cell by this peculiar behavior, she began to disrobe, first taking off her blouse, then her tight bodice, baring her round white breasts. She bounced them a few times, causing a chorus of *ahs* among the gaping jailers, who stared at her hungrily, swallowing hard. A few laughed, encouraging her to take off more. She gyrated, smiling and squeezing her breasts, her eyes blinking seductively while she prayed that Golden Rooster would take action before she was obliged to take the next step—removing her pantaloons.

Watching her and almost driven insane by such a sight were all the guards except the Triad member. He opened the large cell door quietly and led the prisoners to the guardhouse. When the guards discovered the jailbreak, it was already too late. The pirates had grabbed Western weapons from the guardhouse and started firing at the panicked jailers. Firing and running, the pirates escaped through the back door. Golden Rooster rescued Su San-mei, threw his tunic over her and they followed the others. David Brown brought up the rear, firing two pistols at the few guards in pursuit.

Outside the prison compound dozens of Triads were waiting. They whisked the escapees away to a hiding place nearby. It was the Five Blessings Inn, the secret meeting place of all the secret societies.

Meanwhile, hundreds of spectators gathered on the docks to witness the public burning of the opium that had been seized on the Sea Hawk. The fire licked the sky and the smell reached the whole city of Canton. Sniffing with her wrinkled nose in the Five Blessings Inn, Su San-mei said, "Opium? It smells more like burning cow's dung."

"It is cow's dung," Golden Rooster said, puffing calmly on a borrowed bamboo pipe. "The Triads already have the real merchandise. They have to burn something."

16

Hung found the aborigines in Kwangsi Province congenial, honest, and trusting. They made a living by catching snakes in the mountains and selling them to the Cantonese, who believed that snakes were one of the greatest tonics in the world.

The West River, the main waterway between Kwangtung and Kwangsi, was full of junks and barges, with small inns and eateries providing necessities for snake traders on both banks. During the past several years, Hung had traveled along the river many times with Feng, spreading the gospels of Jehovah and making a few taels of silver buying and selling snakes on the side.

In Kwangtung, their religious efforts had often met with angry rejection. Run-kan, who had made friends with the foreigners, told them that they must revise their gospel teaching to include the worship of ancestors. He said that years ago a British Jesuit priest, Father Hansen, had been bodily thrown out of Canton because he accused the Chinese people of worshipping dead ancestors and idols. For a while Hung and Feng preached Christianity without attacking idol worshipping; thus they were able to convert more people and instigate a few small peasant rebellions against their landlords. Some worried landlords started a rumor, as Hung's reputation grew, that he had written many subversive songs, such as: "Days Are Hard," "Soup Is My Meal," and "Death to the Emperor." Another rumor detailed how he had made a peasant girl pregnant, and her father, unable to marry her off, had been obliged to sell her into prostitution. A third rumor was the most damaging, saying that he was spreading a foreign religion, which required a ritual bathing in the river in the nude.

When some border district yamens of both Kwangtung and Kwangsi learned about his subversive activities, they issued an order for his arrest. That was when he and Feng left Kwangtung and moved farther inland.

After roaming along the West River for three years, they finally settled in Jin Tian, a small mountain town where the aborigines embraced Christianity happily. Hung preached a Kingdom of Heaven full of everlasting happiness where all believers in God would eventually go; he described the demons in this world that God had mandated him to slay with the holy sword. He claimed that he had seen God both on earth and in Heaven, and God had made him His Second Son, next to Jesus Christ, who had redeemed a sinful world by sacrificing himself. A Bible in hand, both Hung and Feng preached and recruited Christian soldiers to fight the demons who had usurped the Chinese throne and brought endless misery to the Chinese people.

Jin Tian was poor; it had three streets and a hundred-odd stores, the largest being a pawnshop and a hotel. The rest were unkempt little stores selling local fabrics, rice, sweet potatoes, salt, and other daily necessities. They all had glorious names written on shabby signboards. There were several nameless shacks; from the smell one could easily tell they were opium dens.

Hung and Feng lived in one of the better houses on the main street. It had a tile roof and brick walls and was owned by a prosperous blacksmith named Ironwork Yeh, who had become a God-worshipper.

Run-kan was still in Canton, sending Hung frequent reports on local and national affairs. In most reports, Run-kan wanted Hung to draw his own conclusions. Hung knew that Run-kan always avoided expressing his own opinions for fear that he might prove wrong and unduly influence Hung's judgment. But it was not difficult for Hung to draw conclusions; the reports on the recent Opium War had given Hung a clear picture of the Manchu Dynasty. It was the picture of a molested opium addict, his broken limbs shriveled, his sallow and sickly face black and blue, his voice feeble, groaning in pain. To Hung it was an encouraging picture; England had weakened the demon so much that it would not be difficult to slay.

Run-kan reported again:

> In Mr. Lindley's office I heard many foreigners argue about the Opium War. One such person, a Mr. Gladstone, was sympathetic to China. He shouted that the Opium War was unjust; it brought England disgrace. For that, he got a black eye from

an opium trader, who said that the war killed no more people in China than did excessive drinking in England. Here in the foreign concession Gladstone's voice is weak. Please draw your own conclusions.

Hung drew his own conclusions and wrote them at the bottom of the report: "More silver will be drained and people will become more desperate. On the other hand, since the British have such powerful fire ships and big cannons, the demon might give away more extraterritorial rights and seaports in exchange for British arms to quell local rebellions. This unhappy situation must be prevented."

Feng was not worried. He said that England would remain neutral in the civil war, for the Imperial Court had humiliated Queen Victoria by insisting that Her Majesty's envoys must still give the Manchu Emperor three kowtows during an audience. Such face-saving stupidity would serve the God-worshippers' cause nicely. Hung hoped that Feng was right.

Run-kan reported:

This report is from Chinese sources. In order to win the British conqueror's favor, Ki Shen, Emperor Tao-kuang's uncle who signed the Nanking Treaty, has been learning Western ways. During a recent banquet entertaining Admiral Elliot, Ki Shen confided to the British admiral that Chinese men really like the buxom golden-haired English beauties more than those stringbean Chinese women teetering on lily feet. Draw your own conclusions.

Hung scribbled on the report, "Too trifling for comment."

But Feng concluded that Ki Shen's remark would work in the God-worshippers' favor. Such gibberish from an Imperial uncle would only evoke the foreigners' scorn. England would have no respect for the Manchus. And there was no fear of England exporting buxom golden-haired beauties to China like opium; the white man's racial prejudice would prevent it. Hung agreed.

Regarding respect, both Hung and Feng analyzed it carefully. First, with less than ten thousand men England had cut through China's heart as easily as a knife cutting through bean cake. Second, the emperor was only a face-saving fool, surrounded by ignorant cousins, uncles, and concubines. Third, most of the generals in the Imperial Army were opium addicts; some of them had even enriched themselves enormously by drawing pay for nonexistent troops. And finally, the Imperial Court had no foreign policy; foreign affairs were discussed as though people were haggling in a coolie bazaar.

Final conclusion: The foreign powers would treat the Manchu government as a joke. Time was ripe for the big rebellion.

Every day, Hung and Feng preached at market fairs, drawing more people at each gathering, mostly aborigines. One day a crippled aborigine came to the house and begged Hung to save his only son, who had been arrested for not paying the land tax. The family had been ordered to pay within three days and their tax must be paid in silver. It was a mistake, the old man claimed, because they owned no land and it was impossible to find silver. He was a middle-aged mountain man clothed in rags, his blue cotton turban hanging on his scabby head, about to fall off.

"What if you don't pay?" Hung asked.

The man sank to his knees, tears creeping down his creased leathery face. "They will beat my son until his bottom flesh is split and his legs are broken," he said in a trembling voice. "He will never be able to catch snakes again. We will all starve."

Hung looked at the wretched man, his hands covered with snake bites, one leg crooked and shorter than the other. Hung thought for a moment. There was nothing he could do, but the injustice angered him so much that he helped the man to his feet and declared, "Go home. Heavenly Father will save your son."

After the man had left, Feng looked at Hung inquisitively. "How are you going to save his son?"

Hung looked blank. They had handled landlords, but they had not yet dealt with government officials, who had armed guards and jails and their word was law. Beheadings were as common as buttock-beatings.

But they were sitting in a roomful of people in Ironwork Yeh's house, attending a meeting. Hung did not want to appear helpless.

He remained calm. After the meeting, he told everybody to follow him. They marched to the local magistrate's yamen and asked to see the magistrate. When the yamen guard refused to admit them, Hung produced two documents: the paper that certified him as a Qualified Student and his pass to the Talent degree examination. The guard's expression immediately changed. He looked Hung up and down and studied his gown. Satisfied, he took them to the magistrate's office.

Lying on his daybed in his office, the magistrate, fat with a sallow face, was enjoying his afternoon pipe of opium. After a glance at Hung's papers, he rose from the kang and greeted Hung with a slight bow. The yamen was old and shabby, for Kwangsi was a poor and backward province. Hung knew that a seventh-ranked magistrate in a small county would be impressed by a man who had passed the Qualified Student examination and had participated in the Talent degree examination at a provincial level. Knowing the mentality of government officials, Hung always carried these papers with him, just in case. If he had had a Talent degree, he was sure that the magistrate would have bowed lower and would have offered tea and refreshments.

Without bidding them to sit down, the magistrate asked Hung the purpose of his visit. Talking like a scholar in the style of the eight-legged essay, Hung told the magistrate about the injustice the aborigine had suffered. He quoted Confucius' passage on kindness as one of the eight virtues and embellished it with some flowery words that impressed the magistrate.

"Times are bad," the magistrate said, his voice kind and gentle. "The foreign devils are to blame for such bad times. The Imperial Court has issued edicts stating that all government officials everywhere must increase land taxes and collect them in silver. But if this poor family has only one son and the father is crippled, and this year being the Year of the Snake, their tax can be excused. Heaven has eyes. I am not an unreasonable man, and I pray that the future years will be better and the foreign devils will stop robbing the Imperial treasury."

Coughing his opium cough, he padded to his desk. He used his largest brush and wrote on his official stationery these characters: "Tax excused due to illness of the only son." Then he put his official seal on it and handed the document to Hung with a nod and a grunt, designed to show his authority.

Leaving the yamen, Feng could not help admiring Hung's skill. "What if that turtle's egg had refused to excuse the man's tax?"

"Do your best," Hung said with a smile. "But leave the result to Heaven."

It was big news in Jin Tian when the aborigine's son returned to his village, a free man. The family could not stop praising the power of Hung, the second son of Jehovah. The Hans began to treat Hung and Feng with more respect. Many started to attend Hung's sermons, praying and participating in baptism in the nearby creek. In the meantime, he and Feng studied Sun Wu and other authors on military history and strategy. They discussed how an army should be organized and commanded. Now they were ready to turn their Christian followers into an army to fight a holy war.

As more aborigines flocked to Hung to seek the Kingdom of Heaven, more Hans also began to believe in this foreign God with the big beard and the white halo. Every morning, Hung shouted to a crowd in front of Ironwork Yeh's house, waving his Bible: "A house cannot build itself. How can Heaven and earth and creatures of all kinds create themselves? Such great works cannot just happen! There must be a creator. This creator is God, and God created everything and governs everything. God has commanded that the demons must be slain, that all those who obey Him will go to Heaven where food is abundant and happiness is everlasting. There is no sickness, no death, no debt, no misery, no famine, no bad government officials. For Shangti, God in Heaven, is the supreme ruler and He sees to it that all the demons who bring famine and misery and injustice to people are exterminated. Men in every country revere Shangti and worship Him alone. He needs no golden temple built with men's sweat, nor tall statues set up to worship. Men can worship Him anywhere, on the street, in the fields, and He will look after men's welfare everywhere and bless those who believe in Him."

Having introduced God, Hung then introduced himself as God's Second Son who had the Heavenly mandate to lead an army to slay the demons. He had not yet openly declared who the demons were, but the listeners had easily guessed, for the demons had usurped the crown and had brought untold misery to the Chinese people. Then he opened the Bible and with reverence read of Isaiah and the story of creation.

In a voice trembling with fear, he read the Beatitudes. Finally, he introduced his Heavenly Elder Brother, Jesus Christ, who spoke to him every day from the printed pages of the Holy Bible. At the end of the sermon, he sank to his knees and prayed. All his prayers concerned China's problems, which had been caused by the demons. While praying, he often cast secret glances at his audience. He was happy to see that the sea of bowed heads was getting larger every day and the *Amen* was louder and clearer.

17

Hung finally heard from his brother-in-law, Yang Shiu-ching. Yang and his wife had settled in Thistle Mountain, a town famous for its charcoal. The town was supported by charcoal-making, and Yang had unionized the industry's two thousand workers. He invited Hung to visit him.

It was a two-day trip. Hung and Feng started early to catch the first boat to Kwei Ping, a busy city on the West River. It was a fine day with a gentle breeze that cleared the fog. The warm sunshine dissipated the morning chill as the junk sailed downstream. The boatman sculled steadily with powerful strokes while his wife and teenage daughter cooked at the bow and his other two children, an eight-year-old girl and a twelve-year-old boy, helped wash vegetables and feed the ducks and chickens, which squawked noisily in separate bamboo coops.

The food was simple, served in big rice bowls—a dish of vegetables and bean cake cooked with minced pork, garlic, and red-hot peppers. While the family was partaking of the meal with the passengers inside the cabin, the teenage daughter handled the boat, singing as she sculled. Her clear trilling voice reached far and a fisherman responded in the distance, singing in a longing and haunting voice. On the banks, women were busy washing clothes, beating them on rocks with wooden clubs. Some naked children were playing on the pebbly beach nearby.

The large junks, with their tall sails full, sped by, loaded with bales, all clearly marked "machine-manufactured cloth," in both Chinese and English. There were also crates without markings. Some bore a red seal. The boatmen said they were crates of "black earth." Hung knew it was opium.

While enjoying the meal, Hung and the boatman chatted. Besides carrying a few passengers, the boat also carried some light merchandise on its return trip—mostly leather goods, herbs, dried mushrooms, deer's horns, and live snakes for the health-conscious Cantonese customers.

"Deer's horns are popular among newlyweds," the boatman said with a laugh. "Married, Mr. Hung?"

"Yes. But Mr. Feng here is still single."

"I am devoting my life to God's gospel," Feng said quickly.

As he started to preach, the boatman interrupted him and continued to discuss the potency of deer's horn. "Best to drink it in powdered form, dissolved in *hsiao hsing* yellow wine. By drinking it, it is not uncommon for an eighty-year-old man to still father a son or two." Then he introduced the best all-around elixir he ever transported: snakes.

"The largest snakes are from Thistle Mountain," he went on. "Ever hear of the place?"

"That is where we are going," Hung said.

"Arm yourself with heavy sticks," the boatman advised. "The large ones can swallow a man or a cow whole. But you can fight them off by hitting them on the head. They are powerful but slow. After you have hit them on the head a few times, you can easily outrun them."

He said that some snakes had a hooked tail and spat out a vapor that could intoxicate a man. Such snakes were most precious; their galls were expensive tonics, their skins made the best drums, their meat prevented colds, reduced fever, and stopped vomiting. "You Cantonese believe in it. You Cantonese want more children and more energy to make more money." He laughed.

The boat arrived at Kwei Ping the next morning. The city was much smaller than Canton, but it had everything—old palatial buildings that housed the district yamen, a Confucian temple, a shrine to Kwan Kung, the god of war, and one to Kwan Yin, the goddess of mercy. The main street was lined with shops and colorful signboards, some painted red with gilded characters, selling silk and foreign fabrics, canned food from Canton, furs from Peking and Shantung, fireworks from Hunan, and tung oil from Yunan. The smaller stores sold local products, mostly groceries. There was also a pawnshop, a hardware store, and an iron-works with a blacksmith hammering knives and scissors outside. Push-carts clattered on the pebbled street; traveling barbers carrying their shops on their shoulders rang small bells energetically; fortune-tellers and professional letter writers sat in their stalls, picking their teeth while they patiently waited for customers. The city was full of aborigines from Thistle Mountain, selling monkeys, wildcats, armadillos, and snakes. The men wore turbans and were armed with broadswords; their women were dressed in colorful tunics with embroidered sleeves and aprons. Sturdy as men, they carried heavily loaded bamboo baskets balanced on their shoulders on bamboo poles while they walked over rocks and thorns barefooted.

Hung and Feng hired an aborigine guide to take them to Thistle Mountain. The guide, Shao Chou-kwei, was a quiet, muscular young man, but when he talked about Hung's brother-in-law he became animated. Obviously Yang was popular among the aborigines and had recruited many of them to work in the charcoal factory. For the first time Hung learned that his brother-in-law had an unusual background. He had been an orphan, a beggar boy. He had worked at many odd jobs and was handy with tools as well as weapons. He was a brutal fighter, capable of crippling a man twice his size with a single kick. He had worked as a bodyguard for traveling merchants on the West River; he knew some of the most notorious bandits and pirates, and they addressed him as "older brother."

But after he had come home with a wife a few years ago, he had abandoned all his illegal activities and become a charcoal maker at Thistle Mountain. When Shao talked about Yang admiringly, he was so animated that he became a totally different man. Then and there Hung decided that his brother-in-law was a natural leader; he must recruit him for his rebellion. He had never dreamed that his sister had married such a man. He had liked him, but his first impression had been of an eloquent boaster who was handy with carpenter's tools. Hung had suspected that the squat pockmarked Yang was probably not even a good husband. Now, from talking with Shao, he formed a totally different opinion of Yang and he could hardly wait to see him again.

Thistle Mountain had several peaks, one rising behind the other, the tallest hiding in layers of haze. The road was narrow and twisted, but well hardened by the aborigines' bare feet through hundreds of years of hunting and wood-gathering. The jungle was dense, with sturdy vines hanging from banyans like enormous snakes. In the thick brush hidden animals moved quietly; Shao said they were likely snakes hunting for food. As they climbed, Hung felt the thin chilly air and shivered. Feng kept blowing on his hands. Both were quiet and breathless, but Shao seemed energetic, his sturdy legs bouncy; he walked with large strides, his broadsword in hand, his eyes glancing right and left. Leading the way, he said that they had reached the snake-infested area.

As they trudged up the steep road, crumpling fallen branches and dead leaves underfoot, large birds flapped their wings, flying from one tree to another. A bird's piercing cry startled a rabbit, which darted across the path and disappeared into the thick brush. The jungle was getting darker and more eerie. Hung wanted something to eat. He wished aloud that he had brought some meat buns. Feng suggested that they stop and spend the night. Shao agreed. He spotted an area where people had camped before. He slashed the brush with his sword and gathered some wood, with which he built a small fire.

While Hung and Feng warmed their hands over the fire, Shao went to hunt for rabbits for food. But he came back with a large live snake instead. Holding the ten-foot snake in one hand, his sword in the other, he stood between Hung and Feng and asked them if they were thirsty. Both said quickly, "No."

Hung asked if he was going to drink the snake's blood. Without an expression on his muscular face, Shao nodded. "I am," he said and casually chopped the snake's head off with his sword. As the snake twisted and curled and blood spurted out, he stuffed the cut section into his mouth and sucked. Taking a breath, he continued to drink the blood until the snake stopped struggling. "It is better to drink snake blood when it is warm," he said. "If not, you drink it with some warm wine. Now let's eat the snake."

He skinned the snake, cleaned it of its entrails and roasted it over the fire. Hung and Feng, raised in Kwangtung, enjoyed snake soup in a restaurant, but having watched Shao drink the snake's blood in such a manner, they were no longer hungry. Shao ate the snake ravenously, tearing the meat apart with his hands and chewing it noisily, groaning with pleasure.

Yang, Hung's brother-in-law, lived in a mountain valley with his wife, Little Treasure, and his seventeen-year-old sister, Winter Flower. He had the largest bamboo house in a cluster of smaller houses, surrounded by tall bamboos. Most days the area was covered by thick fog. By the time the dogs started barking and roosters began to crow early in the morning, the inhabitants in the valley had already finished their breakfast and were ready to go to work at the charcoal factory at the foot of the mountain, a short distance away. During the day, the village was quiet, and cooking smoke did not trail up until late evening, for almost the entire village—men, women, and children—worked at the factory, which produced the best charcoal in Kwangsi Province.

When Hung, Feng, and Shao arrived, a flock of barefooted children rushed to meet them. It was rare to have visitors from the outside world and they constantly watched the twisting mountain road, hoping to see strangers arriving.

Yang and his family had just finished their evening meal. Winter Flower had lit an oil lamp in the middle room where Yang was relaxing and chatting with a few neighbors. He was a popular man and union leader, who also functioned as the village head, settling problems and arbitrating quarrels.

The biggest quarrel was often about women. Because of a shortage, they were guarded jealously by fathers, brothers, and husbands. A little harmless flirting would arouse suspicion and a quarrel might occur with the involved parties winding up at Yang's house to air their complaints. If a young man was found emerging from behind a bush with a young woman, her father or brother might demand a pledge of marriage from him. If a man flirted with someone's wife, the husband would roll up his sleeves and threaten him with violence. But it was usually only a lot of shouting; Yang rarely had to separate people because they had come to blows.

Yang and his close friend Square Head Liang were enjoying a cup of tea and a pipe of Fukian tobacco when his seven-year-old son rushed in and reported excitedly that three strangers had asked about Yang Shiu-ching.

"Father, is that your name?" he asked. Children in the valley rarely knew their parents' given names because grownups always addressed each other by their nicknames or simply called each other "Older Brother."

Yang came out of the house just as a neighbor was guiding the visitors to him. In the moonlight, Yang recognized his brother-in-law and Feng immediately. He greeted them warmly with repeated little bows while he misquoted an old Confucian saying, "What a happiness when relatives come afar!"

Hung grimaced and laughed. He introduced Shao, who bowed deeply and flatteringly told Yang that his name had been rumbling in his humble ears like thunder. Yang liked the good-looking aborigine right away and called his sister to make tea. He wanted to see if his sister's eyes would sparkle when she saw Shao. He had been worrying about Winter Flower's single status.

Inviting the visitors to the middle room, Yang inquired about everybody's health in Happy Valley. Hung discovered that his brother-in-law had changed a lot; his spirits were high, his face glowed, and his voice was cheerful and forceful. Despite his pockmarks he even looked handsome in a rugged way. Now the house was full of activity. Hung's sister brought in a basin and a bucket of warm water for the visitors to wash their feet. Ti Ti, Yang's son by Little Treasure, had invited his playmates into the house to watch the three strangers. They stared at them wide-eyed as though they were odd creatures. Yang laughed and tried to shoo them out, but not until Hung had given each of them a brass coin. When Yang saw his sister's eyes sparkle as she served Shao a cup of tea, he happily introduced her to everybody, lying about her age a little.

"She will be sixteen next spring. She is called Winter Flower because she is a late comer, born in the Year of the Rabbit, when our parents were already over thirty. But she is a spring flower. She is so choosy that I am afraid she will never look a man straight in the eye."

Blushing profusely, Winter Flower cast her brother an accusing glance. She was a beautiful young woman, dressed in aborigine fashion, wearing a sleeveless black jacket over her red blouse, a black skirt that reached to her ankles, with flowers embroidered at the bottom. On her neck hung a large silver necklace.

"Our mother was an aborigine," Yang said. "Winter Flower inherited all her clothes. They don't sting my eyes, so I let her wear them." He cast Shao a quick glance. When he found Shao following her boldly with his eyes, he knew that he did not need a matchmaker.

After the guests had had hot tea and washed their feet, Little Treasure served dinner. Yang ate again out of politeness. Hung was glad that his sister looked happy and robust, even pretty. Back home, the family had worried about her future. Like the two older brothers, she was not good-looking and seemed a bit slow-witted. Now she talked and laughed like everybody else and she was several months pregnant.

The dishes she served were strange but tasty. Without asking what they were, Hung ate with extra noises, sucking air, smacking his lips, and belching to show his appreciation.

The family kept two domesticated monkeys that came and went freely, chirping and leaping onto Yang's shoulders, demanding to be fed and looking for fleas in Yang's hair. Yang showed great affection for the animals but sternly forbade them to grab food from the guests' rice bowls. "They like all delicacies," Yang said with a laugh. "If you don't shake a finger at them, they will devour everything on this table, especially the fried wasps and the steamed mountain ant eggs."

After dinner, Yang asked, "Brother-in-law, you are a man full of books and wisdom. I am a charcoal burner with dirty hands. It is a great honor that you should care to take such a long journey to visit me. My stupid mind tells me that you would never have come unless you had something world-shaking in mind. If that is the case, what is it?"

"Yes. Besides visiting my sister," Hung said, "I have something to discuss with you . . . something that is indeed world-shaking!"

Hung spent three days telling his brother-in-law about his world-shaking mission. He also converted him.

18

The gong sounded. More than two thousand charcoal workers poured out of the charcoal factory and stood in front of the main brick building at the foot of Thistle Mountain, ready to hear the gospels of the Universal God Jehovah. The factory owners were happy to let the workers out a little earlier than usual this evening, for Yang had told them that this new God was a demon slayer. He could protect the factory against all kinds of evil spirits and increase production as much as tenfold if all the workers were converted. Recently, one of the dozen factory buildings had caught fire and a Taoist priest had said that the wind and water of the factory had changed from good to bad because the old pine in front of the main building had died. The pine, over a hundred years old, had been the factory's door god, warding off evil spirits for years. The owners had replaced the dead tree. To play safe, they also wanted this new God Jehovah to bless their business. A silver mine had been discovered ten miles away and charcoal was in great demand there. To increase production, the factory needed the blessings of all gods, even this strange God Jehovah.

Hung, standing on a stool and waving a Bible, shouted to the curious crowd in his sonorous voice, "Brethren, all men are the God's sons, all women are the God's daughters. We are all the God's children! Jehovah treats everyone equal. Jehovah welcomes everyone to his Kingdom of Heaven, where people enjoy everlasting happiness ... no hard work, no famine, no misery, no tax, no sickness."

"Amen!" Feng, standing behind Hung, responded loudly. "Say Amen if you agree."

"Amen!" many of the workers in the crowd shouted.

Hung opened the Bible and read a passage from it. "Here is God's command. He says: 'Let the oppressed go free. Break every yoke. Feed the hungry and clothe the naked. Do not worship images of evil gods.

Carry out the will of the one and only Heavenly Father, who is the God called Jehovah.' "

"Amen!" Feng shouted. The crowd all shouted, "Amen!" after him.

Hung went on to introduce Jesus Christ, the First Son of God. He told the story of how he, himself, had seen God in Heaven in a dream, how God had made him His Second Son and entrusted him with a holy sword to slay the demons.

"Our Heavenly Father, God Jehovah, has also made me the Viceroy of China. Those who follow me will be my soldiers and be blessed. Together we will exterminate all demons, bring prosperity, peace, and happiness to everyone on earth."

"Amen!" Feng and the crowd responded in unison, a loud clear roar that echoed in the mountains. Now the crowd was fired up. Everybody was anxious to follow a man—any man—who could change their lot. Hung knew it and concluded his sermon with a prayer that was designed to please the poor and the oppressed. When he had finished, the crowd responded with an explosive *Amen*, which sounded like a bugle blast—a signal that the holy war had started.

At night, while having dinner, Hung told his brother-in-law that he had another mission, a bigger and nobler mission that needed outstanding leaders to carry it out. Hung asked Yang if he was interested in learning about it.

"You don't have to ask," Yang said with a laugh. "I already know."

Hung looked at Yang, surprised. "How did you know?"

"When you preached the gospel of Jehovah, you never stopped talking about the demons and your mission to slay them with your holy sword. It is not too difficult to guess who the demons are. Am I right, eh, my wife's brother?" He looked at Hung with raised eyebrows and a wicked little smile.

Hung laughed. "Your cleverness and analytical power tells me that you are a man of leadership timber, but I hesitated to reveal my heart because I was not sure of yours, even though you are my relative . . ."

"Let me tell you a little more about myself, my wife's brother," Yang interrupted, his voice more serious, the broad smile disappearing. "I traveled the West River up and down for many years as an escort for many merchants, some selling opium, others trading foreign fabrics, and one man a snake dealer. They were all robbed by bandits and secret societies. As their escort and bodyguard, I was supposed to protect them. I could, for I knew most of the robbers, but I only faked a little fight and let the robbers get away with most of the merchandise and cash. But the only man I really protected was the snake dealer. He is Mr. Liang, the man you met the day you arrived. Now he is in the poultry business, raising prize geese at his farm, not too far from here. Why did I protect him? Because he was dealing in merchandise that was beneficial to people. When the robbers insisted on robbing him, I fought. I killed one and wounded three, but there were more than a dozen of them. The turtle's eggs stabbed Liang three times and me five times. They threw us into the muddy river, thinking that we would go to Yen Lo. But we didn't. Why did I let them rob the others? I hated opium and foreigners' goods. Besides, the robbers took the merchandise straight to the Triads, the Heaven and Earth members, the White Lotuses, the Big Swords. These secret societies all have one common purpose—to slay the demons and return the throne to the Hans."

He paused to drink a large mouthful of tea, then flung a finger at Hung and went on, "I know why you hate the demons, my wife's brother. You failed the demons' examination because you did not have money to bribe the 'teeth and claws.' Years ago I worked as teeth and claws of a magistrate's yamen. I collected taxes, I arrested people, I watched other teeth and claws beat people's bottoms until flesh and blood were flying. One day I couldn't stomach it anymore. I decamped. If they had caught me, they would have beheaded me. So I joined many secret societies for protection. I drank a lot of chicken blood and my own blood. My wife's brother, I don't know if I am of leadership timber or not, but I've got a lot of blood to shed. I will join your mission and follow you until you drive the demons over the Great Wall to the place they came from. Since I became a charcoal maker, I have renewed my friendship with many people I met during my vagabond days. Some of my friends have failed, some have succeeded in whatever they are doing, but all of them are frustrated in trying to get rid of something, like a man squatting in an outhouse grunting and groaning."

He poured and swallowed another mouthful of tea. "Do you know why Square Head Liang is raising geese? Because he is also making weapons. The geese are so noisy that nobody can hear the hammering.

Luckily both his fat geese and his weapons are money-makers. His swords
and spears are in big demand by secret societies, his goose feathers are
in big demand by foreigners. I have no idea why the foreigners want
goose feathers. I hear that the foreign devils eat a lot of odd things.
You don't suppose they eat goose feathers, do you?"

They all laughed.

Yang enthusiastically learned the skills of preaching. A naturally
eloquent man who used earthy language that was easy to understand,
he soon became a popular preacher of the gospels of Jehovah. In a short
time he converted many secret society fighters into God-worshippers.
After he had introduced the Kingdom of Heaven and all its glory in his
sermons, he would tell his audiences emphatically, "To join the Kingdom
of Heaven, you need not pay cash dues. There are no initiations like
drinking chicken blood or your own blood, or walking on fire to test
your courage. To become a genuine Christian, the only ritual you need
follow is to walk into a river and get wet. You do that anyway, don't
you, when you take a bath? The Christian bath not only washes your
dirt away, it also cleanses your soul, gets rid of your sins, and makes a
new man of you."

He knew that most of the secret society members had sinned. This
baptism ritual would certainly draw a lot of sinners. Hung liked what
Yang was doing and he approved of his strategy to attract sinners. The
more a man sinned, the more eager he was to join them.

The Dragon Mountain Silver Mine was expanding. In two months
the number of miners had increased from four thousand to five thousand.
Hung wanted Feng to go there and convert miners. Feng accepted the
assignment eagerly.

The mine, owned by Master Kao, was situated beside the Snake
River in the County of Kwei. The Dragon Mountain supplied water,
which ran into the river in torrents each summer. With ample water
and abundant charcoal supplied by Lucky Charcoal factory, Master Kao
considered himself a man blessed by his ancestors, who had been government officials through many generations. He worshipped only his
ancestors, burning incense and offering rare delicacies on their altar in

his ancestral hall. He lived lavishly in his palatial mansion at the county seat, served by a horde of servants and entertained by six concubines, who had all been trained on Pearl River flower boats.

Of his children, he only counted the number of his sons, which totaled fourteen; he was not sure how many daughters he had, and he did not care. Most of his miners were farmers from the nearby counties where soil was poor and famine was a regular curse. It was a blessing that Master Kao owned the mines and had been expanding them. He was good to his workers.

But a banquet never lasts, as the old saying goes. Master Kao, having discovered opium, decided to retire. Between his opium and his concubines, he hardly got out of bed three days in a week. Red Eye Kao, his eldest son, happily took over the management of the mine.

He ruled it like a feudal lord. He forced the miners to go deeper and worked them in two shifts. Sometimes a shaft would collapse and dozens of men would be hurt or buried. Red Eye made the miners believe that it was their fate. He built a small shrine to Kwan Yin nearby and told the miners to burn incense and pray to the goddess of mercy for a better fate.

Since the victims never collected any compensation and Kwan Yin did not seem to offer any protection, the miners were unhappy. But it was not until Red Eye reduced their pay from a string of one thousand brass coins a month to eight hundred coins, that they began to grumble.

When Feng arrived and started preaching, the miners treated him with suspicion. He wore a long gown, and coolies always dreaded long-gown wearers. To them, long gowns represented the upper class that always exploited the poor. But when they listened to Feng's sermon they began to relax. A smile replaced their knitted brows and tight lips.

Feng had prepared his sermons well; every word touched his listeners' hearts and echoed their problems. He eloquently built a Heavenly Kingdom that everybody could hardly wait to get into. He preached day and night—whenever and wherever he gathered a group of listeners.

The miners lived in shacks along the river and in caves at the foot of the mountain. Their gathering place was the marketplace of the area, where some small shops and stalls formed a narrow short street and sold food and daily necessities. The pawnshop was the most prosperous.

Next door was a tea house, owned by the same merchant. It was a happy business combination, for the pawnbroker often found some of his money returning to the teahouse shortly after he had loaned it out in the pawnshop. The more desperate a man was, the more thirsty he became. It was no secret that the teahouse was the next-most-prosperous business in the marketplace. Feng preached most often in front of it.

The number of his listeners grew every day. In the middle of the third week, Red Eye Kao arrived with a servant and confronted Feng, demanding that he move on. He said that no monkey players or storytellers were allowed in the County of Kwei.

"Sir, I am not a monkey player or a storyteller," Feng said politely, waving his Bible. "I am preaching the gospels of Jehovah, the Universal God from Heavenly Kingdom." He began to deliver a sermon trying to convert this young man with bloodshot eyes in the rich blue silk gown, but Kao interrupted him.

"Fortune-tellers are blood suckers," he shouted. "Move on, move on! Go suck blood somewhere else!"

"I know you, sir," Feng said, smiling. "You have done a lot of things that you should not have. The Lord Almighty God said in the Bible, in chapter six, verse thirty-one of the Book of Luke, 'Don't do anything that you don't want others to do to you!'"

Kao glared at him. "What have I done that I should not have? How dare you criticize me!"

"May I answer?"

"Say your piece and be gone!"

"You reduced the workers' salaries. Why?"

"Because the government increased my tax."

"It was your tax, not theirs. The God Almighty said in the Bible . . ."

"Your God be damned!" Red Eye Kao shouted. He snatched the Bible from Feng's hand and tore it up angrily. Feng watched, his face red and breath short, trying to control his anger. "Ah Lo," Kao said to his servant, "kick him out of the marketplace!"

Ah Lo rolled up his sleeves, ready for action. Feng stood his ground. Cursing and spraying saliva, the servant started pushing Feng on the chest. Feng kicked him on the shin. The servant immediately took a kung fu stance, one arm extended and the other in a fist, ready to strike. When Feng turned to walk away, Ah Lo leapt forward to strike. Without even looking, Feng swung a leg backward, his foot striking Lo on the side of his face, knocking him down. As he got up and lunged at Feng again, Feng kicked him in the groin. Lo doubled over, groaning in pain.

"Rebellion, rebellion!" Red Eye Kao shouted, running away and waving his arms. "Send for the guards! Rebellion!"

19

The Dengs, the Weis, and the Lius were the richest families in the County of Kwei. Master Deng had made his fortune by operating gambling and opium dens. Every New Year, when he saw the two characters *wealth* and *nobility* posted on his front door, he felt that half of his life was still empty; he had never reached nobility status. Since he was over fifty, the possibility of his holding a government position was already past. As a gambler, he had never studied the Four Books and Five Classics. But his eldest son, Deng Pi, was young and clever, and had passed the Qualified Student examination. When the government started selling positions, he bought a seventh-ranked magistrate title for Deng Pi.

It was an excellent investment. Now Deng Pi was the magistrate for the County of Kwei and lived in an old palatial yamen with two secretaries—one responsible for administration and the other for finance. Both men were longtime family confidants. Deng Pi also commanded a squadron of three hundred yamen guards, including one executioner, two bottom-beaters, and a dozen jailers.

It was a bright morning. Deng Pi, feeling lethargic, ordered a second cup of ginseng tea in his sitting room. When a slave girl brought the tiny cup on a lacquered tray, she also brought in a visitor, Red Eye Kao. Even though the two men were family friends, they were not close and secretly despised each other. Deng Pi, at thirty, was a few years older than Kao, but for polite reasons he addressed Kao as "Older Brother."

He greeted Kao with a bow. "Older Brother Kao, what wind has blown you over to this humble yamen?"

"Bad news," Kao said, plunking down in a seat without being invited. "A Cantonese man has arrived in the village and is spreading a foreign religion. He is also trying to instigate a rebellion."

Deng poised his ginseng cup in midair, surprised. "Instigate a rebellion? How do you know?"

"He urges my miners to follow him to the kingdom of a foreign god. Together they will slay all the demons. If this is not rebellion, what is it?"

"Who is he? Where does he live?"

"His family name is Feng. Nobody knows where he lives. By the time my militia arrived, he had already escaped. Besides being fleet-footed, he also knows some kung fu. He beat my servant black and blue."

"What does he look like?"

"Medium height, not bad-looking. About thirty. He wears a long gown."

"Wears a long gown?" Deng Pi said thoughtfully. He took a sip of ginseng and rubbed his short chin, a traditional mannerism of magistrates. "Hm, he is either an imposter or a man of importance. We will have to be careful."

"I suggest that we throw him in jail first. Fifty strokes of bottom-beating will squeeze out a confession."

"He wears a long gown. I don't want to treat such a man so harshly without investigation," Deng said, shaking his head.

"Why such lenient treatment?" Kao asked, looking worried.

"We don't know who he is. Suppose he knows our background. Suppose . . ." He stopped.

Red Eye stared at him. "Suppose what? I pay you bribes regularly in the name of increased taxes."

Deng rose to his feet abruptly, upsetting his ginseng cup. "Older Brother Kao," he said, his face reddened, "when you reduced your workers' pay, you blamed it on increased taxes. It was very indiscreet of you to say a thing like that publicly."

"I am not intimidated by a stranger who wears a long gown," Kao said heatedly. "I am going to deal with him, long gown or no long gown." He marched toward the door. At the door, he turned. "But remember, Older Brother Deng, that we are in the same boat!"

Feng bought two lanterns. With his brush he wrote BE RESPECTFUL on one and BE QUIET on the other. Then, one afternoon he hired a sedan chair with four bearers and rode to the magistrate's yamen. He also hired two men to precede the sedan chair, carrying the lanterns. They were supposed to be the "road openers" of an important government official investigating injustice in a low-ranking district.

Deng Pi was awakened from his afternoon nap by his administrative secretary. "Your Honor," the secretary said, "a fifth-ranked official is here to see you."

Flustered, Deng Pi asked, "Fifth-rank? How do you know?"

"He came in a four-bearer sedan chair and with two lanterns. One says 'Be Respectful' and the other 'Be Quiet.' "

Deng Pi knew that such an official was at least fifth-ranked. He quickly threw on his official gown of seventh-rank and hurried to the yamen hall to receive his visitor. Feng had already seated himself in the magistrate chair behind a table, and two yamen servants were busy serving him tea. Deng Pi walked to the table and studied Feng briefly. His instinct told him that the man indeed looked like a man of nobility, even though he did not wear an official gown.

Bowing deeply, he said, "Your Honor, your visit is such a surprise that I did not have time to extend a proper welcome. I beg your forgiveness."

"I came on other official business," Feng said, his voice loud and sonorous, full of authority. "But I have since heard a rumor that local taxes have been increased. Since the province has just suffered a three-month drought, I am not sure if the increased taxes were collected for famine aid. If not, a more thorough investigation will be carried out so that justice will be served and the district's name restored, you understand."

Feeling a chill in his spine, Deng Pi gave Feng another deep bow. "Your Honor, my humble district never collected higher taxes during the famine year. The rumor was created by discontented mine workers. The mine owner can testify to that, either before or after the welcome banquet which we will extend to you in your honor."

"That is not necessary," Feng said with a smile. "But allow me to ask you some questions for the record. You may sit down."

"Yes, Your Honor," Deng Pi said and ordered a chair, which a servant placed below the dais in the spot where bottom-beating punishment was administered to prisoners. As he sat down, he secretly wiped his wet hands on his official gown. In a tremulous voice he answered a string of questions about his background, his connections with Red Eye Kao, and his salary. Feng, quoting Confucius, finally questioned the wisdom of reducing workers' salaries when hungry people were obliged to eat grass roots and tree bark and sell children during the famine. Using classical language, he also drew as an example an historical figure who had suffered terrible consequences because of greed. As Deng Pi listened, his face paled and beads of sweat appeared on his forehead.

"But disaster can be avoided," Feng concluded with a smile. "It all depends on my report, you understand."

"Yes, yes, Your Honor," Deng Pi stammered. "I shall let my secretaries know about this." While he consulted with his secretaries, the servant refilled Feng's teacup and another served him tidbits and watermelon seeds.

Deng Pi extended another banquet invitation. Feng again declined. When he left the yamen in his sedan chair, he discovered a heavy lacquered box beside his seat. He opened it and found that it was full of silver. As the sedan chair bearers trotted toward Thistle Mountain, Feng found the coolies smiling and their legs more energetic and bouncy. He knew then that everybody's palms had been greased.

Feng arrived at Yang's house that evening in the hired sedan chair, which caused some disturbance among the charcoal makers. Dogs barked, chickens cackled, and people darted into their huts to hide their valuables. The visit of an official was bad news, even worse than the arrival of bandits. It usually meant more tax collections or that someone was in serious trouble. Yang was surprised at first, but the moment he saw Feng get out of the sedan chair his family rushed over to make sure that it was he.

"What happened?" Yang asked, staring at Feng.

Feng stretched himself after the long ride and cracked his knuckles. He picked up the red lacquered box.

"The county magistrate paid the chair bearers well and they volunteered to carry me here," he said. "Since it is dinnertime, we might as well feed them."

"Shao just bagged a porcupine," Yang said. "We have some left-overs."

He ordered his wife and sister to prepare food. Feng followed Yang into the hut while the coolies squatted outside smoking a pipe.

"Where is Older Brother Hung?" Feng asked.

"He went to Canton to raise money for firearms," Yang said in a lowered voice. "Why did you visit the county magistrate?"

"To raise money for firearms," Feng said, placing the red lacquered box on the table. "Five hundred taels."

Yang opened the box and stared at the silver, wide-eyed. "Don't tell me you have converted that fat pig, Deng Pi, and he donated the money!"

"I blackmailed him," Feng whispered back with a smile. After he had told Yang what had happened, Yang threw his head back and guffawed.

20

The rebellion in Kwangsi was well planned. But in Kwangtung, Hung had a busy schedule. He was to meet the leaders of some secret societies to discuss coordination, then Run-kan was to take him to Mr. Richard Lindley, the arms dealer, and to the Reverend Mr. Issachar Roberts in the foreign concession. Finally, he would pay his family a visit in Happy Valley.

The day Hung arrived in Canton, Emperor Tao-kuang died. People in China were ordered to mourn the death for three days by not eating meat and by burning paper gold and silver, which was sold everywhere. Hung heard people say that Emperor Tao-Kuang levied taxes even in death.

Hung was happy to see that Run-kan was looking well. He still lived in the same flat near the foreign concession in Canton. Although foreigners were free to preach and trade in China after the Opium War, they still preferred to live by themselves, enjoying their own people, their own customs and food.

By working with the foreigners, Run-kan had adopted many Western ways. He was tanned and had put on weight, filling his Western clothes nicely. In conversation, he often mixed his Cantonese with foreign words, and to Hung's amazement, it was perfectly understandable. His small flat was decorated with Western oil paintings and a large calendar featuring a buxom blond woman.

"The viceroy's favorite," Run-kan said, pointing at the woman's large breasts. "They are selling the calendar everywhere. Now I have become very fond of . . . uh . . . those mountains and valleys. They look better than the skinny flat-chested Chinese women. Mr. Lindley is just the opposite. He will have flat chests and tiny feet anytime." He laughed.

While having a cup of coffee on a Western sofa, Run-kan briefed Hung about the news from Peking. "The new emperor is Hsien-feng,

125

a twenty-year-old weakling, who is controlled by his favorite concubine, Tse-hsi, a frightfully ambitious woman. I will bet you a string of a thousand brass coins that she will one day seize power and become the empress. She is a fox spirit disguised as Kwan Yin, pretending to be kind and merciful. Recently she ordered all the caged birds in the palace released. That was her first act of mercy. Rumor has it that all the eunuchs in the Forbidden City have already started recapturing those poor birds so that this Imperial concubine can continue to enjoy her merciful acts.

"By the way, I have arranged two meetings for you, one with the Reverend Issachar Roberts, the other with Mr. Richard Lindley, my employer. Tonight we will meet the leaders of the secret societies interested in a united front. Remember Old Man Wong?"

"Yes," Hung said. "The owner of the Five Blessings Inn."

"He arranged tonight's meeting. His inn has always been a front for secret societies. It is a miracle that the government has never found out."

"It just shows how inept the government is," Hung said with a chuckle. "They cannot see beyond two feet. This is good news, Run-kan. Things are going well. We have converted a few thousand aborigines, plus three thousand charcoal workers at Thistle Mountain, where we have established a solid footing. Older Brother Feng is busy trying to convert five thousand silver miners, who have been grumbling about the mine company's ill-treatment. People's discontent is our blessing. We find Kwangsi the best place to start the big one. That province is full of backward feudal lords and oppressed people."

He asked Run-kan about the Reverend Mr. Roberts.

"He opened a church in the foreign concession," Run-kan said. "Every Sunday, about two hundred people attend his services. One third are Chinese. He baptized me and made me a member of his choir. He had heard of you before I mentioned your name. He thinks he can make you an ordained minister. Of course, he will have to baptize you first. Anyway, he will discuss that with you tomorrow.

"By the way, he is the one who protected your family while you were in Kwangsi instigating rebellion. Chi Yin, the new Viceroy of Kwangtung and Kwangsi, has turned from a foreigner-hater to a foreigner-worshipper. To him, a foreigner's word is as good as an Imperial edict. Today, working for a foreigner is better than having a Talent degree. But don't go to the countryside. People in the countryside still can smell the blood shed by those who volunteered to fight the foreign invaders. They also have heard rumors about foreigners eating children's eyeballs."

"How about this Mr. Lindley? Is he still sympathetic to our cause?"

"He certainly is," Run-kan said. "But pocketbook and lip service do not necessarily go together. He may say all kinds of good things about a cat, but if you ask him to keep a cat, he may hem and haw and change the subject. So do not depend on him for a donation. Right now he has nothing to donate but sympathy."

"We are not going to ask for charity," Hung said with a frown, his voice tight. "Will he sell arms to us?"

"As a businessman, he will sell anything to anybody if the price is right. The secret societies have been buying arms from him, even though he knows that most of them are engaged in banditry or piracy. I must say he is one of the rare foreigners who will bang the table and curse when opium is mentioned. He has written numerous letters to the *London Times* protesting his country's opium policy."

Hung smiled. Lindley obviously had a soft spot in his heart . . . he was a man with a sense of justice. Touching the right man's heart at the right time and at the right place would bring help and rescue during times of disaster. He hoped that one day both these two foreigners would serve him in some capacity.

"By the way," Run-kan said, "have you ever tasted foreign food?"

"No, I have not," Hung said with a slight grimace. He had heard that foreigners ate raw meat and drank cow's milk.

"I have learned how to make a few foreign dishes. I will cook you a foreign dinner before you go to attend the meeting at the Five Blessings Inn."

"What dishes?" Hung asked hesitantly, not too keen about eating them.

"Boston hash and New Orleans chicken," Run-kan said, jumping up eagerly to prepare the food. "They taste a bit fishy, but you will like them if you sprinkle enough soy sauce on them."

Hung liked Run-kan's foreign dishes. A lot of garlic and soy sauce disguised the fishy smell. After dinner, he took a walk along the Pearl

River before he went to the meeting at the inn. Like everything else, the waterfront street looked older and the people shabbier. There were beggars sleeping in the doorways of dilapidated buildings. The stench from the gutter, mixed with opium smell, was overwhelming. The river was almost dark, with a few lights gleaming here and there. Most of the flower boats were gone, as were the colorful lanterns, the eerie music, the singing, the giggling, and the laughter. He missed the gaiety, even though his experiences on the river had not been pleasant. He looked for Half Moon Pavilion, the flower boat on which Su San-mei had lived and worked. He only found a few shabby ones still in business. There were many empty spaces along the river now. Some had become temporary docks with fishing junks and sampans tied to sturdy posts, knocking against each other on the undulating water.

He asked a few passersby about the Half Moon Pavilion, but they all looked at him glassy-eyed, shaking their heads. Suddenly he was hit hard by a wave of nostalgia and loneliness. Standing at the empty spot where Half Moon Pavilion had docked, he stared at the river and thought about Su San-mei, wondering where she was. Was she living or dead? What was she doing now, if she was still alive? When the new moon emerged from behind a dark cloud and reflected on the dark water, it brought back old memories. He couldn't stand to look at the river anymore; it was too painful. With a lump in his throat, he hurried away.

21

Twelve people sat at the round table in the Five Blessings Inn. Old Man Wong went around busily pouring tea into their large tea bowls. Most of the men were rough-looking, their hands scarred and callused; they were not accustomed to sipping tea from tiny cups. Hung, sitting in the honored seat that faced the entrance, studied them one by one. Two oil lamps flickered on the table, casting shadows on their rugged faces. He recognized two of them, Golden Rooster and Master Li.

Having poured everyone a bowl of tea, Old Man Wong placed a large plate of watermelon seeds in the middle of the table and took a seat. A dozen hands reached for the seeds. For a moment there were only noises of tea-sipping and the cracking of melon seeds. Everybody was waiting for Hung to speak. Obviously they regarded him as the leader.

"Brethren," Hung finally said after clearing his voice, "the purpose of this meeting is twofold: One, it is time to establish communications among the secret societies and the God-worshippers' Association. In Kwangsi we have recruited many leaders and thousands of Christian converts. We are of one mind: Put the Triads, the Big Swords, the White Lotuses, and the God-worshippers together and we are strong. One chopstick, you can break easily; twelve chopsticks together, not so easily. So you see, we must unite and establish communication; we must standardize our signals and coordinate. Timing, brethren, is of prime importance. Coordination and timing are the essence of our success.

"Second, weapons. We have plenty of traditional weapons, but swords and spears are no match for modern firearms. We must either buy firearms from the foreigners or manufacture our own. But it takes money. The God-worshippers have established a close relationship with the foreigners. Since we believe in their God, they will be sympathetic. But still it will take money to buy their weapons. These foreigners are businessmen. They will not die or donate money for our cause, but they may sell us their arms for less profit—perhaps at cost.

"We God-worshippers can supply manpower and the weapons source, but we depend on you to supply the funds." He looked around and smiled, knowing that most of these men were either pirates or bandits. "All your lives you have robbed the rich and fed the poor. It is time to keep the revolution alive . . ."

"Older Brother Hung," Golden Rooster interrupted, "let's say we borrow from the rich to help the revolution."

All the others responded with nods and grunts. Hung raised a hand. "Agreed. Only monsters rob the people . . ."

Before he could finish his sentence, Run-kan burst in, pale and breathless. He rushed to Hung and whispered into his ear, "Older Brother Feng has been arrested."

Hung rose to his feet quickly. "Brethren," he said grimly, "there is an emergency. Let's continue this meeting tomorrow night."

As he hurriedly left the room with Run-kan, he heard Golden Rooster shout after him, "What happened, Older Brother Hung? Can we help?"

Hung did not respond. He did not want to show the secret societies any weakness or adversity at this stage of the game.

Back in Run-kan's room, Shao, the messenger, was waiting. He was still sweating and his clothes were covered with dust. He grabbed Hung's hands and said, his voice urgent, "The county magistrate accused Older Brother Feng of treason. He threatened to deliver him to the Fu yamen for trial. They don't try rebels . . . just cut their heads off. We must fight! Can you get firearms? We'll fight!"

Hung pinched the bridge of his nose as he paced back and forth. Run-kan knew that this was extremely serious. When Hung had had problems in the past, he used to look blank. Soon the solution would come to him. Pinching his nose and pacing indicated despair.

"If we can find firearms," Hung said, "still it takes time to train our men."

"Then we'll fight with what we have—hoes and rakes," Shao said. "The goose farmer has some swords and spears . . ."

"We will think of a better way," Hung interrupted, still pacing.

"The turtle's egg Deng Pi said he'll send Older Brother Feng to the Fu yamen in six days. The moment he arrives at the Fu yamen, they will hang his head over the city gate."

"He is right, cousin," Run-kan said. "You must go back and see what you can do. I shall cancel your meetings with the Reverend Mr. Roberts and Mr. Lindley."

Hung thought for a moment and decided to go back immediately, paying a brief visit to his family on the way. If Feng was executed like a common criminal, it would be the end of the Christian crusade and the rebellion. In no way would he allow that to happen.

When Hung returned to the Five Blessings Inn, the leaders of the secret societies had gone. He found a bag on his bed. Attached to it was a note: I borrowed a thousand taels yesterday.

Below the message was the drawing of a rooster.

Arriving home, Hung took off his coolie disguise and greeted his wife, two children, and two brothers, who all looked thinner and wore white arm bands in mourning. "We are not mourning the death of the demon king," Run-ta, his eldest brother, said. "Our father died last month."

Hung sat in the middle room staring at the ancestral altar, trying to control his emotions. As waves of sadness subsided, he allowed his family to pamper him. He was glad that nobody pumped him with questions about what he had been doing in Kwangsi. His son, a quiet little boy of six, squatted in front of him and helped him wash his feet in the wooden basin. His eight-year-old daughter served him tea and tidbits. In the kitchen both his mother and his wife were busy chopping and stir-frying food. Soon a spicy aroma drifted into the middle room and Run-mo, his second older brother, laid the table for dinner.

Hung asked the children what they did to help with the family chores every day. The boy was shy and the girl answered all the questions. They did everything, including carrying water and night soil. Run-ta and Run-mo told him about the animals and the crops. They brought their own children in for Hung to inspect. Their wives were so fruitful that Hung gave up counting their broods, from toddlers to adolescents, all wearing hand-me-down clothes with patches. It made Hung angry.

Although poor, his family had never worn patched clothes or looked undernourished and hungry before. Now what he saw was a starving family in rags.

When dinner was served, Run-ta, now the master of the house, took their father's seat. "We are not eating meat during the mourning period," he said, heaping vegetables on Hung's bowl. "We have told the dead demon emperor that we're mourning our own father, not him."

Depressed by his father's death, Hung ate very little. He looked at his family and felt another wave of sadness that moistened his eyes. He had neglected his mother, his wife, his children, and above all he had failed his father. He decided that the first thing to do in the morning was to visit his father's grave.

"You are so thin," his wife said, staring at him with a worried look. "We will feed you nothing but meat after three more days of mourning."

Hung did not have the heart to tell her that he was leaving home the next day.

"Yes," Run-mo said. "We have been catching rabbits and porcupines. We also have some salted catfish stored for the New Year."

"Papa," his son said shyly, "will you teach me to read and write?"

"The Confucian temple is not the same since you left for Kwangsi," Run-ta said. "It is dilapidated and empty. Nobody has money to hire another teacher. But you are different. When they hear that you are back, they will scrape their rice barrels to come up with something to start the school again."

"Oldest Brother," Hung interrupted. He took a deep breath, trying to tell the truth. "I cannot stay. I must leave home tomorrow. But I will send for you . . . all of you."

"Where are you going, Papa?" his daughter asked, looking crushed.

"Back to Kwangsi Province," he said. Shaking off his sorrow, he decided to be cheerful and paint a pretty picture of the future. "Kwangsi is a beautiful place, the people are friendly and brave. Your father will build a Kingdom of God there. Give me a year, two years, you will join me. There will be no more famine, no more poverty. You will eat nothing but the best cuts of pork. I will fatten all of you and nobody will slave for the demons anymore."

He stopped, glancing from one face to another. Nobody was smiling. Nobody seemed excited about his Kingdom of God.

"Shiu-chu'an," his wife said, her eyes full of tears. "I want you to stop fighting the demons. Your father died because you were fighting the demons. They arrested him and forced him to tell them where you were."

Hung was stunned. Nobody had told him of his father's arrest. "Did they torture him?" he asked.

His mother nodded, tears creeping down her pale, wrinkled cheeks.

"He died from bottom-beating," Run-ta said grimly.

Hung closed his eyes and fists tightly, trying to suppress a rising fury that was choking him. His children stared at him; the adults looked away. When his anger subsided, he took a deep breath and opened his eyes.

"Why did nobody tell me this sooner?" he asked, his voice still trembling with emotion.

"We have not told you everything," Lotus sobbed. "Father is gone. What is the use?"

"They said you were a rebel," Run-ta said. "Run-kan asked a foreigner to tell the government that you were not a rebel, only a preacher of the gospels of a foreign god. The government is afraid of the foreigners after the Opium War. Otherwise, they would have confiscated our land and our house."

"You are safe now, Shiu-ch'uan," his wife said tearfully. "We can stay together and rebuild our lives . . ."

"Yes," Run-ta said, "and you can preach the foreign religion anywhere now."

"We will stay together, Lotus," he said to his weeping wife. "We will rebuild not only our lives but our country as well. It is a promise!" His voice was firm, his jawbones working, and his reddened eyes glaring. He was more determined than ever to overthrow the Manchu Dynasty.

22

Golden Rooster had gone to Canton to buy weapons and to meet Hung. He had been gone for almost a week now. Every day, Su San-mei wondered if he had seen Hung. In the past she had always avoided talking about Hung, but never got tired of discussing the God-worshippers, hoping that she could learn a bit about Hung in a round-about way.

This time she expected Golden Rooster to bring back a lot of information that would satisfy her secret yearning for news. As the years had gone by, her grudge against Hung had gradually dissipated, but still she would never go to him like an amiable puppy begging to be loved. Her ambition was to do something courageous to benefit the God-worshippers, some deed so glorious that Hung could not possibly fail to notice her and would have to come to her begging to be loved. She had cherished such a dream ever since her miserable Pearl River days. This time she hoped that Golden Rooster would not only bring news about Hung but also provide her with the opportunity to earn Hung's admiration.

When she had thought about Hung years ago, she had mumbled to herself, invoking the ghost in hell: "Go see Yen Lo and see if I care, you turtle's egg!" Years later, as her grudge started to fade, her thoughts softened accordingly to, "I'll show you, you heartless goat!"

Now, as she sat in Golden Rooster's rattan chair on the deck of the Sea Hawk, she thought of Hung and said with a smile, "You are the king, I am the pirate. Remember me?"

Golden Rooster returned to the Sea Hawk in one of his speedy junks. It was early in the morning. Su San-mei had already made some rice gruel and fried a few eggs. Pretending that she was not anxious for information, she made him sit down at the dining table in the main cabin and served him breakfast. Golden Rooster was quiet, looking worried.

Su San-mei, her heart beating, was still trying to avoid talking about Hung. She asked, "You went to Canton to buy foreign weapons, but you come back empty-handed and look like a wet chicken. What happened?"

"I gave away my weapon money," he said with a sigh.

"Gave away a thousand taels of silver? To whom?"

"To Hung Shiu-ch'uan. He needs it more than we do."

Hung's name gave her heart a tug. She was anxious to know why Hung needed the money, but hid her anxiety and asked casually, "Why? Is he marrying off his daughter and has to borrow the money to buy a dowry?"

"The God-worshippers are ready to march," Golden Rooster said. He stopped, picking at his food without appetite. It was not like him; he had always talked, laughed, and eaten ravenously.

Su San-mei began to worry. "Are you ill, Father?" she asked.

"He talked about marching," Golden Rooster went on. "But he left the meeting abruptly. He said there was an emergency. Later I learned that Feng, the priest, had been arrested. I wish I had bought the weapons."

Su San-mei kept quiet. She knew that Feng was in danger and that Golden Rooster was thinking of rescuing him. All the secret societies had vowed to help the God-worshippers in their rebellion. She had never seen Golden Rooster so depressed. The problem must have been terribly serious. She wondered how she could help. Suddenly she remembered Tall Horse Liu, a rich landlord who had recently organized a five-hundred-man militia to protect his property and to act as the local official's "teeth and claws." Levying a local tax, he had bought some modern weapons for his militia, which he commanded himself.

"Father," she said, "if you will allow me, I think I can get you some foreign rifles."

Golden Rooster looked up sharply. "You? Where? How?"

"Give me two hundred men and I will deliver the weapons. We will rob Tall Horse Liu's militia."

Golden Rooster threw up his hands. "Su San-mei," he said despairingly, "I am not in the mood for bad jokes this morning."

"Who is joking? I have a plan."

Shaking his head, Golden Rooster said with a deep scowl, "Listen, Tall Horse Liu has five hundred men equipped with five hundred modern rifles. How can two hundred men with primitive weapons rob them?"

"Why not?" Su San-mei argued. "We will not only get their rifles, but their new shiny boots, too."

Golden Rooster looked at her with narrowed eyes, still shaking his head. Su San-mei stamped her foot in agitation. "I am serious, Father!"

"Two hundred men," Golden Rooster said with a long sigh. "What are they going to do, spit and try to drown Tall Horse Liu's militiamen with saliva?"

Su San-mei swallowed a mouthful of rice gruel. She said with a devilish smile, "Father, Old Sun's new crop of watermelons is ripe. We'll buy a few hundred melons from him. We'll also borrow some water buckets from the townspeople. That is all I need for the job."

"No, no, no!" Golden Rooster said firmly. "We are not going to poison Tall Horse Liu's militiamen with watermelons. Or hit them with water buckets, if that is what you have on your foxy mind."

"Father," Su San-mei said heatedly, stamping her foot again, "you still think I am a good-for-nothing stupid little girl!"

"Yes, I do! And naughty, too!" Golden Rooster barked.

Tall Horse Liu was the biggest landlord in Sin An County. A first cousin of the Fu magistrate, he often acted as "teeth and claws" for his cousin and other well-connected officials. Recently, he had not only equipped his men with foreign rifles but had bought them shiny leather boots. He enjoyed riding around on his white stallion showing off his modern militia, who marched behind him in their new tunics and squeaky boots, imitating the Japanese army's goose steps.

Tall Horse Liu was a squat middle-aged man with a long narrow face; he always rode on his horse to appear tall and it earned him the nickname that he liked. However, he preferred to have people call him Commander Tall Horse Liu, a title granted by the Fu magistrate. His number-one enemy was the secret societies, which often harassed him and stole his pigs and water buffalo. Yet he hated to fight them, especially the Triads, who were like shadows and hard to identify. When chased, they simply melted into towns and villages without a trace.

When he heard a rumor that the Triads had retreated from Feng Tan, a nearby town, he saw a golden chance to earn government praise without much work. He would simply march to Feng Tan and claim the credit for driving the rebels out of Sin An County. After occupying the town, he would post some notices on the walls informing the townspeople that they were now under his protection. The Manchu government had issued orders to all private militias to help quell the rebellions. From his action he might even get a cash reward plus a red-buttoned cap from the Imperial Court. When he thought about it, he became so excited that he immediately ordered his militia to get ready to march.

Feng Tan was one of the Triads' secret headquarters. Almost 80 percent of the townspeople were Triad members. When Su San-mei heard that Tall Horse Liu had fallen into her scheme and was marching toward Feng Tan, she was ready. She had assigned various duties to her two hundred men. Hiding on the roofs along the five-block-long narrow street, the only thoroughfare in Feng Tan, her men waited for Tall Horse Liu's arrival. Meanwhile, the women in the houses were busy boiling water.

When Tall Horse Liu and his men marched into the town, the Triads hoisted buckets of boiling water up to the roofs and poured it down onto the street. Badly scalded, the militiamen panicked. Their screams shook the roofs. Tall Horse Liu ordered a hasty retreat. As the frightened militiamen started retreating from both ends of the street, hundreds of pieces of watermelon began to shower down on them. The men slipped on the crushed watermelons, tumbled and fell, crawling on all fours in a frantic attempt to escape. Most of them abandoned their rifles and ammunition. They fled, screaming. Tall Horse Liu was thrown from his horse. He struggled on the slippery melon rinds in his shiny boots, unable to get up, his short arms flailing and his bowed legs thrusting about like an overturned crab. On the roofs, two hundred men were still pouring boiling water into the street, beating drums and gongs and yelling, "Sha, sha, sha!"

When finally the militiamen had all escaped, the Triads climbed down from the roofs and gathered the abandoned rifles and ammunition belts. The townspeople happily cleaned the street of crushed watermelons and congratulated Su San-mei for a clever job well done. They all hated the "teeth and claws" of the Manchu officials and were sorry that they had not used boiling oil instead of boiling water.

Back on the Sea Hawk with the new supply of modern weapons carried in two sampans, Su San-mei found Golden Rooster relaxing in his rattan chair on the deck, puffing on his bamboo pipe. He had already learned what had happened and had had a good laugh. But he did not want to spoil Su San-mei with too much praise.

"What happened?" he asked quietly. "Did you beat off Tall Horse Liu with your watermelons and water buckets?"

"Look at the foreign weapons in the sampans, Father," she said, pointing. "You could not have bought so many for a thousand taels of silver."

Golden Rooster glanced at the weapons and opened his eyes wide in fake surprise. "I didn't know Tall Horse Liu would be so gullible," he said, clucking his teeth. "If I were he, I would not have exchanged such good weapons for your rotten melons."

PART TWO

THE
HOLY
WAR

23

Back in Thistle Mountain, Hung found that the arrest of Feng was the only topic people discussed. They wondered if the Universal God, Jehovah, would protect him. Those who had become God-worshippers were confident that Priest Feng, as a messenger of God, would walk right out of jail when the time came.

Feng had accomplished a great deal during Hung's absence. He had tirelessly preached the gospels of God and built up Hung's image as God's Second Son, who had been appointed as demon slayer on earth. He would rule as the Emperor of the Heavenly Kingdom on earth, where there would be no famine, no poverty, no misery, and above all no taxes ... where all men and women would be equal, share equally food and wealth, and be blessed with permanent peace and happiness. When a God-worshipper died, he would go from the Heavenly Kingdom on earth directly to the Heavenly Kingdom in Heaven ruled by God Jehovah. To the people in the famine-devastated land where political corruption was rampant, the two Kingdoms of Heaven were shelters too good to be true. Hung knew it, and he would do anything to protect what Feng had accomplished.

During an urgent meeting with Yang, Shao, Ironwork Yeh, Square Head Liang and a few other recruited leaders, Shao and Liang advocated armed rescue. Yang insisted that Hung go to the magistrate and negotiate Feng's release peacefully. With his long gown and the certificates of his scholarly achievements, Hung would certainly impress a seventh-rank official, as he had done once before in Jin Tian. Yang's argument against armed rescue was that the charcoal makers, although trained in traditional weapons of swords and spears, would be no match for the yamen guards who were armed with bird guns and Western rifles. Hung's "three-inch tongue" would be a much better weapon.

Before the meeting was over, Hung made his decision. He would go to the yamen and use his "three-inch tongue" to free Feng. It was so urgent that he would go immediately, for the magistrate had threatened to send Feng to the Fu yamen in Kwei Ping in six days, and there was only one day left. Even if there was a trial, the result would be certain death by decapitation.

Without food and with a hasty change of clothes, Hung, accompanied by Shao, who disguised himself as a servant-bodyguard, started for Deng Pi's yamen. At the yamen, Shao struck the large iron bell three times to announce an urgent appeal for justice. The yamen door opened and two uniformed guards came out. "Too late for appeal," one of the guards said. "Come tomorrow."

Hung stepped forward and fished out a tael of silver from his sleeve. "Please inform His Honor this is an urgent appeal, a matter of life and death."

After a quick glance at the silver, the guard cupped a hand without extending it. "His Honor has already retired to his living quarters," he said in a softened voice.

Hung quickly stuffed another tael of silver in the guard's cupped hand. "Please inform him that Hung Shiu-ch'uan of the God-worshippers' Association is here to see him."

"You wait here," the guard said and withdrew.

Shao looked worried. "Ease your mind," Hung said with a smile. "I have thought everything out. This is the only way to speed things up."

"What about the God-worshippers' Association?" Shao asked. "Older Brother Feng is a preacher and is accused of treason."

"That is just a threat by an ignorant magistrate in a backward province. He does not know that even the emperor has issued an edict to allow the preaching of the foreign religion, thanks to the Treaty of Nanking. I have brought proof. He will be enlightened."

Hung and Shao waited for almost half an hour in the audience hall in the old yamen before Deng Pi waddled in from the back door, coughing and sniffing at a snuff bottle. He was followed by a secretary and two armed guards wearing uniforms with BRAVE sewn on their chests. The guards stood below the dais, each holding a sword and a bird gun. Deng Pi took his seat on the dais behind his large, black lacquered desk that was decorated with an embroidered red silk apron.

The secretary, a dried-up stooped old man, took a chair behind a smaller desk below the dais.

"Kneel," he said in a birdlike weak voice.

Hung sank to his knees. He knew that this was only a yamen ritual that he must observe. One day he would receive nine kowtows not only from such sesame-size officials but also from ministers of first rank.

"State your appeal," the secretary squawked.

In an even voice, his face without expression, Hung first stated his name, his scholarly background, and his Christian religion. Then he quoted Chi Yin, the Viceroy of Kwangtung and Kwangsi, who had granted the God-worshippers' right to preach the gospels of the foreign God in both provinces. Having sufficiently impressed the magistrate, he then requested the release of Feng, one of the preachers of the foreign God.

Customarily he would have made the statement with his head cast down, but such a posture would indicate admission of a crime or wrongdoing. He decided to strike an upright posture, stare at the magistrate straight in the eye and wait.

Deng Pi sniffed at his snuff bottle a few more times. After an explosive sneeze, he hit his desk with his gavel. "Hung Shiu-ch'uan," he said, "your foreign religion is blasphemy to our own Buddha, Confucius, and the Jade Emperor in Heaven—but since the foreign devils have won the Opium War, both the foreign religion and the foreign tobacco have been forced on our shores. It is indeed beyond my power to stop them. But, Feng Yung-shan, using this foreign religion as a shield to plan a rebellion, has committed a crime punishable by decapitation. It is my duty to send him to the Fu yamen for trial. There is nothing I can do and therefore your appeal for his release is denied." With a nod of finality he gave his desk another bang with his gavel.

"Your Honor," Hung said, his voice steady, his stare unyielding. "Feng Yung-shan is also performing his duty. Besides spreading the gospels of the foreign God, he is also trying to acquaint himself with the officialdom in this district so that he will know how to conduct himself correctly . . ."

"His conduct has already proven him a cheater, impersonating a government official. He is a criminal beyond redemption, with suspicion of rebellion."

Knowing that further argument would be futile, Hung quickly fished out a bank certificate from his pocket, rose to his feet and placed it in front of Deng Pi. "Your Honor, may God bless you."

Deng Pi picked up the certificate and looked at it through a pair of eyeglasses which he did not need. Taking his time, he returned the glasses to their embroidered case and laughed a long laugh that Hung could not interpret. He did not know if it was an expression of delight or anger. He had heard such laughter in Cantonese operas, but it could mean either good news or bad, a prelude to promotion or decapitation.

As Hung wondered, Deng Pi threw the certificate at him and barked, "Hung Shiu-ch'uan, what do you take me for, a muddle-headed corrupt official? You are blind! Guards, throw him out!"

Hung picked up the certificate and allowed the two guards to grab his arms and steer him out of the yamen unceremoniously. Shao followed closely, his eyes glaring and nostrils flaring. But Hung's warning look stopped him from violence.

Back at Thistle Mountain, Hung was depressed and his willpower weakened. Feng was his most trusted right-hand man. There was no one else able and sophisticated enough to take his place. For the first time in his life he began to feel pessimistic about his mission.

Shao and Liang became more militaristic, claiming that the only way to rescue Feng was a midnight attack. With five hundred charcoal makers well trained with swords and spears, they could whisk Feng away as easily as fishing a carp out of a fish bowl. Yang was wavering. As Hung was pacing restlessly, wringing his hands, a charcoal maker rushed in and breathlessly reported that a sedan chair had arrived.

Hung and Yang looked out through the front door and saw people hurrying out of their huts to watch. An arriving sedan chair was always big news. The chair was preceded by a lantern bearer. A large-character MAO was printed on the lantern. Obviously the visitor, Mao, was someone of considerable importance. Hung instructed Yang to bring the visitor in. Striding toward the crowd that was gathering around the sedan chair, Yang wondered who Mao was.

Without lanterns bearing the characters "Be Respectful" and "Be Quiet," the visitor could not be an official of high rank. Perhaps it was someone below the seventh rank. He shouldered into the crowd just as the visitor was stepping out of his sedan chair. It was the stooped old man with the birdlike face and birdlike voice.

"I am the secretary from the magistrate's yamen. I have come to see Hung Shiu-ch'uan."

"Follow me," Yang said, hoping that Feng's fate had turned for the better, for the secretary had come without armed guards.

Hung had watched everything through a window. When Secretary Mao stepped in, he rose and bowed, feeling that a stone had been lifted from his heart. He asked the secretary to sit down as he ordered tea.

Secretary Mao took a chair with a grunt, glanced around the small room and coughed, an unnecessary cough of authority that all yamen officials had practiced and used at appropriate moments. He took a sip of the hot tea that Yang's sister had served. With a sigh he said, quoting an old saying, "If sufficient incense is offered, there is no fear that the Buddha will not nod."

Hung grasped the meaning of the quote immediately. He spread his hands with a bitter smile. He said, "But in the yamen His Honor threw the 'incense' back at me and gave me a scolding. Everybody present witnessed it."

"Of course," Secretary Mao said with a smile. "With everybody watching what else could he do? The yamen is the wrong place to offer incense. That is why I am here."

Hung had a mouthful of satirical remarks to say about the magistrate and his office, but he swallowed them. He knew that he must do everything to speed up Feng's release.

"Yes, yes," he said amiably, "forgive my stupidity. I should have known better. Here is the same certificate for five hundred taels of silver, deposited at Forever Prosperous Bank at Kwei Ping." He tried to hand the piece of paper to Secretary Mao.

Mao glanced at the certificate and shook his head, raising both his hands, all ten fingers extended.

Hung looked at the ten bony fingers and knew that the old man demanded a thousand taels. He fought a strong desire to return the magistrate's scolding by giving the whole yamen a piece of his mind. But he took a deep breath and swallowed his wrath. Since the secretary kept his ten fingers up and his expression looked so determined, Hung knew there was no room for bargaining. It was a matter of life and death, and the yamen had the upper hand. He took Yang aside and asked him if he could raise another five hundred taels.

Yang nodded. He went to his bedroom, pulled a box out from under his bed and carried it to the middle hall where he placed it at the feet of the secretary. "Another five hundred—please count."

After the secretary had left in his sedan chair with the money, Hung asked Yang where the five hundred had come from.

"Older Brother Feng fleeced it from the magistrate. It was earmarked for gunpowder. Now it's being returned to Deng Pi. The turtle's egg doubled his money, but it saved Brother Feng's life."

Hung smiled. When Lindley's shipment of firearms arrived, the God-worshippers would raid the yamen and get all the money back plus more. He wondered how much silver and gold Deng Pi had stored under his bed.

The next day the news was not all good. The magistrate had refused to free Feng. He had returned the prisoner to Kwangtung under guard, with orders that Feng was never to come to his district again to preach the gospels of the foreign God. If caught in his district again, he would be sent to the Fu yamen for trial on grounds of treason. The magistrate had already posted such a public notice on the city wall.

The bad news was soon followed by more bad news. Many converted silver miners clamored to withdraw from the God-worshippers' Association, saying that if God Jehovah could not protect Preacher Feng, how could He protect the others?

Hung, Yang, and Shao held an urgent meeting. "What are we going to do?" Shao asked.

They all looked blank. "God will show us the way," Hung finally said. He turned to Yang and asked, "Where else are people unhappy in this county?"

"Elephant Valley," Yang said. "A new tax is being levied there to rebuild Kan Wang Temple. It is a rich men's temple. Rich people flock to the temple to ask Kan Wang to wash away their sins and wrongdoings, and yet the poor are forced to pay for the temple's improvement."

"How far is it?"

"Ten miles."

Hung had a plan. He wanted to know more about this Kan Wang, an idol he had never heard of. His plan might not work, but he must adhere to his motto: "Do your very best, and leave the result to God."

The hundred-year-old Kan Wang Temple was situated at the foot of Elephant Mountain in Kwei Ping District, surrounded by old pines and banyans. The massive building was freshly painted red, and the yellow glazed tiles had been recently replaced. The eaves were refurbished with newly carved dragons and phoenixes, and two stone lions were added to guard the front vermilion gate. It looked more like an Imperial Palace than a temple.

Inside, the statue of Kan Wang, ten feet tall, was sitting in a dragon chair with his feet apart, one hand resting on a knee and the other holding a long sword. It was an ugly idol with bulging eyes and porcupine whiskers. According to legend, he was a cruel rich man who had murdered his own mother and donated his sister to a Fu magistrate in return for protection. As a result, he got away with all his crimes. A local soothsayer had even declared that Kan Wang was destined to be a king. After his death, the rich and the powerful built a temple for him, believing that Kan Wang could protect anyone who was sinful and had committed a crime. Supported by the rich throughout the province, the temple had always been prosperous. Money and food offerings were constantly piled up on its altar; incense and candles never stopped burning; its keeper lived in luxury at the back of the building, fattened by rich food offerings and courted by landlords and local officials who needed Kan Wang's blessing. The keeper became a man of power locally; he would do anybody a favor if the bribe was attractive.

According to Yang's report, recently a rich man, Master Fei, wanted to buy a young widow in the next village but her brother refused to sell. Master Fei asked the keeper's help. The keeper declared the next day that in a dream he had been told that Kan Wang wanted to marry the widow. Nobody dared refuse Kan Wang's wish, so a marriage ceremony was arranged between the spirit and the widow. During the wedding ceremony, the widow was carried to the Kan Wang Temple in a sedan chair, and Master Fei, disguised as Kan Wang's spirit, performed conjugal love several times in the keeper's quarters. In the morning the widow hanged herself.

When the widow's brother discovered the fraud, he sued Master

Fei in the district court. The district magistrate studied the suit and concluded that Kan Wang, being a spirit, naturally could not perform conjugal love with a living person; therefore it was not unreasonable that he delegate a living being to perform it on his behalf. Case dismissed.

The widow's case made the people in Elephant Valley unhappy. But it was not until the new tax was being levied on them that they aired their complaints openly.

Yang's report about Kan Wang made Hung burn with anger, but at the same time he was glad. "It is God's will that such a scandal happened at this opportune time," he said. "I have a plan. If we can carry it out, we shall regain people's faith in the God-worshippers' Association.

In the afternoon, Hung, Yang, Shao, and dozens of charcoal makers, armed with sticks, shovels, and rakes, marched toward Kan Wang Temple like a small army.

Outside the temple there were several sedan-chair bearers squatting and smoking bamboo pipes. A few lay in a corner puffing opium. Inside the temple, their masters were kowtowing to Kan Wang, praying and offering money and food on the altar. Candles flickered and a thick incense smoke trailed up in front of Kan Wang's red scowling face. The God-worshippers burst in. Without a word, they bodily threw the Kan Wang worshippers out.

Hung brushed all the incense bowls, candlesticks, and bowls of food offerings off the altar with one violent swipe of his heavy stick. Then he mounted the dais and hacked the Kan Wang statue with a hatchet, first splitting its face, then cutting off its arms and, with one final heavy blow, smashing the torso. The rest of the God-worshippers were busy defacing the walls, destroying the latticed windows, and beating the keeper. In less that twenty minutes the temple was a shambles and the bloodied fat keeper lay on the ground twisting and groaning with exaggerated pain.

A big crowd was gathering in front of the temple. When the God-worshippers came out, dusting their clothes and hands, people gaped and cheered. Hung climbed on one of the large stone lions that guarded the gate. Surveying the crowd, he raised his hands to quiet them.

He shouted, "Brethren, Kan Wang is the worst evil idol in Kwangsi Province. Only criminals, cheaters, and sinful folk worship him. He represents the greedy landlords and corrupt government officials. Is he a real spirit that has power over us? We have destroyed him. Will he destroy us? Wait and see. Nothing will happen to us. The rich and the powerful only use superstition to exploit the common people. I, Hung Shiu-ch'uan, have the Heavenly mandate from God to demolish this evil place, destroy the demon Kan Wang, and forbid the demon worshippers to rebuild it. From now on the new tax is voided. All those who refuse to pay this unreasonable tax will be under the protection of God Jehovah. To spread the gospels of our God, I urge all of you to join the God-worshippers' Association. Together we will form a formidable holy army and smash all the demons, all the blood suckers, and all the corrupt officials. Together we will build a Heavenly Kingdom on earth where there will be no taxes, no famine, no misery . . ."

Before he finished, the enlarged crowd—more than a thousand strong—raised their hands and clamored to join.

24

When the news of the destruction of Kan Wang Temple spread, the people in the villages and towns within a radius of five hundred miles began to send representatives to Thistle Mountain to show support. More people asked to join the God-worshippers. The doubting silver miners all changed their minds about withdrawing. In a few months, the membership records increased from a pile five feet high to ten feet high.

Meanwhile, Ironwork Yeh's weapons factory in Jin Tian and Square Head Liang's goose farm in Thistle Mountain increased production. New shipments of gunpowder arrived. Money started pouring in from some disgruntled well-to-do local people. Hung discovered that quite a few rich families also were interested in becoming God-worshippers for one reason or another.

A Wei family, one of the richest in the County of Kwei, joined without solicitation. Wei and Liu were two feuding families in the district; their enmity could be traced to their grandfathers. Grandfather Liu had passed the Imperial examination of Advanced Scholar degree and had been appointed a fifth-ranked Fu official. He became the head of a leading family with a high door, lived in a palatial home and was served by a horde of maids and male servants. The other rich man, Grandfather Wei, made a fortune in the salt trade and also became a large landowner. But he was unhappy about his lack of scholastic status. He bought an Associated Advanced Scholar title to boost his prestige. To show his new status, he hung a large black lacquered board over his gate saying in gold characters, MANSION OF ASSOCIATED ADVANCED SCHOLAR.

Both families were large landowners. During drought they always fought each other for water, sometimes resorting to open battles. They

armed their servants and hired mercenaries to do their fighting; sometimes their sons and grandsons joined the fray. Each time a relative was
wounded or killed, the family feud deepened. Now the families were
controlled by the eldest grandsons, Wei Ta and Snake Head Liu, who
had earned his nickname by being sneaky. Both men were in their late
twenties, both were restless, itching for a fight, even without a cause.

One night, Snake Head Liu and a few servants sneaked to Wei's
house and replaced the signboard with another. The new signboard said,
MANSION OF ADVANCED SCHOLAR. Three days later the Fu yamen sent a
dozen guards to Wei's house and arrested the father, accusing him of
falsifying his family title. When the father argued that the family had
never claimed the title of Advanced Scholar, only Associated Advanced
Scholar, the court produced the new signboard as proof of guilt.

The father protested that somebody else had replaced it, but the
Fu magistrate laughed. "Who would bother to replace somebody else's
signboard?" he asked sarcastically. Ignoring further argument, he sentenced Wei Ta's father to fifty strokes of bottom-beating and six months
in jail.

The loss of face was so devastating that the Wei family decided to
declare war. But with less land, less status, and fewer connections with
local officials, Wei Ta changed his plans. The God-worshippers had just
sacked the Kan Wang Temple, an act that even he himself would not
have dreamed of committing . . . a feat of tremendous daring. Without
consulting his family, he paid Hung and Yang a visit and requested that
he be allowed to join the God-worshippers immediately. He also offered
a donation of two thousand taels of silver, with more to come if needed.
Other minor landlords, tired of bribing officials, quickly followed suit.

Since the Opium War, foreigners seemed to be more powerful than
the Manchu Emperor. The people believed that worshipping the foreign
god certainly would bring some protection, if not prosperity. Besides
following Wei Ta's suit and joining the God-worshippers, some of them
also added the bearded foreign God to their god collection. They placed
a picture of Jesus Christ on their family altars alongside the Buddha,
Kwan Yin, Kwang Kung, and assorted other gods and goddesses.

The Governor of Kwangsi was alarmed. He alerted many border
generals, county magistrates, and Fu magistrates, and other government

contingencies and ordered them to suppress this dangerous tide. But all of them lacked funds for firearms because the foreigners had drained the country of silver.

The Fu magistrate managed to raise an army of two thousand men. He ordered them to march to Thistle Mountain to see if Hung Shiu-ch'uan was arming his God-worshippers. If so, he wanted his troops to bring Hung's head back. He wanted to be the first one to claim that he had quelled a rebellion.

Having learned of the Fu magistrate's movements, the God-worshippers prepared for the first large-scale government attack. To recruit more leaders, Hung studied the lists of potential candidates and the detailed maps which Feng had compiled before his arrest. Hung discovered two men on the lists who were highly qualified as future commanders.

The first was Shih Ta-kai, a transplanted Hakka from Kwangtung Province, orphaned at an early age, self-educated, who had made a small fortune in farming and trading water buffalo. Quiet and upright, he detested corruption and injustice. He was widely read and well trained in martial arts—a man to be wooed.

The second was Hu Yi-huang, thirty-four, a Kwangsi native, immensely rich, a well-read man with a degree of Talented in Military Strategy. He was generous and sociable. Repulsed by corruption, he refused to pursue officialdom in the present government.

To recruit these two men, Hung paid each a visit as a humble man seeking advice. Both men had already heard about the God-worshippers and their heroic deeds. While conversing with Hung, they found that they were all frustrated idealists with a secret ambition to overthrow the Manchu Dynasty. Without much persuasion Hung converted them and promised them leadership positions in his future Heavenly Kingdom.

One winter night a violent gale blew outside Hu Yi-huang's palatial home. Trees bent in the wind and windows banged. Inside the large middle hall five men were kneeling in front of a portrait of Jesus Christ; eight candles were flickering on the altar. The five men were Hung Shiu-ch'uan, Yang Shiu-ching, Shao Chou-kwei, Shih Ta-kai, and Hu Yi-huang. They were making a pact as the founding leaders of the God-worshippers' Association.

After three kowtows to Jesus Christ, Hung offered a prayer: "Oh, God almighty in Heaven, the God-worshippers, under your command, have assembled more than ten thousand faithful followers. We are all of one mind, determined to slay the demons and build a Heavenly Kingdom on earth, where people will worship only one God; all people will be sisters and brothers enjoying peace and prosperity and equally blessed by you. We five worshippers pledge our devotion to you and will carry out your command to start the holy war in your name. We shall follow the road opened by you for Moses, and march forward to the promised land, singing your praises. We shall execute your commands without fear and regardless of personal sacrifice, like eldest brother Jesus Christ, who sacrificed himself for the good of common men. Oh, God almighty, we seek your direction and blessing in this holy war which, we five, your most devoted servants, solemnly swear to lead. Amen."

After the swearing-in, the five men moved to a large hardwood long table, seated themselves in carved ancestral chairs, and discussed each man's duties and responsibilities. The ritual of praising each other's talent and ability and nominating each other for the highest positions took considerable time. Finally, the highest five positions were filled:

(1) Hung Shiu-ch'uan, the absolute leader of the God-worshippers' Association; (2) Yang Shiu-ching, the Commander in Chief of the holy war; (3) Hu Yi-huang, Minister of Food and Weapon Supply; (4) Shih Ta-kai, Minister of Military Training; (5) Shao Chou-kwei, Army General. They also appointed Feng Yung-shan, the absentee leader, as the Prime Minister, and Run-kan, another absentee, the Foreign Minister. They chose Hung's birthday as the date for the Kwangsi uprising. They named their kingdom Taiping Tiankuo, the Heavenly Kingdom of Great Peace.

Using Feng's detailed maps, they discussed their basic strategy. They would first capture Kweilin, the provincial capital of Kwangsi Province, then march north to Hunan, Hupei, Nanking, and finally to Peking. If the government defense was strong, they would use back roads to avoid major clashes; if weak, they would occupy cities and large towns to replenish supplies and recruit new soldiers. They also designated Jin Tian as the place to start the uprising. From the maps, the City of Yun An and the provincial capital were the most formidable yet strategically the most important. Shih Ta-kai was ordered to gather all the information about the two cities' defenses, their supplies, and their commanders' backgrounds.

The following day, the five men disappeared to their hiding places to work out the details of their duties. Meanwhile, the hammering of weapons at Square Head Liang's goose farm increased, but the noise was still drowned out by the ear-splitting cries from some two thousand well-fed geese. In Jin Tian, Ironwork Yeh's blacksmith shop had also expanded and gone underground.

Jin Tian suddenly became a place of activity. Women were busy making banners, tents, and uniforms; all the roads were full of men carrying hidden arms and supplies. The eastern part of Jin Tian had been designated as the camps for men and the western part as the camps for women. Families from the surrounding villages were willingly abandoning their homes to join the camps. Mountain caves were cleaned, tents were pitched, and bamboo huts went up everywhere. The soldiers were trained in nearby mountain valleys. Messengers bearing goose-feather arrows darted from command post to command post on fast horses. Children and the elderly were kept busy cooking, washing, and fetching water while dogs, pigs, and chickens roamed freely, barking, honking, and cackling amid singing and laughter. Jin Tian had become a happy settlement for more than ten thousand people, a sample of what was to come—the promised Heavenly Kingdom of the God-worshippers. But behind the peaceful facade a war was fomenting in mountain valleys and hideaway huts.

The Fu magistrate who had planned to attack Thistle Mountain changed his mind. He appealed to Hong Yun, Governor of Kwangsi, for help. Hong appointed two Imperial army commanders, Chu and Tao, to deal with the God-worshippers. Chu and Tao assembled five thousand men and marched to Ping Nan County with a secret war plan.

The Imperial troops spent a day in the county seat making preparations for a surprise attack on Jin Tian the next night. The commander of the Fu yamen guards, along with the Fu magistrate, played host at a banquet for the officers of the Imperial troops. The drinking and eating was noisy and full of festivity. The officers had already worked out the strategy for a sneak attack.

The open road from Ping Nan to Jin Tian was twenty-five miles, but there was a short cut—an intestinelike path going through a mountain gorge, which was only half the distance. The path had been well beaten by thousands of aborigines' feet for hundreds of years; the life-threatening wild animals, poisonous snakes, and mountain evil spirits along the way had long since disappeared. The men believed that this invasion would be like a pleasure trip.

Full of confidence, the two commanders and the Fu magistrate played the finger-guessing game and consumed several dozen jars of mao-tai and *hsiao hsing*. After the banquet Commanders Chu and Tao retired to the yamen guest house, still feeling high from the liquor. Chu suggested that they send for two local singsong girls to spend the night with them. Tao was hesitant, saying that they should not underestimate the God-worshippers. He had heard rumors about their magical powers; they had destroyed quite a few temples, including the infamous Temple of Kan Wang. It was no secret that those who had offended Kan Wang would always wind up sick or suffering from loss of properties; in serious cases, even loss of loved ones to violent death. Yet nothing had happened to the God-worshippers.

Chu laughed. "Their bad luck is coming, can't you see?" he said, belching from too much food and wine. "By tomorrow night their heads will fall like rotten melons!"

"But they have more than ten thousand people," Tao said, looking worried.

"Half of them are women and children," Chu said with another laugh. "Since when have you become henpecked . . . so frightened of women? Listen, we are not going to fight all ten thousand men. Remember the old saying: 'To wipe out a horde, aim at the chief; to kill a man, aim at the head. When the head is gone, all the rest becomes useless.' "

"But how to find their heads?"

"All rebels love banners. Haven't we found that out? Each sesame-size chief has a banner flying outside his camp, bearing his name and title. We simply sneak into the quarters of their "heads" and *Cha!*" He made the gesture of chopping several heads off with the edge of his palm, then smiled smugly. "The God-worshippers will be no different.

If we get lucky and capture Hung, the war is over before we even fire a single shot. How about two aborigine girls? They say the aborigines are good and clean."

Commander Chu said he always loved to spend the evening with a woman before a battle; if he was lucky, he might even deflower a girl, for a virgin's blood was a lucky color and it always brought victory to his troops.

Commander Tao was not too sure. He said that the God-worshippers were different from the Triads, the Big Swords, the White Lotuses, and all the other rebels; they had the backing of foreign devils. Furthermore, he added, the Imperial Court had issued an edict stating that no one was to interfere with the preaching of the gospels of the foreign God. "What if the God-worshippers have a few foreign devils among them and we chop off a wrong head or two?"

"Ease your mind, older brother," Commander Chu said. "There are no foreigners among the God-worshippers. The foreign devils have blue eyes, yellow hair, pale skin, and a nose three times as big as ours. I have never seen one, but if such creatures are found anywhere near here, don't you think that we would already have heard about them?"

Commander Tao was finally convinced that there was nothing to worry about. His confidence regained, he rubbed his hands together and said with a smile, "Two singsong girls? Why not? In history, heroes and beauties are always mentioned in one breath."

The night was foggy. Commander Tao and Commander Chu were sound asleep in their adjacent rooms. Lying beside them were their aborigine singsong girls, who had hardly slept because of the two men's heavy snoring. Outside the yamen, five thousand government troops slept in large tents and barracks, with colorful banners hanging limply on bamboo poles outside the officers' tents. The air was dead. Nothing disturbed the still night except the chirping of crickets and the men's snoring.

Five hundred God-worshippers, headed by General Shao, appeared from behind houses and shops. When they reached the yamen, they fanned out in several groups. They were dressed in yellow tunics and red turbans, with a broadsword strapped on their shoulders. Some carried local-made firearms. Two men scaled the yamen wall and presently the gate opened and Shao gestured with his broadsword. One of the groups poured through the gate. Soon pandemonium broke loose; yelling and battle cries sent a shock wave through the area. Some of the Imperial guards inside the yamen rushed out of their rooms with their weapons but were instantly hacked down by the God-worshippers. The two aborigine girls were hysterical, running in circles and begging for mercy. Inside the guest house the two commanders leapt out of their beds, wondering what had happened. Tao, in a daze, groped for his clothes, but before he could throw his trousers on, two God-worshippers grabbed him and threw him down. They bound his hands and legs and dragged him to the courtyard, where Commander Chu was already lying on his face, his hands and legs similarly strapped with sturdy rope. Lying beside each other, they turned their heads to each other and stared.

"What did I tell you?" Commander Tao said. "Never underestimate an enemy."

"If each of us had had a virgin last night," Commander Chu replied, "we wouldn't have had such bad luck."

Outside the yamen, the noise of fighting quickly subsided. Most of the government officers had been either captured or killed. The soldiers surrendered without a fight; only a few escaped with little clothing on. The surprise raid provided the God-worshippers with a large amount of weapons and food supplies. Before dawn, they had disappeared with the bounty as quietly as they had come, taking with them a dozen captives, Tao and Chu among them.

The night raid was the God-worshippers' first victory against the Imperial troops. It boosted the morale of every man and woman in Jin Tian; their energy doubled and their activities were carried out in the open. In Thistle Mountain, the hammering noise in Mr. Liang's weapons factory increased so much that even the hullabaloo raised by thousands of geese could no longer hide it. Knowing that the swift maneuvering of Shao had struck fear into the Imperial troops, Hung ordered many notices posted in surrounding towns and cities offering amnesty to those who surrendered with their weapons.

As a northward march was being readied, Hung issued another order instructing all the converts to pack their clothes, food, salt, and other properties, set fire to their shacks and come to join the community in

Jin Tian. Many people in the surrounding counties did so, and the community doubled.

On a bright morning, the captured officers from the Imperial troops were offered amnesty if they would join the God-worshippers. Those who refused would be sentenced to forty-nine days of hard labor. Then they would be released and sent home. Tao and Chu, knowing that their lives were being spared, chose the forty-nine days. Hung was glad, for he wanted the two men to become a propaganda tool for the God-worshippers, carrying stories back to their camps, telling what they had seen and experienced . . . messages that would strike more fear into the enemy.

To boost morale, the God-worshippers decided to have a victory celebration before the northward march. During the day of festivities gongs, drums, and firecrackers were heard through the valley. Cooking smoke trailed up and the aroma of roasted pigs drifted to the river on an east wind, which was unusual, since the wind always blew in the other direction toward the mountains. A geomancer from Ping Nan announced that it was an excellent sign; it meant that even the Chinese gods approved of the deeds of the foreign God.

While feasting in their headquarters, Hung, Yang, and the other leaders did not forget Feng and Run-kan. Two empty places were set at the head table. Hung poured wine and filled two empty bowls with food as though Feng and Run-kan were present. At the banquet, Hung conducted prayers twice, once at the beginning and once at the end, thanking Jehovah the Heavenly Father for the food and the victory. Then everybody joined in a chorus, singing a Chinese version of "Marching of the Christians," a holy song Hung had learned from Run-kan and had taught the others to sing:

> Onward God-worshippers,
> Marching to Kingdom of Heaven;
> With the cross of Jesus,
> Slaying all the demons.

Just as the singing was reaching its crescendo, a guard rushed in breathlessly and shouted, "Priest Feng has come back!"

Everybody stopped singing and turned toward the door. Smiling pleasantly, Feng walked in, covered with dust, a bundle of clothing slung across his back. He was followed by the two yamen guards who had been ordered to escort him to Kwangtung. They were also travel-worn, their faces darkened by hard weather. Hung rushed forward and took both Feng's hands.

With happy tears in his eyes, he cried, "Elder Brother Feng! This is a miracle! God has answered my prayer!" He cast a quick glance at the guards and added hesitantly, "Is this a good dream or bad?"

"Good," Feng said, still smiling. He gestured for the guards to come forward.

The two guards sank on their knees in front of Hung. The older, a man about fifty, said respectfully, "We are indebted to Priest Feng for enlightening us about the God-worshippers' Kingdom of Heaven. Through the long journey to the Kwangsi border, he taught us the gospels of Jehovah. He told us about the creation of the world in six days, the big flood, the big march, the big famine, the crossing of the crimson sea, the pillars of cloud and fire, and finally the promised land. During the journey, we shared food and water. Together we swatted flies and mosquitos, we evaded pirates and bandits. Everything that we did together gave us more faith in the brotherhood of the God-worshippers. Today it is a great honor to meet with you face to face, Second Brother of Jesus Christ. From now on we shall follow you as your soldiers, obey all your commands, slay the demons, and build a Heavenly Kingdom of eternal happiness."

"Amen," the other guard said. Both gave Hung nine kowtows, the utmost salutation, which was reserved only for an emperor.

25

The God-worshippers were ready to march. All the secret societies had been alerted and Golden Rooster had accepted a mission that had been bothering him for several days. The God-worshippers' planned route was along the south side of the West River; there were numerous towns on the north side where the Imperial armies had built strong forts with cannons aimed at the river. Some of the cannons were big enough to destroy ships and cause havoc among the marching troops on the opposite banks.

Golden Rooster had received a request to seize a town called Han Shan on the north side. It was a small walled city fortified with cannons on all sides. All four city gates were closely guarded in the daytime and closed at night. The gate on the south side was the city's main outlet; traffic was heavy but restricted. Dozens of Imperial soldiers were posted at the gate, questioning all the people who entered the city. Sometimes the soldiers searched them thoroughly. To seize the town was a difficult task; most of the two-thousand-man garrison was equipped with modern rifles. Golden Rooster regarded the job as almost impossible, but his love for a challenge prevented him from saying no. Su San-mei asked him what was bothering him.

"Annoyed by bedbugs," he said, reluctant to tell the truth. Su San-mei always had clever solutions to difficult problems, but this was war, and he did not want her to meddle with it.

"Father," Su San-mei said, "if you are really annoyed by bedbugs, I cannot help you. But if you want to seize Han Shan, I know what your problems are. I would like to reduce your scowls with a few suggestions."

Golden Rooster's scowl deepened. "So you know?"

"Fire cannot be wrapped with paper," she said. "Why hide it? Let me tell you what your problems are. If I am wrong, I shall seal my mouth and never say a word again. Number one, Han Shan is on the north bank and you cannot move your men across the river without ships or a bridge. Yet all your ships are engaged in transporting merchandise, except a few small sampans, which are not enough to move a lot of fighting men. So you scowl.

"Number two, you cannot attack a walled city without modern weapons, but most of your foreign rifles and cannons are being used to defend your ships. So you scowl some more . . ."

"All right," Golden Rooster interrupted. "Since you are clever enough to guess all my problems, you might as well tell me all your foxy ideas for solving them."

"Number one," she said rapidly, having already thought out all the answers, "most of the villagers in this province have coffins. These people are poor but they don't want to die without a coffin. This is an age-old tradition of the southerners, you know that."

"You don't have to tell me about traditions. I assume you want to borrow some coffins. Go on."

"We will borrow a hundred," she said, "and ask the villagers to carry them to the river's edge."

Golden Rooster watched Su San-mei explain her plan. She sounded so confident that he listened without interruption. When she had finished, she held her breath, waiting for his reaction.

He lighted his bamboo pipe and puffed on it leisurely, his rugged face expressionless. It irritated her and she blurted out, "Father, in three days it will be Kwan Yin—worshipping day. Hundreds of peasant women will pour into the Kwan Yin temple in the city to pray for more baby boys. The sentries will not ask too many questions. If you do nothing but puff on your smelly pipe, we'll miss this golden opportunity to seize Han Shan!"

"I don't like the idea of disguising our men as women. No Triad is pretty enough to get by with it. If a man is pretty, he cannot be a very good fighter."

"We need only a dozen men in disguise. They are going to pray for babies, not join a beauty contest for Imperial concubines."

Golden Rooster knew that Su San-mei had all the answers. If he continued to argue, she might accuse him of trying to pick bones from an egg. So far, she had not failed in her schemes. Besides, the plan she suggested sounded vaguely familiar. It seemed to be a plan derived from Su San-mei's Book of Military Strategy. She had probably borrowed it from old tales told by teahouse storytellers.

He finished his pipe, knocked the ashes out deliberately on the deck and sighed. "All right, but if you fail we will need all the coffins to bury ourselves in."

Within three days, the Triads collected a hundred coffins from three nearby villages. They were good sturdy coffins, all black laquered and built out of heavy blackwood. The southerners all believed in life after death; for a better life in the next world they all wanted to be carried to their graves in the best coffin they could afford. Sometimes they starved themselves to save money for such a coffin.

Each coffin was at least three feet wide and seven feet long. Spaced correctly, a hundred coffins could cover the distance between the West River's north and south banks at its narrowest place. Working feverishly on a moonless night, two hundred villagers, mostly Triad members, carried the coffins to the river, fastened them with sturdy ropes and speedily built a floating bridge three feet wide. Before dawn, a thousand fighting men had crossed the river quietly and camped in the pine forest south of the city.

At dawn, a dozen Triads disguised as women approached the main gate with numerous other peasant women who were trying to enter the city. They carried incense, candles, and food offerings in baskets that hung from bamboo poles. The twelve Triads walked mincingly in their loose women's clothes, their faces rouged and eyebrows painted. The sentries found them rather attractive. Flirting a bit, the Triads fluttered their fingers at the soldiers as they followed the other baby-seekers on their way to the Kwan Yin temple, their long weapons hidden inside their bamboo poles and their small weapons inside their food offerings of chicken, pork, and tubs of rice.

In the evening, as soon as the city gates were closed, two hundred Triads appeared in the distance, out of gunshot from the eastern wall. They waved flags and banners and made a terrific din by beating drums and gongs while screaming, "Sha, sha, sha!" They sounded like a big army bearing down on the city of Han Shan.

The garrison commander immediately ordered his troops to the eastern gate, ready for an enemy assault. To boost their own morale, the troops fired the big guns and small firearms aimlessly, frightening all the birds away, causing chickens to cackle and dogs to slink off with their tails between their hind legs. The townspeople bolted their doors and windows; babies cried and mothers yelled their missing children's names fearfully, creating a bedlam that the townspeople had never experienced before.

Meanwhile, the twelve Triad "baby seekers" sneaked to the south gate and overpowered the few guards there, slitting their throats. The dozen guards who were on the wall heard cries and rushed to their comrades' aid, but were brought down by the Triads' rifle fire. When the Triads threw the south city gate open, hundreds of Triads emerged from a nearby pine forest, shooting their guns and brandishing hatchets and swords. They poured through the city gate.

The moment the defenders of the eastern gate heard the noise and found that they were being attacked from inside the city, they panicked. Some dropped their weapons and ran; others threw up their hands and surrendered. Golden Rooster was leading the attack from the south gate. Su San-mei was one of the "baby seekers." They met at the eastern gate.

Surveying the rows of Imperial troops begging for mercy on their knees, Su San-mei asked Golden Rooster what he was going to do with them—take them prisoner or let them go? Without hesitation, Golden Rooster ordered them to go. He had no use for opium addicts and Happy Buddha bellies.

The cache of modern weapons was enormous. "What now, Father?" Su San-mei asked triumphantly. She hoped to conquer a string of other towns to impress Hung Shiu-ch'uan. But Golden Rooster had no such ambition.

He said, "If the mayor has a good cook, we will have a victory banquet in his yamen, then vacate the city before the God-worshippers arrive."

"Why are we in such a hurry?" Su San-mei asked, disappointed.

"I don't want to hear them preach the gospels of their foreign God."

"Why not? Don't you want to hear about all the good things in Heaven?"

"They say that Heaven is closed to all sinners," Golden Rooster retorted. "What good is it to hear about the good things? Let's go sack the mayor's yamen."

26

Since Snake Head Liu had secretly replaced the signboard on Wei Ta's front gate, the Wei family had never recovered from the humiliation of being wrongly accused of falsifying their family title. Wei Ta felt some relief, however—even excitement, when he joined the God-worshippers. He was sure that by belonging to a strong organization, his chances for revenge were much better.

Now that the God-worshippers were getting stronger every day, he was eager for an appointment. But after donating two thousand taels of silver, he did not hear from Hung again. When he heard that the God-worshippers had again recruited many insignificant local "dogs" and "cats" as important "tree trunks" in their army, he was terribly upset, cursing and banging on tables with his fist. His four children and three concubines avoided him.

Only his wife, Ching Ching, ate breakfast with him this morning and tried to soothe him. At the carved teakwood dining table, staring at his food, Wei breathed hard, his nostrils flaring. His rice bowl was full. His wife picked up another morsel of pork with her ivory chopsticks and placed it on his soy sauce dish.

"Try this morsel, my son's father," she said gently. "It is the gristle part, your favorite."

"Don't urge me to eat," he said hotly. "I have no appetite, can't you see?"

His wife, at thirty-two, was four years older than Wei but looked at least five years younger. She almost never lost her temper, but Wei's loss of appetite, her father-in-law's sickness, and the worsened family feud with Snake Head Liu was beginning to worry her. With Deng Pi's backing, Snake Head Liu's harassment was getting worse and there was not much the Wei family could do. But the Wei family was still rich and powerful, owning a thousand acres of land and a private militia of over a hundred men. Why was her husband getting gloomier every day?

She asked, "My son's father, one day you are excited and happy, another day you look as gloomy as Yen Lo. Why?"

"Why!" he answered, throwing down his chopsticks angrily. "Because one day I am praised and respected, another day I am treated like cow's dung!"

"Who treated you badly, besides Snake Head Liu?"

"The God-worshippers. When I donated two thousand taels, all I got was a string of praise words from Hung Shiu-ch'uan. He even baptized me. Now that they are ready to march, have I heard from him? Not a word! My two thousand taels were tossed into the water without causing even a ripple!"

His wife was quiet for a moment, picking at her food. She had never thought too much of the God-worshippers. Like her father-in-law, she felt that the foreign God's picture hanging on the wall beside the ancestors was an eyesore; it made her uncomfortable, as though a total stranger had moved in and taken the master's seat in the family's middle room. It had sickened her father-in-law so much that the old man had never stopped grumbling about it.

"What did you expect Hung Shiu-ch'uan to do?" she asked.

"He gave every cat and dog a position but me," Wei said unhappily. "He made a charcoal worker the commander in chief, an aborigine snake-catcher a general, a goose farmer a minister. I, Wei Ta, a well-bred man from a family with a high door, am ignored and forgotten! He did not even inform me when he declared the holy war against the Manchu Emperor! My two thousand taels have been thrown away on a heap of cow's dung!"

"Withdraw from this God-worshippers' Association, my son's father. Ask for your money back. It will make your father happy and cure his illness."

Wei ignored her. He grunted and groaned, banging on the table. Suddenly he rose, went to the window and stared.

The peach trees in the garden were in full bloom with bees and butterflies hovering over thousands of pink flowers. Birds chirped happily in the lush elms and pines. In the pool, fat goldfish swam leisurely among the lotus leaves. Through the moon door he saw clusters of bamboo sway gently in the breeze. The view was like a beautiful watercolor painting by a Ming artist, a lovely scene, poetic and soothing. Yet, beyond those massive red walls was chaos, hatred, a hundred-year feud with the Lius that had caused bloodshed and death every year.

When he thought of the feud, his resentment against the God-worshippers was overwhelmed by his anger against Snake Head Liu. He threw his fist against the brick wall. It hit with a sickening thud. Seeing blood creeping out of his fingers, Ching Ching became alarmed.

"My son's father," she cried, running to him. "Why must you hurt yourself? Let me put some cobweb on your wound."

Wei pushed her aside and stalked out of the room.

"Follow him!" Ching Ching said to two servants who were standing nearby, staring stupidly.

"I said follow him!"

In consternation the two servant-guards trotted after Wei, their large pigtails bouncing over the character WEI on their tunics, which were tight kung fu uniforms that Wei had designed for all his employees.

Hung and his leaders were having their daily meeting at their temporary headquarters. Ironwork Yeh personally served them tea and tidbits, playing host but not participating in the discussion. He was a good blacksmith but always considered himself a man who followed others . . . a man with clever hands but not a clever mind. He listened to his leaders' discussions, admiring their knowledge and ideas. They constantly quoted famous sayings, especially from *The Book of Strategy* by Sun Wu. As they planned their next big move, Yang advocated caution and patience. Once more he quoted the ancient Sun Wu: "Know yourself and the enemy; a hundred battles will be fought and a hundred battles will be won."

General Shao said that he had already studied the enemy; he had examined the strong points and the weaknesses of both sides and had come to the conclusion that if a hundred battles were fought now, the God-worshippers would win every one of them.

He explained why: The Imperial armies were commanded by inept officers who indulged in decadent ways of life; their soldiers had no discipline and were despised. The militias, which were recruited from vagabonds, vagrants, and opium addicts, were even worse. To protect their own benefits and positions, the commanders never reported their weaknesses and failures to the Imperial Court. Most of the local officials, especially district and Fu magistrates, had bought their positions with cash. They would hide any calamities until they had recouped their investments. He believed that the recent easy defeat of the Imperial troops was a good example. Their increased numbers, therefore, should not be a cause for concern.

Hung agreed. "We are God's army," he said. "Even if we die in battle, we will all ascend to Heaven. But God never indulges us. He does not want raggle-taggle vagrants and vagabonds in His army. In God's army we are disciplined soldiers who obey our commanders and God's Ten Commandments."

Now that the date for marching was drawing closer, Hung decided to hasten preparations. He wanted posters put up on as many city walls as possible, urging nonbelievers to join the holy crusade. He drafted the main message himself. It read:

Come over to the God's side. Together we shall slay the Manchu demons and build a kingdom of eternal happiness.

He knew that eternal happiness was the greatest lure to the common people, who had known nothing but misery.

The activities in the community doubled. Hundreds of posters went up everywhere. Men and women in colorful new uniforms drilled. The hammering of weapons was heard all over the valley. New recruits were registered and classified, food and supplies collected, hundreds of mule carts and horse carriages built. The holy war was declared. The activities excited everyone and most men could hardly wait to start the march.

Wei Ta, wearing his own uniform—which he had designed along the lines of the God-worshippers'—walked with long strides, his sheathed sword hanging at his side. He bowed to Hung, ignoring the others.

"Older Brother Hung," he said, "I have come with a proposal. I will not waste your time, so I will come right to the point."

Hung and his leaders were discussing the forthcoming march. They were surprised by Wei's intrusion. However, Hung smiled. "We are always willing to listen to new ideas, Older Brother Wei," he said amiably.

"In this county there are three families whose combined wealth would be enough to support the holy war for an entire year," Wei said proudly. "My family is one of them."

He looked from face to face at the dozen leaders in the middle room, waiting for a response. Hung, Feng, and Yang glanced at each other.

"I am a resident of this county," Yang said. "The names of Wei, Deng, and Liu are like thunder in everybody's ears. What is your proposal?"

"I cannot speak for the other two families," Wei said, squaring his shoulders. "But if you think that I can be useful, the entire Wei family will join the God-worshippers. I shall sell my one thousand acres of land and donate the proceeds to the God-worshippers' treasury. My two hundred tenant farmers, my militia, my servants and their families, and all my family members—a total of at least five hundred mouths— they will all follow you in this campaign. This will be done only if you think I can be of use. It is up to you to decide." He stopped again, waiting for a response.

Knowing that Wei was seeking a position, Hung studied him for a moment. He knew something of physiognomy and in the past had used it to determine people's character. He found that Wei's eyes, slightly bulging, permanently bloodshot and shifty, were most interesting. They indicated greed and hunger for power. His large nose and thin lips also meant determination and ambition. If he was an able man, Hung thought, he would make a good leader. Since the God-worshippers needed leaders, he was inclined to say that he would be useful. He asked, "In what capacity do you think you would be useful?"

"I am a man of action," Wei said. "I am sure I can contribute my share in the military."

Hung again glanced at Yang, who was smiling. He decided to let Yang accept him or reject him. But it was Hu, the treasurer, who spoke first.

"Older Brother Wei," he said, "it is God's will that you should come here today and propose to donate your entire wealth to the cause of the holy war. It shows that you are a man of great wisdom and courage. I am sure there is room for you in the military. Since this is a war, military talent is equally as important as money." He turned to Hung and added, "Older Brother Hung, I highly recommend that Older Brother Wei be recruited as an inner member of our organization and that a high position be offered to him."

"Older Brother Yang is the commander in chief," Hung said. "It is up to him to decide."

"I have already decided," Yang said with a smile. "With your nod of approval, I shall appoint him as my deputy, with the title of full general."

Wei's face brightened instantly. He looked at Hung, waiting for his nod of approval.

Hung nodded without saying anything.

Commanding a thousand men, with banners flying, Wei Ta rode toward Snake Head Liu's house at a fast pace. He had ordered his troops to march quietly, making as little noise as possible. It was late at night. The moon was shining on the winding road, frogs were croaking noisily in the rice fields, a few lights gleamed weakly in the distance. He knew that the Liu family mansion was not far away, for only the very rich could afford oil for all-night burning. As he rode silently at the head of his men, he felt unusually courageous; he also felt a tremendous sensation of gratification mixed with an exciting desire for vengeance. His chest out, his right hand on the handle of his long sword, he slowed the pace to further reduce the marching noise.

The thousand men, armed with traditional weapons as well as Western arms, followed him closely, almost tiptoeing, waiting for his signal.

Reaching the Liu mansion, Wei unsheathed his sword and waved it over his head. "Sha!" he cried. It was his signal for attack. Suddenly torches were lighted, drums and gongs roared, guns were fired, and battle cries shattered the still night air. The front gate was battered down and the thousand men, in three groups according to prearrangement, poured in. One group surrounded the buildings, one group attacked the guards and the militia, a third group searched for treasure.

The Liu family was caught totally by surprise. The militia, roused from sleep, surrendered without a fight. A few guards grabbed their weapons but were instantly shot to death. Wei went directly to Snake Head Liu's bedroom, where he slept with one of his concubines. He pulled Liu out of bed. Liu, still sleepy-eyed, finally recognized him.

"Ah, old . . . Old Brother Wei," he stammered. "What . . . what is this? Am I . . . am I having a nightmare?"

Before he had finished, Wei let his big sword fall. As Liu's head rolled, the concubine rushed out of the room, shrieking. Wei raised his sword again, but he quickly changed his mind. He was not going to waste any of Snake Head Liu's concubines; they were God's best creations.

The surprise raid was over in less than an hour; Wei still had time to attack Deng Pi's yamen. When he thought of Deng Pi, he saw blood and money in one glorious picture. His hatred for the district magistrate was no less than his hatred for Snake Head Liu, and he felt an even stronger desire to personally chop Deng Pi's head off. He had always wanted to make a urinal out of the magistrate's skull.

On his way to Deng Pi's yamen he instructed his men to loot and kill without mercy, but all the loot must go to the God-worshippers' treasury. The opportunity to raid a magistrate's yamen excited him so much that he felt fearless and powerful—even heroic. Ignoring his sneak attack plan, he kicked his horse, which reared and snorted and galloped in the direction of Deng Pi's yamen. Banners flying, the God-worshippers disappeared in a huge cloud of dust.

It was late in the afternoon. Hung and his leaders were holding a meeting at their temporary headquarters, discussing the necessity of occupying a few strategic towns and seizing some yamens. They needed more modern arms, food, and money. Yamens usually had hidden treasure which had been stored away by rotten officials. They also needed more able-bodied men. Some of the yamen prisons were full of them, mostly wrongfully convicted and jailed. They discussed the possibility of releasing all the prisoners from local jails and converting them to God-worshippers. With their built-in hatred for the local officials, they would all make good fighters against the Manchu government. Those who could not fight could work as laborers and supply carriers.

Each yamen had a small contingency of armed guards. Some were trained in modern weapons. But Hung was not worried. He had received numerous reports that most yamen guards had smiling Buddha bellies; half of them were addicted to opium, and when they fought, they usually fired their weapons at a safe distance, making only noise. When they sighted an enemy, they usually dropped their weapons and ran.

"Let them run," Hung said. "We will not pursue them—just pick up their weapons. The weapon catch is more valuable than war prisoners with Happy Buddha bellies."

The leaders all agreed and decided on a policy. When fighting the Imperial Army, only capture their weapons and supplies. No Buddha-bellied prisoners.

Shih Ta-kai, the newly appointed minister of military training, had once served in the Imperial Army. He said, "We need horses, and the Imperial Cavalry is a good source." He said that the Imperial Cavalry enjoyed galloping about, waving their sabers. In an engagement, they often retreated without a fight. But their battle cries were deafening— some frightened birds never returned. Their horses were all Mongolian ponies, not very big but sturdy and easy to manage. Wounded or crippled they made good stew.

It was decided that the first stage of the campaign was to collect supplies and horses to carry them. Hung emphasized that all this knowledge about the enemy should be made known to all God-worshippers to boost their courage. He also wrote a few rules:

> Don't be frightened by noises and battle cries, for our enemies have a habit of slapping their own faces swollen to look red and healthy.
> Avoid unnecessary killing and pursuit.
> Build goodwill with the local people and let them spread the good word.

"We must convert people as we march," he added, "and take those who are willing to follow."

As Hung talked, noises were heard outside, first drumbeats then shouting mixed with horses' hooves clattering on the pebbled street.

"Don't tell me we are being atttacked by the Imperial Cavalry," Feng said, somewhat disconcerted.

"The Imperial Army would not shout, 'Long Live the God-worshippers,'" Hung said. "Ironwork Yeh, please find out what is going on."

Just as Ironwork Yeh was about to investigate, General Wei Ta marched in, his gaudy uniform dusty and blood-stained, his face darkened with dirt and a five-day stubble on his chin, but his eyes gleamed and his mouth stretched in a wide triumphnt smile.

"Older Brother Hung," he said, bowing low. "Mission promised and mission accomplished. I thank God Jehovah for His blessing."

Hung looked surprised. The dozen other leaders in the middle room glanced at each other. Wei had only requested a thousand men for field training. Nobody had said anything about a mission.

"What mission?" Hung asked.

"The mission of liquidating the rich and sacking a yamen," Wei said. "Excellent field training for our fighters."

"Who have you liquidated?" Hung asked.

"As I told you, there are two other rich families besides mine— Liu and Deng. I liquidated them. And I also sacked Deng Pi's yamen. All their wealth has now become the property of the God-worshippers. Here is the list." He stepped forward and submitted a short list of assets to Hung, who glanced at it and handed it to Hu, the treasurer.

As Hu read the list, his face beamed and his eyes widened with excitement. He read it aloud in a triumphant voice. "Three thousand acres of rice fields, twenty thousand taels of silver, five hundred taels of gold, a hundred and twenty tenant farmers, four hundred militiamen, forty-two male servants, twenty-five serving maids, and sixteen con-cubines."

"I confiscated them all!" Wei said triumphantly.

"How about casualties?" Hung asked, looking grim.

"Only a few. I raided them at night. All their 'teeth and claws' surrendered without much of a fight. Deng Pi looked pitiful. He knelt before me trembling and begging for mercy in his yamen, like hundreds of others have knelt before him trembling. I got a few drops of blood on my clothes. That is all."

"What did you do with the Lius and the Dengs?"

Originally, Wei had planned to place the heads of Snake Head Liu and Deng Pi on a plate and present them to Hung as victory trophies, but when he remembered Hung's Christian sermons, he changed his mind.

"I have personally sent Snake Head Liu and Deng Pi to visit Yen Lo. I ask you to decide what to do with their family members."

Hung scowled and made the sign of the cross in front of his chest. "Release them and let them go home," he said. "The God-worshippers do not confiscate homes. As for their tenant farmers, militia, and servants, they have a choice of remaining in Kwangsi or joining the holy war. As for those who have gone to Yen Lo, bury them in a decent coffin with a cross on their graves. We consider them converted, so they can also go to Heaven."

After Wei had left, looking disappointed and confused, Hung said, "I have reservations about this man."

"My wife's brother," Yang said, his eyes widened in surprise, "this man has brought us thousands of acres of land and thousands of taels of silver and gold. He liquidated two powerful families and sacked a yamen in one night without losing even one God-worshipper. He has demonstrated an ability that is rare to find. He is God-sent!"

27

Now that the God-worshippers were in open rebellion, those who were natives of Kwangtung sent for their relatives to join them. Hung sent a cousin to bring his family, and instructed him to disguise them as beggars escaping a famine. The main forces remained in Jin Tian.

Everytime the God-worshippers seized a town, they were polite to the townspeople; when they withdrew, not a chicken was missing. But they ordered the children to beat drums and gongs for a few days to give the impression that the town was still occupied. By the time the enemy discovered the ruse, the God-worshippers had already left and occupied another town. In anger, the Imperial troops often sought revenge on the natives, raping, killing, and looting. When other towns learned of the differences between the two sides, they knew what to do. Everytime the God-worshippers withdrew from a town, the towns-people would pack and follow them with all their possessions; a line of push carts, donkey carts, pigs, and water buffalo stretched for miles, following the crusaders.

Having learned of Hung's success, the secret societies also came out into the open and uprisings were reported in all the southern provinces—Kwangtung, Kwangsi, Hunan, Hupei, Fukien, and Kwei-chow. They all had their own banners and uniforms. It was a war of colors and hand-to-hand combats mixed with looting, but they all had one purpose—exterminating the Manchu Dynasty and restoring the Ming Dynasty.

To unite the secret societies, Hung dug up a Ming heir and established him as a symbol of the Ming Dynasty. He named the fat young man The Celestial Virtue. He proved to be a nuisance and a burden because the scion of Ming demanded all the benefits of royalty, especially wives and concubines. Hung tolerated the young coxcomb and his whims;

he had him married to six wives, thinking that one day he might have to take as many wives himself when he landed on the throne in Peking. It was a three-thousand-year-old tradition.

With the secret societies united, he gained their complete trust, especially the Triads, the largest and most powerful, now under the command of Golden Rooster. But almost all the secret societies refused to embrace the foreign God, for they detested the discipline, especially the Ten Commandments.

In January of 1851, the God-worshippers throughout Kwangsi Province were ready to acclaim Hung Shiu-ch'uan the emperor. They decided that the day of crowning should coincide with the Chinese lunar New Year in February. In the camp at Thistle Mountain a pavilion was built. Since Feng had written the protocol, Hung appointed him President of the Board of Rites. He also appointed Yang, the Commander in Chief, as the East Prince, Shao the West Prince, Feng the South Prince, and Wei the North Prince. As for himself, he accepted the title Heavenly Emperor of Taiping Tienkuo.

In February all was ready. In front of the pavilion a huge platform was built. It faced a mountain valley that was large enough for thousands of people to witness the coronation. The stage was decorated with colorful lanterns and banners, the floor carpeted, and a Dragon Throne placed on a dais.

Hung had ordered that all God-worshippers grow their hair long, without a queue, as a gesture to defy the Manchu regulations. He also designed the uniform—yellow tunics and red turbans, with red waistbands and ankle bands. In action, the hair must be neatly twisted into a knot at the nape of the neck and covered by the red turban. Tunic buttons were sewn onto the front rather than at the side, as was the Manchu custom. Across the men's chests were black characters to identify their units. The officers were distinguished by cassocks bordered with yellow stripes. Their standard-bearers carried triangular pennants. The high officers, such as princes and generals, had square flags planted outside their quarters or carried by bearers who accompanied them. They wore helmet-shaped hoods; their padded jackets and long gowns were all yellow without decoration of any other color.

Before dawn, all the coronation preparations had been made. There was a sea of lanterns and torches burning brightly in the mountain valley. Amid them, red turbans bobbed. Gongs and drums thundered, waiting for the Heavenly Emperor to appear at sunrise. When the sun emerged from behind a mountaintop, Hung Shiu-ch'uan, regally dressed in a yellow silk robe that was elaborately embroidered with a dragon and a phoenix, was carried to the platform in an open sedan chair by sixty uniformed porters. The princes and generals greeted his arrival by sinking to their knees and remaining there until the Heavenly Emperor had mounted the platform and taken his seat on the throne, facing south. Then the highest officials rose to their feet and climbed up to the platform in order of their rank. To the Heavenly Emperor's left, closest to his scarlet umbrella, stood Yang, Commander in Chief and Prince of East; to his right stood Shao, Prince of West. In front of him, Feng knelt down, taking the Southern position as Prince of South; behind the throne stood Wei, Prince of North, and the other princes and generals. Below the platform the representatives of the five armies cheered. Hung handed the kneeling Feng a scroll, which Feng received after one kowtow. Then he rose to his feet, turned to face the audience, and read in his sonorous voice the edict from the Heavenly Emperor:

> The Kingdom of Heaven has come. It is named Taiping Tienkuo, the Heavenly Kingdom of Great Peace. The Heavenly Emperor, Second Son of God, has the holy mandate to lead you to slay the Tartar demons in the north, thus the Heavenly Kingdom of Peace will be restored to its proper place, the Forbidden City in Peking. So the Heavenly Emperor has spoken.

As Feng stepped aside, Yang, the commander in chief, came forward and stopped a few feet away from the Heavenly Emperor. He stood erect, his legs slightly apart, his hand on the handle of his broadsword. He surveyed the troops with narrowed eyes for a moment, then spoke in his deep cracked voice.

"You Taiping braves, fierce as tigers, will march north under the Taiping banners without fear and with one heart. Everywhere your swords fall, Tartar heads will fall. As the evil demons flee, the Golden Age will begin. I, your Commander in Chief, will lead the battle. There will be no retreat. In death we will all go to Heaven. In either direction we will be blessed. I want you to say Amen after me. It will be your pledge to the Heavenly cause. Amen!"

The crowd all said, "Amen!" after him. It was so loud that it echoed in the mountains and valleys, and all the birds took flight from the nearby trees.

28

George Gordon was an avid reader. His hobby had been astronomy; the stars and space had always fascinated him, but since he had discovered that China was stranger than mysterious space, he had been spending much of his leisure time in the local library, searching for any material about China. Allergic to dust, he often came out of the book stacks sneezing, his arms loaded with magazines and brownish books that smelled of mildew.

Sensitive and emotional, he was not a quiet reader. When deeply involved in a story, he often reacted openly with sighs and chuckles, turning people's heads in the reading room. Lately, he had studied China's religious revolts, muttering comments to himself. Sometimes he closed his eyes, fantasizing that he was in China getting involved. In his imagination, he participated in many of the secret sects' uprisings, drinking chicken blood during initiation ceremonies and conducting guerrilla warfare against rotten Manchu officials.

In his research he had met many strange characters. The leader of the Eight Diagrams Rebellion of 1813 was a seven-foot-tall giant who could lift a cow over his head. It was said that he had once killed a tiger with his bare hands. He had established a pattern for sacking government yamens. First he killed the local officials then looted the treasuries, burned the government buildings, and finally freed all the prisoners to rectify the injustices of misgovernment.

Other leaders who interested Gordon were the Great King of Red Heaven in Honan, the Great Prince of Black Earth in Szechwan, and the Great Emperor of Red Mankind in Kwangtung. From the descriptions of the secret societies he found in his readings, Gordon even drew pictures of the fascinating leaders and hung them on his bedroom walls.

He followed the travels of Thomas Meadows closely, a Britisher who often reported his adventures in obscure religious magazines. Meadows had first arrived in Canton in 1842, having studied Chinese at Munich University. A descendant of Viking stock from Northumberland, he was a bear of a man, heavily bearded. He traveled to inland China in his own boat, befriended many rebel leaders, and studied all phases of the ancient Chinese culture which European merchants chose to ignore. He was the first European to report the rise of one of the biggest secret societies, called the God-worshippers.

Gordon discovered that there was also a white man's colony in China, a community of Jews in Kai-feng in Honan Province. They had come to China through Persia in the second century A.D. The Chinese Jews had been awaiting the arrival of the Messiah; but when he had not come, they had gradually forgotten the prophecies but had kept the Sabbath. When they heard about the God-worshippers, they felt a special kinship with them and prayed for their arrival, expecting to hear their interpretations of the Messiah's teachings.

One night Gordon found an article in *China Mail* that read like an adventure story. It was about an Englishman named James Callahan, who tramped around the Orient seeking fortune and romance. He had left London with hardly any money in his pockets and took a freighter to Hong Kong where he was robbed and kidnapped by a pirate ship from Macao. Believing that all white men were rich, the pirates forced him to write a ransom note. An orphan, he composed several ransom letters to nonexistent relatives.

One was to his "rich" grandfather in London, demanding a million pounds for his freedom. The pirates were delighted, treating him like a money tree. They pampered him with the best delicacies and rare wines, dressed him in silk, and entertained him with kidnapped singsong girls. He took the luxury in stride, ready to enjoy life as the pirates' honored guest as long as the promise of "a big fortune" remained credible.

The pirates did not mind a long wait, knowing that a letter to the foreign land beyond the vast ocean took time. Callahan estimated that it would take a year or two, and the pirates believed him, for dreams of a million-pound windfall would make even the most brutal murderers patient, gentle, and kind.

But Callahan's good luck ran out after three days when the pirate ship was robbed by another pirate ship from Hong Kong. The raiders slaughtered everybody except Callahan, convinced that a white man was useful on a ship; he could offer protection if they were raided by a customs boat in the China Sea.

This second pirate ship was also engaged in the slave-girl trade, selling girls to Hong Kong's virgin market. Jane, one of the slave girls, was an English-Portuguese young woman who spoke several languages. She offered to translate for the pirates. A beauty at sixteen and born in the Orkneys, Jane had been kidnapped in Macao. She and Callahan met and it was love at first sight. Conversing in English, they swore devotion to each other and plotted their escape.

When they reached Kowloon, Callahan miraculously freed Jane and they escaped. While fleeing, they joined a strange crowd of people who wore blue turbans, often talked in sign language, and practiced kung fu. They worshipped the sun and claimed that they were invulnerable to weapons, fire, or drowning. Jane, understanding Chinese, said they called themselves White Lotus. Their leader, Celestial Bamboo, smoked opium and sucked blood from beheaded snakes. She reported that the members of the White Lotus Sect were on their way to join the God-worshippers in Kwangsi Province.

Traveling in the mountains, Callahan soon died from a poisonous snake bite. In Kwangsi Province, Jane was adopted by the God-worshippers, and their priest, the Reverend Mr. Joseph Edkins, took good care of her. Jane helped Edkins preach the Gospel by singing hymns and beating a tambourine. They were chased by Imperial troops, who massacred many God-worshippers, hung their heads on poles, and sold their flesh to roadside inns to make meat buns.

The Reverend Mr. Edkins supported the God-worshippers because Yeh, the Governor of Kwangtung, enjoyed drinking mao-tai as much as he enjoyed killing. The Manchu official had boasted that in the space of six months he had decapitated seventy thousand rebels—men, women, and children. As there were not enough baskets in Kwangtung in which to send the heads to be counted by his superior, the Viceroy of Kwangtung and Kwangsi, he gave orders that only right ears be sent instead. As the emperor in Peking had demanded a quota from each province, Governor Yeh had executed many innocent men and women to meet that quota. In Canton eyewitnesses reported that the governor's yamen guards had been doing nothing but count ears.

When George Gordon read about this in the article, he became so incensed that he banged the table and uttered a loud curse, which brought the librarian hurrying over to shush him. All heads in the reading room turned and two school girls sitting nearby giggled.

Next day, George Gordon sent his sister Augusta a letter in which he swore that he was going to China to join the Reverend Mr. Joseph Edkins.

| 29 |

After a fortnight of discussion and argument, the Taiping leaders finally decided on the route of their crusade. They would first take Kweilin, the provincial capital, then go north and march straight to Hunan Province. From Hunan they would follow the Hsiang River and Tung Ting Lake to reach the great Yangtze that ran through the heart of China. They would occupy Nanking at the mouth of the Yangtze and establish the Taiping capital there. From Nanking they would march north until they seized Peking and overthrew the Manchu Dynasty. Like the children of Israel, they would not consolidate their conquests, but march on to the Promised Land, as described in Exodus.

Every morning Hung conducted a prayer. He preached a sermon every Sunday and ordered that the Bible be the only required reading. The Four Books and the Five Classics were banned and idolatry forbidden. Only Jehovah was the sole God, whose words would be spoken through the chosen Taiping leaders. Yang, the East Prince and Commander in Chief, often spoke God's words in a trance, which was properly recorded in Heavenly decrees and kept in the Taiping archives.

Forty-thousand-strong, the Taipings marched . . . first the fighters, then the porters of supplies, followed by the female soldiers, with the elderly and children bringing up the rear. At intervals Commander in Chief Yang gathered the troops around him, stared at Heaven and spoke, his voice trembling, his body in a trance, as if he were possessed by God. "Oh, my children, this is God speaking. I have sent down my Second Son, the Heavenly Emperor, to guide you to the promised land. Every word he speaks is a heavenly command to be faithfully obeyed. Forget small losses in battle. Always march forward!"

Through the mouth of Shao, the West Prince, God also issued the following commands: "You must not rob or steal. When you have money, you must make it public. You must love your brethren. You must not commit adultery. Above all, you must not retreat!"

As the well-disciplined Taipings marched eastward, their banners flying, drums and gongs thundering, the Governor of Kwangsi was greatly alarmed. He gathered his commanders in his yamen and held an urgent meeting. He first spoke to Chu and Tao.

"When you returned, you boasted of your success. You claimed that you killed thousands of God-worshippers, even though you lost all your own men. You claimed that after their defeat, the rebels would hide in their lair at Thistle Mountain to lick their wounds and never again dare to attack the Imperial troops beyond Kwei Ping. Now what has happened? They are marching toward the capital!"

Angrily he waved a piece of paper in the air and went on, "Look at this dispatch from the magistrate of Siang. It says, 'The whole country swarms with God-worshippers. Our troops are few. To quell this rebellion would be like trying to extinguish a big fire with a cupful of water.'" When he finished, he banged his fist on the table and demanded, "What do you say to that?"

Tao was trembling with fear, unable to say anything. Chu, high on an early pipe of opium, coughed apologetically. "Your Excellency," he said haltingly, "the bandits and pirates from Kwangtung Province have joined the rebels. The governor of Kwangtung is responsible. He should not have driven the undesirables to our province."

"Rubbish!" the governor retorted. "I have always suspected that you gave me a false report about your victory, considering the condition you were in when you returned. You were in rags, your queues were cut off, and you looked miserable. If you returned in triumph, where were your troops? Where was your war booty? You came back without your queues, your trousers full of holes, and your mouths packed with lies! I have a good mind to have you executed and your corpses displayed as a warning to other rotten officers in the Imperial Army!"

The governor's last remarks sent a shock wave through the audience room. Their faces paling, Tao and Chu sank on their knees and knocked their heads on the floor. In trembling voices they begged for mercy.

Yao, a county magistrate and a close friend of the two commanders, quickly got up and bowed. He said, "Your Excellency, I suspect that the rebels have foreign aid. The foreign devils must have supplied them with foreign firearms, which have more firepower than the locally made ones. The Opium War certainly proved that. In fact, I suspect that Hung Shiu-ch'uan is not a Chinese at all. Nobody has taken a good look at him. According to recent sightings, he wore a yellow hood and a yellow robe, with a big sword hanging at his side. He was too tall for a Chinese. I would not be surprised if he is found to be a foreign devil disguised as a Chinese . . . a barbarian of some sort . . ."

"Rubbish!" the governor retorted, again banging his fist on the table. "He is a peasant from Flower County in Kwangtung Province, a lunatic who suffered nightmares and destroyed temples and insulted our sage, Confucius. For that alone he should be fried in oil and fed to the wild dogs."

"Your Excellency," the Mayor of Kweilin said, rising to his feet, "This Hung Shiu-ch'uan is real. I hear that he is not a fool. He has studied Sun Wu's *The Book of Strategy* and is familiar with the ancient military arts. Based on Sun Wu's book, he first conceals his strength, then he advances if he finds us weak. He retreats if he finds us strong. So far he has been winning at a rate of three victories against one defeat. Recently one of the rebel books fell into my hands. Besides a lot of gibberish about the foreign God, it describes the organization of their army, which has a general to command a division, a colonel for a regiment, a major to lead a company, and so forth. Now they have fifteen thousand fighting men and women, well trained in martial arts, fierce and wild, unafraid of death, for in death they are supposed to fly to Heaven on wings. Your Excellency, this is a formidable enemy . . . not like our own troops who are lazy and cowardly. Some even bring opium pipes to the front. This is a true picture, which many commanders and local officials have been hiding. We must appeal to the Viceroy of Kwangtung and Kwangsi for help. Without massive reinforcements we are lost!"

As the governor listened, the color of his face turned purple. He glared at the mayor; his breath suddenly became short and his lips trembled. The commanders and other local officials held their breath, fearing for the mayor who had had the audacity to criticize the Imperial Army.

The governor banged the table again. He pointed a long fingernail at the mayor and said, "You seem to know the God-worshippers better than any of these empty rice tubs here. You will write the appeal to the viceroy, detailing what you know about the Taiping rebels, and request what we need in help to quell the rebellion in this province. Make the message urgent. Emphasize that we are limited in funds and manpower. Unless we have massive aid from the viceroy, Kwangsi Province will be lost!"

Banging the table once more, he rose and withdrew to his private quarters, sighing heavily and shaking his head.

30

The Taipings took their first large walled city, Yungan, an important area surrounded by a great wall twenty feet high, with four gates between gate towers. The Imperial garrison of ten thousand surrendered after a two-day assault from all sides by fifteen thousand Taipings. After the city's surrender, another fifteen thousand Taipings poured in from both land and river, a sea of yellow and red colors, drums and gongs thundering, pennants fluttering in the wind. The Heavenly Emperor entered the city in triumph, carried in his Imperial sedan chair by sixty porters. As he passed through one of the wide city gates, the civilians prostrated themselves on the street and dared not look up. In the mayor's yamen, a throne had already been set up. The yamen was to be the Heavenly Emperor's temporary palace.

Many more people had joined the Taipings. One of them was Li Shu-chen, a twenty-four-year-old man with a good education, from a middle-class family in a nearby village. When the fleeing Imperial troops looted the village, Li burned his own home, took his wife and mother, and headed for the river. But on the way the family was swept up by the invading Taipings. Knowing that the Taipings were disciplined, Li volunteered and allowed his wife and mother to be taken into the female regiment. Inside the city he had expected a massacre, but what he witnessed was the most lenient treatment of the captured Imperial troops. He saw Taiping posters everywhere reiterating God's Ten Commandments. Walking among the polite Taiping soldiers, he felt a peaceful and comforting sensation that he had never experienced before. And it touched him deeply that in such chaotic wartime, his mother and wife were safe.

Like all other new recruits, he was issued a uniform and a Bible; he was given a nickname, "Faithful," which was sewn on his uniform. He dutifully read the Bible. An intelligent man, he quickly grasped its message and meaning. He memorized all the proclamations, the regulations, and the rituals, and he learned how to pray. He was determined to be a good Taiping soldier. Soon he learned how the army was organized. There were a total of nine armies. Each had five divisions, and each division had five regiments. He was assigned to a regiment commanded by a colonel who trained his men in sword and spear fighting. As a good martial artist, he excelled and attracted the immediate attention of the commander in chief. Soon he was made an instructor. But he knew that no matter how good a man was with those weapons, he was no match for an enemy armed with a musket. During training sessions he told his men that the best way to fight a man with a firearm was to avoid direct confrontation . . . to lie low and then finish him with a sneak attack. "Forget the battles cries," he emphasized. "They only alert the enemy. And a bullet is fast and deadly."

Li Shu-chen readily agreed that food and money taken from an enemy must be turned over to the common treasury, according to army regulations. Eventually, in the Heavenly Kingdom of Great Peace there would be no rich or poor; all men and women were brothers and sisters, equally blessed by God. He had no quarrel with that; he had always thought that his wife was smarter than he, a frustrated woman chained by thousands of years of tradition. He also had no objection to the Heavenly decrees that God Jehovah was omniscient, omnipotent, and omnipresent. Since his youth, Li had always been bored by the different rituals of the various gods and spirits. Even a fox spirit demanded the burning of spirit money and food offerings; and he was tired of kowtowing to the Buddha, the Kwan Yin, the Lo Han, the Kitchen God, and a string of dead ancestors. One God was enough; he was glad that from now on he would not have to knock his head on the ground to every cat and dog.

Everything went well with the Taipings in the occupied city. Hung ordered Taiping coins to be minted and paper money printed. With the silver and gold confiscated from the Imperial yamens, he forgot about Lindley's firearms, which had never arrived. He had sent a messenger to Canton to urge Run-kan to join him in his temporary palace. He told him to leave Lindley's service, since the foreigner had proven unreliable.

Meanwhile, Hung's family arrived, having evaded the Imperial troops and experienced many narrow escapes. His wife did not mind his two concubines, since she knew that an emperor was entitled to numerous wives to assure the country an heir. Only recently Hung had selected two women out of the female regiment, married them, and given them the title of royal concubines.

He kept close contact with the secret societies, and requested their services to tie up the Imperial troops in the surrounding provinces so that, when the time was ripe he could march again without hindrance. The Triad Society, the White Lotus Sect, and the Big Sword Brotherhood all agreed to harass the Imperial troops if the enemy attempted to encircle the Taipings. He continued to convert people and recruit leaders of various ranks. He had an eye on Li the Faithful, believing that the young man had great promise, a potential leader of the army. He even thought of giving him a title ... perhaps The Faithful Prince ... but not until Li had shown that he deserved it.

Yang and Shao had proven to be excellent leaders, the emperor's right- and left-hand men. Hung had given them the authority to do things without his approval. To prove that God appeared before the Taiping leaders, the eloquent and clever Yang would often start trembling and walking in a trance, as though he were seized by a mysterious power. He would babble in a strange voice, declaring that Hung, the Heavenly Emperor, had received orders from God to perform various duties. He would sweat and tremble and report God's mandate to unite all the oppressed, slay the demons, and invade Peking on a certain date. Thousands of doubtful Hans were convinced that Hung had indeed received a mandate from God to save them from Manchu slavery. Many more peasants and small businessmen sold their shacks and small plots of land to join the crusade.

Hung granted more titles to his close associates and ranked them with numbers of years. He, the emperor, was addressed as Ten Thousand Years; Yang, the East Prince and commander in chief, was called Nine Thousand Years; Feng, the South Prince, Eight Thousand years, and so on.

The news of the Taiping Rebellion finally reached the Imperial Court in Peking. The young emperor, following the advice of his favorite concubine, issued edicts to the governors and viceroys in the southern provinces and ordered them to quash the rebellion within two months, or all the commanders would be beheaded. Viceroy Chi Yin of Kwang-tung and Kwangsi, dreading such a responsibility, reread the Kwangsi governor's appeal, which he had ignored for some time. Now the appeal seemed indeed urgent. He quickly dispatched a reply, promising an immediate aid of a hundred thousand taels of silver and ordering him to build up defenses and train new recruits.

Chi Yin was glad that Hung had spared Kwangtung and moved to Kwangsi to start this revolt. He would let the Kwangsi governor do all the fighting. Raising money by taxing people was a lot easier than fighting the God-worshippers, who might indeed possess some magic power bestowed upon them by the mysterious foreign God. The for-eigners worshipped the same God and had not lost one battle during the Opium War.

When Hong Yun, the Governor of Kwangsi, received the viceroy's dispatch from Canton, he spent a sleepless night wondering what to do. The hundred thousand taels of silver was a huge amount, but it would take time to train new troops, and the Imperial edict wanted him to quell the rebellion within two months.

He got up before dawn and called an urgent meeting. Five com-manders, a county magistrate, a district magistrate, a Fu magistrate, and the Mayor of Kweilin arrived, some still yawning from lack of sleep. In the great audience hall, Hong Yun read the viceroy's dispatch. Then he scanned the room with his bloodshot eyes, waiting for anyone to speak up. The officials, sitting in two rows of ancestral chairs below the dais, avoided his eyes. Nobody dared to express an opinion.

The governor shook his head with a loud sigh of disappointment. "Since nobody has any good ideas," he said, "I must call upon myself for a solution to this life-and-death matter. Luckily, during a sleepless night, I thought of several solutions. As the old saying goes, 'Money can make even a ghost mill grain.' We have a hundred thousand taels of silver, but very little time. So, the solution is ..." He scanned his audience again, waiting to see if any of the empty rice tubs could guess what he had in mind. Nobody uttered a sound. Again he shook his head slowly to show his disappointment and scorn.

"If money can motivate even ghosts," the governor went on, "there is no reason why the desperadoes and assassins in this province would not render us a service, would they not?"

Now all the government officials suddenly became enlightened. They looked at each other and grunted with approval.

"Excellent idea, Your Excellency!" the Fu magistrate said with admiration. "Hung Shiu-ch'uan's head is worth at most a thousand taels. With his head falling off his neck or a dagger in his heart, all the other bandit chiefs are worth nothing. The war can be won with merely a thousand taels of silver. What a brilliant idea, Your Excellency!"

The governor pulled at his whiskers and smiled. "I will put two thousand taels on his head," he said. "I want you to paste the reward poster on every city wall."

The next day, the poster went up everywhere. Two thousand taels of silver would be awarded to anyone who could bring Hung Shiu-ch'uan's head to the governor's yamen. Or better still, capture the bandit chief alive and deliver him in a cage.

For ten days the governor waited anxiously for a response, but no one came to claim the reward, not even a desperate mountain thief who would murder his mother for a string of brass coins. While the governor was nervously counting the days in his private quarters, sipping a bowl of ginseng soup, a servant came in and said that someone wanted to see His Excellency. He was a large, ugly man who was interested in the reward money.

The governor stopped his spoon between the bowl and his mouth. "Good news," he told himself excitedly. Some brave man has finally shown up to do something for the Great Manchu Dynasty. "Tell Secretary Tung to see him first. If the man is real, call me."

After the servant left, the governor finished his ginseng and waited restlessly in his armchair, hoping that this man was not a prankster or some drunkard who did not know what he was doing. Just as he finished his second pipe of Fukien tobacco, he was sent for by Secretary Tung. Ordinarily the governor would have dilly-dallied for a while before he made his appearance to show his importance, but this was urgent.

He hurried to the audience hall and took his seat on the dais. The large, ugly man did not kneel. The governor stared at him and he stared back. He was over six feet tall, broad-shouldered, with a big stomach over which a black sash loosely rested. His blue cotton coat reached his knees, his breeches were tied at the ankles, and his straw sandals were muddied. His rugged face had been pitted by smallpox, but he was clean-shaven, deeply tanned, and leathery.

"He is a boatman from the West River," Secretary Tung said, rising to his feet from his chair below the dais. "Golden Rooster is his only name. He was an orphan born into this world by an unknown mother. He is a Triad chief, unhappy with Hung Shiu-ch'uan. I have questioned him thoroughly. He seems to be sincere in his heart, and judging by the looks of him, he also seems to be capable of doing such a job. But he demands more money, Your Excellency."

The governor studied the man, looking at him up and down a few times. "How much do you want?" he asked.

"For Hung Shiu-ch'uan's head, four thousand taels. Two thousand now and two thousand when his head is delivered."

The man spoke without kneeling and his voice lacked emotion or respect. Ordinarily such a man would be thrown out without a hearing. But this was an unusual job. The governor knew that a sissy or a polite man would be unfit for such a job.

"Four thousand?" he said, trying not to sound scornful. "It is enough to send an army to capture him. He is not the only chief. It takes money to exterminate the rest of the maggots. The government is not a bottomless well of money . . ."

He stopped, regretting that he had become a bit chatty. He was talking to a Triad chief . . . a desperado and a killer.

There was a moment of silence. Golden Rooster took a deep breath and said with a slight smile, "Your Excellency, I understand your difficulty. I shall offer you a better deal. For five thousand taels of silver I shall not only deliver the head of Hung Shiu-ch'uan, I shall also deliver the city he has occupied."

"You mean recapture Yung An?" the governor asked, raising his eyebrows expectantly.

"That is right, Your Excellency."

"How are you going to do that?"

"I am a head of the Triads, with three thousand men under my command. I have an alliance with the God-worshippers, and I know all Hung Shiu-ch'uan's strong points and weaknesses like his own mother does. For five thousand taels of silver I shall return Yung An to you along with the heads of all the God-worshipping chiefs."

"Your Excellency," Secretary Tung chimed in. "He is speaking the truth. I have heard his name before. He even fought the foreign devils during the Opium War and won some battles against the foreigners. He has no real allegiance to anyone but money."

Golden Rooster nodded with a smile. "That is true," he said. "And I hate the foreign devils and the foreign devils' God!"

That was what the governor liked to hear; hating the foreign devils was the man's real credentials. "All right," he said to Secretary Tung. "See to it that he signs a pledge."

Hiding his excitement, Governor Hong Yun returned to his private quarters. He took out his stationery and personally drafted a letter to the Viceroy of Kwangtung and Kwangsi requesting the money the viceroy had promised.

31

Golden Rooster returned to the Sea Hawk, his flagship on the West River, all smiles. Su San-mei was waiting for him with dinner ready on the deck. She had cooked a snapping turtle, Cantonese style, Golden Rooster's favorite. The river was busy with traffic, mostly large junks transporting cotton, timber, livestock, and foreign fabrics. Half of Golden Rooster's fleet of twenty-two vessels was gainfully engaged with such freight, but was also smuggling arms to various secret societies. The other half was riding at anchor, fully armed, ready for action. His assignment was to engage the Imperial Army in Kwangsi, waging small battles to tie it down so that the Taipings could speedily march eastward as originally planned.

"For the first time your terrible scowl is gone," Su San-mei said, dishing out food. "It means good news."

"Good news, you clever woman."

Golden Rooster sat on a stool heavily. "The turtle's egg fell into the net like a fat snapping turtle."

"Here is a goblet of mao-tai, Father," Su San-mei said, offering him the wine.

"Let us not celebrate too soon," he said. "The money will have to come from the viceroy in Canton."

"How much?" Su San-mei asked anxiously.

"Just as you suggested. Five thousand taels of silver. He didn't even bargain."

Su San-mei smoothed her chin with her fingers thoughtfully, a mischievous smile on her deeply tanned face. Golden Rooster looked at her and shook his head. "What now?" he asked. "When you smile like that, something else is fermenting in your foxy mind."

"I have another idea," she said.

"Don't overdo it, Su San-mei," Golden Rooster said quickly. "Your

193

first idea was good and successful. Let's wait for the peach tree to bear fruit. Another idea might ruin everything."

"The second idea will be just as good, Father. You carried out the first, let me take care of the second."

"Tell it to me first," he said, finishing the mao-tai in one big gulp.

Su San-mei glanced around then whispered something into his ear. Golden Rooster scowled.

The governor read the viceroy's long-winded reply twice, making sure that he had not misread anything. He had learned that in official dispatches, messages between the lines must be examined and reexamined, for a little misinterpretation could mean the loss of one's red-buttoned cap. At his age he could not afford the loss of his position, for the loss of face alone would be devastating to the reputation of his gentry-official family ... one with the highest door in Kweilin. The viceroy's letter said:

> To raise half a million taels is not as easy as picking up a morsel of food with chopsticks. The foreigners have drained silver from Kwangtung for more than a decade. Taxing the people who have little left is as painful as wringing a man's guts out. For this reason, the entire amount will be raised in several installments, even though the matter is urgent and your suggestion seems workable. To contract someone for such a job is not what I had in mind, but it provides a shortcut that might uproot the poisonous plant with one swift stroke. It is worth a try without informing the Imperial Court in Peking. But if you fail, I want you to know that fire cannot be wrapped up with paper. The reaction from the Forbidden City will be in a turtle's shell ... only a fortune-teller can predict the consequences. However, after a careful study of your proposal, I have decided to advance five thousand taels to meet this unusual request, hoping that the scheme will be successful and a huge amount for future military campaigns will be saved. In any case, the rest of the money will be raised, for the locusts must be exterminated one way or another. It is hoped that you will dispatch a reliable representative to Canton to receive the five

thousand taels and transport it to your yamen under proper protection.

Seal of Chi Yin,
Viceroy of Kwangtung and Kwangsi

Below the viceroy's name were two more impressive official seals. It was a letter with many anxiety-causing questions. The governor's scowl deepened as he pondered those questions. The last one was most worrisome. He must send someone to receive the money in Canton; obviously the responsibility for the money's safety would fall into his hands.

"The crafty old goat," he mumbled as he folded the letter and began to ransack his mind to find someone reliable enough for such a job.

He had only two close subordinates, Tao and Chu. He liked to use people he knew best, even though their ability might be questionable. He wished that he had had among his subordinates a Ju Kwo-liang, the cleverest man of the Three Warring Kingdoms in the third century A.D., who could come up with instant answers to the most difficult problems.

He sent for Chu, who waddled in with a worried look. The governor showed him the viceroy's letter and asked him to suggest a man to transport the silver. Chu read the letter twice, his lips moving.

"Your Excellency," he said with a broad smile. "You have just found the right man for the job. It is so different from the last. Transporting five thousand taels of silver is not like fighting five thousand God-worshippers."

"So you recommend yourself?"

"Who else can you trust, Your Excellency?" Chu said. "I shall take every precaution and hire the sturdiest ship. The silver will be guarded by two dozen of my most trustworthy soldiers, personally selected by me. Give me six days, round trip."

"Only six days?" the governor asked, scowling.

"Yes. I'll find a ship with five sails and twelve oarsmen. I expect to cut the sailing time in half. In transporting money, speed is essential. I know."

A thirty-foot junk with five sails and twelve oarsmen arrived in Canton in two days. Twenty bales of cotton were swiftly loaded in two special compartments and the ship sailed within two hours of its arrival. Besides the twelve sailors and a captain, it also carried two dozen fully armed soldiers and Commander Chu. The ship's captain, nicknamed Golden Eagle, was a slim man in a loose blue cotton tunic. He had a dirty face, which was always half covered by a large straw hat. He seemed to be deaf and dumb, but an excellent sailor. When Commander Chu had sent word out that he wanted to hire a ship to transport twenty bales of cotton, a speedy ship with his specifications, he had found one with surprising ease. At first he had had some doubts about its captain, but when the ship arrived in Canton in two days, all his doubts evaporated. He had nothing but praise for the dirty-faced captain.

The return journey was even faster than he had expected. On the fifth day, the ship was nearing Kweilin. The five sails were full in the wind and the oarsmen sculled vigorously, grunting with each powerful stroke. Sometimes they sang in unison, like soldiers on a march. The Imperial guards, armed with both swords and modern rifles, kept a close watch in three shifts. Commander Chu spent most of his time playing chess with his men inside the main cabin, his worry and concern decreasing steadily as the ship sped toward its destination. During the past several hours, he had even felt confident, expecting to regain the governor's full trust after this successful errand.

Most of the time the captain was sitting at the stern behind the back cabin, steering the ship with its rudder. Inside the back cabin, a woman cooked and washed; she was actually the ship's first mate, a man in disguise, who communicated with the others in a river dialect that the land people did not understand.

It was late in the afternoon of the fifth day when the ship developed problems. Commander Chu had just finished his evening meal in his cabin. When he heard excited yelling and loud conversation in the strange dialect outside, he stepped out to ask what was wrong. A sailor told him that the ship had sprung a leak and water was pouring into one of the storage cabins in the forward section. Chu rushed to check. The cabin was already half full of water, with ten bales of cotton already submerged. The ship was slowly sinking; water was bubbling out of the storage cabins. It had happened so fast that the soldiers were unable to remove the cotton.

Commander Chu ran around in circles, directing his men to salvage the cotton bales in the other storage cabin at the back of the main cabin. Again it was too late; water was pouring in, soaking the cotton. With the wet cotton and the silver that was hidden inside, the bales were too heavy to move. The soldiers heaved and shoved until they were almost neck-deep in water. Finally Chu ordered his men to abandon ship. Like a heroic man, he was the last to jump, but not until he was assured by one of the sailors that the cotton would be safe. They would fish them out and transfer them to another ship. It happened that they had a sister ship that was nearby and it was coming to help.

Wet and shivering, the soldiers clambered ashore, their teeth chattering. They borrowed some wood from a sampan and quickly built a fire. Commander Chu sat close to the fire and watched the sailors climb on the other ship. Yelling and talking loudly in their own dialect, they proceeded to salvage the cotton. Tied to long sturdy ropes, a dozen of them dived and swam to the sunken ship. One by one they emerged to take a breath, then disappeared again. Those on the second boat waited for signals. When a diver came up with a raised fist and thumb, two men on the other boat pulled on the rope. Presently a bale of cotton emerged. It was a grueling job, but with almost fifty boat people working, the cotton bales were quickly fished out and loaded onto the other ship. Commander Chu watched closely, counting every bale.

It was almost midnight before the job was done. A sampan took the soldiers to the second boat, which sailed almost immediately in the bright moonlight, having lost only half a day's sailing time.

When the cotton was delivered to the governor's yamen, it was midafternoon on the sixth day. The governor was at the yamen gate, smilingly watching the bales unloaded from two mule carts closely guarded by his soldiers. He praised Commander Chu for a good job well done, and the commander acknowledged the praise with a deep bow.

"Your Excellency," he said, his voice trembling with pride, "it is under your blessing that nothing has happened to the merchandise except that it has gotten a bit wet. Every bale is here. I have counted them carefully three times."

"You have my full trust," the governor said, smiling broadly. "Time to have a jar of mao-tai to take the chill off your bones. Come, Commander."

The governor entered the yamen, followed by Chu, who was thinking of a raise in rank and an increase in salary.

While the governor was having a drink with Chu in his private quarters, the bales of cotton were piled up in the audience hall under the supervision of Secretary Tung and the captain of the yamen guard. The yamen treasurer was also there, account book open and writing brush in hand, ready to count the silver and enter it in his books.

When the governor had finished the first jar of mao-tai, laughing and talking, he ordered another. "Commander," he said, "the job is only the beginning. But it is a good beginning. With money, even a ghost will do our bidding, as the old saying goes. Now, tell me, what will be the next step?"

"Your Excellency," Commander Chu said somewhat drunkenly, "the next step would be for me to give Golden Rooster five hundred taels of silver . . ."

"But the turtle's egg has demanded five thousand . . . half now and half when he delivers."

"Ease your mind, Your Excellency," Chu said expansively. "I know how to deal with thieves and bandits. When he sees silver he can hardly wait to lay his hands on it, regardless of how much. But I will invite him to the yamen to take a look at the rest of it. A mountain of glittering silver will be his if he can capture the City of Yung An with Hung Shiu-ch'uan's head hanging on the city gate. If he fails to do so, all we will have lost is five hundred taels, not two thousand and five hundred. In dealing with thieves and bandits one has to be . . ." With a mischievous grin he jabbed his head a few time with his forefinger and finished the sentence, ". . . one has to be smart."

"Yes, yes," the governor agreed. "It takes brains to think ahead. I am glad you have them. Kan pei, bottoms up!" Chu downed his drink in one gulp and the governor started to pour again. But before he had filled Chu's goblet, Secretary Tung rushed in breathless and looking terribly upset.

"Your Excellency, Your Excellency," he cried. "Five thunders have struck! There is no silver in the cotton! Not one single tael!"

"What?" the governor said, feeling faint. "What is in the cotton?"

"Rocks, Your Excellency. Nothing but rocks."

The governor sank to the floor and everything blacked out.

| 32 |

The deadline specified in the Imperial edict was approaching fast, but luckily the Taipings remained quiet—there was no drum or gong beating and no yelling of, "Sha, sha. sha!" The governor had no idea whether the enemy's activities were in hiatus or they were making secret preparations for a major assault on the local yamens and then Kweilin. The thought of it even spoiled his appetite for his shark's fin and bird's nest dinner.

The good news was that the viceroy was able to scrape up more silver in Kwangtung. The second installment of the hundred thousand taels had arrived without mishap. He had covered up the last theft nicely, reporting that the assassin had lost his nerve and he had trained more troops with the first batch of money. In the meantime, he had appealed to the Governor of Fukien, a close friend, to send three thousand troops to help him prevent the God-worshippers from marching toward Fukien. The Governor of Fukien was rushing the troops to Kweilin in the hope that the rebels would never attack his own province. He was gratified that the Governor of Kwangsi was so thoughtful and he told him so in a long-winded letter written in perfect eight-legged style. Governor Hong Yun replied with a similar lengthy letter on the theme of "that is what friends are for."

In early April, activity in the captured city of Yung An was reported again. The Taipings, in quick succession, had sacked two more towns, looted the yamens, executed the local officials, and urged the townspeople to join their holy crusade. According to a spy's eyewitness report, some Taiping leaders, in a trance, had passed the word from God above to potential converts that those who joined the crusade would be able to withstand swords and spears. He said that some God-worshippers had even demonstrated the magic. Trembling and sweating, they had planted their feet on the ground in kung fu fashion and cried, "Sha!"

Men holding broadswords had hacked them on the chest but there had been no wounds or blood . . . only a white mark on the spot where the sword had struck.

Governor Hong Yun immediately sent out several more spies and each of them returned to report a different story. But the truth was that the Taipings were looting government treasuries, collecting food and weapons—a sure sign that a major invasion was pending. Thousands of tents had been pitched outside the captured city, flags and pennants rose like a bamboo forest, horses galloped around, and soldiers in colorful uniforms moved about like ants. Governor Hong Yun called an urgent meeting.

"The spies have brought various stories about the God-worshippers' magic power," he told his officials. "I let them go in one ear and come out the other, for all of us are fantasy storytellers after having read too much of such nonsense. But they all agreed on one thing—the rebels are ready to throw their dice on one big gamble—taking Kweilin. This is a life-and-death matter. I want all of you to come up with an idea to defend our city and repel those locusts. We have a garrison of five thousand men. Three thousand more are on the way from Fukien. It is only a few drops in a cup compared to the Taipings' fifty thousand wild animals. Anyone?"

"Speaking of animals, Your Excellency," Commander Tao said, "we all know that during the three Warring Kingdoms period one small country used water buffalo to defeat a large country. It is called the fired buffalo strategy." He stopped and waited, unsure of the governor's reaction.

Hong Yun had already lost confidence in his two closest subordinates. He scowled, but on second thought he saw a sparkle in the dark tunnel. In ancient history a small army had invented the "fired buffalo" tactic and routed an army five times as big by sending a thousand water buffalo stampeding toward the enemy camp. Each buffalo had a burning torch tied to its tail, and the frightened beasts had finally overrun the enemy camps, trampling troops and setting fire to their tents and buildings. It was such a famous battle that even today, storytellers in teahouses retold it with relish. He scanned the room. His officials all looked excited, but none dared to speak, probably for fear of saying the wrong thing, for it was no secret that Chu and Tao had both fallen out of the governor's favor.

The governor heaved a long sigh. After an unnecessary cough to show his authority, he said to Tao, his scowl deepening, "You two empty rice tubs should have been thrown in jail after so many bungled jobs. But, considering that you had no part in the last disaster, I may allow you to regain your lost merit by doing something useful. If we adopt this 'fired buffalo' tactic, what do you suggest that we do? Speak up!"

Tao's face brightened instantly. The favorable response was more than he had expected. "Your Excellency," he said, his voice louder and more confident, "We shall have eight thousand men, including the three thousand from Fukien. That is more than we need for this battle. The God-worshippers are concentrated in an area outside the eastern gate of Yung An. Such a concentration is an ideal target for fired buffalo tactics. It will be hard to find a thousand water buffalo in such a short period of time, but five hundred will pose no problem. We will simply borrow them from the farmers in the nearest three counties under the control of the Fu magistrate. Each buffalo needs only two soldiers to arm it. Sharp knives will be tied to its two horns, a torch tied to its tail. When everything is ready, the other soldier will light the torch and let go! The cavalry will accompany the frenzied animals, keeping them in line so that they will run directly to the enemy camp. I can see the result already, Your Excellency. Blood will be spilled by the knives . . . flesh and bones will be smashed by trampling hooves. Thousands of God-worshippers will be running and crying for mercy in a sea of fire. It will be a memorable victory with your stamp, Your Excellency. And it might spell the end of the Taiping Rebellion once and for all."

As Tao talked, he looked so excited that his hands waved and saliva flew. The governor was equally excited, but he tried to hide it by pulling a long face.

"Since you seem to be delighted with this foolish idea, are you willing and capable of carrying it out?" he asked.

"Yes, Your Excellency!" Tao said. "Give me a thousand men and cavalry. I will wipe out the God-worshippers. I never underestimate an enemy, Your Excellency, but this time we will turn them to ashes. And the buffalo will be returned to their lawful owners in good condition

... perhaps with partially burned tails. I suggest that a nominal compensation be paid to each owner."

The governor turned to his other officials. "I want to hear your opinions," he said. "I like to hear both pro and con. Speak up!"

All the officials spoke at once. All agreed that it was an excellent idea. They all spoke with conviction except the Fu magistrate, who saw the burden of collecting five hundred water buffalo and it depressed him.

33

After Su San-mei had sent the substitute bales of cotton to Kweilin, she had the original bales fished out and the sunken boat floated and repaired. On Golden Rooster's Sea Hawk they counted the silver. Not a tael had been lost. They did not worry about government raids because they knew that the governor would keep the theft a secret to save face.

"Father," she said, still laughing, "this turned out even better than I had originally planned."

"Guess you are right," Golden Rooster said, puffing on his bamboo pipe happily. "Your fox mind always worried me. Robbing a government boat always invites an open attack. That is why I scowled on your second idea after you suggested the first. But the Jade Emperor in Heaven has taken good care of you. I suggest that from now on you be a little less foxy and offer the Jade Emperor a few incense sticks."

"Father," Su San-mei interrupted, "luck comes in streaks. Have you heard about the governor's 'fired buffalo tactics' in their next attack? They are confiscating buffalo everywhere."

"That is Hung Shiu-ch'uan's problem, Su San-mei," Golden Rooster said. "We have saved his head once . . . let him protect himself the next time."

"But we made money by saving his head," Su San-mei argued. "If luck comes in streaks, who knows what luck will come out of our attempt to save him again?"

Golden Rooster looked at her askance. "Su San-mei, a cat is not concerned about a dog's safety. Why are you so worried about him?"

"Let him boil in oil and see if I am worried," she snorted. "But we have an alliance, have we not? Even pirates obey a code to help each other."

Golden Rooster heaved a long sigh. He was glad that Su San-mei was not a shifty woman. "Even a fox talks about codes," he said, shaking

203

his head. "All right, what do you intend to do about the governor's 'fired buffalo tactics'?"

Sewing a button, she glanced up with a mischievous smile. "Leave everything to me, Father."

He looked at her indulgently, wondering if she was going to involve herself in a major war. She was too young to risk her life. The secret societies were not equipped to involve themselves in a major conflict. He blew out a mouthful of smoke, pointed his bamboo pipe at her and chided, "A woman's place is washing, cooking, and sewing buttons. You have done enough man's work. Fighting 'fired water buffalo' is not a woman's job."

"I have fleeced the government of five thousand taels of silver. You said that was not a woman's job either."

"Cheating a stupid turtle's egg is a lot easier than butting your pretty head against a thousand frenzied water buffalo with knives on their horns and burning tails. No! You have nothing to do with this! Let the Heavenly Emperor take care of his God-worshippers."

Su San-mei stopped sewing. She had never forgotten Hung, her old flame. This was a chance for her to show that she hated him for being so heartless and never attempting to redeem her. She was determined to show him that she was not a weakling to be abandoned and forgotten so easily.

"Father," she said, her voice beseeching and urgent, "I need to do this. And I promise that I will not be so foolish as to butt my head against those buffalo. I have already worked out a way that will make the Heavenly Emperor feel grateful. I want him to thank you and me for saving his life!"

Golden Rooster was surprised, but did not want to laugh off Su San-mei's remark as a joke. She had never failed him in the past. "Tell me," he said, "what are you going to do this time?"

Su San-mei, a smile on her face, whispered something into his ear. Golden Rooster threw his head back and laughed.

"Father," Su San-mei said teasingly, "when you laugh, more and more you sound like an old rooster crowing."

"Yes, an old rooster heralding daybreak," he said, chuckling. "Every day is a new day full of your foxy ideas."

"Will you please not tell Hung about this?"

"Hung has ears and eyes everywhere. He will probably save his own life before you can save it."

"He is busy enjoying being the emperor," she said grudgingly. "He's probably surrounded by concubines and his ears and eyes are deaf and blind to everything but women's whispered sweet words." She stopped, ashamed to show her jealousy so blatantly.

Again Golden Rooster looked at her askance; he was beginning to suspect there was a love-hate relationship between her and Hung. "You ought to tell him where you are," he said seriously. "You are as far as a thousand miles away and as close as right in front of him. How far or how close . . . let him decide. I have no objection to being one of his fathers-in-law."

"I'll never tell him where I am," she said heatedly, her voice bitter. "But I'll let him know . . ." She stopped, looked at Golden Rooster and demanded, "Will you let me do it or not?"

Golden Rooster kept puffing on his pipe and blowing out his smoke without saying yes or no. "I know," she said, "you'll think about it. You'll think about it for the next ten years!" With a little snort, she got up and started toward the cabin with her sewing. Golden Rooster watched her fondly, shaking his head. He was worried.

It was a dark night. Stars were shining brightly beside the new moon. Suddenly, hundreds of lights gleamed in the distance like little fireflies. Su San-mei and her one hundred chosen horsemen recruited from the secret societies were watching beside their Mongolian ponies on top of a hill near the West River. Half of them were armed with modern rifles while the other half carried firecrackers and gongs. Below the hill, stretching for miles toward the city of Yung An were the drought-ravaged rice fields. Luckily the rice had been harvested before the fields were completely dried and caked. A dry autumn had brought little wind; there was no sound except the cicadas making a din in the scattered, half-barren ash trees and sycamores. Su San-mei strained her eyes at the distant lights, which soon started moving. Waving a long sword, she gestured at her horsemen, who nodded and mounted their scrawny restless horses and reined them in tightly, waiting.

The distant lights became bigger and clearer. Soon hooves thundered on the dried rice fields and five hundred water buffalo were seen bearing down toward the low hill, their horns shining with swords, their nostrils flaring and snorting, their eyes wild. The burning torches, tied to their tails, bobbed up and down like waves in a sea of fire.

Su San-mei, silhouetted against the dark sky on her stallion, made another gesture. Her horsemen, armed with rifles, galloped down the hill toward the Imperial Cavalry, which had been assigned to keep the stampeding buffalo on course. They met the cavalry head on, firing and shouting. Many Imperial soldiers fell off their horses; others made an attempt to fight with their swords, spears, and muskets, but they were no match for the Triads armed with modern rifles. In a few moments the Imperial Cavalry turned on their heels and fled.

Meanwhile, the other half of Su San-mei's horsemen were heading the maddened buffalo off to a valley nearby, beating gongs and exploding firecrackers. Soon they drove the beasts into the valley, which was surrounded by low hills. Another hundred men on the hills were ready. They slaughtered the animals with rifles and spears. The gong beaters dismounted quickly, pulled out their daggers and helped finish the massacre and cut up the meat. Half of the animals had already been frightened to death by their own torches, which the Triads gathered and used to build hundreds of fires. Over the fires they roasted the buffalo meat, laughed, talked, and had a feast. Su San-mei ordered tons of meat salted and smoked. At dawn she had enough salted meat to last several winters, for which she thanked Hung Shiu-ch'uan, without whom no such windfall would have come down from Heaven. Indeed, it was a lucky streak. One of these days, she would like to let Hung Shiu-ch'uan know that a mysterious woman had not only warded off a "fired buffalo attack" to save his life, but was also sending him a thousand catties of smoked water buffalo meat.

The great march was announced. The army was now swollen with new recruits, rich with food and silver, oil, and salt which had been confiscated from district yamens, local officials, landlords, and rich merchants. Morale was high, boosted by God's promise of a happy future and an easier life. The sea of colorful square flags and triangular pennants fluttering in the wind, the new weapons shining in the late-afternoon sun were all spirit-lifting. They sent waves of excitement through the city and the camp. Every Taiping, man or woman, was eager for action.

Hung was enjoying all the trappings of an emperor. His six concubines were supervised by his Empress, who had gracefully accepted the extra ladies and helped adorn them with pearls and jade. She believed that an emperor without a well-dressed harem would look strange to his subjects—like a peacock without feathers.

A few of the princes and generals had also acquired harems . . . especially Wei Ta, the North Prince, who had appointed himself as the rear guard in charge of the ladies' sedan chairs. He already visualized his future palace with massive red walls and yellow tiles, his dragon-adorned robes of silk and satin. One day he would also have the Heavenly mandate to be God's spokesman, trembling, sweating, and talking in a trance as Yang often did. He suspected that Yang had an insatiable ambition and wanted the people to have a superstitious belief in God. He was already envious of Yang's power, being the commander in chief and addressed as Nine Thousand Years, privileged to pass out God's words, even to the Heavenly Emperor himself.

Hung dispatched a message to Run-kan and instructed him to join the great march in Kweilin, the capital city of half a million inhabitants. He intended to seize the city within a week. From Kweilin the Taiping Army would march across the provincial border to Hunan. Along the way, from all sides, the distant secret societies would swear allegiance to him. Golden Rooster, who had commandeered a large fleet of ships and small boats, was already a formidable ally. He hoped to appoint the pirate chief commander of the Taiping Navy as soon as they occupied Changsha, the capital of Hunan. From Kweilin to Hunan, the vast plains would be an easy passage, but it would be even easier to take the waterway from Changsha all the way through the big lakes and the Yangtze to Nanking. With his skill in seamanship, Golden Rooster would play an important role in this holy crusade, even though it would be hard to make him a God-worshipper.

Under two oil lamps in the dark yamen audience hall, Hung pored over a map and discussed the details of the march with Feng and Yang. Outside, the other princes and generals were all busy discharging their respective duties. As the time drew closer, the entire Taiping population felt an increasing tension, as though they were a giant arrow about to be shot from a bow.

It was midnight when Hung finished his work. Both Feng and Yang were ready to retire to their own quarters for a good night's sleep. Before dawn, a cannon would be fired and the march would start. All the details had been worked out, orders issued and regulations proclaimed. The Heavenly Emperor smiled benevolently, thanking his closest friends and relatives, Feng and Yang. Liquor was forbidden, but Yang suggested that they send a guard to buy a bottle so they could propose a toast to the Heavenly Emperor and to themselves.

Hung had just reluctantly agreed, when Shao came in with a piece of paper. "Heavenly Emperor," he said, "a woman has sent you one thousand catties of buffalo meat. Here is the message: 'A gift to the Heavenly Emperor.' Signed, A Woman."

"A woman?" Hung asked. "What woman?"

"The porters did not say."

"Hm," Hung grunted with a shrug. "Feed a piece to a dog first."

"I already had a piece," Shao said. "It is safe. It is delicious, freshly salted and smoked!"

"A thousand catties," Hung said thoughtfully. "It's a lot of meat. Well, we shall all have a buffalo meat midnight supper. A bottle of mao-tai will go nicely with it."

"Aren't you curious about who this woman is?" Yang asked.

Hung shrugged. "Whoever she is, she is rich. That is all I want to know."

"I agree," Yang laughed. "Rich women are not necessarily pretty or young. Why be curious?"

34

Hong Yun, the Governor of Kwangsi, called Secretary Tung to his audience hall. His commanders had reported that the God-worshippers were rolling toward Kweilin like waves of a big flood. The three thousand Fukien troops had fled and all his own troops had withdrawn into the city, ready for a last-ditch fight. Hong Yun had never had much faith in his own troops and saw the imminent fall of Kweilin.

"Secretary Tung," he said quietly, his hands resting properly on his knees, as though he were posing for a painting, "Heaven has eyes. A curse is in the fate of Kwangsi and myself, probably because of an inexcusable sin either committed by myself or by my ancestors. The curse is a lesson to teach the sinful. As the Buddha has well said, 'Cause and effect go in a circle, hand in hand.' So it is time to accept the curse, which will redeem my sins and spare my people. This is my decision: Please have a rope tied to the ceiling. The moment I hear gunfire, I shall climb on a chair, put my neck in the loop, and be on my way to see Yen Lo."

"No, no, Your Excellency!" Secretary Tung cried, sinking on his knees. "You must not go to such extremes to spare the people. I hear that the God-worshippers will not loot or kill after they occupy a city. Nine kowtows to their leader, Hung Shiu-ch'uan, is enough to humor the enemy. All they want is money and food, Your Excellency."

"You know that Kwangsi is a poor province," the governor said with a sigh. "We never have much in our warehouses or treasury. All my life's savings do not amount to more than five hundred taels of silver, even though I have often slapped my own face swollen to look healthy and taken two concubines after the death of my wife. Taking only two concubines looks very shabby, but the truth is that I cannot afford another. The fact that I do not have an heir is another proof of the curse that I deserve. Time is short, Secretary Tung. I want the rope ready when I return. Meanwhile, I must arrange a settlement for my concubines and have a last meal with them. It also takes a little time to change into my official robe to pay my last respects to the emperor."

Looking sad and sighing, he rose, bowed to the secretary and returned to his private quarters. Secretary Tung, tears washing his wrinkled bony face, kept knocking his head on the ground until the governor had disappeared behind the door that led to his small living quarters.

Back in the middle room, which also served as the dining room, a table of food had been readied—four dishes and one soup, almost cold, waiting for the governor. He wandered in, looking grim. His two concubines, Fei Fei and Chi Chi, rose to their feet quickly from the glazed porcelain stools and greeted him with a low bow.

"Dinner is getting cold," Fei Fei said with a faint smile. "Please take your seat at the table."

"I shall pour wine," Chi Chi said, hurrying to pour *hsiao hsing* wine into tiny cups. The table was set for three, and the two concubines took their usual seats flanking the governor. They were dressed in their best for this special occasion—Fei Fei in a silk blue Manchu gown and Chi Chi in red, their hair piled high, hidden in embroidered Manchu fanlike hats.

Never forgetting to cough at an appropriate moment, Hong Yun cleared his throat and took the master's chair that faced the entrance. He picked up his wine cup and toasted his two concubines according to their rank—Fei Fei Number One and Chi Chi Number Two. After the toast, Fei Fei picked up a morsel of red-cooked pork with her silver chopsticks and put it on the governor's rice bowl; Chi Chi did the same, picking up a piece of chicken giblet, the governor's favorite.

"In Kwangsi, delicacies are in short supply," Hong Yun said, helping himself to a spoonful of cucumber soup. "The simple dishes are shabby, but it is the occasion that counts."

"What occasion, Your Excellency?" Fei Fei asked. "Are you being promoted?"

"No, no," Hong Yun said quickly. "Since I must tell you sooner or later, I might as well tell you now. This is our last meal together. I have five hundred taels of silver saved up. After the meal, you may divide . . ." He choked, unable to go on.

The two concubines' faces whitened. They were stunned for a moment. Finally, Fei Fei found her voice. She stammered, "Y . . . Your Excellency, do you want to send us home? If we are no longer wanted, please tell us why!"

"It is not our fault that we did not give you a son, Your Excellency," Chi Chi said, looking hurt.

"No, no!" the governor said, wincing with emotion. "Not that, not that! It is my fault . . . all my fault that I do not have an heir. The reason I ordered our last dinner is because . . . because I shall leave you tonight."

"Where are you going?" Fei Fei asked fearfully. She had suspected that it was not a pleasure trip, for Hong looked so depressed.

"I am going to visit Yen Lo," he said, trying to sound normal. "The God-worshippers are coming. I, as the top official of this province, cannot face the enemy, so I have arranged my demise to redeem my curse. By doing so, I hope that the people can be spared any suffering that the curse may cause. But I hear that God-worshippers are not rapists or killers. I am sure they will not molest you . . . especially if they see my dead body."

Before he had finished, the two concubines rushed to him, grabbed his hands and wept, one pleading with him not to die, the other begging to go with him. Finally both begged to die with him. They tugged at his sleeves, touched his face and banged the dining table in agony. But Hong Yun sat in his chair stoically, determined to be unmoved. He knew that the women were genuinely heartbroken, but taking them both to see Yen Lo was unfair and unjust. He must bear the curse alone.

The city was dark and quiet. General Shao, the West Prince, riding ahead of his troops, signaled his men to stop. The first to reach Kweilin, he surveyed the city walls from one end to the other and wondered why the city was so quiet. He suspected that the enemy was using the Empty City Strategy of Ju Kwo-liang, the wisest man of the Three Warring Kingdoms, who invented the strategy to lure the enemies into the city and then ambush them. But when Ju had used it, he had kept his city gates open. Now none of the gates was open. Shao rode quietly to the nearest gate and pushed. The gate was locked. Having made sure there was no ruse, he ordered his men to scale the walls. Five hundred

Taipings, some using ropes and others using ladders, scaled the walls quietly, making as little noise as possible. When the first dozen men had gone over the wall, they quickly threw the gate open and the main force poured in without firing or shouting or beating drums and gongs. They fanned out inside the city and found that the defenders had gone and the houses were dark. Obviously, the Imperial Army had already abandoned the city and the population had locked themselves inside their houses, waiting for whatever fate Heaven had designed for them.

Still cautious, General Shao rode directly to the governor's yamen. He dismounted and went in, followed closely by his personal guards. The yamen was also dark and quiet. Shao took a torch from an aide's hand and held it high as he walked into the audience hall.

In the semidarkness, he found a man and two women dressed in their best, sitting in three chairs on the dais, their eyes tightly closed. Above them were three nooses hanging from the ceiling. Shao mounted the dais and coughed. The governor opened his eyes. When he saw Shao, he looked surprised.

"Who are you?" he asked.

"I am Prince West of the Heavenly Kingdom of Peace," Shao said. "From your clothes, I assume that you are the Governor of Kwangsi, are you not?"

"Yes. But why was there no fight? I have not heard one single shot."

"Either your troops have all escaped or they are hiding themselves as civilians." He glanced at the hanging nooses and looked at the governor quizzically.

"Oh, those," the governor said apologetically. "The answer to my curse. If we had heard one single shot, you would have found us hanging on these ropes. It seems that Yen Lo has rejected us."

Rising to his feet, he gave Shao a low bow and added, "God-worshippers, let these two women go. I place my life in your hands."

After the fall of Kweilin, the God-worshippers' long march was almost unhindered, until the Taipings reached Hunan Province; they had overrun the towns and villages between the two provinces as easily as splitting a bamboo. Along the way they had converted many more people but had collected little food or livestock. Hung was disappointed that Kweilin, the capital, was so poor and so shabby, but he was gratified that the Taipings had taken it without firing a shot. He was also glad that Shao had converted its governor and the governor's two concubines.

But Hunan was different. The Changsha garrison put up such a stubborn resistance that it took twenty thousand Taipings fifteen days to break down the defenses. Most of the thousand men scaling the city walls were burned to death by boiling oil that was poured down by the defenders; half of those who broke down the city gates met with ambushes inside the city.

Hung usually remained outside a city when it fell, but Changsha was so important that he went in with his troops. When he walked into the governor's yamen, he was shocked to see that the governor and his entire family had hanged themselves in the audience hall. On the governor's large mahogany table he found a suicide note written in perfect eight-legged style, stamped with the governor's official seal. It said that his whole family, a total of twelve members including a wife, four concubines, and six growing children, had all sworn to die with the city. The note also indicated that the governor was the first to hang himself. He was dressed in his best embroidered official robe with horseshoe sleeves, his queue newly braided and oiled, his red-buttoned cap set properly on his head. Hung, out of respect for this scholarly official, personally took down the body, laid it on the mahogany table and gently closed its eyes. He ordered General Shao to give the whole family a decent burial.

The fighting did not stop even days after the occupation. Feng was ambushed and fatally wounded with three bullets in his stomach. Heartbroken, Hung rushed to him, squatted beside him and held his hand. As he lay dying on the street in a pool of blood, he said to Hung with a smile on his face, "Heavenly Emperor, I have accomplished my mission on earth. I am ready and happy to ascend to Heaven to serve God in person."

He had been Hung's closest and most trusted associate, and the most devoted Christian. Every time Hung thought of him, he felt a large lump in his throat.

Hung had expected Changsha to fall grudgingly, for Hunan was a tradition-laden province, deeply rooted in Confucianism, Buddhism, and ancestor-worship. But it was a rich province. The war bounty was enormous. It included dozens of warehouses and armories full of food and ammunition. Besides horses and mules, the livestock would provide meat for the Taiping fighting men for several months.

For the march toward Hupei, Prince Hu, the treasurer, arranged to have most of the supplies transported through Tung Ting Lake to the great Yangtze on ships and barges of all sizes and shapes, guarded by the Taiping Navy under the command of Golden Rooster.

During the march, Hung was dressed in his Taiping army uniform and armed with a sword and musket. He rode on a tall white stallion with golden trappings, followed by five hundred personal guards and a square yellow banner that was twice the size of the other banners. The character HUNG on the banner was his own calligraphy, written with bold strokes and each stroke indicating strength and character. Everybody bowed to his banner; it was the symbol of a kingdom to come.

General Shao and his army remained in the front as vanguard, followed by Yang, the commander in chief. Following Hung and his retinue were Hung's family members in one group, and the other officers' families in another, with the noble ladies and the elderly women riding in sedan chairs. Two thousand porters, singing in unison to prevent fatigue, carried light supplies, which swung from their shoulders on poles. Thousands of mules and water-buffalo carts followed the coolies, carrying heavy loads of food supplies, cannons, and ammunition. Bringing up the rear was General Wei and his men, most of them carrying modern firearms. The marchers stretched for ten miles, and their lines grew longer every day as they moved toward Hupei Province. Wuhan, the twin city in Hupei, was their next destination. By occupying Hupei, the Taipings would be able to control most of central China, the country's richest rice bowl.

Between Hunan and Hupei the Taipings again took towns and villages as easily as splitting a bamboo. In many counties the Imperial garrisons dropped their weapons and ran. Hung watched townspeople welcome him with firecrackers. The young volunteered to carry the Taiping Army's newly collected supplies; the elderly offered water, eggs, and even chickens to the soldiers on the streets.

After a long day's march, the Taipings pitched tents wherever they could find sufficient space; many spent a few hours sleeping in temples and ancestral halls. Others dozed under melon trellises and in mountain caves. Hung had seen to it that no Taiping soldiers ever occupied people's homes. By the time they reached Hupei, more people had joined the crusade and the march had grown to fifteen miles long.

But Wuhan's defenses were strong. A major battle was fought on both sides of the wide river, on which the twin city was built. Thousands of armed junks and sampans were mobilized, with the Taipings and Imperial troops fighting simultaneously on water and on land. Traditional weapons clashed, cannons roared, and bird guns popped. Those armed with modern weapons raided the government warehouses, ammunition dumps, and yamens. The battle lasted three days with huge casualties ... thousands killed and wounded. Houses on both banks burned for days. On the fourth day General Shao and his men were hopelessly surrounded by the enemy's main force. Facing imminent defeat, he ordered his men to kneel down and pray to God for His blessing. After a brief prayer, he and his soldiers leapt up and charged, breaking the siege and sweeping to victory. But in the end, the West Prince, leading the charge, fell off his horse with a bullet between the eyes. It was the last bullet the Imperial Army had fired during the defense of Wuhan. When they fled, Wuhan fell and the Taipings seized the second-most-important city in south-central China. Their losses were heavy. In Wuhan, the entire Taiping armed forces prayed for Shao's spirit; another Taiping leader had ascended to Heaven to serve the God in person.

Not long after the Hupei victory, the Taipings' luck ran out again. They began to suffer a series of almost fatal adversities on their march to Nanking. First they were plagued by sickness, then by bad weather and an acute shortage of food because of a recent famine in the area. Hung prayed every day, and eventually God came to his aid. Numerous secret societies arose from nowhere to break the Imperial Army's encirclement and rescue many trapped Taiping divisions. Some of the secret societies Hung had never heard of—Straw Planters Sect, the Green Grass Cutters Sect, the Firewood Gatherers Sect, the Red Spear Society, and so forth. They had come suddenly and disappeared suddenly. Hung ordered a mass prayer, thanking the Lord Almighty for His blessing, comparing the rescue to God's opening of the Red Sea.

Once again the march continued smoothly, the cities and towns falling easily. Nearing Nanking, Hung mounted to the top of a hill where he watched the advance of more than a million God-worshippers marching toward their destination, a glorious sea of yellow banners and red turbans stretching as far as the eye could see. He felt such a marvelous sensation of triumph that he thrust his sword into the air and sang:

> Onward God-worshippers,
> Marching to Kingdom of Heaven,
> With the cross of Jesus,
> Slaying all the demons.

35

Charles George Gordon read avidly about the Taiping Rebellion in China. He regarded Hung Shiu-ch'uan, the rebellion leader, a Christian warrior, a hero of heroes. He had always been sympathetic toward the oppressed. To him, any revolution trying to overthrow an oppressor was glamorous, romantic, moral, and religious.

The education he had received at Woolrich had not satisfied him, and his career had not excited him until he was ordered to fight in the Crimean War in 1854. But his hopes were soon deflated, because he was sent to war as an engineer instead of an officer of artillery. He wanted to see action as a highly spirited soldier. In the Crimea he did see some exchanges of fire in the trenches, but it was nothing compared to raising his saber and charging at the head of a company of courageous men fighting for a cause, like Hung Shiu-ch'uan of China.

As soon as he returned from the war, he plunged into the study of the Taipings again. He had read about Hung's personal life, his devotion to God, and his heroic deeds. All were described in detail by sympathetic reporters who had witnessed the civil war and reported from various Chinese cities. Since the 1851 uprising in Kwangsi Province, Hung's Taiping armies had swept through six southern provinces and triumphantly occupied Nanking with an army of one million men and women. In early 1853 he had proclaimed himself to the world as the first Christian Emperor of China, and Nanking as his new capital.

As Gordon read about his conquests and triumphs, his blood boiled with excitement. He could hardly wait to visit the new capital of the new Christian nation—the Heavenly Kingdom of Great Peace. He would volunteer his services in whatever capacity the new nation needed. He inquired about such possible services at his own government offices in London.

He was surprised to find that nobody in the government knew much about the Taiping Rebellion. Those who had heard or read about it simply dismissed it as secret societies trying to seize power. England was not concerned, except that the rebellion might disrupt trade with China. The export of opium and wool fabrics to Canton and Shanghai had increased since the signing of the Treaty of Nanking. Britain had become one of the most favorable nations, along with France, America, and Russia. In 1855 Britain was the leading trading country in China; her tonnage was the biggest. Of all the foreign ships reaching Shanghai, more than half of them flew the British Union Jack.

Gordon was unhappy about his government's disinterest in the Taipings. "We are making money in China," one official in the Foreign Office told him. "Why upset things by aiding a rebellion?"

Soon it was no secret that England had issued strict orders to the British troops in China to remain neutral. But when the Taipings began to march north and threaten the city of Tientsin, the foreign powers became alarmed. They could no longer sit on the wall, test the wind, and do nothing. The wind had started blowing in the wrong direction, making the Western trading countries uneasy. If the Taipings occupied all the free trading ports, would the foreign powers still enjoy all the extraterritorial rights? If Peking fell, would the Treaty of Nanking still be honored? Even though the Heavenly Kingdom of Great Peace was a Christian country, their foreign policy might be totally different from that of the corrupt Manchu regime.

There was some heated debate among the policymakers in London and in the press. Charles George Gordon followed them closely, chewing every word to draw his own conclusions. Morally he still wanted to help the rebellion, for the Taipings were fighting for China's independence. It was obvious that the foreign powers were trying to colonize China and perhaps divide the country like a big melon, then fight over it. Selling opium to China had always repulsed him; forcing China to buy wool fabrics and other overproduced merchandise for which China had no need also rubbed his conscience the wrong way. On the other hand, he was British, and he had to think as a patriot, if not as a Christian.

He remained a second lieutenant in the Royal Engineers. As soon as he had returned from the Crimean War, he was ordered to Pembroke Docks to assist in the construction of a series of useless forts. Increasing frustration made him more religious and more anxious to go to China to do something worthwhile, or to spread the gospels of God. He was glad that his sister Augusta, now a spinster of thirty-three, had also become more pious toward church and God, and they often exchanged ideas in letters, which helped change his whole outlook on life. His compromise with frustration and unhappiness made him almost fatalistic.

He still had his officer's uniform from the Crimean War, even though he detested its gold braid and scarlet coat. He believed that he would one day wear it again in China. Somehow he believed that it was his fate.

His father had been promoted; he was now in command of the Royal Artillery, a rather influential position in the military. George, growing increasingly restless, wanted his father to pull some strings.

"For what?" the general asked.

"Have someone send me to China," he said.

"To do what?" the senior Gordon asked.

"To see some active service, sir," George said. "You know some bigwigs in the War Office. A word or two from you would probably get me on an oceangoing ship."

"My dear boy, I have not heard a great deal about your ambitions. What exactly do you want to do in China?"

"Preach or fight. It doesn't make any difference, sir."

"Fight? Fight what?"

"I would like to fight in any way that is good for Britain. There's bound to be something that I can do."

General Gordon peered at his son, somewhat amused. "I have heard that Marco Polo said the same thing. He wanted to go to China. He said the same thing to his father. 'I want to go to Cathay and do what is good for Venice.' And by Jove, he did! He lived in the Chinese Imperial Court for ten years and almost married a Chinese princess. Is that what you have in mind?"

"No, sir."

"Well, that's not what Marco Polo had in mind, either. But the trip did revolutionize the Italians' cuisine. He brought back some Chinese foods that have become the Italians' main staples—spaghetti, pizza, and ravioli. My dear boy, I have no objection to your going to China, whatever secret desire you may have, but British cuisine is the bloody best in the world, and we British have an almost evangelical tradition that cannot be tarnished by pagan cultures. Wherever we go in the Orient, we go with a Bible in one hand and a sword in the other, not hoping to marry Oriental princesses or introduce shark fins and bird nests into our menu."

"Sir," George said, "I've always kept my army uniform pressed and my boots shined. If I go, I will go with a Bible in one hand and a sword in the other! That is exactly why I want to go, sir!"

General Gordon took a deep breath and looked at his son fondly. "Well, I'll write to Sir John Burgoyne and see what he can do. China is the area that all the foreign powers have their eyes on. I do hope that you can do a lot of good for England while gallivanting in China."

George did not think that Sir John Burgoyne, semiretired, would do much for him. Perhaps his father had just used him as an excuse to end the conversation. Perhaps he should write to some missionaries again. Mission work still had the strongest lure ... more than rattling sabers on horseback.

He continued to study British relations with China. The more he studied the more confused he became. Britain had not stopped chastising the Manchu government with little wars. Only recently British forces had occupied Taku forts near Peking; before that an Anglo-French force had ravaged that area and the Manchus had been obliged to fight two wars, one against the Anglo-French forces and another against the Taipings. Yet, at the same time, the Western powers were ready to aid the Manchus to crush the Taipings' rebellion, even though they insisted on remaining neutral. He suspected that England was just as confused as he. Since the accession of Queen Victoria, Britain had fought numerous small wars in China for the security of British trade, including their trade in opium. Twice the French had joined the battles as Britain's ally, although Napoleon III was not much interested in trade. Gordon suspected that France only desired to achieve some cheap military glory at half cost. The Manchu forces also seemed diverse and confusing; some of their commanders were pro-foreign and anti-Taiping, others were anti-foreign and anti-Taiping. The anti-foreign forces even massacred missionaries and kidnapped foreign envoys, rousing the foreign powers' anger and provoking retribution. All was a terrible mess and Charles Gordon was extremely vexed. He wrote to Augusta: "It is all very amusing, but my conscience forbids me to laugh very hard at this China comedy."

In the spring of 1859, Charles George Gordon, at the age of twenty-seven, was finally ordered to Peking.

36

Sitting on the golden dragon throne in his glittering Palace of the Heavenly Kingdom of Great Peace in Nanking, Hung Shiu-ch'uan, the Heavenly Emperor, felt depressed. The princes and generals had withdrawn as soon as the morning audience was over. Most of them had been people whom he knew very little; quite a few of his closest associates had died in battle. The death of Feng and Shao still pained him. Yang the East Prince, Wei the North Prince, and Shih the Shield Prince were the three remaining old associates who had gone through fire and high water with him from Kwangsi. For years he had watched them bickering with one eye open and one eye closed. Lust and greed had set in, in the new kingdom; power struggles had raised their ugly heads. Luckily he had nurtured Li the Faithful; he had cultivated him and pruned him like a young plant that had grown into a sturdy tree. He hoped that from now on he could depend on this tree for shelter against the sun and rain.

He had never realized that being an emperor was such a lonely and isolated job. Close friends distanced themselves; some even built a wall between them as though they were afraid of a man whose word was law. Only those who had secret ambitions prostrated themselves at his feet trying to be close. Even his family had changed. He missed the intimacy, the small talk, the little teasing. Now his mother and older brothers behaved like polite guests, his wife and concubines acted like slaves, saying nothing but *yes* and doing all his bidding without question. Sometimes, when he was surrounded by concubines and ladies-in-waiting, he still felt lonely. Yet he wanted to be alone.

Each morning, after the audience, he remained on his throne and reminisced about those memorable struggling days. Even the humiliating failure of his two Imperial examinations in Canton had become fond memories. The triumphant entry into the City of Nanking six years ago had been especially unforgettable. Carried on his Imperial sedan chair by sixty porters, he had been obliged to duck under many gates. The banners, the noisy beating of gongs and drums, the firing of ceremonial cannons, and the cheers of the Taipings still rang in his ears. Everyone had been honest and faithful, devoted to him and to God.

He had heard people call the Taipings Long Hairs. He had liked the nickname and its implications. The Taipings had grown long hair on the shaven part of their heads and had gotten rid of the queue in defiance of the Manchu rule. With the symbol of slavery gone the men were proud, for the name Long Hair had become symbolic of freedom and the people's salvation; it represented fighters against oppression, corruption, and extortion by government officials. In many provinces the people had prayed for the arrival of the Long Hairs.

But recently their good name had begun to change. Some people had started calling the Long Hairs bandits. In remote areas people thought Long Hairs were ghosts who ate human flesh, who had invented the most cruel tortures such as "five horses tearing a body," "a thousand cuts," and "boiling in oil."

During bad times the people had always helped uprisings. After the burning and pillaging by bandits, the officials always scraped up what was left, then drought or flood followed, giving the people only two choices: death or rebellion. And they often chose rebellion. Not anymore. Today most would rather choose death. After the Kwangsi uprising the Long Hairs had enjoyed such popularity that during the long march from Kwangsi to Nanking, people had cheered, cried, brought flowers, water, and food which they could hardly spare. Not anymore.

Yes, those were the glorious days. He had enjoyed his own immense popularity. The Heavenly Kingdom of Great Peace had had ideology, organization, equality, and justice. His armies' triumphs over the demoralized Imperial troops had been praised in books and poems. Teahouse storytellers had told of Taiping victories, battle after battle. Not anymore. What he saw today was inner strife among his leaders. He saw the gradual breaking up of the fine fabric of his government. The infighting between Yang and Wei was beginning to worry him the most. It made him wonder who would eventually fight the Heavenly Emperor himself.

Many times he longed for Run-kan to return. He had given Run-kan the title of prince and reappointed him foreign minister. Run-kan, fluent in many European languages and having adopted many foreign habits, seemed to enjoy the foreigners' company in Canton and Shanghai. His associations with the foreigners was sometimes rewarding, feeding Hung with knowledge and advice which Hung had no way of obtaining otherwise. Run-kan had warned him that although Taiping's Christian ideology had aroused the foreigners' sympathy, the revolution had gradually made them fearful. They were afraid that a new China might emerge to threaten the privileges they had obtained after the Opium War. Run-kan even predicted that Britain and France might openly cast their lot with the Manchu Dynasty. This prediction had been another rock weighing heavily on Hung's heart.

But nothing bothered him more than the signs of disappointment expressed by the general population. He had lately examined his revolutionary programs and found them unsatisfactory, the cause of the people's unrest:

(1) There was no private property; everything belonged to a common bank and a government granary. He wondered if this system would kill people's incentive.

(2) All the land was divided and distributed equally to the population according to the size of the family. All people were treated equally. He wondered if all people really were created equal. If not, those more capable than the others should be allowed to cultivate more, creating competition and increasing production.

(3) The equality of men and women also created problems. Chinese traditions died hard. Many women were reluctant to join the army and do men's work. Monogamy was obligatory. Yet the Taiping leaders, including himself, had taken many wives. He had already heard people grumbling, quoting an ancient saying: "The officials are permitted to set a fire, but the people are not allowed to light a lamp."

(4) The Taipings were devoted only to a foreign God and intolerant of other religions. They had destroyed pictures, statues, and temples of Buddhism, Taoism, Confucianism, and ancestral tablets. The gentry was unhappy. He heard that in Hunan a retired gentry-official, Tseng Kuo-fan, was organizing an army to fight him.

(5) His promise to create a heaven on earth had not materialized. The nation was still war-ravaged, people were still dying of famine and

disease. The gap between the poor and the rich had even widened despite the doctrine of equality. The Taiping leaders seemed to represent the only rich class in his kingdom.

(6) He attributed his military success mostly to the weakness of the enemy. His own strategies had been really very simple, all borrowed from Sun Wu's Military Tactics, a moth-eaten book in existence for thousands of years. The essence was simple: "Hit the enemy at his weak point; avoid strong, well-fortified positions; mislead the enemy and ambush him." It also emphasized that, "To defeat a better-equipped enemy, the poorly armed army must have better discipline, morale, and organization." That was all there was to learn from Sun Wu. So Hung had no great secret for winning battle after battle in this holy war. Now, sitting on his throne, thinking of the past, he did not really feel very proud of his achievements.

He sent for Li the Faithful. The young general came in and bowed. He had won many battles and had never boasted of his accomplishments. It was one of his characteristics that Hung found endearing, a sure sign of honesty . . . perhaps a sign of loyalty also. He had predicted the young man's future in Kwangsi, a foresight that had made him trust Li and give him the nickname, Faithful.

"Faithful," he said kindly, his voice a little tired, "the Heavenly Kingdom of Great Peace is not as perfect nor as peaceful as I had expected. A formidable foe is rising in Hunan. The province is famous for hot peppers, soldiery, and passionate women. You can blame it all on the hot peppers. But this new Hunan army worries me. It is not like the Imperial troops, half of whom are rotten and addicted to opium. This Hunan army is organized and financed by the gentry-landlord class. They are fighting for a strong cause to preserve Chinese culture and the Chinese way of life. It is led by a scholar-general called Tseng Kuo-fan and his younger brother, General Tseng Kuo-chuan. Have you heard of them?"

"Yes, Heavenly Emperor," Li said. "Tseng Kuo-fan is reportedly a military genius. His brother is known as the Hunan Tiger. Indeed, a formidable foe!"

"How to repel this enemy? Do you have any suggestions?"

"Since their slogan is to preserve Chinese traditions and Chinese culture, their cause will have popular support. To counteract it we should first relax some of our own restrictions. End the separation of men and women. Disband the women's regiment in the army and send the women home to their husbands. Stop destroying other idols, especially those of Confucius. The Hunan Army has no allegiance to the Imperial Court. In fighting them we should emphasize one point: We aim to overthrow the Manchu Dynasty, not destroy Chinese culture."

Hung had questioned Li to find out more about the young man's knowledge and analytical ability. Li had answered to the point without exaggeration or unnecessary flowery explanations. Grunting in satisfaction, Hung said in an equally even voice, "Faithful, six years ago, when you were a young soldier, I recognized you as leadership timber, and you have proven it. Now that Feng the South Prince has ascended to Heaven, I feel that I have lost a leg and an arm. I am anxious to find someone to take his place as my most trusted aide. Today I want to give you a title. From now on you will be addressed as Prince the Faithful. I also want to appoint you as the deputy Commander in Chief of all the Taiping forces. Yang the East Prince will have no objection. He is now busy bickering with Wei the North Prince. I want someone who will be busy tending to affairs of the nation, and I hope it will be you."

Li bowed. "Thank you, Heavenly Emperor. I hope that I can live up to your expectations. With my limited ability, I shall do my very best not to fail you."

After Faithful had withdrawn, Hung nodded with a deep sigh. It was refreshing for Hung to see someone straightforward and down to earth, not too proud nor too humble. Another man would have trembled with excitement, given him nine kowtows, then exaggerated his own abilities and promised to fulfill his every desire, including reaching for the moon.

PART THREE

CHINA
GORDON

|37|

Charles George Gordon arrived in Peking after France and England had won another war in China. Punishing the Imperial Court for not honoring some of the terms of their treaties, the French troops destroyed the Imperial Summer Palace outside Peking. Gordon was elated. Being sympathetic with the Taipings, he wanted the Western powers to fight the Manchus and help the Taipings overthrow the Manchu Dynasty. At twenty-seven, no more than five feet nine inches tall and slight, he felt tireless and energetic even after a long tedious ocean journey. He was eager to argue, to fight . . . to do anything to correct the wrongs in this mysterious land that had fascinated him since childhood.

It was a chilly afternoon in October, 1860. He found his contingent encamped under the walls of Peking. The Gobi wind was blowing, churning up dust and autumn leaves everywhere, stinging his eyes. But Peking impressed him. He had never seen such beauty in architecture, especially the Forbidden City with its massive red walls and shiny yellow tiles gleaming in the sun. He marveled at the ingeniously carved eaves and endless marble steps that stretched into the Imperial Palace, where only a few white men had entered. He had heard that the emperor's summer palace in the northern suburb was even more magnificent. Eager as a child in a candy store, he seized an opportunity to visit it that afternoon.

He took a rickety carriage drawn by a bony horse. When he arrived, he was horrified by its destruction. The palace grounds extended for several square miles and contained more than two hundred houses of great beauty, but most of them had been burned to the ground, their carved beams, lacquered pillars, latticed windows, and yellow tiles fallen into heaps of debris. It pained him the most when he saw antiques of museum quality lying in pieces—porcelain, cloisonné, lacquer, and jade carvings, all smashed or trampled. He was astounded and revolted by this unnecessary vandalism by a civilized Western country; it was so offensive to his aesthetic sensibilities that he was almost in tears. He later learned that the summer palace had already been extensively looted by the French before it was destroyed. He wrote to Augusta:

> ... we are still pillaging the place and picking up pieces to sell. A gold ornament can bring £48. A French soldier sold a string of pearls to an Englishman for sixteen shillings, which the Englishman sold the next day for £500. You can scarcely imagine the beauty and magnificence of the palaces we burned. It made one's heart ache. It was wretchedly demoralizing for the army. Everyone was wild for plunder.

He was assigned to engineering duties in Tientsin under General Stavely, his brother-in-law, husband of his second sister, Mary. When he learned that it was his own father who had talked Stavely into recruiting him, he began to feel uncomfortable. It seemed to him a blatant case of nepotism; he always fiercely disapproved of such backstairs influence.

Again he wrote to his sister Augusta to air his complaint, hoping that she would indirectly acquaint their father with his son's character and beliefs. He and his father had never been very close and he always felt that they did not know each other very well.

General Stavely's office was in a yamen that belonged to a Manchu prince, a rambling four-acre park dotted with pagodas, stables, servants' quarters, miniature gardens, and artificial hills. The British had seized it after the Opium War. George Gordon visited the General one day as a relative, not as his subordinate.

The general was quite a bit older than he, tall with military bearing, meticulously dressed, his chest covered with decorations, his scanty hair graying. Gordon hardly knew his brother-in-law, but his sister Mary seemed to be happy. Stavely shook his hand rather stiffly.

"I hope I can get on well with you, George," the general said as soon as Gordon took his seat on a hardwood ancestral chair in the sparsely furnished gloomy room.

Gordon knew what his brother-in-law meant; even his own father had hinted that he was a keg of gunpowder. "You certainly will, General," he said amiably. "But I'm not thrilled about engineering work."

"You have always been a restless man, George. But you have missed the action. We have won every bloody war. The dragon has now become a lamb. However, if the rebels slay the lamb, we may have war again. We can't let that happen, can we?"

"You mean England will quell the rebellion?" Gordon asked.

"Look, George, we've put money in the bank and are drawing handsome interest. You don't want some bandits to rob it, do you?"

"But the Taipings are not bandits," Gordon protested. "They are revolutionaries trying to overthrow a tyranny."

General Stavely stared at him with a condescending smile, shaking his head. "George, I had hoped you would study China more thoroughly before you came. The Taipings are nothing but a bloody horde of vagabonds and riffraff, headed by a political fanatic who dreamed of crowning himself Emperor of China in Peking. Thank God he could only go as far as Nanking! Listen, what you have heard about this pseudo-Christian is all his own propaganda. To cheat the godless Chinese he invented a vision. He waved the Bible and declared it was a vision of God. He saw himself as the son of God and the younger brother of Jesus Christ, chosen at God's command to exterminate the poor Manchus. This man is a fraud, George."

Gordon looked shocked. He had never expected such a strong negative reaction from his brother-in-law, which undoubtedly represented the general opinion of the British government. He was not convinced. He argued, "Hung Shiu-ch'uan has written beautiful poems and books about the Christian religion. How can you . . ."

"Have you read them?" the general interrupted.

"Of course not. I don't read Chinese."

"Then how can you tell they are beautiful? From his propaganda pamphlets, which he has scattered freely to gain sympathy, he has only a superficial idea of Christianity. I'm told that he has received some Christian education from an American priest from Georgia . . . a Reverend Mr. Roberts. This chap was kicked out of his hometown for some unsavory business he had committed. Believe me, this Christian Heavenly Emperor knows our religion no more than you and I know how to cook a shark's fin dinner. He only uses Christianity as a pretext to seize power. Yes, he talks about the Ten Commandments, but he violates most of them himself. When asked why he has so many wives, his answer was, 'Solomon had six hundred. It's all in the Bible.' "

Gordon cut the visit short. He did not want to hear more negative remarks about Hung and his rebellion. It was like listening to someone criticize his own family. Without any excuse, he rose, shook his brother-in-law's hand and bid him an abrupt good-bye. The general seemed to know him well, and grinned.

After Gordon had left Stavely's office he felt depressed. If Stavely had not destroyed Hung's reputation completely, he had done considerable damage. The disillusionment was devastating. But he decided not to jump to conclusions. He must learn more about this Heavenly Emperor. He had not thought too much about Hung's vision before, but now he began to have some doubts. If indeed Hung had declared himself the younger brother of Jesus Christ, that alone would be enough proof that the man was a fraud and committing blasphemy.

He gave Tientsin an extended tour. He did not like the workman's city; it was full of shabby buildings, crowded, and smelly, and lacked anything that appealed to the senses. But it was an important port, bustling with activities involving defense, transportation, and industry . . . nothing intellectual or aesthetic except for some opera houses and a few massive buildings that belonged to the rich and powerful.

To absorb knowledge of the city and its people, he visited a local market and ate some hot stew of unknown substance at an open-air restaurant. The stew tasted odd but he finished it. He had been told that Chinese food, especially the coolie kind, was made of gristle and bones, mixed with herbs. It soothed a man's nerves. But this bowl of stew seemed to make him restless. At night he tossed on his bed, unable to fall asleep at all.

His roommate in his quarters, a young lieutenant, asked him in the morning, "Say, Mack, what was wrong with you last night? You rocked the damn bed all night. Thought it was a bloody earthquake."

Gordon shrugged with a grin. "Just something I ate at the coolie market."

"Ah! Wildcat!" Lieutenant Shaw said. "The best aphrodisiac in the world, I am told. It supports the Tientsin red-light district. The Chinese are very clever. They always make one business to help another."

Gordon avoided conversation on such a subject. Without comment, he walked out with his toilet articles. The lieutenant shouted after him, "Say, old chap, I know where to go if you need something to neutralize the wildcat meat. It'll make you sleep like a baby."

The engineering unit was still awaiting orders. Gordon decided to spend more time exploring the city of Tientsin. Knowing that most of the Chinese cities had a main street named after the city, he asked passersby where Tientsin Boulevard was. Many hurried away as if they were afraid of a white man; others shook their heads with a bow. Finally, an old man who understood a few words of English directed him to a wide street with two-story buildings.

It was a busy thoroughfare full of pedestrians and carriages. Most of the shops had glittering signboards and sold everything from groceries to foreign fabrics. He dropped into a nice clean restaurant and ordered something by pointing a finger at random at an item on the Chinese menu. He was adventurous, but hoped it was not wildcat again.

The customers in the restaurant looked well-to-do; many dressed in gowns of good material and had good table manners, holding their chopsticks with the small finger extended like a flower petal. He had read in articles about China that such behavior indicated good breeding.

His order arrived. It was a steaming bowl of noodles with some meat and vegetables heaped on top. He watched some of the other noodle-eating customers and ate his noodles in the same manner, first pouring some soy sauce on the noodles from a jar, then mixing the noodles with his chopsticks. When they were well mixed, he lifted the noodles with his chopsticks, blew on them a few times, and sucked them into his mouth in one big breath. The action was noisy, but he heard sucking noises all around him amid a bit of groaning with pleasure.

Before he finished, a middle-aged man wearing a long gown spotted him and hurried over, all smiles. He spoke a little English. After a low bow he said, "Foreigner, sir. You have English paper?"

Gordon stared at him, wondering what he really wanted. "What English paper?" he asked.

"Or English book? Any English book. I buy! I have money." He fished out a handful of brass coins from his pocket and bounced them on his palm. "You have? You have?"

"Yes, I have, but I don't have them with me."

"You go get? I wait. Or maybe I go too? Two coins buy paper. Ten coins buy book. How many you have?"

"Sorry, my books are not for sale," Gordon said, returning to his noodle eating.

"So sorry, so sorry," the man said, hurrying away.

Gordon wondered if the man had orders to buy papers and books. Or was he a fish monger buying paper to wrap fish with? When Gordon paid and walked out of the restaurant, he was still puzzled.

Sauntering along the street he soaked in the sights and sounds and felt lucky that he had finally landed in the mysterious Orient. It was so different from England and Western culture. Only he wished that he could speak the native tongue. On a street corner he saw a large crowd trying to buy something from a vendor, waving their money, shouting and pushing. To his surprise, those who had come out of the crowd all carried old English-language newspapers or dog-eared books in English. He stopped and watched the crowd curiously, wondering what in blooming hell was going on. In a little while the crowd had bought all the papers and books, and the vendor hurried away, his pockets heavy with brass coins. He continued his little tour, shaking his head. The land was indeed a mystery. He would like to write to Augusta about it.

When he reached another street corner, he saw people running and hiding valuables in their hats and shoes. He looked around and discovered that a robbery was in progress at a bank across the street. The robbers, all dressed in the uniforms of the Imperial Army, ran out of the bank shooting. By now the street was almost deserted. Gordon backed into a doorway just as a merchant was closing the door and bolting it. There were half a dozen soldiers running across the street toward the spot where Gordon was standing. But the robbers ran past him and disappeared around the corner. When the last soldier passed by him, he caught a glimpse of his face. He was a white man in a Chinese uniform—a tunic reaching his knees, with a Chinese character sewn on his back. Gordon could not believe his eyes, but he swore that it was a white man with a large Roman nose, blue eyes, and white skin, and wearing a Chinese soldier's rice-bowl cap at a jaunty angle. From his glassy eyes and red face, he seemed a bit drunk.

"I'll be damned," Gordon muttered, staring after him.

38

Nanking, or Southern Capital, had been the capital for many Chinese dynasties. Built on water, surrounded by rivers and canals which connected with the great Yangtze, it was a large city with a population of more than a million. The city walls, almost fifty feet thick, were built of sandstone, with an enormous gate on each side. But there were numerous tunnels and secret gateways that had been built by emperors and warlords during thousands of years of unrest. Within the city, countless bones and skeletons had been buried during political upheavals, murdering rampages, palace intrigues, enemy massacres, and plundering. Yet the city had not lost its beauty. The parks were lush with trees and flowers, brilliantly purple in winter and pleasantly green the rest of the year. Like Peking's Forbidden City, many palatial citadels housed the families of the emperor and the princes, guarded by bannermen in colorful uniforms. Because the Mings had made their last stand against the Manchus in Nanking three hundred years ago, General Wei, the North Prince, hoped that one day he would remain in Nanking even after the Taipings had seized Peking. In fact, he hoped to drive the Manchus out past the Great Wall and become the Heavenly Emperor himself.

Secure in this great city with its huge fortifications, with several armies fighting the Imperial forces on several fronts in the surrounding provinces, he worried more about his enemies within the city than he feared the enemy outside. Yang, the East Prince, was his number-one worry. During the past several years he had found that Yang was getting increasingly ambitious, acting as if he, not Hung, were the true spokesman of God. He considered Yang a dangerous foe, with the majority of the Taiping forces still under his control; his tactics were ruthless and his intrigues unpredictable. A direct confrontation with Yang would be suicidal. Furthermore, Yang was the Heavenly Emperor's brother-in-law, a relationship that offered him extra protection. But there had been signs of disharmony between Hung and Yang in recent months. Perhaps he should take advantage of that and try to alienate them further, using Hung to get rid of Yang or vice versa.

After a few days of toying with the idea, Wei decided to pay Yang a visit. He would take the first step toward compromise with Yang, build up his ego, and hint that he was in a precarious situation in the kingdom. Yang had been grumbling about Hung's change of direction in policy. Some of Hung's new appointments had also infuriated Yang, especially the promotion of Li the Faithful.

Yang's palace was the most luxurious, after Hung's Imperial Palace. It was built like Hung's except smaller. It had all the trimmings: glazed tiles, vermilion doors, thick red walls, massive pillars, carved eaves, and marble walkways with carved balustrades. The gardens were designed like those in Suchow and Hangchow, famous for their delicate beauty —with fish ponds, bubbling waterfalls, miniature mountains, and pagodas. Wei had always been envious of Yang's princely life and his title of Nine Thousand Years, a title with built-in power and prestige. Each time he visited Yang he felt a burning envy that was gradually turning into pure hatred.

Yang received him in his garden. Outwardly still polite, they chatted in the pavilion overlooking the goldfish pond. Two serving maids trotted back and forth serving them tea and tidbits.

Wei had already prepared the course for the discussion to follow. Knowing of Yang's resentment, he avoided the usual beating-around-the-bush and came to the point. "Nine Thousand Years," he said, "the promotion of The Faithful has troubled me. First, he was made your deputy without your permission. Second, he is a quiet man. I never trust quiet men . . ."

"Why do you tell me all this, Prince North?" Yang interrupted him.

"Why? Because I have always been grateful to you. You were the first man who sponsored me and brought me into the inner circle in Kwangsi. Without you I would not be here today, a prince in this kingdom. But the kingdom is in danger. The Heavenly Emperor is losing his grip and popularity. People are looking for someone strong who can lead the kingdom back to the proper course." He stopped and took a sip of tea, waiting for a reaction.

Yang sighed. Obviously he agreed with him. "Who do you think this man should be?" he asked.

"Who else but you?" Wei replied quickly, his voice firm with conviction. "Everybody in the kingdom thinks you are the true spokesman of God. And you were the first one to enter Nanking when it fell. Your record of victories is better than that of any other general or prince." He stopped again; he did not want to sound too eager and arouse Yang's suspicion. He filled the gap by taking several sips of tea.

"If you think so," Yang asked, "what do you suggest that we do?"

Wei smiled. Yang was using the word *we*. It was a good sign. He cleared his voice and said, "Increase your personal prestige and power in the kingdom. Do something that will make you look superior to the Heavenly Emperor. I have thought this over carefully, Nine Thousand Years. If you need my help, I shall be happy to submit a plan."

Yang looked at him without any expression on his smallpox-pitted face. Wei knew that Yang did not trust him but was reluctant to say so.

"Nine Thousand Years," he went on, "I don't blame you for doubting my intentions. My intentions are selfish. I want the best man to be emperor and I want to serve the best man. Otherwise, what future do we have? The moment the enemy gets stronger, the kingdom will be finished. I hear that the enemy has already hired a foreigner to organize a foreign army to fight us."

"Yes, I have heard that, too," Yang said, looking more relaxed. "They have hired an American vagabond to lead a horde of Shanghai vagabonds and named them the Ever-Victorious Army." He laughed. "That does not worry me."

"But still this foreigner, vagabond or not, may get more foreign weapons. That is our weakness. Most of the Taipings still fight with bows and arrows."

Yang seemed to agree with him again, but did not say so. He rubbed his rugged face with his stubby fingers and turned up his eye heavenward as if seeking advice from God. With a heavy sigh he finally said, "Prince North, tell me your plan."

Recently Hung had heard a great many rumors. The one that concerned him the most was that the Manchu government had created the Ever-Victorious Army. It had been the idea of Li Hung-chang, the

Viceroy of Hopeh and Shantung, and the new army had been placed under his control. Li had hired an American soldier of fortune named Townsend Ward to command it. Hung had heard that the army had already won a few small battles against the Taipings in Kiangsu Province. Since the creation of the Hunan army of Tseng Kuo-fan, this Ever-Victorious Army had become another chicken bone in Hung's throat.

Hung missed Feng, his confidant, with whom he could talk freely and consult in times of trouble. Once in a while he had a talk with Run-ta, his eldest brother. But Run-ta was no Feng. He was like a dried-up orange; no matter how it was squeezed, there was not much juice in it. After Hung had become the Heavenly Emperor, Run-ta had become a "yes man," even worse than dried-up fruit. But Hung needed someone close to talk to this morning; he sent for his brother.

Run-ta, having grown fat, waddled into Hung's study and announced his arrival with an artificial cough. Hung invited him to sit down. With a grunt, Run-ta sat on an ancestral chair heavily, filling the chair from arm to arm. Hung winced. If Run-ta grew a little fatter, there would be no chair in his palace to fit this meatball, he thought.

"Eldest brother," he said, "to boost the Taiping Army's morale, I am thinking of relaxing some restrictions, such as disbanding the women's regiment and becoming more liberal toward religious beliefs. What is your opinion?"

"Yes, yes, I agree with you a hundred percent," Run-ta said, nodding and fanning himself with a small folding fan which he carried in his collar. "Perhaps you should start rebuilding the Porcelain Pagoda and all those golden Buddhas that our troops destroyed when Nanking fell. Yes, yes, it is about time to ..."

"What rumors have you heard lately?" Hung asked.

"Nothing much, nothing much," Run-ta said. "The old rumors are still rumbling like distant thunder. It is all Yang's fault. When Nanking fell he chopped off some heads. The facts have become so exaggerated by our enemies that the executions are described as a massacre. Twenty thousand innocent people perished, they say. Blood ran on the streets like rivers, they say. Pigtailed people knelt in the dirt crying for mercy, they say. Taiping swords fell and heads rolled like watermelons during harvest time, they say ..."

As Run-ta rambled on about old rumors, counting them off on his fingers, Hung interrupted. "Eldest brother, have you heard about the Ever-Victorious-Army?"

"Oh, yes, yes," Run-ta said. "A foreign devils' army, they say. Obviously the Manchus believe in the foreigners' fighting ability because the white men won all the battles in China. Besides big cannons, the sight of a white man with red whiskers and green eyes riding around rattling a saber is enough to make a Manchu soldier flee in his wet trousers. That is why the Manchus have hired foreigners to fight on their side. But the Taipings are not to be intimidated."

He paused to take a deep breath, then holding both thumbs up, he continued proudly. "We have the people's support. We have an eighty-thousand-man garrison, well fed and trained, armed with plenty of cannons and small arms. There is no reason why we should worry about a handful of foreign devils. If they are foolish enough to attack, we will make them float on the mighty Yangtze like a thousand dead fish. Remember your Dragon Boat, Ten Thousand Years?"

Hung wished his family members would not address him as *Ten Thousand Years*, but it was a habit they had formed and he had stopped correcting them. "I remember," he said. "What about it?"

"Ah," Run-ta said. "I still remember the glorious day vividly, the triumphant day your golden Dragon Boat docked outside Nanking. As you stepped onto the landing platform, all the princes and generals sank to their knees to receive you. Floating near your Dragon Boat were quite a few swollen bodies of the enemy. They represented the demons we had slain, but you were kind enough to say that they made you feel such revulsion that they almost spoiled the joy of your triumph. That night, when you sought comfort in the Bible, you ordered all of us to reread the chapters in which the children of Israel slew the Amalekites and Moses swore perpetual war against them in the name of God. I studied everything carefully you had ordered. Ask me anything about the holy Bible. See if I . . ."

"I am glad, Run-ta," Hung said, rising to his feet. "I shall send for you when I need your advice. Thank you for the visit."

Run-ta was reluctant to leave, but Hung had already reached the door. At the door Run-ta said with a bow, "I am a devoted Christian, Ten Thousand Years. Every morning I make food offerings and burn incense sticks before God." With another bow, he left, waddling like a Manchu government official and coughing with authority.

Hung returned to his chair feeling more depressed. He regretted that he had not put a stop to idolatry toward God; he regretted that he had allowed the people to burn incense and even ghost money in front of God, as they had done in front of the Taoist idols. Now it had almost become a custom, a religious ritual, reducing the sacred image of God to an object of superstition. He blamed it on Yang, whose trembling, sweating, and speaking in a trance was a sacrilege; but since it had helped spread the gospels of God he had not objected. Now it was another of his regrets.

To cheer himself, he thought about the bright side of things. He had covered almost fifteen hundred miles during his successful long march. He had taken the capital cities of four rich and densely populated provinces. Now he was the ruler of almost thirty million people, with two million troops under his command. Some of them were still winning battles in several provinces. Despite all his troubles, he must do every-thing to consolidate the cities he had conquered. There were only two generals who were trustworthy and capable of doing that—Li the Faithful, and Shih the assistant prince whom he had promoted to Shield Prince. He would always miss Feng, his closest confidant and adviser, who had died too soon and too young. Without Feng the Taipings would never have marched out of Kwangsi; they would still be in Thistle Mountain, hammering out primitive weapons and eating snakes and porcupines.

It was a sunny day. The fog had lifted unusually early. His mood changing from gloomy to slightly cheerful, he took a walk in his garden. He wanted to be alone, to think and sort out his priorities. The palace he had built looked magnificent, with bright green and yellow roofs and red walls; two minarets rose into the sky, visible all over the city, a symbol of triumph. The wall enclosing it was decorated with his religious proclamations, which he had personally written on yellow satin and signed with brush and red ink. Walking amid dwarf trees and miniature mountains in his garden, he tended the flowering shrubs and trimmed off a few withered flowers. As the warm sun shone on him, he felt more relaxed . . . even happy.

Outside the courtyard one of the two gongs sounded suddenly. He tensed. It meant that someone desired an audience. When giving an audience, he usually rode to the audience hall in his sedan chair. But today he decided to walk, forgoing even his attendants and his colorful umbrella.

Arriving at the audience hall, he found Yang and Wei already there with their retinues. Wei told the Heavenly Emperor that Heavenly Father had brought a message from Heaven through Yang. Hung was stunned. He had never expected the two men to become so friendly that one would support the other in such a manner. Yang, standing in the middle of the hall, had started trembling and sweating. In a trance, he blamed Hung for having stopped the Taiping armies from destroying idols of other gods.

"There is only one God," Yang spoke as God the Father. "Are you aware of that?"

Hung hesitated. He could not deny such an edict. He was not convinced that Yang was really speaking in the person of God—but if he destroyed Yang's image as God's spokesman, it would also wreck his own credibility. Observing his own holy rule, he reluctantly sank onto his knees in front of Yang and replied, "Oh, Heavenly Father, your unworthy son knows he has made a mistake. He is hereby humbly begging the Heavenly Father's forgiveness."

Now Yang was trembling more violently, as though God were showing His wrath. He said, his voice hollow and distant, a voice from Heaven, "I order you to receive fifty blows, here in your own Imperial Court, in front of everyone." He stopped, sweat pouring down his face, his bulging eyes staring. People looked at him in awe.

It took a second for the words to sink in. There was a loud catch of breath in the audience hall, which was now filled with people—officials, attendants, and guards. Everyone looked shocked, their mouths agape.

Wei immediately prostrated himself in front of Yang and pleaded with God for a remission of the sentence. But through Yang, God refused and instructed the Heavenly Emperor to order the execution of such punishment on himself. Wei tried to beg for a reduction of the punishment, but Hung quickly stopped him and submitted to God's order.

"Guards," he said, prostrating himself on the floor, "fifty strokes on the bottom of the Heavenly Emperor. If anyone is found to show mercy, he will be subject to the same punishment."

The two guards whose assignment was the execution of such orders looked at each other in consternation. "Do it!" Hung said, his voice stern.

The guards picked up their five-foot-long split bamboo sticks and hit Hung's buttocks alternately. The split bamboo made a loud noise. Hung received the humiliation and the pain stoically, without expression. But everyone else in the audience hall grimaced. Many looked away with tears in their eyes. A few openly wept.

The shocking scene was abruptly interrupted by Li the Faithful, who marched in and announced that an important victory had been won by Shield Prince Shih Ta-kai near Tientsin, the gateway to Peking.

"Here is General Shih's message," Faithful said, waving a piece of paper.

The gloom dissipated instantly and sad faces broke into smiles. Amid cheers, the Heavenly Emperor mounted his throne. "Read his message," he ordered.

The Faithful Prince read the message in an even voice, hiding his excitement:

> The Taipings have taken many towns east of Tientsin after a week of stubborn enemy resistance. We also beat back a ten-thousand-man contingent called the Ever-Victorious Army. Our braves survived this army's superior firepower and ambushed its foreign commander, killing him instantly. When this foreigner fell, the Imperial troops fled and now we are marching toward Tientsin without much enemy resistance.
>
> The fleeing Manchus call our Bible *goblin books*. We saw refugees carrying goblin books and begging for mercy, hoping that we would not harm them. We heard that in Tientsin, English goblin books are collected and sold. People buy them for protection. Some people even paste pages from them on their doors, as Taoist incantations are posted on doors to ward off evil spirits. If we spare their lives, we might have many more converts. We expect Tientsin to fall in a few days.

When Li the Faithful finished reading, there was another loud cheer. Hung silenced them and conducted a prayer, thanking God for correcting his wrongdoing and for the important victory near Tientsin. Then he ordered Prince Faithful to write a reply to Shield Prince Shih in the Heavenly Emperor's name, congratulating him and wishing him well. When Faithful bowed and withdrew, Hung caught a glimpse of Yang glaring after the young general. It was a glare of intense hatred. Now he realized why Yang had wanted to humiliate him, for it was obvious to everyone that he had already designated Faithful as the next commander in chief. With a smile he dismissed everybody.

39

Li Hung-chang was one of the few Hans serving in the Manchu Imperial Court who wore a high-ranking red button on his cap. After Emperor Tao-kuang died, Tse-hsi, the weak young emperor's favorite concubine, almost seized power. She liked Li Hung-chang, even though he was a Han, a second-class citizen. He was small, but Tse-hsi believed that his brains weighed twice as much as those of any of the Manchu Imperial ministers, most of whom were fat royal relatives. Secretly she called him Ju Kwo-liang, after the cleverest man in Chinese history.

But today Li Hung-chang was worried . . . especially after the morning audience in the Imperial Palace. He came out of the Forbidden City looking pale and tired. Riding in his sedan chair he felt that he was holding his life in his hands. He even envied the simple life of his eight sedan chair bearers who had no worries, no complications. Nobody cared what they were thinking; a full stomach was enough to make them happy. He thought of the morning audience and shuddered. It had gone badly.

Ordinarily Tse-hsi sat behind a screen and let the young emperor talk. But this morning the young emperor had been indisposed and Tse-hsi had faced the ministers directly. The young emperor sometimes had ideas of his own; Tse-hsi never liked his liberal ideas. Whenever there was something that was urgent and important to discuss, Tse-hsi would often prevent the young emperor from giving his opinion. Once or twice she had pointed a bejeweled finger at His Majesty and said, "I don't want you to poke around with your inexperienced finger. Be quiet or be off!"

This kind of rebuke in front of all the ministers had pained Li Hung-chang; he wished he could find the right answers to all difficult problems and spare the young emperor such humiliation.

This morning they had discussed a life-and-death problem: the

Taipings were coming. The majority of the ministers had only one suggestion: the Imperial family must take immediate refuge in the northern province of Jehol. During the discussion, the ministers had been in a state of panic, whimpering and arguing. Some had blamed Li Hung-chang for having wasted money on the Ever-Victorious Army; others even suspected that he had secret ambitions, supporting a Hunan army that had no Manchus in its ranks.

Li Hung-chang had his supporters, too. The two factions had called each other's proposals "mending the fence after the sheep had escaped." The barbed arrows flew and Li was often caught in between. This morning Tse-hsi had held a neutral position. Her face expressionless, she had listened and rolled two jade balls in her left hand, switching her sharp eyes from one man to another. Li had learned that this was her nervous habit, but he admired her outward calmness. Finally, holding a long face, she had ordered the ministers to stop bickering. Pointing a long fingernail at Li, she had said, "I want you to find the solution. Report to me before I leave for Jehol."

As he rode along Chien Men Street outside the Forbidden City, he saw people running toward a large crowd. He stopped his sedan chair and ordered Ah Hing, his attendant, to find out what was happening. A few moments later Ah Hing returned and reported breathlessly that people were buying "goblin books." Li had heard about the "goblin books." Feeling more depressed, he hurried back to his yamen and told his attendants that he would not see anyone. He must think.

He could take the easy way out, buy a goblin book himself and let the God-worshippers take over. After all, he was a Han.

As he paced restlessly in his study, pinching the bridge of his nose and racking his brains for a solution, he heard noises outside that sounded like an argument in two languages. It was odd. He wondered who could be speaking such coarse English. It must be a foreigner. Li knew bookish English quite well, but this man's English was hard to understand.

Now the foreigner was shouting at his secretary, whose Pidgin English, mixed with Chinese Mandarin, was even more incomprehensible. The argument became more heated, then stopped suddenly. Presently Mr. Soo, his secretary, came in, his face still red with frustration.

"Your Excellency," he said, "a foreign devil insists on seeing you. He says he'll shoot me if I don't let him in."

"Who is he?"

"He is an officer from the Ever-Victorious Army. He is half drunk; his liquor breath could fumigate the entire yamen. Shall I call the guards and throw him out?"

Knowing that the foreigners had special privileges in China since the Opium War, Li hesitated. Roughing up a foreigner could violate a term in the Treaty of Nanking and bring unpleasant consequences. "Bring him in," he said. "I'll see him."

Looking relieved, Mr. Soo withdrew quickly. He, too, did not want to cause an international incident by throwing a foreigner out, especially when the foreigners' "goblin books" were in such great demand. Everybody was seeking foreigners' protection.

The big white man staggered in. Right away Li recognized him as the deputy-commander of the Ever-Victorious Army, an American with an odd name: Burgevine. He saluted Li and took a seat without being invited. He was a squarely built giant with a large paunch, sloppily dressed in a British colonel's uniform, jacket half buttoned, his chest bedecked with ribbons and medals. Li took the seat farthest from him and waited.

Burgevine swallowed a couple of times, as though he were trying hard not to vomit. "Me Colonel Burgevine," he said in Pidgin English. "General Ward, him die, sabe?"

"Yes, I have heard," Li said quietly.

"You want good man take place General Ward?"

"Yes, I want a good man to take General Ward's place," Li said, using proper English and hoping that Burgevine would stop using his Pidgin English. "Do you have any suggestions?"

"I have good man," Burgevine said with a grin. "He velly good shooter . . . velly experienced. He win big battle alla time guarantee. Better than General Ward!" He gestured wildly, making shooting gestures and jabbing at his own head with a finger. "Him good head!"

Li held a long face. He did not want to encourage conversation, nor did he intend to hire anyone so strongly recommended by this drunkard. But he did not mind hearing who the man had in mind . . . undoubtedly his own brother or best friend.

"All right," he said. "Tell me who he is. I will consider his qualifications and decide."

"Me!" Burgevine said with a broad smile, stabbing his hairy chest with a thick thumb. In proper English he continued, "Five years in the French Foreign Legion. Fought in Africa, the Sudan, Southeast Asia. You name it, I was there, shooting and bayoneting enemies. Sir, you can't find a better man to replace General Townsend Ward!"

After he rid himself of Colonel Burgevine, Li analyzed the crisis. If he let Hung Shiu-ch'uan overthrow the Manchu Dynasty, as a nationalist Hung might void the unequal treaties the Manchus had signed with the foreign powers—perhaps even burn all the opium in China. To protect their extraterritorial rights and the opium trade, England, America, and some other European countries might overthrow Hung just as quickly. If that happened, China would be colonized by the foreign powers and suffer the same fate as India and Burma. Then characters like Colonel Burgevine would flock to China as scavengers. He shuddered. It was a choice between a rotten Manchu Dynasty and a colonized China. Suddenly the choice became easy. He must do everything to save the Manchu Dynasty.

The first person who came to mind was the British Consul General. He must tell him the urgency of the situation and why it was so important to defeat Hung. Consul General Johnson was his closest foreign contact; it was he who had helped him recruit the foreign officers for his Ever-Victorious Army. Johnson would be happy to recommend a new commander. With British firearms and a good British officer to direct the war, the little army was his best hope.

He stopped pacing and ordered his sedan chair.

| 40 |

Charles George Gordon was ordered to Shanghai. He was shocked by its poverty. He saw beggars dying by the roadside, coolies who were nothing but skin and bones laboring like animals—pulling carts, digging ditches, staggering with heavy loads on their backs; they were scolded, whipped, kicked, and spat on. He had been glad to leave Tientsin, but Shanghai depressed him so much that he almost requested his brother-in-law to give him another assignment. His new job was to head a group of engineers studying the British concession's defense works. But when he arrived in the British concession, the world suddenly changed.

He had not seen the other Shanghai—the Shanghai for the foreigners and for the rich Chinese. It was a world of tall brick buildings, wide boulevards, and lush gardens. The gap between the rich and the poor shocked him.

He had barely settled down in the British concession's government guest house ready to work on the defense project when General Stavely sent him a wire asking him if he was interested in becoming a Chinese general.

Gordon was taken aback by such a ridiculous question at first, wondering if his brother-in-law was drunk when he sent the telegram. But the next day the general arrived and they met at British Consul General Johnson's office. Gordon's first question was, "What do you mean, 'Chinese general'?"

"To head an army called Ever-Victorious Army. Its commander was killed in action recently. They are fishing for a replacement."

"Killed in action?" Gordon asked. "Killed by whom?"

"By the rebels, of course. He was a mercenary ... well paid ..."

"Sorry, I'm not interested," Gordon interrupted. He wasn't interested in money. Besides, he was still sympathetic with the rebels, even though Hung Shiu-ch'uan had disappointed him; the man's hero image had been marred by the many unsavory rumors he'd heard.

"I thought so," General Stavely said with a smile. "But no harm in asking. It would be quite an adventure, you know. A less reckless bloke with better discipline wouldn't get himself killed in China."

The discussion ended there. But on his way to work, Gordon couldn't put his brother-in-law's proposal out of his mind. Hadn't he always been attracted to adventure and action? Compared to building defense works for a small British concession, being a Chinese general at twenty-seven years of age commanding an army was so infinitely more adventurous ... even romantic ... even though the name Ever-Victorious repelled him. The whole thing still sounded preposterous. But deep down in his heart he yearned for this kind of job, even though his moral sense still told him *no*.

He took a handful of army engineers and surveyed the concession area, but his mind was not on the job. It was a pleasant day. He heard eerie music in the air, he smelled rich pungent food, saw horse carriages clippety-clopping on the wide street, and well-dressed Mandarins carried in sedan chairs with servants trotting behind them. He saw foreign goods displayed in stores with colorful lanterns and glittering signboards.

In his mind's eye he also saw the contrast of the slums. Without revisiting the area he could almost smell its decay, see dirty water poured at his feet from doorways, naked children rummaging in garbage, and beggars dying in gutters. Such disparity offended him so much that he once again felt the strong urge to do something about it—something more important than just building bunkers, fortresses, and trenches to defend the privileged few.

He received a letter from his sister Augusta. In his guest house room he read it again and again, chewing every word like an animal ruminating its cud. While reading, he could almost hear her speaking, her voice stern, chiding yet comforting.

George, I understand your complaint about Father putting in a word for you and getting you a job, but nepotism or backstairs influence is a time-honored convention. There is no point to fighting it. Nowadays everyone uses a little private influence or blood relationship to get ahead in life. I had hoped that you had grown out of your delicate sense of honor. You always disliked being praised. When Mother proudly displayed your Crimean sketches to her friends, you were so offended that later you tore them up in a fit of temper, remember? That was totally uncalled for. In defending your own sense of propriety you offended another person's sensitivity. A coin has two sides, dear George. There are people who will think one side is prettier than the other and vice versa. One man's favorite food can be another man's poison. Knowing your idiosyncrasies, I worry about you. I do hope that you get along with General Stavely. He is older and our brother-in-law. Please do seek his advice. In a strange land you will always find a mixture of fascination and horror. You must make adjustments and balance your views. Relax the reins of your Puritan conscience. Enjoy China, George, and don't let unnecessary worry or anger get you down. Do whatever is good for England.

Before he blew out his bedside lamp, he narrowed all his reservations and made one simple decision: *Do whatever is good for England.*

On Gordon's way to see Li Hung-chang, Lieutenant Mah, a young officer from the Ever-Victorious Army, briefed him about the man. Gordon hoped that he could deal with Li as easily as he had with General Stavely.

The small scholar-general with a thin goat beard received him in his Spartan office, which was in an ancient yamen in Peking. He had recently been appointed Viceroy of Kiangsu and Chekiang Provinces, strategically the most important area to be defended, because the Taipings had turned more attention to seaports, especially the largest, Shanghai, in Kiangsu Province.

Li was cordial, speaking scholarly English with a slight accent, his voice small and polite but precise and full of authority. After repeating the praise of Gordon's moral character and good reputation in General Stavely's recommendation, Li welcomed him into the service of the Great Manchu Dynasty. Then he explained what he had hoped the small Ever-Victorious Army would accomplish: He had wanted it to win small battles to harass and dishearten the rebels with superior firepower. Now, however, the army was in disarray without leadership. He gave Gordon two weeks to get it into shape.

When the briefing ended, he sent for General Ching and introduced them. General Ching was a tall thin man in his fifties, well groomed in a modern military uniform, complete with assorted medals pinned on his chest. They saluted each other smartly in Western fashion. Li said that General Ching of the Imperial Army would supply Gordon with an additional two thousand new recruits to replace those who had deserted or joined roaming bands of bandits.

Li hardly looked at Ching when he spoke. Gordon detected a bit of humor in Li's voice, as though he felt that this foreign devil and Ching would have a lot of fun together and he could hardly wait to see the fun. But Li also had penetrating eyes that gleamed through two slanting cracks, searching and studying, making Gordon feel naked. Out of his usual Chinese sereneness he smiled faintly; but it was a faint smile of sincerity, not like General Ching's perpetual grin, which bothered Gordon. Grinning and saying, "Yes, yes," was all the general had done during the thirty-minute meeting.

"From now on, you two gentlemen will be fighting side by side," Li kindly said to Gordon, rising to his feet. "Being unfamiliar with Chinese situations and topography, you will consult General Ching whenever you feel the need. Both of you will answer to me. I am your commander in chief."

He walked Gordon to the door and bade him good-bye with an endearing smile.

As Gordon left, he heard General Ching talking, pouring out Chinese like firecrackers. He wondered what Ching was talking about. He decided that he must watch out for this grinning cobra.

Gordon had been given General Ward's white Arabian stallion, a nervous horse that was hard to control. Luckily he was a good horseman. The way he handled the stallion impressed Lieutenant Mah, the officer assigned as his adviser and aide. Riding beside Mah, he learned more about the so-called Ever-Victorious Army, a name he hated.

The Army had engaged the rebels in some small battles without shedding much blood. The rebels, mostly armed with Chinese weapons, had done more shouting than fighting, and the Ever-Victorious Army, armed with modern rifles, had made even more noise by shooting from out of range.

"But General Ward was killed," Gordon said. "There must have been some serious fighting."

Lieutenant Mah spoke good English after serving as a houseboy for many British generals and missionaries in China. "He was ambushed," he said. "We still don't know if he was killed by the rebels or by our own men. We are only permitted to say that he was killed in action."

Gordon was quiet for a moment, wondering if his own life was in danger. "How much training have the men had?" he asked.

"Oh, not much. Some precision marching, that's all. Most of the men have fought before and know how to pull a trigger."

"How about the officers? Don't they care about training?"

"Well, not very much," Mah said with a shrug. "Most of the officers are white men—English, American, and French. A few have no nationality. All bearded, all look alike."

"No training, no drilling. What do you do when you aren't fighting?" Gordon asked, flabbergasted.

"Well . . . a bit of plundering," the Chinese officer said with another shrug. "But not all of us steal. I don't."

"I hope not!" Gordon said angrily. He remembered the Chinese soldier with the white man's face who had robbed the bank in Tientsin. He was sure those robbers had been members of the Ever-Victorious Army. If he found that Roman nose again, he would box his ears before he spoke.

The small army was stationed in a large compound with rundown buildings and barracks. Of the three thousand men left, about 10 percent were of different nationalities. Two thirds of the officers were Europeans and Americans. When Gordon inspected them, the men, wearing leftover Imperial Army uniforms and discarded European officers' uniforms, were scattered around the drill field, some standing talking in groups, others squatting on the trash-littered ground smoking cigarettes. Some officers were sitting in the shacks playing poker or throwing dice. He inspected the area briefly, then ordered the lieutenant to have the men assemble in front of his office, a large rundown bungalow. After the bugler had blasted a few notes repeatedly, the men slowly drifted to the bungalow.

Colonel Burgevine came last, buttoning up his uniform. He eyed Gordon up and down and saluted him sloppily. "Colonel Burgevine reporting," he said casually. "Glad you've taken command. These chicks need a hen."

Gordon ignored him. He had already been told that the deputy commander was a pain in the ass. With a deep frown, he scanned the crowd of riffraff in their assorted uniforms.

"Men," he shouted, "I am General Charles George Gordon, your new commander. First, I don't like what I see. You are nothing but a bunch of vagabonds who need a bath. Second, my rules: From now on, no squatting around smoking, no spitting, no gambling, and above all, no plundering!"

"Hey, Mack," Colonel Burgevine spoke up. "What army doesn't do a bit of plundering in its spare time?"

Ignoring Burgevine, Gordon shouted, his tone threatening, "If I find anyone stealing as much as a Chinese brass coin, I'll shoot him personally! Just remember that!"

There was some groaning among the officers. Gordon ignored them and went on. "We have been ordered to Shanghai in two weeks. Before we leave, I want to see a well-trained, well-dressed, disciplined army. I want every one of you to live up to this army's name, Ever-Victorious! I want brave fighting men who always obey my orders. Anyone who retreats without my orders will have me to deal with. If I don't shoot you, you'll be thrown into the tank until you rot. Colonel Burgevine, are you listening?"

The colonel spread his hands in answer. Gordon repeated, "I asked you, are you listening?"

"Sure, I'm listening, Mack," the colonel said. "Good stuff. You and I together will win some wars."

After he had dismissed the men, Gordon marched over to Colonel Burgevine and mumbled, "Burgevine, I want to see you in my office."

When Burgevine arrived in Gordon's bungalow, Gordon wanted to make the meeting as short as possible. "Burgevine," he said, his voice cold and ominous, "you're through. I want you to pack and get out of here within the hour. Is that clear?"

Burgevine stared at him incredulously. He started to argue, but Gordon's glare stopped him. With a shrug he walked out.

* * *

During his fortnight stay in Peking while he trained his troops, Gordon had reservations about the war he was involved in. Every day he witnessed head-chopping executions on Peking streets. He was told that all the Long Hairs were executed without a trial, and that the captured Imperial troops suffered a similar fate in Nanking. It was a long war in which two million people had already died.

Before he led his new Ever-Victorious Army to Shanghai, he laid down three conditions to both Li Hung-chang and General Stavely: (1) he did not appreciate interference; (2) he wanted to end the war as soon as possible so that he could stop further bloodshed; (3) unnecessary killing would not be tolerated. General Stavely readily approved. Li Hung-chang handed the handwritten conditions to General Ching for response. General Ching's response was a repeated, "Yes," and continual nodding of his head, a toothy smile on his long bony face. Lieutenant Mah told Gordon that such a response did not mean yes; it only acknowledged the receipt of his request.

"Blast it!" Gordon said. "It's not my request. It's my demand!"

"Play it by ear, General," Mah said. "It's the Chinese way. *Ma ma fu fu, comme ci, comme ça.* Right?"

Gordon controlled his temper, remembering what Augusta had told him in her last letter: "Make adjustments. Balance your views . . ."

It had never occurred to him that he would command a navy as well as an army. Both were tiny. Since the war was to be fought along the intricate waterways of Kiangsu and Chekiang Provinces, troop movements would be easier and swifter by boat. He liked his flagship, an old fifty-foot British gunboat, freshly painted white and blue, like an old woman heavily made up to look young. But it had several good guns, six sails, and a tall smokestack that put out black smoke. He had been trained as a gunner and was satisfied with the boat's firepower. The other vessels were an assortment of small steamboats, junks, and sampans . . . enough to carry the five thousand troops from one port to another without difficulty. His orders were to recapture Cha Ding, about thirty miles from Shanghai, then take Chin Pu on the west.

Disguised as a Chinese fisherman, he reconnoitered the area in a sampan. He had learned in the Crimean War that accurate reconnaisance always saved lives. With a small group of men all dressed as fishermen, he landed in enemy territory and darted from one cover to another, making sketches and taking notes.

The next day, before dawn, he attacked. Quietly, two thousand men crossed the moats that surrounded Cha Ding. Gordon personally directed the scaling of the city walls and took the city without much fighting. It was almost a bloodless success.

That night, occupying the mayor's yamen, he wrote a letter to Augusta:

> I am sitting in a *tai su* chair, one of those terribly uncomfortable chairs with an elaborately carved straight back. I'm scribbling this letter to announce my first victory in China. If I had commanded a regular army, this victory would not have meant much. But what I had was a few thousand men, a mixture of ignorant peasants and the riffraff of Shanghai, officered by a collection of white desperadoes and mercenaries from Europe and America. I booted my deputy out, but the rest of the officers were still a jealous and quarrelsome lot, so treacherous that sometimes I worried about turning my back to them. Lieutenant Mah, my aide, told me that the whole force was constantly on the verge of mutiny. God, I never saw such a rabble! I'm still wondering if their last commander was killed by the enemy or by one of his own men. But don't worry, I feel safe now. After the initial victory, all of the rats became respectful. Some even started saluting me smartly and addressing me as "sir." Because I direct the war with a cane instead of a saber, the soldiers think I have a magic wand. They have become diligent, obedient, and trustworthy. With Mah on my side to translate their gibberish, I think I have become their little God."

|41|

The Faithful Prince did not care much for the trappings of royalty. Since he had become a prince his subordinates had started kneeling in front of him when addressing him. He also thought that the ceremonial platform built in his headquarters was too garish and pretentious. Sitting on it under an umbrella made him feel like an actor in a comic opera. All this power put wild ideas into the minds of some of the other generals who wanted to be princes or even the emperor. For some, the trappings were an appetizer. Hung had already hinted that something was brewing, but The Faithful had been too busy to notice.

One of his spies had returned. A trusted aide, dressed like a peasant, he came in and sank to his knees in front of him. The Faithful quickly stopped him and told him to take a seat. He felt more comfortable when people spoke to him sitting down, especially if they were old friends or longtime associates. The spy obeyed and reported what he had learned about the new commander of the Ever-Victorious Army.

"Another foreigner," he said. "It is rumored that he has a cat's green eyes, which can look through walls. He has boasted that he will defend all the seaports by directing his war from a boat and will crush the rebellion in six months. He did a thorough survey of Shanghai and all the waterways in Kiangsu Province. He has requested many armed steamboats, which the British government will supply. He has ordered new uniforms for his men, now numbered at five thousand all told. And he has selected three hundred men as his personal bodyguards. The men seem to like him, probably because he has raised their pay. Now he is steaming off Shanghai to relieve a town on the estuary of the Yangtze River."

"Hm," Faithful Prince said, thinking. "What is his name?"

"Everybody calls him China Gordon. He likes to wear Chinese clothes and eat with chopsticks."

This foreigner will be Golden Rooster's biggest headache, Faithful thought. He had already ordered the Taiping Navy to capture some of the ports along the Yangtze, especially Shanghai. It was strategically important that the Taipings take Shanghai in order to control the entire east coast. "How strong is this foreigner's navy?"

"He has a flotilla of British gunboats, cargo vessels, and five thousand men. His flagship has several big cannons. One of them is a thirty-two-pounder. They say this foreigner has a big temper. He is as energetic as a wild horse. He eats one meal a day and sleeps two or three hours a night. He can take a cat nap standing up. He is not armed . . . only carries a cane. People believe it is a magic wand. Holding it, he can ward off bullets. Nothing can hurt him . . ."

"All right, that is enough," Faithful interrupted. The moment he heard such superstitious nonsense he knew that the report was not reliable. Still, this China Gordon was a formidable foe.

He decided that he must go see the Heavenly Emperor. Ordinarily when a prince went to see the emperor, he rode in his sedan chair carried by eight bearers, accompanied by guards and attendants carrying pennants and lanterns. But he preferred a fast horse, which could reach Hung's palace across town in half the time.

Hung was in his study composing a poem, as he often did, his brows knitted in concentration, his brush flying over his rice paper swiftly. He was proud of his writing and caligraphy, which showed dexterity and strength.

> The Heavenly Father sits on the throne in Heaven.
> The Heavenly Elder Brother sits on His right.
> By grace of Father the Heavenly, Second
> Brother sits on His left.
> United as one we reign. There is no other God.
> Disobeying the Three-in-One will be struck
> down by five thunder bolts.

He wrote the poem as an edict, hoping to strengthen his position as God's Second Son. He had been reluctant to counter his own orders, especially the one about ending the destruction of idols, for fear of appearing weak and indecisive. To emphasize that there was only one God would be better than ordering the Taipings to resume sacking temples and idols. Besides, continuing to denigrate Confucius would drive more people to the Hunan Army's side, especially in the conservative provinces of the central plains. Because of the war and other important affairs, he decided not to pay too much attention to Yang.

He had heard that the young emperor in Peking was not stupid, only totally controlled by his favorite concubine, Tse-hsi. He had heard that Tse-hsi believed the Hunan Army was the major force to stop the Taipings. She had even issued an edict in the emperor's name, to Tseng Kuo-fan, the Hunan Army's commander saying:

> You are to be commended on organizing the Hunan braves. With you leading them, it will not be difficult with one roll of the drum to sweep these wretched vagabonds from the face of the earth.

When Hung thought about Tse-hsi's edict, he could not help chuckling. A typical communication from a shrew, an impatient and frivolous woman. He had heard that she was also cruel, suspicious, and licentious, having already started collecting handsome actors under the pretext that she loved the Peking Opera. It would be unthinkable for such a woman to rule China.

When he thought of Tse-hsi, he wondered if he himself was being corrupted by power. He had neglected his family, especially his old mother and his uncomplaining wife, a kind woman who never spoke ill of anyone.

He remembered the old days in Happy Valley. His wife had washed for him and sewn his clothes. At the dinner table she had always selected the best morsels of meat and heaped them on his rice bowl while she herself ate only the skin and gristle. Yet, during those struggling years he had denied her warmth and love, confiding to Run-kan that there was no sparkle in his marriage, only a relationship of "same bed, different dreams." It was not until after he had made her empress that he had showered her with gifts; he had done so not out of love but because of his feeling of guilt.

He also remembered his mother's devotion . . . how she had always worried about his health and welfare . . . how her hair had grayed rapidly because of his failures at the Imperial examinations and her subsequent long illness caused by them. Yet, since he had become Heavenly Emperor he had hardly visited her; his concern for her health and welfare was expressed only by providing her with more gifts and luxury. She must have been terribly disappointed.

While brooding on his negligence and indifference, he felt a sudden rush of warm feelings toward his family. He decided to make amends no matter how busy he was or how bad the country's fate turned out to be. Luckily his daughter and son had grown without blemishes. Both were good-looking and respectful . . . only a little uncomfortable in his presence. It was one of the disadvantages of being an emperor; being a father was bad enough; a distance always grew between father and children when children were grown. How he missed the intimacy they had had during their childhood years, rocking them on his knees, pinching their plump cheeks, joking and laughing.

If he had known all the regrets, the unhappiness, and the pressures of being emperor, perhaps he would not have . . . He shut out such a thought quickly and sat up on his throne. One thing he should never regret, he thought, was the rebellion.

The Faithful came in unannounced. Hung tolerated the young general's idiosyncrasies since he was one of the most trusted men left, so hard-working that he often neglected small ceremonies.

"Heavenly Emperor," he said after a bow. "The British are no longer neutral. They have appointed one of their officers to command the so-called Ever-Victorious Army."

"I already know that," Hung said.

"But this man has turned a horde of vagabonds into a regular army, with ships and guns, discipline, and new uniforms. They have orders to cut the waterways and stop us from taking the seaports. We must send Golden Rooster to deal with him."

"Golden Rooster is fighting that bookworm, eight-legged essay-writing Tseng Kuo-fan."

"Tseng is still in Hunan," Faithful said. "He has not even reached the Twin City in Hupei Province. I consider the east coastal cities strategically more important than the central plains, where the land has been devastated by famine and the people drained of energy and money.

Tens of thousands have died in the war. It will only be a burden for us. But the coastal provinces are rich. Without them we cannot survive."

"Golden Rooster," Hung said reflectively as he paced back and forth, almost forgetting the subject Faithful had brought up. "I have not seen him for years. People swear that he has never robbed a poor man or killed an innocent man. I don't believe it. No red-eyed pirate has such a clean record."

He remembered the subject and returned to his chair. "I trust his ability but he has never fought a foreigner. He is still a backward old-school warrior, fighting with Chinese traditional weapons more often than with modern firearms. All right, order him to deal with this foreigner. Do what you think is right."

As Faithful was leaving, Hung said, "Oh, by the way, Wei just visited me. He says that Yang wants to be called 'Ten Thousand Years' instead of 'Nine Thousand Years.'"

"Grant him Ten Thousand Years," Faithful said. "Hope that he can live that long."

Without further comment, he walked out.

42

The old fortune-teller had kowtowed and left. Yang, the East Prince, savored what the soothsayer had said. "I see clouds and rain in your horoscope. Clouds and rain signify the arrival of the dragon. You will be the real dragon, East Prince. You will be the one who will soon sit on the throne in Peking. It is all in your horoscope."

According to Wei, the North Prince, this fortune-teller was the best in Nanking; people called him a *pan-sheng-shan*, meaning half man and half spirit, who could predict fortunes or misfortunes with uncanny accuracy.

Everything seemed to confirm this *pan-sheng-shan*'s prediction. The throne in the Forbidden City had been hovering in Yang's mind's eye; now he could almost touch it. Wei had been instrumental in planning the coup. It had become public knowledge that the East Prince was God's real spokesman. Wei had even convinced Hung that the East Prince should be addressed as Ten Thousand Years, and now half the nation had started referring to him as such. His two trusted generals were doing exactly what he had planned. General Hu, his old friend, was consolidating his positions along the Yangtze. General Shih, another Kwangsi native, had almost advanced to Tientsin, and Peking was now within his grasp. But he had restrained him, telling him to hold back. He did not want Hung to enter the Forbidden City in triumph; he wanted to lead the Taiping Army into the Imperial Palace and mount the dragon throne himself. Wei would be his prime minister, Shih his commander in chief. He would declare China a new Christian nation, with all the foreign powers coming to congratulate him and celebrate with him the dawn of a new era.

Yang and Wei had been planning the coup for some time now. It was not until the punishment of Hung that events had started to move rapidly. Hung had been submissive after the bambooing. He had become almost a yes-man, yielding the title of Ten Thousand Years without an argument. His weakness was an omen, like a sick man about to die. Wei had said that they could probably stage a coup without bloodshed. The only obstacles were The Faithful, and Yang's own domestic problem. His wife, Hung's sister, had not spoken to him since he humiliated Hung. So far she had not found out about his plans for the coup. If she were obliged to choose sides, Yang had no doubt that she would choose her brother, and have the coup smashed. By then, his own head would probably be dangling over his own yamen gate.

Thinking of the coup, he remembered the numerous secret meetings with Wei in Wei's yamen. Today he was obliged to see Wei again.

He changed into his best embroidered silk robe and ordered his carriage. He hated his sedan chair; it was too confining and too slow. Riding in an open carriage drawn by eight horses was more awe-inspiring; he liked the sound of the horses' hooves, which struck the ground like drums beating. Accompanied by fifty horsemen as his personal guards, he always felt thrilled as he watched banners flying and horse hooves churning up a huge cloud of dust.

He was surprised to see Wei's yamen so well guarded this morning. Hundreds of soldiers, carrying modern firearms, surrounded the palatial building. The soldiers saluted him as his carriage passed the front gate into the enormous courtyard. He visualized a royal reception with people kneeling, heads bowed without daring to look up. Such a sight would soon become commonplace, he thought as he alighted from his carriage.

Wei came out of the main building and smilingly met him. He led him into his audience hall where many of Wei's subordinates were waiting. They all rose to greet him, but nobody knelt. It is coming, he thought as he was taken by Wei to the honored seat opposite the host's chair.

The audience hall was not elaborately adorned, like his own, but glittering enough to befit the position of a prime minister. It was furnished with carved hardwood chairs and tables that were decorated with embroidered aprons and seat covers. All the palace lanterns were lighted. Chinese traditional weapons held by ceremonial guards shone under the bright lights.

Wei urged Yang to eat some of the delicacies that were arranged on the table in front of him. Yang nodded. After taking a bite from a braised goose foot, he said, "North Prince, have I come to enjoy a banquet? I thought it was only a private meeting between you and me to discuss a private matter."

"There is nothing more to discuss now, Ten Thousand Years," Wei said, smiling graciously. "Everything is well arranged. The wood has already been carved into a boat. Nothing can change it now. Try some of the bear's palm. It is a rare delicacy."

Yang picked up a piece of the stewed bear's palm with his ivory chopsticks and took a bite. It was as tender as bean cake, and he praised it, smacking his lips to show his appreciation. An attendant filled his teacup.

"I am glad everything is well arranged," he said with a laugh. "Do you mean that the arrow is on the opened bow, ready to go, eh?" He laughed again and took another bite of the bear's palm.

"Exactly," Wei said, laughing with him. "In a short moment it will all be over. Enjoy everything while you can, Ten Thousand Years. Try some of the ants' eggs, the old aborigine dish from Kwangsi. I have missed it all these years, haven't you?"

"Yes, yes," Yang said. "Soon we shall be able to enjoy anything our hearts desire, won't we?" He helped himself to a spoonful of the white eggs. As he chewed he went on, "I assure you that all your dreams will be fulfilled, North Prince. Perhaps this is a preliminary celebration, is it not?"

"Exactly, exactly," Wei said, lifting his teacup in a Triad manner. It was a secret sign and Yang recognized it. His face started to pale. Just as he looked around to see if his own guards were present, two assassins leapt onto the dais. One grabbed him and the other slashed his throat with one swift stroke, almost severing his head.

Hung was waiting in his study, pacing as usual. It was a habit he had developed when he had problems. He used to tend his garden when he felt nervous, but now he had no privacy there because his wife and concubines always offered to help him, thinking that an emperor should never touch dirt. Besides, he should never bend his waist except to God.

Wei arrived late. Hung admitted him and locked the door.

"It is done," Wei said, laying a red lacquered box on his desk.

"What is that?" Hung asked.

"Yang's head," Wei said, grinning.

Hung turned his head away, closing his eyes tightly. "Why do you bring it here?"

"For you to take a look. He almost killed you. What do you want me to do with it?"

"Bury it with his body."

"No, I think we ought to hang it over the city gate. We have killed a chicken to warn the monkeys, so to speak . . ."

"No!" Hung interrupted. "Bury it with his body. Give him a decent funeral. What happened to my sister?"

"She is safe with my wife," Wei said soothingly. "She will not be told anything until you have declared the successful crushing of the coup. She will understand."

Hung sank into his chair, his face ghastly pale and his lips trembling. He stared at the red box on his table, his eyes full of tears. "If I had known that this would happen . . ." He stopped, so choked that he could not continue.

"This is God's will, Heavenly Emperor," Wei said. "If you had known all this would happen, you would not have gone to Kwangsi and we would not have had the revolution."

After Wei had left, Hung ordered his attendant to send for his sedan chair; he must see his sister and personally invite her to move into his palace. Perhaps seeing the rest of the family every day would soothe her pain.

He remembered those lean years in Happy Valley, how the whole family had worried about her single status. She had been plain and undernourished, and the family had lacked money to provide a dowry. She had been so innocent that she had seemed ignorant of her own seemingly doomed future, yet she had remained quietly happy, a beam of sunshine that warmed the entire household.

He remembered the gown she had sewn for him before his trip to Canton for the Imperial examination. It was the best gown he had ever owned in Kwangtung. When he saw her again in Yang's house at Thistle Mountain years later, he was pleasantly surprised to see how healthy she had become. Against all expectations her marriage had turned out to be a success and Yang had proved to be a good husband.

Yang had made her a happy mother, a plain woman who had even become beautiful. Her change had touched him so much that he had decided to strengthen his ties with Yang and make him his number-one aide in the rebellion. Now, with all the glory, their lives had turned out to be a terrible tragedy. How was he going to tell her that he, her own brother, had participated in her husband's murder?

When tears crept down his cheeks, he wiped them away quickly. He closed his eyes tightly, trying to suppress his tumultuous emotions. He did not want any attendant to catch the Heavenly Emperor crying.

43

Charles George Gordon divided his time between his headquarters in the British concession in Shanghai, and his flagship, Hyson. He enjoyed sleeping in his cramped cabin on the ship, for everything was within reach, and the gentle rocking of the boat helped his sleep.

He had given his five-thousand-man army a month of intensive training. With new Imperial Army uniforms and discipline, they no longer looked like a horde of bandits. He got rid of the gaudy banners and encouraged his European officers to wear their own European army uniforms. He did not want any of them to plunder in the disguise of a Chinese soldier, as he had once seen in Tientsin. Besides, Mah had told him that European officers in their own European uniforms were more feared because the Opium War had convinced the Chinese soldiers that foreign devils never lost wars.

Actually, Gordon hated to see his two dozen European officers appear at his headquarters in all sorts of uniforms, from sergeants' to colonels'. When they were together, the assortment of clothes looked even more ridiculous because most of them were from different countries. But if that was what China needed, he was not going to change it. All he wanted was to win battles.

Since he had taken over command and finished the army's intensive training, he had won some easy battles against the Taipings. He was pleased with his troops' performances; they handled their modern weapons skillfully, followed his orders, and demonstrated courage. The officers looked like comedians, but on the whole they were experienced and behaved well, except when they were drunk. Drinking was a problem, but Gordon tolerated it because during a recent campaign he had discovered that the tipsy ones were more courageous.

This morning he called his European officers to his quarters for a meeting. They arrived in groups and lined up in front of his desk, waiting for him to speak. Gordon thought it was an enormous improvement in discipline. Before, the Europeans had come in chatting and laughing, some belching from overeating.

Gordon inspected the two dozen officers. Their hair was neat and their beards trimmed. One of them still had a cigar in his mouth. Gordon reached over, removed it, and tossed it out the window. Pacing in front of them, he began to speak.

"Men, I want you to know that I'm rather pleased with your service, but the small battles we've fought were no harder than bagging a frightened deer. There is nothing to brag about. But I hear that we will soon face some major enemy forces. One of the groups is commanded by a man called Golden Rooster, who has had a lot of experience fighting the British during the Opium War. When we engage this character, I don't want any cracking of knuckles, stretching, or yawning. Every man must be alert at all times and never for a moment underestimate this Golden Rooster's ability."

He stopped pacing and looked at the row of bearded faces. They stared at him, at attention. The pause seemed to make them even more alert. He went on, waving his cane for emphasis, "Men, the little warm-up engagements are over. In major battles, I want you to follow my tactics, or philosophy, or whatever the dickens you call it.

"First, preparation. In every engagement a thorough investigation of the enemy's strength. Careful reconnoitering of the area is absolutely necessary. No hasty shooting or running.

"Second, surprise attack. Only with knowledge can you surprise an enemy and catch him unprepared.

"Third, save energy and lives. Avoid unnecessary killings. The last battle was a good example. We did not confront the enemy. Instead, we sneaked up behind them and subdued them with half the possible bloodshed. Massacres are absolutely forbidden. Urge the defeated enemy to surrender. I'll treat all prisoners well. I'll even recruit them to fight on our side. Remember, the Chinese soldier has little ideology. He usually fights for a bowl of rice. If we offer him two bowls plus a chunk of red-cooked pork, he will fight for us."

After he had dismissed the European officers, he confined himself to his cabin trying to devise a plan to deal with this new enemy, Golden Rooster.

* * *

Gordon held more meetings, waiting for Golden Rooster to deliver the first blow. He was itching for action. Meanwhile, he was fighting another battle—Shanghai poverty.

Lieutenant Mah told Gordon that he would become immune to Shanghai's poverty and its bad smell in time. Gordon said that he had already begun to like the smell of salted fish and the blackened thousand-year-old eggs. He boasted that getting used to Oriental food was never much of a problem for him. He ate only one meal a day, anyhow. And he didn't care what he ate. When bread became stale, he just dipped it in a cup of strong coffee and ate it without knowing the difference.

But poverty was something else. The sight of a hungry child rummaging in some garbage for food, or dying of disease in a dirty doorway, gave him heart murmurs and headaches. It made him angry, unable to sleep; it became hard for him to swallow.

He treasured his blue eyes, which were perfectly clear most of the time. They were his best feature. With his well-trimmed mustache he considered himself rather good-looking. He did not want anything to mar his looks. But the Shanghai poverty was giving him bloodshot eyes and other ailments. For selfish reasons, he told Mah, he had to do something about it.

Lieutenant Mah recommended a Chinese eyedrop and a "cure-all" ointment. Gordon chose another cure: He started a charity for poor children in Shanghai. He began to raise money among his countrymen and his own officers, regardless of the amount . . . even a few pennies were acceptable.

Every morning, before going to his office, he rode to the slums on his white stallion and scattered coins among the wretched street urchins. Running with their dirty hands outstretched, trying to catch the flying coins, the children trampled each other. One morning, to Gordon's horror, two skinny boys were trampled to death. He immediately stopped the practice and set up a rice-soup station.

With the help of Mah, he hired a cook and a server who dished out a hot rice gruel at a temporary stall on a street corner. The children brought their own rice bowls. Gordon, if time allowed, saw to it that the child ate the gruel right there, instead of taking it home for the adults. His charity was for children only. When money ran out, he donated his own salary to tide it over. Two large caldrons of rice gruel, cooked with pork liver and chicken wings were a day's ration. Sometimes Lieutenant Mah would chip in some money to save face, for he did not want to look too stingy while a foreigner was so generous.

Occasionally, a rich British merchant whom Gordon had met socially would make a handsome donation. Once or twice a week a high-ranking officer from the British Officers Club would palm a few pounds into his hands, like a master tipping a servant. Such windfalls always brought special treats to the starving children—an extra meat-filled bun or a bag of peanuts . . . sometimes a whole chicken leg or a few tea-soaked hard-boiled eggs, the children's favorite. The charity, to Gordon's own pleasant surprise, cured the symptoms of many of his own ailments.

There was a long lull in the war, but it often flared up again without warning. Gordon learned from Lieutenant Mah that the Taipings had problems. A coup had failed and the commander in chief had gone to Heaven without his head. The Heavenly Emperor had changed many of his policies, replaced half of his advisers and generals, and created many more titles. Now dozens of generals were titled, some living in luxury in occupied cities. Lieutenant Mah was sure that whenever there was a lull, there was a new problem developing in Nanking. Gordon wished that one day the Heavenly Emperor would have a problem too big to handle, throw up his hands and give up.

Lieutenant Mah said that the Taipings' biggest problem was probably the Hunan Army, which had recently taken the Twin City. If it had not been for Golden Rooster, the Hunan Army could have seized every town along the Yangtze and reached Nanking already. Mah said he would hate to fight this pirate chief, a tricky giant with a loud laugh that sounded like a rooster's crow heralding the sunrise. His laughter was the death knell for his enemies. Gordon had heard many such stories, which resembled folklore, and he took them with a grain of salt.

Meanwhile, his own fame was spreading rapidly in China. His Ever-Victorious Army had finally lived up to its name. So far it had not lost a fight. A few of his soldiers had tried to loot, but Gordon had stopped them by shooting an officer dead in front of the others, just as he had warned.

Once a group of new recruits had become boisterous, demanding better food and better pay, yelling and firing their guns, on the verge of mutiny. Lieutenant Mah said they were a Shanghai gang called Bi San. They would stab their own mothers without blinking an eye. Mah suggested that the army get rid of these killers . . . too dangerous. Gordon only grinned. Without a word, he marched to the rioters, grabbed the leader's pigtail, pulled him out into the open, and began to cane him savagely until the man sank to his knees begging for mercy. After that public display of authority, Gordon found that discipline was never a problem again.

Out of admiration, Mah tried to emulate him, but he quickly gave up, knowing that he did not have the foreigner's gall. Gordon always wanted to set a personal example, no matter how dangerous the situation was. He seemed to attract danger. In the heat of battle, he would thrust a cigar between his teeth and head straight for the point of greatest peril, yelling orders and waving his cane. Mah had to admit that the only thing that he had copied successfully so far was to thrust a cigar into his mouth.

Mah went to Li Hung-chang's yamen to make his weekly report. When he arrived, Li was enjoying his water pipe and his mild coughing. He was glad to see Mah, for he was always curious about Gordon and wanted to know how the foreigner was faring as a Chinese general.

"Your Excellency," Mah said, "you have hit a bull's-eye in choosing this foreign devil to lead the Ever-Victorious Army. He is a very strange creature, tireless and never seems to get hurt. He works all the time, planning by night and executing by day, planning by day and executing by night. Every move is a surprise to the enemy . . . everything well planned ahead. He is a glorious fellow, Your Excellency!"

Li Hung-chang nodded with satisfaction. "Indeed he is Heaven-sent," he said with a sigh. "I hear that he will go all day without food. At night he will just suck a dozen eggs. Is that true?"

"And two pots of black coffee," Mah said. "When he goes to bed he hardly takes his clothes off. He likes to sleep on his boat. He crawls into his bunk and starts snoring right away. In two or three hours he is up, making coffee and sucking eggs. But he always looks tidy and spruced-up."

With a happy smile, Li smoothed his thin beard. "Some say he is half human and half spirit. I wonder."

"Sometimes he is soft as Kwan Yin," Mah said. "I saw him cradle a wounded man in his arms and shed tears. Another time he held a half-dead boy in one arm and directed operations with his cane. Men fell on his right and left but he never got hit. Probably he is half spirit."

"He met quite a few Mandarins," Li said, trying to remember the occasions. "You could tell he did not like them, but he put up with them. He even won the affection and confidence of a few members of the royal family. They put in some good words for him . . . except when he demanded more money."

"He never wants more money for himself," Mah said. "He only complains about the low pay for his men. Whenever the pay is late, he jumps up and curses. Once the pay was a week late. He gave General Ching a terrible time. Besides talking about sending in his resignation, he even threatened to hand the captured cities back to the Long Hairs."

Li shook his head with a sigh. "In spite of all his good points, I can see that this foreigner has all the airs and superiority of the others. I hate all foreigners, but it is not wise to let them know. General Ching has told me that Gordon's never-ending demands for punctual pay are very tiresome. Someone ought to tell him that irregular troops like his always clamor for punctual payment when they are not permitted to loot. By the way, I hear that the Long Hairs are sending their navy to the east coast. Is it because of this China Gordon?"

"No doubt about it, Your Excellency," Mah said. "The Long Hairs' navy commander is an old pirate called Golden Rooster. This man, I've heard, has fought foreigners during the Opium War. He is itchy to fight another foreigner, and has volunteered to break Gordon's winning streak.

Li thought for a moment, took out his snuff bottle and waved it under his nose a few times. After a loud sneeze he said with a sigh, "I don't mind if the Golden Rooster beats him initially. It might dampen his superior air. And it might also save some Chinese face. But I would not worry. With the British navy behind him, he will eventually roast this golden rooster. You will see!"

44

The Yangtze was much wider than the Pearl River, but the night with its half moon and sparkling stars in a dark cloudless sky reminded Su San-mei of the older days when she and Golden Rooster had robbed opium boats on the Pearl River. During the past two years, she and Golden Rooster had been defending the Twin City in Hupei Province against the Hunan Army's repeated assaults. Without the Twin City, the central plains would be lost and the Hunan braves could sail straight to Nanking. It was as simple as one two three, yet Nanking had ordered Golden Rooster to withdraw. The Heavenly Emperor wanted the Taiping navy transferred to Kiangsu Province to fight a foreigner, who had won every battle against the Taipings.

Golden Rooster came on deck to watch the stars. He squatted beside Su San-mei and filled his bamboo pipe. The half moon reflected on the undulating water, like something one could scoop up with two hands. The flagship was sailing downstream easily, steady and fast. Following behind it were over a hundred sampans and junks, the flotilla stretching out for miles. They looked like fishing boats, but every one of them was heavily armed. In close combat the sailors used Chinese traditonal weapons; at long range they fired muskets, modern rifles, and cannons, all British-made and sold to the Taipings by the foreign gunrunner, Mr. Lindley.

Su San-mei broke the silence. "I think the emperor has made a mistake. The Twin City is more important than Kiangsu Province."

Golden Rooster did not respond right away. He puffed on his pipe a few times, inhaled deeply and sighed. When Su San-mei heard older people sigh, she could not tell if they were sighs of happiness or sadness. She supposed that sighing was merely a habit, like coughing.

"Su San-mei," Golden Rooster finally said. "The Heavenly Emperor must have his reasons. Those who make stupid moves never become emperor. So just trust his judgment."

"Well . . . we'll have to fight foreigners again."

"I like it," he said. "Fighting foreigners is easier than fighting Hunan braves. They are less tricky."

There was a moment of silence. Su San-mei knew that Golden Rooster admired Hung and had never said a bad word about him. Because of that, she often refrained from criticizing him, even though she still held a grudge against Hung for having abandoned her. After she had saved his army from the "fired buffalo" attack and later sent him two thousand catties of buffalo meat, he had never even attempted to find out who she was. She still felt hurt, and had sworn that she would never become a God-worshipper.

"Father?" she asked. "Why did you become a God-worshipper?"

"Su San-mei," Golden Rooster said deliberately, as though he were afraid of giving the wrong answer, "in Heaven we have the Jade Emperor. In hell we have Yen Lo, the king of ghosts. Knowing that I will go to hell, there is no point in worshipping anybody in Heaven. But there is no harm in becoming a God-worshipper."

"Why are you so sure that you will go to hell?"

"To tell you the truth, we all go to hell when we die. The only difference is whether you will suffer in hell or not . . . whether you will become a dog, a pig, or a rat in your reincarnations—or not."

"Do you really believe that, Father?"

"I do. But you never can tell until after you die. Anyway, don't do anything against your conscience in this life. Even though you kill, you don't kill an innocent man. If you rob, be sure to rob a stinking turtle's egg who has robbed the poor."

"If not, Yen Lo will punish you, I suppose."

"Yen Lo is a just ghost king. Those who did things against their conscience will be fried in a big wok of boiling oil. And that is not the end of the punishment. In their reincarnations, they will return to this world as dogs, pigs, and rats."

"Why do we fight for Hung Shiu-ch'uan?" she asked after a long silence.

"Because I want to see a Ming Emperor sitting on the Dragon Throne in Peking. I thought Hung might be the one."

"Do you think differently now, Father?"

Again Golden Rooster did not answer immediately. He finished his pipe and knocked its ashes out against the deck. "The Heavenly Emperor has climbed a mountain," he finally said. "He was called a God-worshipper when he started. He was going to build a Heavenly Kingdom for everybody. When the kingdom was established in Nanking, people called the God-worshippers 'Tai Pings.' It was the height of the Taiping kingdom. Then when misery and unhappiness persisted in the Taiping kingdom, people started calling them 'Long Hairs.' It is like climbing a mountain. You climb up, reach the top and come down the other side. That is the history of the Taiping kingdom."

"What will happen?" she asked after she had fully digested Golden Rooster's analogy.

"That will depend on what we can do in Kiangsu Province. If we cannot defeat the Imperial troops there, we will have no more mountain to climb. We shall be buried and wait for reincarnation."

For a moment, Golden Rooster looked sad. It was the first time that he had sounded so pessimistic. Su San-mei put a hand over his and said, trying to sound cheerful, "Father, we are going to fight a foreigner. You like to fight foreigners, remember? Through the years you have taught me how to fight a strong enemy and win. If you don't feel like fighting, let me do it! You can sleep through it if you like. When you wake up, a victory banquet will be waiting for you in the provincial capital . . ."

"Don't give me such foolishness," Golden Rooster interrupted. "You sound like a five-year-old girl. By the way, how are you going to win a war against a strong enemy?"

Su San-mei was glad he had asked. In the past she had fought battles against only incompetent, muddleheaded Manchu officials and had won them easily. But in a real battle against a formidable foe, she had never had a chance to test herself. Now at least she could do it in words and receive a grade from her old master. As though she were taking an oral examination, she told him how a weak army could win a war against a strong one. She drew the example of Ju Kwo-liang, the cleverest man during the three Warring Kingdoms. Ju defeated a strong enemy by using the Empty City Strategy. Having no real defense for his city and outnumbered in troop strength, he kept his city gates wide open. When the invaders marched in thinking that he had already fled the city, he ambushed them with showers of arrows and watched the panicked enemies trampling themselves to death.

Golden Rooster listened quietly, his face expressionless. When she had finished, he sighed. "You are a good storyteller," he said. "The story has been told a million times, but you still make it interesting."

"Is that all?" she asked, disappointed.

"Su San-mei," he said seriously, "no fool will fall into the 'empty city' trap again, just as nobody except fools will use the 'fired buffalo' tactics again. But there is a basic strategy for a little man to win a battle against a big man."

He refilled his pipe with tobacco, lighted it, and went on. "When I was a young rascal in Shantung Province, I did a lot of street fighting and I always won because I was big and strong. My fist carried a thousand catties of strength. A blow from it could knock down a horse. Everybody was afraid of me. One year we had a terrible famine. One beggar challenged me to a fight at a rich man's birthday party. The rich man wanted the fight to entertain his guests. The winner was to take all the prize money.

"The beggar was a skinny little fellow called Iron Head, supposed to be a famous fighter in his prime, but hunger had made him take this fight. I was hungry, too, even though it was against my conscience to fight this little grasshopper. I could squash him with half a punch.

"During the party, the rich man and his guests drank and ate and enjoyed themselves while they watched us fight, as though they were watching two dogs trying to kill each other. But I could never touch this Iron Head. He was here and there, on my left then on my right. If I punched, he was at my back. If I turned, he was somewhere else. He was like a shadow. He never punched with his hands, for they could not possibly deliver a blow more than fifty catties strong. They would have been like mosquito bites. He fought with his feet and his head. When I missed him with a punch, his foot flew up and hit me anywhere he wished, knocking me sideways. When I tried to avoid his kick by stepping back, he rushed me like a bull and rammed his head into my unprotected stomach, knocking the wind out of me. His head, with all his weight behind it, was what defeated me. In the end, I sat on my big behind in the dirt, my head spinning, my body aching, breathless and exhausted. I said respectfully, 'Master Iron Head, you win.'

"You see? I was beaten by a little grasshopper. But I learned a lesson . . . the same lesson that was taught by Sun Wu's book thousands of years ago. This is the way we are going to fight in Kiangsu. Our enemy is a foreigner. His yellow hair and colored eyes are already very intimidating. With the Imperial Army and the British gunboats behind him, he will be like me in Shangtung. I'll be like the little Iron Head. I'll be here and there, in his front and in his back. He won't be able to touch me. When he backs up, I will ram him. I will win!"

General Ching was unhappy about Gordon's inaction. The Taiping Navy had already sneaked into the vicinity of Shanghai. They looked like a group of scraggly wet chickens struggling on the water, not daring to come into the open. Gordon's waiting irritated Ching so much that he confronted him on his flagship, Tyson.

Gordon watched the agitated Chinese general, amused. It was the first time that Ching had not kept saying, "Yes, yes," and nodding with his perpetual smile. Gordon considered Ching a good soldier, but the general tended to be brave at the wrong times. Both Ching and Gordon were impatient with the Imperial Army's lethargy, incompetence, and corruption, but Ching was brave without tactics. He was proud of his new firearms, which had recently been purchased from his new friend, Mr. Lindley. He could hardly wait to try them on the Long Hairs. But he must coordinate his actions with Gordon's.

Gordon understood his irritation, but he believed in preparation prior to battle. He always studied the enemy's position, its weaknesses, its strengths, and its maneuverability. But to General Ching, it was a waste of time. The Ever-Victorious Army had the firepower; all Gordon had to do was to confront the enemy and pulverize those little boats with his big guns.

As he continued to argue, finally Gordon had to shed his studied Chinese politeness and tell him with a long face and cold voice, "General Ching, I have already laid out my conditions in this war. One of them is that I will not have unnecessary killing. The way you want to do this is to massacre our enemies as well as innocent fishermen."

"But it will shorten the war," General Ching said, still unsmiling.

"I will conduct this war my way. Do you want me to tender my resignation?"

General Ching grimaced. The word *resignation* stung his ears. He smiled quickly for fear he might hear Gordon's ultimatum, "If you don't do it my way, I'll return the captured cities to the Long Hairs." Such words from a Chinese general would have brought an executioner's sword down on his neck; but Gordon was a foreigner. He was protected by the Treaty of Nanking. He could say anything he liked. Even Li Hung-chang was obliged to nod and smile. With a bow, Ching left the Tyson, without further argument.

Golden Rooster was familiar with the intricate waterways of Kiangsu Province. He laid a map on the table in his cabin and showed Su San-mei how to conduct mobile warfare. The Taiping ships would remain in the small rivers, where the enemy's big gunboats could not enter but the Taiping boats could come and go, harrassing the enemy with sneak attacks. It would keep the enemy on the move and cut their strength more than half, because more than half of their boats could only maneuver in the deeper and wider rivers.

"We will first exhaust them" Golden Rooster said, "then take the chance of wiping them out. If this China Gordon is arrogant, as most of the foreigners are, he may believe that we are afraid of him, always trying to escape. So he will follow close at our heels. When they catch us, he will discover that he has caught some unarmed fishing boats. Suddenly, guns will start shooting from the shore or from hidden boats. He will be a dead goose."

Su San-mei was not convinced. She was getting nervous. "Father," she said, "we have zigzagged east and west, north and south for many days now. The enemy has not followed us. They have not fired a gun yet."

"Patience, patience," Golden Rooster said. "Foreigners are usually lazy. They will have three bottles of whiskey before they eat breakfast. I have learned that much from robbing their opium ships." After a short laugh, he traced the map with a finger and added, "We will have time to set a decoy here and hide our main force in this willow grove just outside this little town. When they charge our decoy, our concealed forces will quickly close in and mete out heavy punishment, which will cause great confusion. When they attempt to flee, they will find that there is no way out, for we will already have encircled them."

He made a big circle on the map with a finger. "The enemies in this entire area will be in our pocket. I hope this foreigner will be among them."

Su San-mei was convinced that Golden Rooster knew what he was doing.

About thirty miles out of Shanghai, the two sides finally exchanged some gunfire. But nobody got hurt. It was hard to tell which was a Taiping boat and which was a fishing boat. The big Taiping boats were in the small waterways and the big British boats were in the big waterways. Su San-mei watched the British boats maneuvering. They reminded her of the billy goats she had seen in Kwangtung trying to mount a sheep, but the sheep always eluded them. Golden Rooster said that this was only an onlookers' war ... something for the public to enjoy. In reality, it was a maneuvering to mislead the enemy. Now he was ready for the real war, to be waged quietly in the darkness.

Every night he would change into some light clothes, almost skin-tight so that he could swim easily if necessary. He and two other men, similarly clothed, would go out in a heavily armed sampan and return before dawn. Golden Rooster refused to say what he was doing. Su San-mei guessed that he was trying to assassinate the foreigner. One night she offered to go with him, but he firmly said, "No." He said that in a few days it would be all over and that the less she knew about it the better. Whenever he was gone, she could not sleep. She would wait nervously until he returned. Every night he returned; nothing happened. After a few more nights she relaxed and slept.

One night she was awakened by explosions. She leapt out of her bunk and rushed on deck. Nearby there was a ball of fire, and a burning sampan was sinking. There was a full moon. In the bright moonlight, she saw the boat submerged in the yellow water, with the fire still burning. Suddenly she recognized it. It was Golden Rooster's shabby boat. Nearby, two bodies were floating. One was struggling, one arm flailing above the water. She could tell it was Golden Rooster.

She dove in and swam madly toward him. When she reached him, she put an arm around him and flipped him over onto his back, then started towing him toward his flagship. Several seamen had already jumped in to help them. They carried him into his cabin and lay him on his bed. Su San-mei almost vomited when she found a hole in his stomach and one leg missing. She quickly covered him with several blankets and ordered mao-tai. With the help of the others, she fed him a few spoonfuls of the spirit and tried to clean his wounds. When he became unconscious, she shook him and called him, keeping him awake. Experience had taught her that if a wounded man drifted away he may not wake up again.

After a few more spoonfuls of mao-tai, he opened his eyes again. She cuddled him in her arms, rocking him gently to keep him awake. "Father, Father," she called. "You are back. I am Su San-mei. We will dress your wounds and make you well."

Golden Rooster tried to focus his glassy eyes on her face. "Su San-mei," he said weakly, his voice hardly audible. "My time has come. I have met a clever foreigner. I could not lure him to the shallow waters. I tried to dynamite his boat, but he got me first." He swallowed hard and grimaced.

"Father, don't die," she cried. "Please don't die!"

He managed a weak smile. "When a man's time has come, it has come. The foreigner's cannonball said so. A bull's-eye. My dynamite sank my own boat. It's Heaven's will."

He stopped again and gasped for air. She kept rocking him, tears pouring down her face. "Father, don't go! Your time has not come! Please!"

His eyes were showing white, but he struggled to keep himself awake, trying to focus. "Don't worry," he said, his breath getting shorter. "When I go, Yen Lo will not fry me in oil. When I return, I will not return as a pig . . . or a rat."

He stopped, dropped his head and was gone. Failing to wake him again, Su San-mei buried her head in his blood-soaked clothes and broke down, her body shaking with heartrending sobs.

|45|

Lying on his wide canopied bed in his palace, Hung turned and looked at the nude body of Jin Jin, one of his numerous concubines. The sublime shape of the young woman, her smooth ivorylike skin, her long dark hair falling on the yellow silk pillow, and her fragrant body did nothing to him. He had become sexless. Like a man who had been invited to three banquets in a row, his stomach was so full that he had lost his appetite, even for the rarest delicacies. Depressed and wanting to be alone, he woke her and politely sent her away.

He stared blankly for a while, trying to empty his mind of all his regrets. His greatest regret was the assassination of Yang, his own brother-in-law. He had learned that Yang's attempted coup had been instigated by Wei, the North Prince. Yang had been an excellent general, but vain—loving gaudy clothes, royal trappings, and splendor. By boosting Yang's ego, Wei had successfully alienated Yang from Hung. Now Hung saw clearly that he had been fooled.

Thinking of Wei's intrigue, Hung was appalled that he had been so naïve and so stupid as to let it happen, resulting in the murder of his own brother-in-law, a really harmless man who had only loved titles and honors.

The more he thought about it the more repentant he felt. He also felt threatened. Shuddering, he got up quickly and ordered his stationery. Secretly he sent a dispatch to Yang's trusted General Shih Ta-kai, the Shield Prince, who was fighting the Manchu forces in Anhui, Chekiang, and Kiangsu. He urged Shih to return to the capital for an urgent meeting.

For several days he mourned Yang's death and had him buried in silk without a coffin so that it would be easier for his spirit to ascend to Heaven. While he waited for Shih's return, he appointed Faithful as the new commander in chief. Faithful immediately turned his attention

281

to the war in Kiangsu and left for that province where the Taipings were losing ground rapidly after the death of Golden Rooster. Hung knew that Faithful was not interested in politics. Faithful was probably ignorant of all the palace intrigues. He had left Nanking without even asking any questions about Yang's death.

Shih returned with only a few personal guards. He went directly to see the Heavenly Emperor. Hung invited him to his study and confided in him about Wei's intrigue and the murder of Yang. Shih, a reliable general, calm and loyal to Yang, controlled his anger the best he could. His face red and breath short, he quietly swore vengeance.

"Heavenly Emperor," he said, "Wei and I cannot exist in the same kingdom and breathe the same air. I request your permission to kill him and make a urinal of his skull. But if he knows that I am back, he will do the same to me. I must take care of my family first."

"I think you should," Hung said. "Send your family away for the time being, and be fast!"

Shih immediately sent his guards home to help his family escape. Meanwhile, he secretly contacted all his trusted officers in Nanking and alerted them to Wei's intrigues and possible coup.

Soon the guards returned with bad news. Wei's troops had already seized Shih's house. His parents, wife, three concubines, and six children had all disappeared.

"I must escape," Shih told Hung. "I shall return with my troops."

It was late at night. Shih rushed out of the city without guards, to avoid attention. On the river bank, he disrobed and left his clothes to simulate suicide. Then he boarded a waiting boat and sailed into the darkness.

Wei did not believe that Shih had drowned himself. When he discovered that Shih had actually fled Nanking, he stamped his feet in fury and shouted, "Those who allow a mountain tiger to escape are guilty! Their heads must fall!" Then he had Shih's entire family massacred.

Soon the news of the massacre reached the Imperial Palace. Sorrow and anger made Hung sink into his chair in his study, bury his head in his hands and mourn. He mourned his own stupidity and helplessness. How could he have trusted Wei, the man whom he had not trusted to begin with? He still vividly remembered how Wei had massacred his enemies in Kwangsi Province. Now Wei had fooled everybody and almost seized power.

Outwardly Nanking remained calm. Obviously Wei was cautious and considered that the time was not ripe to overthrow Hung openly. He still addressed Hung as Ten Thousand Years and kowtowed to him. Knowing that a coup was imminent, Hung alerted his guards and secretly dispatched an urgent message to Prince Faithful, ordering him to return immediately.

Imminent danger suddenly made him regain his senses and his ability to make his way through thorns, to open impossible paths, as he had so often done at Thistle Mountain. For the next few days he was kind to Wei, pretending that he did not know of Shih's escape. He extended an invitation to both Wei and Shih to attend a palace banquet in celebration of Wei's birthday. Secretly he gathered all his Kwangtung men and trusted officers under Prince Faithful's command. He laid out a plan, hoping that both Faithful and Shih would return in time to rescue him if the plan failed. Now he was the old Hung Shiu-ch'uan again, clever, alert and determined.

That evening he wrote two scrolls, one quoting Jesus:

All they that take the sword shall perish by the sword.

The other was a long quotation of Confucius:

Those who have killed others will have themselves killed; those who have saved others will have themselves saved. Who says that the eyes of Heaven are not wide open?

The banquet hall was colorfully decorated with banners, lanterns, and couplet scrolls. The birthday banquet was small and intimate, with twenty round tables of guests served below the dais. Only two tables were placed on the dais. Hung was seated on one side and Wei on the other. In between them, a huge portrait of the god of longevity was hung on the wall, with incense and candles burning in front of it on a long table. Flanking the longevity god were the two scrolls Hung had written the night before, both of which were temporarily covered with rice paper.

During the banquet, Hung gave a glorious report on the war against the Manchu troops. Then he showered praise on Wei, declaring that Wei's contribution to the revolution was greater than that of his own, and that Wei deserved to be addressed as Ten Thousand Years. These remarks did not please Wei; they sounded like a paraphrase of what he himself had said to Yang.

"On this special occasion," Hung said, rising to propose a toast, "we shall all drink to Prince North's longevity. We wish him Ten Thousand Years! Bottoms up!" He downed his drink in one gulp. All the guests below the dais followed his lead.

Wei finished his drink and glanced uneasily to see if his guards were present. None was. He knew then that Hung had been clever enough to provide everyone with food and drink. Wei's guards were probably drinking and celebrating his birthday elsewhere.

"Since Prince North has everything," Hung was saying, "no gift is more appropriate than quotations from Jesus Christ and Confucius." He gestured for an attendant to uncover the two scrolls.

When Wei read the scrolls, his face paled. He made an excuse to wash his hands. Just as he was about to leave his chair, two assassins leapt onto the dais. One grabbed him and the other slashed his throat. He fell dead instantly, just as Yang had died a few weeks earlier.

|46|

After the death of Golden Rooster, Tseng Kuo-fan's Hunan Army advanced rapidly toward Nanking, but the Taipings still held a vast territory of almost seventy thousand square miles with a population of twenty-five million. Hung had lost many of his ablest generals, both in war and through inner struggles. Becoming fearful, he dared not trust anyone with extensive powers except those of his own blood. He appointed his two older half-brothers, Run-ta and Run-mo, as his chief ministers. The two men had wallowed in luxury in Nanking, growing equally fat. They assumed power with aplomb and added trappings and concubines that befitted their elevated positions.

Hung also granted titles to numerous generals who were fighting in Chekiang and Kiangsu Provinces, which he regarded as vital to his kingdom strategically. But the disillusionment with some of his close associates and the advance of the Hunan braves brought on a terrible depression. He read the Bible and prayed fervently every day. His family often heard him cry out in his study, "Oh, my eldest brother in Heaven, help me! Help me!"

For almost six months the Imperial troops had been shelling Nanking. Distant guns boomed day and night, but most of the cannon balls fell in the rice fields outside the walls. The guns were only noise, like dogs barking in the morning. Life went on almost as usual.

On a mild summer day, Run-kan arrived. Hung was delighted. The sight of his cousin—one of his two closest associates—immediately lifted him out of his deep melancholy. The benevolent smile returned to his previously gloomy face. He found food more tasty and his women more voluptuous, even though they were still passive and unexciting. The news from the various fronts was not always bad. Faithful was fighting in Kwangsu; Shih Ta-kai was regrouping his troops in Anhui.

285

Hung had ordered Wei's head packed in a sealed box and shipped to Shih. Since Wei had massacred Shih's family, it was only fitting that Shih be allowed to dispose of his enemy's head any way he wished.

"Run-kan," Hung said one evening when they were alone in his study, "I would like to have a foreign preacher reside in Nanking. Can you think of anyone who is willing to move here as a permanent resident? With a foreign preacher giving sermons every Sunday, it will help change the way we are viewed. Nobody will call us 'contraband Christians' anymore."

"I am glad you asked," Run-kan said. "Before I left Hong Kong, Mr. David Brown inquired about the possibility of coming to Nanking to preach."

"Who is David Brown?"

"He was a navy man before. He accompanied Golden Rooster on many seafaring adventures."

Hung frowned. "A pirate?"

"He robbed a few opium boats, I suppose, but the loot went to support secret societies' uprisings. We sacked quite a few landlords, too, remember?"

"How can he preach? Did he study the Bible?"

"He is an ordained minister now. He must have studied it."

"Hm," Hung said, pulling at his beard, which had turned almost white through the years. "He might do. In the Bible there are examples of sour oranges turning sweet. St. Paul and St. Peter were not exactly good apples in the beginning, and they both became saints. Invite him. We shall give him a royal welcome. A church will be built for him and regular Sunday services will be held. The more foreigners we have in this city the better. And I want my own family to take the lead and go to the foreigner's church . . . and study the Bible. So far, my brothers have only learned how to say grace before dinner."

Run-kan immediately wrote to David Brown in Hong Kong. He had been disillusioned by the Reverend Mr. Roberts, who had changed his opinion of the Taipings and called them 'contraband Christians.' He had also been disappointed by Mr. Lindley, who had made many promises which Run-kan had found to be only bubbles. But in Hong Kong and Shanghai he had made new foreign friends. One of them, a Mr. Thomas

Meadows, visited him in Nanking. This new friend was so enthusiastic about the Taipings' noble undertaking that he had many times requested a visit to Nanking and an audience with the Heavenly Emperor. Finally, he was here.

Hung again was delighted. Thomas Meadows was friendly and a warm supporter. A middle-aged Englishman with thick black wavy hair, heavily bearded, he spoke fluent Chinese and laughed easily. He was a good talker, knowledgeable and opinionated, a strong advocate of a strong independent China. He believed that China was the only country that could counterbalance Russia's ambition to dominate the world. He attacked Britain's policy of propping up the dying Manchu Dynasty; only a nation of four hundred million Bible-studying Christians could bring peace and prosperity to the world.

Everything Thomas Meadows said was music to Hung's ears. He dined and wined this foreign guest and held intimate meetings with him and Run-kan, making grand plans to save the world. Thomas Meadows promised to convince England that it should make a one-hundred-and-eighty-degree turn and treat Hung's Heavenly Kingdom as its closest friend, and to help him overthrow the Manchu government. Then Hung could visit Europe and bring back with him both the Pope and Queen Victoria as honored guests to his Heavenly Capital.

Hung, Run-kan, and Thomas Meadows often talked for hours in Hung's study. Meadows never tired of praising Run-kan, saying that his literary attainments were high, his temper amiable, his knowledge of Christian doctrine respectable. All in all, he was a valued member of Christian society. Hung could not agree with him more.

They laughed and joked; Hung had not had such a relaxed time since he'd become emperor. He urged Run-kan to cook some foreign food. Run-kan agreed readily. He had studied Western culture and adopted many Western habits. Since the Heavenly Emperor could not come and go freely, he ordered a small kitchen built next to Hung's study.

"Western food is really very easy to make," Run-kan announced on the day the kitchen was completed. "The foreigners like their food to have some cow smell. If you can not find butter, a little goat fat will do. It can produce a similar smell in any food."

He cooked his favorite foreign foods in the new kitchen—Boston hash and southern-fried chicken, which Thomas Meadows ate with a slight frown but was polite enough to praise as exotic.

Run-kan dispatched more invitations to his foreign friends in both Shanghai and Hong Kong. Quite a few accepted. The Heavenly Emperor welcomed them with open arms. Besides shaking hands, he also practiced embracing, a greeting that most Chinese abhorred. To many of them, even hand-shaking was too intimate. But the Heavenly Emperor had decided to go Western, in order to win more Western friends. He knew that the Manchu court had been doing the same thing, with many Mandarins entertaining the foreigners constantly in the delightful atmosphere of tranquil Oriental gardens, serving rare delicacies from the high mountains and deep seas. He had heard that Tse-hsi had even invited a foreign lady to paint her portrait. It was obvious that both sides needed foreign help; they especially needed their powerful cannons.

In trying to gain Western sympathy, Run-kan played an important part. He had so many foreign contacts that he wrote and received foreign letters every day. Whenever the Taiping postal service saw any mail with wormlike words on the envelope, they automatically delivered it to Run-kan. Hung treasured Run-kan's contacts and urged him to keep up the good work. If necessary, Run-kan decided, he would have himself baptized in every church when he traveled as Taiping's goodwill ambassador.

Mr. Meadows wrote articles about the Taiping Kingdom using glowing terms. A few were accepted by missionary publications; Meadows carried many of those dog-eared magazine clippings in his breast pocket. He enjoyed reading them whenever there was an audience, regardless of whether they understood English or not. Hung had them all translated, printed, and distributed among his generals and princes, and had them posted on all the city walls. Meadows also began to carry the Chinese version of his articles; his breast pockets were bulging more every week.

One night, Hung, Run-kan, and Meadows were talking in Hung's study and sipping jasmine tea from tiny cups under colorful silk-shaded palace lanterns when there was a sudden thunderous noise. A large cannonball fell through the palace roof, shattering the glazed tiles and carved ceiling. It landed less than a yard from Hung's feet. Family members, guards, and attendants, greatly alarmed, rushed in to see what had happened. They saw the gaping hole in the ceiling and paled. Everybody started talking at once, urging the Heavenly Emperor to vacate the room and take shelter. Hung turned the iron ball with his toe a few times.

"I am familiar with this," he said calmly. "It is from the big river. Almost a bull's-eye. No Imperial troops have such good aim. I guess the Hunan braves have finally arrived."

Mention of the Hunan braves alerted everybody. An atmosphere of war, which had been absent for many years, returned to Nanking, bringing an air of tension immediately.

47

To defend the city of Nanking, the Heavenly Emperor ordered Faithful back from Chekiang Province, where he had recaptured many towns and villages. "Nanking is like a man's heart," he told Faithful. "When the heart goes, everything goes."

Faithful attempted to argue, but in making life-and-death decisions, he considered that Hung was a little wiser. He strengthened the defenses of the city, especially the side that faced the Hunan Army. He virtually ignored the Imperial Army, knowing that they had been wasting their ammunition by shooting out of range.

With Faithful and Run-kan at his side, Hung felt more secure. He appointed Run-kan Prime Minister as well as Foreign Minister.

Nanking was under siege, but life went on. There were seventy-eight minor city gates, half of them blocked and cemented. The others had secret tunnels connecting with the outside world.

Quite a few foreigners arrived: first the Reverend Mr. David Brown; then two adventurers whose nationalities were unknown; followed by a Mr. Wade, a spy from London who had been sent by General Stavely as a representative from the London Missionary Society.

The two soldiers of fortune, having found that there was no fortune to be made, left after two days. The London missionary lasted a week. Faithful found him too nosy and kept a polite distance. Only David Brown stayed and enjoyed a warm welcome. He was warm, gregarious, and knowledgeable, full of energy and enthusiasm in whatever he did. Hung did not build him a church, but he ordered a rice barn turned into a place of God, with an altar and a picture of Jesus Christ nailed on the wall. The Reverend Mr. Brown conducted his services there every Sunday. He allowed the devoted God-worshippers to make food offerings but forbade them to burn incense or ghost money because it smoked up the building in which he also lived. As for the food offerings, mostly chicken, pork, and rice, he fed them to stray dogs and cats at night.

Every morning, in his heavily accented Chinese, the Reverend Mr. Brown was seen on Nanking's streets urging people to embrace Christianity. He baptized people in the Yangtze, dunking howling children in the muddy water, sprinkling holy water on old ladies, and reciting Hung's favorite sermon: God's Words for Exhorting the Age. He ended each sermon with a song composed by Hung himself:

> Wielding a sword three feet long,
> to conquer mountains and rivers strong,
> All monsters and devils we will capture
> and cast into hell.
> People united, land consolidated,
> the sun and moon sing our triumph.
> The tigers howl, the dragons snarl,
> peace rules, endless happiness reigns.

After Run-kan had been made prime minister and foreign minister, he decided that the war must be won at any cost. He immediately instituted some reform programs and made plans to build railroads and steamboats. He started fire and life insurance companies and newspapers. He allowed missionaries to travel, to live and preach anywhere they desired. He recruited scholars to write the Ten Commandments and the Sermon on the Mount on rice paper and had them pasted on all the gates in Nanking.

Soon he discovered a serious problem. The Imperial forces laying siege to Nanking had grown to fifty-thousand-strong, including the Hunan braves. The city only had a garrison of thirty thousand and there was not enough gunpowder. The Heavenly Emperor had no solution, but kept an air of unconcern outwardly, while in private he prayed, placing his fate in God's hands. Luckily, Prince Faithful was an able commander in chief. He battled the Hunan braves successfully and held them at bay. As for the other Imperial troops, he ignored them, for they still shelled Nanking out of range, wasting their gunpowder.

One night, Run-kan called a strategy meeting in the Heavenly Emperor's palace, with Hung presiding. Participating in the discussion were the garrison generals and the top-ranking princes. Poring over a large map, they devised a plan. Hung, the chief planner, used his red ink and drew over the map a head of a lion, tracing the borders of the three strategic provinces, Kiangsu, Chekiang, and Anhui. The beast looked out to sea on the east. Shanghai was its mouth and Nanking one of the ears. At its throat stood Hangchow, the provincial capital of Chekiang.

The plan was to send troops from Wuhu, the beast's other ear, straight down to Hangchow, across the neck, and cut the beast's head off. Since the important trading ports were in the head, the head-cutting strategy would cut the sources of the Imperialists' foreign arms.

All the generals praised the plan and Prince Faithful accepted it as his duty to carry out. He plunged to work. In two weeks he executed the plan with swift precision and threw the Manchu generals into panic. As a result, the siege of Nanking was lifted. Faithful pursued the defeated army and took most of the towns on the way. Unlike other Taiping generals, he adopted a lenient policy toward his enemies, helping the injured and offering traveling expenses to those who desired to return home. He issued strict orders forbidding massacres, allowing farmers to work on their farms, and had decapitated anyone who took farm products without paying.

In Nanking, the Heavenly Emperor gave a banquet celebrating the lifting of the siege and the cutting off of the lion's head, where the Taipings had once again established themselves.

Run-kan decided that he could do more good for the Taipings as a roving ambassador, winning foreign friends for the kingdom. Hung agreed, and wrote a personal invitation to any foreigner Run-kan wanted to invite for a state visit.

"Do you think foreigners like Chinese food?" he asked the day before Run-kan was to depart through one of the secret tunnels.

"Yes," Run-kan said, "but they don't like dirty fingers in their soup."

Hung composed a personal invitation. It read:

Foreign brethren of the Western Ocean, join the Father and Elder Brother and Second Son of the Christian faith. Together we shall extinguish the demons and the reptiles.

From the memorials of the Taiping Officials, we have learned of many Western brethrens' intentions to come to the Heavenly Capital. Come, brethren. We shall welcome you with the utmost courtesy.

He gave the hand-written invitation to Run-kan, who was to have it printed and distributed to worthy foreign friends. At parting, Hung said, "Tell them we don't have delicacies from high mountains and deep seas, but four dishes and a soup will be prepared by the best cooks and served by servants whose fingernails are clean and thumbs not in the soup."

| 48 |

Charles George Gordon was back from a meeting with General Ching in the latter's headquarters. He was in an irritable mood; he wished he could really see into people's minds, as rumors said he could. He could never penetrate General Ching's mind. Except on rare occasions, he always met a smiling face, nodding agreeably with protruding teeth fully exposed. But what was behind that long narrow face? He never knew.

His cabin was tidy and clean, meticulously kept by his two attendants. Lieutenant Mah came in with a dispatch. Gordon sank into his chair quickly. He did not want to stagger, knowing well that the dispatch would bring bad news. He had had nothing but bad news lately.

"From General Stavely's headquarters," Mah said.

It was Mr. Wade's report. Gordon read it carefully, hoping to find some vital information from the spy whom his brother-in-law had sent to Nanking. It read:

> The trip was quite muddy crossing the plains since a storm had caused the Yangtze to overflow. With the help of a Taiping official I borrowed a skinny water buffalo from a farmer and rode through a secret tunnel that led into the city, which, I determined, is as large as London and Paris combined. It is extremely hard to gain entrance since six out of thirteen gates are bricked up. But I did it, using all the ingenuity at my command. Along the way I saw many ruins, especially the Porcelain Pagoda. A shame! For that was one of the magnificent treasures of Nanking.
>
> I was received by the Faithful Prince, a rather good-looking fellow in a princely robe of several colors, similar to those I saw in Chinese operas. He also wore a tall Ming headdress

embroidered with dragons, which looked so foolish that I call it a fool's cap.

He was rather cautious. I squeezed hard but he kept talking about our common religion and emphasized the point repeatedly that we were all brothers of one family. I asked what had happened to Yang, their East Prince and commander in chief. He said that God had called him back to Heaven, which could mean that he had died. I asked him about the city's defenses and the strength of his army. He just smiled. It was, I assume, a sign of confidence. I guess that he probably has a garrison numbering several hundreds of thousands. I heard that the Taipings had four large armies outside Nanking, but I do not believe they are much of a threat to General Gordon, for a third of the Taipings are opium addicts. Besides, their food is always short. They loot and steal despite their fervent belief in God's gospels. They repeat grace before a meal without understanding a word of it. They make wars like Jews and still behave like Chinamen, walking chop chop with their hands hidden in their sleeves, their faces expressionless and inscrutable . . ."

At this point, Gordon gave up. "A bag of wind," he said, tossing the lengthy report onto his desk in disgust. "I can get more information right here in Shanghai."

Indeed there was much talk about the Taipings. Everybody was discussing the Heavenly Emperor in the foreigners' concession. Some called him the "coolie king" and described his way of life as "high life below stairs." Some foreigners even declared that they had seen pictures of the dead East Prince when he was a "tea porter." Others retorted that many of Christ's disciples were simple fishermen of Galilee. They defended the Taipings and disliked the idea of abandoning neutrality. Wandering among the foreigners, Gordon listened to the arguments pro and con, and discovered that Shanghai's prosperity had been mainly due to the increase of trade in the Taiping territories.

Refugees were flocking into Shanghai. Gordon found that the original population of three hundred thousand had swollen to more than a million. The frightened people were sure that the Taipings would arrive any day. Old English-language papers became popular items in the markets. People who had bought them to wrap up fish in the past, now paid high prices for them to paste on their front doors, believing that a foreigner's paper would give them protection. The *London Illustrated News*, being the most popular, was posted everywhere. Some families even hung out yellow flags, a Taiping color, thinking that when the Taipings arrived they would protect their own. But the Imperial troops dragged them out of their homes and decapitated them until Gordon begged Ching to put a stop to this slaughter of innocent people. Ching smiled and nodded but the slaughter went on.

Gordon marched to Li Hung-chang's office and demanded a retraction of Ching's order. Li pulled at his thin beard, listened to Gordon's complaint patiently, but made no decision on what to do. Gordon had no patience with the Chinese official's foot dragging. Forgetting his politeness, he stood up, lay his two hands on Li's desk, and thrust his head forward. "Governor," he said, "the yellow flags have to be ignored. Killing innocent people as suspects must be stopped!"

Li stared at him, as if surprised by such a strong statement. "How can you be sure they are innocent? They fly enemy flags."

"They are not enemy flags . . . just a square foot of yellow cloth. They fly them for protection, Governor."

Gordon found his voice rising. He quickly softened it and went on, "They believe the Taipings are coming. Some even believe they have already infiltrated the city."

"Then there is the more reason to kill a few chickens to warn the monkeys."

"Governor," Gordon said patiently, trying to keep his voice down, "we need the people's support. Shanghai is an arsenal that both sides need. It is the main trading port for British guns and ammunition. Without it, no side can survive, and without the people's support no side can defend its positions. Killing innocent people is no way to win the people's support. It is as simple as that."

He watched Li as he talked and saw Li's face remain blank. Knowing that what he had said had gone in one of Li's ears and out the other, he decided to use his most effective weapon. Sure enough, before he finished the threat to present his resignation, the governor smiled and said, "Certainly, General Gordon. The yellow flags will be ignored. Tell General Ching it is my order."

Word of the yellow-flag episode spread quickly, even reaching the Taiping territories. Some families in Shanghai burned a few sticks of incense for General Gordon in gratitude. Gordon grimaced when he heard about it, but thought it was important that he had built some goodwill on both sides. His idea of ending the war was still through peaceful means.

In the foreign concession in Shanghai Gordon found two factions of foreigners: the Long Hair haters and the sympathizers. The former thought that their privileges and extraterritorial rights in China would be threatened if the Long Hairs brought down the Manchu Government, with which Britain and France had signed several unfair treaties; the sympathizers were mainly influenced by two articles published in two popular magazines at the service club in the British concession.

One was by the Reverend Mr. Issachar Roberts, who had formerly claimed that the Taipings were a bunch of "contraband Christians." But after visiting Nanking, he had changed his mind again. In an article in *China Mail* he said that the Imperial troops burned churches while the Taipings prayed in them. He had met The Faithful Prince and had been impressed. Surrounded by aborigine bodyguards, the prince wore a crown of real gold, not a "pasteboard crown" as most of the Europeans believed. And he wore his dragon-embroidered yellow robe with dignity. He seemed genuinely kind and courteous, and expressed a strong desire for peaceful relations with the foreigners. In concluding his article, Roberts editorialized:

> It is a great pity that two worlds which worship the same great God—the Western Powers and the Heavenly Kingdom—cannot live together. Britain should reconsider its present erroneous policy of helping a Godless government quash a Christian nation.

Another article, published in the *London Illustrated News*, told the story of the Reverend Mr. Joseph Edkins, an elderly widower who had taken a young second wife, Jane, to live in the Heavenly Capital. She was a lady of thirty years, from the Orkney Islands, pretty, gentle, with large dark eyes. She was devoted to both God and her husband, but her health was failing. Even in sickness she assured her husband that all was well. Always smiling, she gallantly helped the Reverend Mr. Edkins spread the word of God. Whenever her husband delivered sermons in the streets of Nanking, she was there playing the hand organ, her frail body shaking with fever. She heard duty call and she could not say no. When her sickness became worse, she lay in her bed and listened to the distant guns. Through the noise, she tossed, lamenting the death and destruction, feeling helpless.

Fearing for her life, Mr. Edkins took her out of Nanking. On their way to Hong Kong, she died in his arms. Her final words were, "Darling, after you have buried me, please go back to Heavenly Kingdom of Great Peace. They need you . . ."

Gordon noticed in the service club that many readers of the article wiped their eyes when they finished. He was sure that the article had turned many Long Hair haters into sympathizers.

While preparing for the defense of Shanghai, Li Hung-chang urged General Stavely to send another spokesman, Harry Parks, to Nanking to extract a promise from the Heavenly Emperor not to attack Shanghai. Meanwhile, Li was meeting Lindley in Shanghai, negotiating a large shipment of arms for the Imperial Army. Harry Parks returned empty-handed. He reported that the Heavenly Emperor had refused because he had received a vision forbidding him to grant such a promise.

"This Heavenly Emperor is not a fool," Gordon told General Stavely as they accelerated the building of Shanghai's defenses. The general agreed.

The building of defenses in Shanghai became feverish. Gordon learned that Prince Faithful had sent one of his most trusted generals, Four-Eyed Dog, to invade Shanghai. It was rumored that Four-Eyed Dog's two bulging eyes equaled four, two in front and two behind his head.

Gordon did not want to bring the war to Shanghai. To defend it, he decided to attack Suchow, the Taipings' headquarters in Kiangsu Province. He summoned and addressed his officers, some of whom were still desperadoes and fortune hunters at heart, but who respected a superior who was always fearless in battle. Waving his cane and braving bullets, Gordon had never failed to impress his men. Sometimes he held a Bible in the other hand while talking or directing skirmishes; it made many of his European officers believe that God was indeed with him, for somehow stray bullets always flew past and hit someone behind him. Quite a few times such incidents had turned sinners into God-fearing men, thereby improving discipline in the Ever-Victorious Army.

"Tomorrow I want you to recapture Chan Su without bloodshed," he told them. "Follow me and obey my orders. God will be with you."

The next day they recaptured Chan Su, a small town on the estuary of the Yangtze, almost without bloodshed, for Gordon had reconnoitered the town's defenses and put the right number of men and effort into the job. He weakened the stronghold with a bombardment, then scaled the wall with ease.

His next target was Taitsan, a short distance from Shanghai. He moved in with his gunboats and cargo vessels, four thousand men, and his flagship, Tyson. First, he used a steamship to drag up the stakes the Taipings had planted as obstructions in the main channel, then he battered down the low bridges with guns. Within two days, the Ever-Victorious Army captured all the defensive stockades.

Gordon never boasted about his simple strategy. Instead he attributed his successes to God. When the Taipings heard about how God had helped this foreigner, they began to wonder about their own God.

Soon after he had captured Taitsan, he set out to take the neighboring town of Quinsan. General Ching, who had followed him with his Imperial Army, now joined him. Wanting to share some of the glory, the general suggested a head-on assault, the only type of fighting he knew, especially since he was bulging with ammunition. But again Gordon vetoed a direct confrontation. He had reconnoitered the area. He did not like the eighteen-pound gun on the city wall nor the lofty hill that rose from the center of the town and the vast number of Taipings defending it. Besides, the purpose of the enemy's occupation of Quinsan, as he had found out, was to defend Suchow, the Taipings' most important stronghold in the province. The link between Quinsan and Suchow was a canal on the west side of the town. He told Ching to ignore Quinsan altogether. General Ching, bewildered and sulky, questioned the wisdom of this foolish strategy.

"How can you get the tiger cubs without going into the tiger's lair?" he asked, quoting an old Chinese saying.

"That is exactly what I mean," Gordon replied. "We are not going to get the cubs, but the daddy tiger and the mama tiger."

Without further ado he steamed westward with his entire flotilla and three thousand men. After a brief shelling, he occupied Chunyi, a small town on the canal, cutting the link between Suchow and Quinsan. He sent four hundred of his own personal guards to pursue the Taipings who were fleeing toward Quinsan while he left five hundred of Ching's men to hold Chunyi. Then, with the rest of his entire force, he set off westward along the canal toward Suchow. The defenders in Quinsan, having heard that the Ever-Victorious Army was on its way, panicked and surrendered to General Ching without a fight.

Gordon, standing at the bow of the Tyson, cane in hand, took firm command of the invasion. Braving wind and stray bullets, he barked orders in his sonorous voice, his curly red hair fluttering and his piercing blue eyes gleaming in the sunlight. To many of his soldiers he was a demigod with magical powers; to a few of his European officers he was a madman. The flagship, carrying six European officers and over five hundred Chinese, steamed steadily along the narrow canal, its thirty-five-pound gun booming and more than a hundred rifles firing.

The Taipings on both canal banks scattered in fright. The foreign ship, tall and slick, with a long stack spitting smoke, made thunderous noises, its whistle letting out an eerie scream that was even more terrifying than its firearms. Many had heard about such foreign ships during the Opium War; a few who had seen one swore that it was paddled by a fire-spitting dragon. The knowledgeable ones said it was propelled by a machine called iron horse. The sight of it began to strike fear into the people who lived along the banks; many of them fled with the defenders, empty-handed.

As soon as the Taipings deserted a fort, Gordon ordered a dozen men to disembark and hold it. After occupying several such forts and taking more than a hundred prisoners, he ordered his troops to halt and turn around. They were so close to Suchow that some of Gordon's officers wondered why he chose to retreat while he was winning. Gordon knew that his European officers were anxious to land, because everyone had heard of the Suchow women, who were delicate and beautiful . . .

more famous than Peking duck in Peking. Anyone who had visited either place and tasted neither would be held up to ridicule. He knew that his "hot pants" officers would risk their lives for a little pleasurable adventure. But an all-out invasion would cost heavily; perhaps he would lose half of his men and ships.

He had never given up his idea of winning the war without much bloodshed. But it would be futile to explain his strategy to the European desperadoes. He simply said to his men that his sixth sense told him to retreat before the enemy blocked the canal behind him. If nothing else, they all believed in his uncanny sixth sense.

On the return trip the big gun continued to boom and the steamer's siren kept screaming. Once again the fire-spitting Tyson struck terror along the canal as it sailed without further encounters.

On reaching Quinsan, he saw his own men and General Ching's troops lined up on the banks outside the city, greeting him with cheers. Many townspeople were also at the city gate to welcome him with gongs and firecrackers. The smiling General Ching boarded the Tyson to offer his congratulations. The general had already won credit for occupying Quinsan without firing a shot. When he saw the hundred-odd prisoners squatting on deck, he gave Gordon an extra handshake, for he could see in his mind's eye many bloody heads hanging on the city wall the next day.

Gordon, through his piercing blue eyes, could also see what the general was thinking. Pacing in front of the dejected prisoners, he asked in broken Chinese if they would like to join the Ever-Victorious Army. The prisoners looked stunned for a moment, then stared at Gordon as though they did not believe their own ears. It was not until Lieutenant Mah had repeated the question in his correct Chinese that the prisoners started knocking their heads on the deck in tearful gratitude. They all clamored to enlist. The shocked General Ching could only gape. When he found his voice he asked Gordon incredulously what he was doing.

"Don't worry, General," Gordon said with a smile. "We believe in the same God. They'll serve me well."

49

Since Golden Rooster's death, Su San-mei had been fighting a depression that had brought back all the sorrow of the old days. Golden Rooster had replaced her own father, making her forget the agony of poverty. He had helped her wash away the shame of her flower-boat days and the loneliness of being deserted by Hung. Above all, he had saved her life and made her live again with meaning and a certain amount of happiness that she had never known before.

Now she was grateful to another man, Prince Faithful, who had given Golden Rooster a decent funeral in Anhui, Golden Rooster's birthplace. He had asked her if she still wanted to serve in the navy. She had met the new navy commander, a man as large as Golden Rooster though not as ugly. But after two weeks, she had asked to resign. Nobody could replace Golden Rooster. She missed his warmth, his kindness, his discipline, his ugliness, his loud laughter. Everytime she saw the new commander sitting in Golden Rooster's old rattan chair, she could not stop tears from filling her eyes.

In Nanking, she was surprised that Prince Faithful did not live a princely life. His palace was modest, with a small courtyard in the eastern city. He was a widower; he did not have a second wife nor concubines. In fact, Prince Faithful did not even have a banner like the ones that flew outside the gates of all the palaces of Nanking's princes.

She found Faithful a good-looking man, medium-size, perhaps even a little shorter than she was. Whenever he was kind and willing to do things for her, she fantasized about another father-daughter relationship; but somehow it did not fit. She was probably older than he. Besides, Faithful was not as relaxed as Golden Rooster had been; he never had time for small talk and he hardly laughed. Regimented like a general, he did everything according to the rules.

He appointed her as a deputy in the women's regiment, which was commanded by Sister Woo, a stout woman about forty who walked in long strides like a man and talked loudly in a slightly cracked voice. The only difference between her and a man was that she had an enormous bosom.

The regiment's headquarters was also in the eastern part of the city, not far from Prince Faithful's palace. It was the farthest from Nanking's waterways and the least threatened by the Hunan braves and the Imperial Army. Su San-mei shared a bungalow with the commander, Sister Woo. As her deputy, she also shared a sparsely furnished office in a two-story building. There was a large empty lot behind the building, but half of it had been cultivated as a vegetable garden, with cabbages and spinach growing in rows in dry dirt, looking limp and undernourished. Sister Woo said that the lot used to be a military drill field, but since the women's division had been reduced to a regiment, more than half of the women had been discharged. Only those unattached ones—singles and widows—were left behind to carry on the soldiers' work. Sister Woo predicted that the regiment would soon disappear, too, if Prince Faithful had his way; the prince believed that women had been designed to do different jobs, and fighting was not one of them.

"He comes here quite often," she added with a laugh. "Probably looking around for a woman who can do the job that only a woman can do—give him babies."

Indeed, Prince Faithful, busy as he was, often showed up at the regiment's headquarters unexpectedly. He never preached the gospels of God. He called brief meetings and gave certain orders pertaining to the defense of Nanking. "It is the women's regiment's duty to keep watch on the eastern city gate," he repeated at every meeting, his eyes always scanning the room where the women officers had gathered to hear him. Su San-mei could not help remembering what Sister Woo had said about the prince's purpose for holding such meetings—to pick a wife.

One morning, after a brief meeting, Faithful took Su San-mei aside and told her that Heavenly Emperor wanted to see her. She had never expected that Hung would want to see her again. The gap between them was like earth and sun. In fact, she had been convinced that he had long forgotten her. Now that Faithful had mentioned Hung, the disturbing memories stirred, like a dead body raising its head. But she felt a desire to find out how he was ... what he looked like.

"How does he know I am in Nanking?" she asked.

"He is the emperor," Faithful said. "He has eyes and ears all over the city. Certainly he knows who the new deputy commander of the women's regiment is."

She had no idea how awesome Hung's palace was. It was closest to all the waterways, guarded by dozens of Taiping bannermen in yellow uniforms and red turbans who held traditional weapons—long handled swords and spears. Large square yellow flags stood beside the main entrance, fluttering in the breeze. Two huge marble lion dogs guarded the entrance with angry bulging eyes. It reminded her of the Forbidden City in Peking, which she had seen in picture books.

Inside the gate was a large courtyard surrounded by massive palatial buildings with carved beams, gleaming red columns, and white marble steps. Between the buildings she caught glimpses of a beautiful garden in the back, with moon doors, miniature mountains, waterfalls, pagodas, and pavilions peeking from behind bamboo clusters and twisted pines. A lady-in-waiting, dressed in a flowing silk gown of the Ming period, took her to the receiving hall in the main building. While passing a door, she also caught a glimpse of the enormous audience hall and the golden throne. The receiving hall, half the size of the audience hall, was furnished with dozens of straight-backed teakwood chairs that had embroidered yellow cushions. In the back was a large chair draped in yellow silk, placed on a carpeted dais, flanked by banners and pots of chrysanthemums. Hanging on the wall behind the silk-draped chair was a large portrait of Jesus Christ nailed on a cross. The room was full of rose-scented air.

Half a dozen young ladies, similarly dressed, rose from chairs as Su San-mei entered. They bowed as she was conducted to a chair beside the large one. She awkwardly took the chair and asked the ladies to sit down, wondering who they were. No one looked familiar; they could not be Hung's relatives. The lady-in-waiting bowed and withdrew. Presently another lady came into the room ... an older woman who was more elaborately dressed and looked vaguely familiar. She approached Su San-mei with quick little steps, smiling.

"You look as young as ever, Su San-mei," she said, taking the chair on the other side of the large chair.

Su San-mei bowed and sat down. She remembered who the woman was—Hung's wife. She had not aged much; her face was still smooth and her smile sweet. Su San-mei had met her a few times in Happy Valley many years ago—a gentle woman who had never said a harsh word to her, even though it was an open secret that she had been Hung's first love. She smiled back, feeling somewhat awkward. She did not know how to talk to an empress.

"When Heavenly Emperor told me that you had agreed to see him, I was excited," the empress said. "It was a pleasant surprise when he saw your name on the new officers' roster. All these years you had been serving in the navy, but we did not know. I am happy that we meet again."

"I am happy, too," Su San-mei said with a nervous little laugh.

Just as Su San-mei began to feel a little relaxed, a lady-in-waiting announced, "The Heavenly Emperor."

All the ladies rose from their chairs and knelt down. Su San-mei knelt after a moment's hesitation. Hung mounted the dais. Their eyes met. He looked much older, his hair graying at the temples and his forehead marked with a few deep lines. With his neat beard and straight posture, he still looked handsome. He had shed his scholarly stoop, which she had always hated, but his usual bright eyes were now clouded with red spots and he had put on considerable weight, sporting a large paunch that befitted an emperor.

"Su San-mei," he said, his voice trembling slightly, "how wonderful to see you again!" He made an attempt to touch her, but remembering that they were not alone, he stopped. "Get up, get up, all of you."

The ladies all rose and resumed their seats. Hung introduced them. They were all his concubines. "You don't have to introduce me," his wife said. "We know each other quite well."

Hung laughed. He took his seat in the draped chair and coughed. Su San-mei could tell that it was a cough of authority, a habit of government officials and rich people. She was disappointed that Hung should have adopted a habit that he used to despise.

"I have studied your service in the navy," he said with a smile. "You served well. How did you happen to join?"

Su San-mei found Hung's voice still the same, sincere and warm, and his smile genuine, except that his teeth seemed longer and not as sparkling. She relaxed and told him about how Golden Rooster had adopted her and how they had transported merchandise for the foreigners. She deleted the part about her attempted suicide. He listened intently. When she finished, he said, his voice tinged with sadness, "You may have heard of the attempted coups during the past year. I don't worry about my own life, but my family must be protected, especially the women. You have a good military background, trained in both traditional and Western weapons. I have always wanted to recruit a military lady-in-waiting who is capable of protecting the empress and the concubines. I want you to fill the post and move into the palace."

She had no great desire to move into his palace. She was accustomed to a relaxed life, unpretentious, where she could speak and laugh freely. But she was curious about Hung's life. His wife seemed happy, the concubines all looked fresh and bright-eyed, even though they were quiet and submissive. The restricted palace life could not be too bad. Before she answered, Hung rose from his chair.

"Think about it," he said with a smile and left. Obviously he was a very busy man.

Su San-mei found life in the palace a shocking contrast to that of the ordinary people in Nanking and a far cry from what she and Hung had gone through during those hard years in Kwangtung. Each of his concubines had her own personal maids and enjoyed her own whims in food and clothing.

A room was assigned to her in the concubines' quarters in the east wing, next door to Little Phoenix, a pretty young woman with large feet, coarse hands, and a Kwangsi accent. Su San-mei knew that she was an aborigine girl from Kwangsi. Little Phoenix loaned her some silk clothing and the two chatted almost all night.

She learned from Little Phoenix that Hung used to have twelve concubines and numerous ladies-in-waiting, who were actually secondary concubines. He used to sleep with a different woman every night. But since the two attempted coups, his life had changed. The concubines hardly saw him anymore. For almost six months now they had waited for his invitation to a night of "cloud and rain."

Knowing that "cloud and rain" was a refined term for sex, Su San-mei asked, "How about his wife? Doesn't he see her, either?"

"No, the empress has not slept with him for two years. She does not mind, since she has already produced an heir. The young prince is almost a grown-up man now.

Little Phoenix was quite chatty. She said that the king's sex life was an open book, for a public invitation must be extended to the chosen one for the night; it was like a ritual. He had dismissed all the jealous ones, who had fought over him like ordinary women, yelling and tearing each other's hair out.

"You are not jealous anymore?" Su San-mei asked, finding that her own jealousy began to disturb her.

"I am sure that many of us are," Little Phoenix said with a smile. "But what can we do? We cannot just march to his bedroom and demand "cloud and rain." We must wait for our turn. Now that the turn never seems to come, we have become resigned to it."

For almost a week, Su San-mei did not see Hung again. She and the six concubines shared the maids and the food; they enjoyed chatting, playing chess and musical instruments together. Su San-mei suspected that some of them must have been high-class singsong girls, who could compose poems and play the pipa and the flute. When there were no maids or ladies-in-waiting present, they talked freely, joking about high government officials and making faces. They all seemed incensed about injustice, quoting the old saying, "The high official is permitted to set a fire but the common people are not allowed to light a lamp."

One night an invitation for "cloud and rain" arrived. A lady-in-waiting brought it into the dining hall just as dinner was being served. Everybody dropped her chopsticks and waited anxiously for the chosen one's name to be announced. The lady-in-waiting opened a red envelope and read the name, "Su San-mei."

Su San-mei accepted the invitation reluctantly. She had mixed feelings about such a visit. It was almost no different from accepting a flower-boat customer. The same lady-in-waiting conducted her through a foyer and several porticoes decorated with Hung's own calligraphy on couplet scrolls. Every room was full of scented air like a rose garden, Hung's favorite fragrance, and there were exotic flowers in large porcelain pots with delicate Ming designs, artistically placed here and there.

Hung's bedroom was smaller than she had expected. She relaxed, for she had dreaded a big dark room, cold and impersonal. It was a relief that the small bedroom was intimate and warm, with a large bed covered by a brocade spread. The yellow canopy made the bed look like an open hearse. In all her life she had never experienced great "cloud and rain"; only in fantasies had she discovered that she was capable of great passion. She knew that with the right man, the right atmosphere, and the right amount of stimulation she would reach *Wu Shan*, the mysterious mountain that all lovemaking couples hoped to attain. Hung had always done the right things. His tenderness, loving whispers, and light touches had made her shiver with tingling pleasure. But that was only in her dreams.

Hung was waiting for her in a yellow silk robe. He asked her to sit in a similar chair beside him. The arrangement seemed to indicate that the room served only one purpose—to perform "cloud and rain."

The lady-in-waiting took away the brocade cover from the bed. She fluffed the two pillows and smoothed the sheet. Then she laid some towels on a lamp stand. With a deep bow, she withdrew, a little mischievous smile on her heavily powdered face. Su San-mei felt uncomfortable again, wishing that the lady-in-waiting had stayed a little longer. Hung took her hand. She looked up and their eyes met again. Hung swallowed hard a few times.

"Take off your clothes," he said, almost like an order given by a nervous man.

Su San-mei hesitated. After he had repeated the order a few more times, she obeyed. As she was undressing herself, Hung sat in his chair watching, swallowing and cracking his knuckles, his face expressionless. He ordered her to lie on the bed with her feet stretched a few inches outside of the edge. She did so and stared at the canopy, feeling nervous and self-conscious about her nude body. She was disappointed that the trip to *Wu Shan* had had a wrong start. She closed her eyes and waited.

Presently, she heard Hung rise from his chair and approach the bed. When she felt him touching her feet, she opened her eyes a small crack. Hung was licking one of her toes, like a dog licking a bone, groaning and humming. When he climbed on top of her she received another shock—he was impotent. After several frantic attempts to penetrate her, he gave up. Crawling around in the bed, he demanded different poses and pecked her flesh like a rooster pecking on grain. Finally he wound up the encounter with a long session of oral sex that she had never before experienced, even during her flower-boat days. With a slight nausea, she left his bed at dawn, determined to find an excuse to move out of the palace as soon as possible.

| 50 |

Gordon tried to explain his philosophy to those involved in the civil war, but it always went in one ear and came out the other. General Ching, his own European officers ... even some of his own soldiers did not seem to understand why in a fight it was best to aim at the head.

"Always try to get the general instead of trying to kill a lot of soldiers," he said to Lieutenant Mah. "When the head is gone, the arms and feet all become useless. Simple as that! Why can't those blockheads understand that?"

"Sir," Mah said, "those blockheads may think differently. A hand may have a gold ring, a foot may have a few diamonds hidden in the boot. A head has nothing but a few fleas hidden in the hair. They are not stupid, sir. They have a different philosophy. Do you really want to get to the head and save lives in this war?"

"Isn't that what I've always been preaching?"

"Sir, if you want to fight this war without looting and bloodshed, there is only one way."

"What is that?"

"Try to conduct a secret talk with some of the enemy generals. Try to turn them into ... what do you call it ... turncoats?"

"How?"

"Well, there is always a way. Some of the Taiping princes and generals are not always happy."

"Find out. We'll do it!"

"But don't ever let General Ching know about this, sir, or you may find my head dangling on the city gate. To him, conducting secret talks with an enemy is treason."

"I know," Gordon said, frowning. "It's a bloody nuisance to find him always so one-track-minded. Tell me, who is the right Taiping head to talk to?"

"Prince Mo in Suchow," Mah said. "He's the commander in chief in Chekiang and Kiangsu Provinces, with orders to take Shanghai. If he surrenders, we'll win a bloodless war, as you wish."

Gordon clapped a hand on Mah's shoulder and said, "Mah, I was told that the Taiping Rebellion had already shed enough blood to fill the Yangtze River. If we allow this war to continue, we'll probably shed enough blood to fill the Yellow River, too. Do anything to end this bloodshed, Mah. If anyone hangs your head on the city gate, I'll demand that he put mine up there, too!"

Mah smiled. "In that case, I'll be two hundred percent safe. Actually, your threat of resignation is enough to guarantee that my head will never leave my neck. Give me a week, sir. The newly arrived Four-Eyed Dog is a bone in the throat. Otherwise three days would be enough to find out if Prince Mo will take the bait."

Gordon frowned. He had heard a great deal about this Four-Eyed Dog. He wanted to know why he was so feared.

"Like General Ching, he's one-track-minded," Mah said, his voice tinged with admiration. "He declared long ago that he will be buried in his gaudy Taiping uniform. Dogs are never stubborn, but this one is. Maybe because he has four eyes." He laughed.

Gordon made several excursions to Suchow, firing about fifty rounds at the city each time. It was not to inflict casualties but to deliver blows to the city wall, exhibiting his gun's firepower and striking fear into the defenders. The Suchow garrison seemed intimidated enough not to return fire. Every sign indicated that the Taipings in Suchow were tired and in trouble.

This was what Gordon had expected and he had timed his move correctly. Lieutenant Mah went to work. Gordon trusted him and did not ask how he was going to do it. In two weeks Mah brought him news. The Taipings wanted to talk. "We've had a preliminary meeting," he said. "In a week we'll hear from them again. By the way, sir, General Ching said the government is going to negotiate a large shipment of arms with Mr. Lindley in Shanghai. He asks you if you have a shopping list."

"Who is this Mr. Lindley?" Gordon asked.

"The biggest arms dealer in China," Mah said. "Do you want to meet him?"

"Why should I?" Gordon said. "I'll just pass him a list of what we need."

"Personal contact has its advantages, sir," Mah said. "This foreigner is a hard bargainer. Knowing his weaknesses you can get a better deal."

"That's not my concern. By the way, what weaknesses?"

Mah was familiar with Lindley's background. "He's an artillery instructor and supplier of guns and victuals. He always wants people to address him as Mister. His fetish is Chinese women's small bound lily feet, which can be cupped in one hand. That's his weakness," Mah concluded with a smile.

"I have no objection to calling him Mister," Gordon barked. "But how in bloody hell can I provide him with Chinese women's lily feet that can be cupped in one hand?"

"That's where the go-between comes in, sir," Mah said. "I know of a man who knows him . . ."

"Forget it," Gordon cut him short. "I'm not a pimp!"

"This gentleman is quite useful, sir."

"Who? Mr. Lindley or the man who knows him?"

"The man who knows him. He has been supplying everything that a foreigner desires in China. He can get just about anything—tall, short, fat, or thin . . ."

Gordon's glare stopped him. "I don't want anything tall, short, fat, or thin," he barked. "I want to meet that bloody prince in Suchow!"

To induce an enemy to surrender, Gordon knew that he must first create fear of total destruction in the enemy's mind. He spent a week completing an encirclement of Suchow, the chief rebel stronghold. It was a beautiful city, and he prayed that he would not have to destroy it. From the Tyson he could see through his field glasses the city's gray walls and turrets, above which shimmering pagodas and green palace roofs peered from lush clusters of ash and pine. His encirclement, he suspected, brought a faster response from the Taiping prince, who agreed to meet him on a designated junk provided by a supposedly neutral party . . . a fisherman.

The junk, shabby but spacious, was anchored a few miles off Suchow. When Gordon and Lieutenant Mah arrived, five Taiping princes were already there waiting: Prince Mo; Prince La, the second in command; Prince Su, Prince Tung, and Prince Hong. Gordon was disappointed that the famous General Four-Eyed Dog was not present. They greeted each other with cold politeness in the main cabin, in which bamboo chairs had been placed. A pot of hot tea stood on a bench in the center of the room. No meeting was ever held without tea in China. Immediately after introductions had been completed, Lieutenant Mah filled seven cups with tea. While sipping, Prince Mo laid out his only condition for surrender: the lives of the princes and generals in Suchow must be spared and the troops treated with leniency. He demanded a guarantee from Gordon before he would hand over the city.

Gordon listened to the roly-poly prince's demands and wondered how he was to guarantee them. General Ching seemed to enjoy massacring his enemies, especially Taiping chieftains, whose heads were his trophies. Knowing that he could not take Suchow peacefully without such a guarantee, he consented and signed his name on a document produced by Prince Mo. The prince passed the document to the others, who examined the strange signature and grunted their approval. While putting the piece of paper into an inner pocket of his yellow silk robe, Prince Mo smiled for the first time and extended his pudgy hand.

"Good, good," he said in his heavily accented English. "We give you Suchow. God bless!"

Gordon and his four thousand men entered the city the next day. He gave strict orders that they march in formation and that looting was punishable by instant death. He personally would shoot any looter. The city was quiet but full of grim-faced rebel soldiers in their colorful uniforms. The shops were closed. Most people stayed home for fear of a massacre; an invasion without a massacre seemed to them a funeral without a coffin. Lieutenant Mah had spread the word that there would be no bloodshed, but nobody seemed to believe him. The Taiping soldiers began to smile after they saw that there were no executions and no gunshots. By the end of the day, all the rebel soldiers had laid down their various weapons. Some even expressed their desire to join the Ever-Victorious Army.

Meanwhile, Gordon informed General Ching of the peaceful capture of Suchow. In the evening, he and Mah rode to the palace of Prince

Mo to see how things were going. The modest palace was full of Taiping high-ranking officers who seemed to be in good spirits. A few were drinking and playing the finger-guessing game. They told Mah that they were satisfied with the peace terms, and with thumbs up they all smiled at Gordon and said, "*Ding hao, ding hao.*"

General Ching, having received Gordon's dispatch, immediately passed the information to his superior, Li Hung-chang. Li wholeheartedly agreed to the peace negotiations, but he demanded that a formal surrender agreement be signed by the Taiping princes. Gordon was irritated by such unnecessary red tape. However, he managed to assemble the Taiping princes and generals within a few hours. At General Ching's headquarters, the Taiping chiefs, commanding a total of one hundred thousand men, signed the agreement without protest. Gordon insisted that the lives of the eight princes and generals be spared and all their troops be treated with leniency. General Ching readily agreed, nodding and smiling.

On the following day, more Taiping troops abandoned the rebel cause—except Four-Eyed Dog, who escaped with his twenty thousand troops immediately after the surrender agreement was signed. General Ching made an attempt to pursue him but changed his mind; instead he declared that the Taipings had negotiated in bad faith and made the surrendered princes responsible.

Gordon, fearing treachery, toured the city to prevent executions. He first went to Prince La's palace, which Four-Eyed Dog had shared as his headquarters. He was too late. Lying in the hall in a pool of blood were three headless corpses. The palace was in shambles. Three princes had been murdered and their heads hoisted over the door. After ordering the bodies buried, Gordon charged into General Ching's temporary headquarters in Suchow, his temples throbbing.

General Ching was having his evening meal when Gordon arrived, the gloomy dining hall choking with garlic and hot pepper smell. The general invited Gordon to share his favorite dish—Suchow fish heads. Gordon declined and angrily demanded to know why three princes had been executed.

"It was an oversight," the general said amiably with his perpetual smile. "The peace treaty will be honored."

"Honored! You have already violated it!" Gordon shouted.

"They have violated it, too," the general said. "One of them escaped, did he not?"

"Four-Eyed Dog did not sign the treaty. He never agreed to sign it. How can you blame the others for his escape?"

General Ching stopped smiling momentarily. With a deep sigh, he said in a voice that resembled a disappointed school teacher speaking to an incorrigible pupil, "We have a saying in China, 'All crows are black.' There are still several millions of crows out there. To kill a few chickens to warn the monkeys is the only way . . ."

Gordon decided that argument would not bring back the lives of the dead princes. He might as well save his breath. Without waiting for General Ching to finish quoting old Chinese sayings, he stalked out. While passing the door, he heard the general call after him, "General Gordon, go back to your boat and relax. Enjoy a good victory meal!"

Back on the Tyson, Gordon tried to relax. He brewed a pot of coffee over an oil lamp. Realizing that he had not eaten all day, he took out a loaf of bread from his tin bread box and broke a chunk from it. The bread smelled mildewed but he did not mind. After dunking it in coffee, he would not be able to tell the difference.

As he was eating, he fumed, thinking of General Ching's victory meal—of his Suchow fish heads. He had done nothing to win the battles except chop heads off of those who had already surrendered. He did not know what to think of him—a clown or an animal?

He had just finished his own victory dinner of coffee and stale bread when he heard gunshots. He took down a pair of field glasses from the wall and rushed out of the cabin. As he looked through the binoculars, he saw a large force of Imperial troops rushing into the city yelling and firing muskets. It was late in the evening; the surrender should have been concluded, enemy arms collected, and names registered according to the surrender terms. He wondered what was going on. Could it be a sort of victory celebration?

Mah was also looking through a pair of binoculars. "It couldn't be a celebration," he said. "The soldiers are shouting 'Sha, sha, sha!' That means 'Kill, kill, kill!' "

More soldiers were pouring into the city, yelling and firing. Soon billows of smoke rose, followed by flames licking the evening sky. Gordon grabbed his cane, leapt ashore, mounted his stallion, and galloped back to the city. Mah followed on his horse.

Suchow was in chaos. Imperial soldiers were running, yelling, "Sha, sha, sha!" Houses were burning and Taipings were fleeing in panic. On the streets Gordon saw numerous corpses lying in pools of blood. They were all Taipings. He galloped to the palace of Prince Mo. As he had feared, he saw the prince's head hanging over the gate and the palace was burning.

He turned and barked at Mah, "Take me to Prince Su's palace!"

He followed Mah, galloping through many deserted narrow streets until they reached another burning palace. The prince and his whole family had been slaughtered, their heads all dangling over the gate— the prince's wife, his parents, and his three adolescent children, a girl and two boys. Gorden stared at the burning building and the bloody heads for a moment, his eyes glaring and his face red with anger. Without a word he galloped back to his boat.

Gordon confined himself to the Tyson and raged for three days. Finally, following Lieutenant Mah's advice, he abandoned his plan to assassinate General Ching. He submitted his resignation. In no uncertain terms he accused Li and Ching of involving his personal honor in their own treachery. All his peace efforts had been wasted and now the war would rage on indefinitely. He washed his hands of the whole affair and returned to Shanghai.

| 51 |

Mr. Lindley went to see his old friend, Run-kan, in Nanking. The arms business was booming since the Taipings and the Imperial Army had increased their seesaw fighting everywhere. The shelling of Nanking was a good sign, especially since most of the cannonballs fell short of their targets. He had learned that the Taipings were hunting for bargains.

Soon after his arrival, he was disappointed to find that Run-kan had gone back to Hong Kong. But another old friend was there to receive him. He and the Reverend Mr. David Brown had known each other since the Opium War, when he was selling British machine-made fabrics and Brown was robbing British opium boats with Golden Rooster. Since there was no conflict of interest in their respective businesses, they had met quite often to drink and talk. Brown knew Lindley's tastes in food and women. He often acted as Lindley's guide and scout. In Hong Kong and Canton he had recruited a few pimps who knew where to find singsong girls with the smallest bound lily feet. Usually such women were high class; their services came with certain requirements, such as tea ceremony, playing musical instruments, and composing poems, with their final service being "cloud and rain." But Lindley would have none of that; and it usually took quite a bit of talking before a girl and her turtle lady agreed to sell the final services without the preliminaries. To Lindley, Brown was a necessary liaison if he wanted to indulge in a bit of pleasure in this peculiar Chinese society.

David Brown was glad to see him. He received him warmly at his church in the eastern part of Nanking, not too far from the Heavenly Emperor's palace. The church was a converted rice barn, but through the years Brown had decorated it the best he could and made it a respectable place of worship. It had a pulpit with a large portrait of Jesus Christ hanging in the back. Specially made benches with low backs filled the hall, enough for a large congregation of five hundred at one sitting. Every Sunday he conducted services in four seatings, two in the morning and two in the afternoon. In the evening, his Bible class also filled the hall.

In the back, he furnished his living quarters with Western sofas and chairs. He loved everything in China except the Chinese furniture, which gave him backaches and was hard on the behind. He had two guest rooms and had played host to quite a few Americans and Europeans. The most recent guest was Burgevine, who had expressed interest in organizing a Taiping Ever-Victorious Army. He had requested that Brown put in a few good words for him with the Heavenly Emperor. Hung was interested and had referred the matter to the commander in chief, Prince Faithful. But Burgevine had demanded such a high fee that Faithful's jaw had dropped. They were still negotiating, although the longer they discussed the matter, the less interested Faithful became, and Burgevine was getting increasingly restless. Nanking was terribly dull; there was not even a public bar where he could have a drink or two.

Brown introduced Burgevine to Lindley and the two met as though they were long-lost friends, chatting and laughing into the wee hours every night. Lindley asked Brown to arrange an audience with the Heavenly Emperor, believing that with his charm and salesmanship he could make a sale big enough for him to retire and enjoy small bound lily feet for the rest of his life in China.

Brown did not want to act as an arms dealer's agent and was glad when Hung refused to see Lindley ... the name had been mentioned several times by Run-kan in a negative tone.

"Too bad Run-kan is not here," Brown said to Lindley sympathetically. "I am sure he could say a few words for you and a deal could be made." Suddenly he realized that Lindley might want to wait forever for Run-kan's return. He added hastily, "The Taiping Kingdom needs an ambassador to promote the country's cause among the foreigners. Run-kan has moved to Hong Kong to do that until the war is over."

"So the emperor refuses to see me, eh?" Lindley said, looking incensed. He seemed to take the refusal as an insult. "Well, I'm not exactly anxious to see him, either. But he certainly can't fight a modern war with swords and spears. If he needs modern weapons, I'm the one to talk to. I hope you'll make him realize that, Reverend Brown. And

I have a policy—I treat a middleman as a business partner. Some easy money can be made, Mr. Brown."

"Mighty tempting, Mr. Lindley," Brown said with a laugh. "But I've forsaken fame and fortune to serve God. For the good of the Taipings, I'll talk to the commander in chief, Prince Faithful. But don't hold your breath. Mr. Burgevine here can tell you that nothing is easy in Nanking."

"Say, Lindley," Burgevine said, already half drunk, "you and I are from Christian countries. God sent us here to save another Christian country. We're here risking our lives, eating grub unfit for dogs, fighting bedbugs, and drinking God knows what. If the host country don't appreciate what we're doing, we'll just do the next-best thing . . ." He stopped to belch.

"Patience, gentlemen," Brown said with a smile. "I'm sure the Heavenly Kingdom will appreciate what you have to offer. Just be a little more patient. Let the Lord make the final judgment."

He rose quickly from the kitchen table. "I'll see you two gentlemen tomorrow." He withdrew to his room with a sigh of relief. While preparing for bed, he wondered what had gone wrong with the Taipings' cause. Unless something started to rot, it would not attract horseflies like Lindley and Burgevine.

After Brown had gone and the number-one boy had cleared away the dishes, Lindley lighted a cigar and asked, "By the way, what's the 'next-best thing' you mentioned a moment ago?"

Burgevine poured himself another drink. Then glancing around, he lowered his voice and confided, "Let's pay China Gordon a visit and make a proposal tomorrow. I have it all planned. If it works, we'll have all the tea in China."

52

Back in Shanghai, Gordon was still brooding, waiting for Li Hung-chang's acceptance of his resignation. The Ever-Victorious Army was deteriorating; the officers were grumbling about the late pay, the men idled, and some Shanghai rascals returned to their old nest without discharges. But discipline in the barracks did not cause much concern; problems so far were limited to loud quarrels, which usually ended with spitting and cursing each other's ancestors. The foreign officers had a few fist fights, but they claimed they were only boxing exercises with a winner-take-all purse. Gordon did not interfere, knowing that the Europeans would bet on anything; even a dog fight on the street would involve some money changing hands.

The war raged on. The Taipings seemed to be getting stronger. Four-Eyed Dog assembled the remnants of the defeated troops in Che-kiang Province and gradually moved into several counties in Kiangsu. With sufficient reinforcement from Anhui, he might be able to take Shanghai.

Gordon slept little and still ate stale bread soaked in coffee. He avoided involvement but kept his ears and eyes open. He played a lot of chess with Lieutenant Mah in his headquarters in the British concession, pretending that he was not concerned.

Lieutenant Mah knew better. The foreigner was only carrying a grudge against General Ching and Li Hung-chang because of the Suchow massacre. Li had been wringing his hands about how to deal with this "temperamental brat," as he called Gordon behind his back. He consulted with Mah frequently, and was anxious to know about his health and mood, somewhat like a father who had a good mind to spank his child but was too fond of him to do so.

Depressed and disillusioned, Gordon remained inactive, his patience wearing thin. The European rowdies quarreled and fought more often and the soldiers started looting. Gordon sent an ultimatum to General Ching. He told him that he was leaving for England by the next ship, whether his resignation was accepted or not.

The next day a Mandarin appeared at his headquarters bearing an Imperial gift of ten thousand taels of silver and a letter of appreciation from the emperor in Peking. Gordon thanked His Majesty but rejected the gift, an unheard-of act. A personal gift from the emperor was a lifetime honor worth ten thousand kowtows. Gordon's European officers wondered if he were indeed crazy. Some of them tried to approach him, suggesting games and cards, but Gordon would not have anything to do with the rowdies. He preferred to spend his time alone in his room brooding or writing to his sister Augusta.

Two days before the next British ship's departure, another emissary from Li Hung-chang arrived in the person of Mr. Hart, customs inspector, who said that the Suchow massacre of the Taiping leaders was Li's fault and Li wanted to apologize. Would General Gordon honor His Majesty by resuming command of the Ever-Victorious Army for another term?

"Listen, my good man," Hart said, puffing on his pipe in Gordon's favorite rattan chair, "this is unheard of in China, an emperor begging a foreign subordinate to keep his job."

"I wash my hands of China," Gordon said morosely. "Let Li Hung-chang hire somebody else to do his dirty work."

Hart stared at him, his graying sideburns moving up and down as he puffed on his pipe noisily. Finally, with a heavy sigh he said, pointing his pipe stem at him, "General, your brother-in-law and I are good friends, and I'm old enough to be your father. This visit is half official and half personal. This job has nothing to do with China. You're doing it for England. We are supposed to be neutral in this civil war, but how can you win without taking sides?"

"Taking sides?" Gordon said.

Hart heaved another sigh. "Listen, we've signed two excellent treaties with the Imperial government, we've gained the status of 'most favored nation' in China, enjoying free trade, extraterritorial rights . . . I even collect customs duties for them. We take sides to protect our own interests . . ."

"I know, I know," Gordon said. The unequal treaties signed between

England and China had always bothered him; they were still rubbing his conscience the wrong way. But he was not about to reveal his true feelings to Hart, who obviously enjoyed his job as China's tax collector. He said, "Let me just say that I'm tired. I wish to go home and take a long vacation."

"At your age?" Hart asked, his bushy eyebrows raised in surprise. "Why would you waste your youth in a blasted country town doing nothing, while here you can change the fate of China and achieve glory for old England? Listen, if you agree to resume your duties, I'll even ask Li Hung-chang to get you a real title. You'll be the first Britisher to own a Chinese title, the equivalent of baron or earl ... something that will stand out on your family tree forever."

Gordon had always hated such empty honors. But discussing his feelings with Hart would have been like suggesting that pipe smoking was detrimental to health. Besides, he was afraid that Hart would toss the word *patriotism* at him. Helpless, he felt he had no choice but to throw up his hands and accept his advice. Hart grabbed his shoulders and kissed both his cheeks.

Li Hung-chang's apology and the emperor's plea for Gordon to resume his command boosted Gordon's prestige so much that the Ever-Victorious Army seemed to be energized at once. The officers shared the honor and boasted about it. One word from Gordon was sufficient to keep his rabble force in line again. In a week, his war against the Taipings started anew in earnest.

Displaying his usual coolness, he continued to direct the war with his magic "victory wand" in one hand and a Bible in the other, reciting the Gospel of St. Luke: "Be not afraid, only believe."

Again no bullets touched him, but finally malaria felled him. He was laid up on the Tyson with a high fever. The concerned Li Hung-chang dispatched his personal physician to treat him. The old herb doctor used an ancient cure; he plastered a dozen fat leeches on Gordon's forehead. Gordon meekly let them suck his blood. He feared nothing, but the little black slimy animals unnerved him. He felt that the sickness was easier to bear than the medicine. But in three days, he thanked God that the leeches had done their job. His fever was gone and he had bounced back to health.

Lieutenant Mah collected the leeches and put them in a glass jar.

"They seem to have doubled in size by dining on your blood, sir," he said. "Would you care to keep them as a souvenir?"

Without a word, Gordon grabbed the jar and tossed it overboard.

The next day, Gordon had two visitors, Mr. Lindley and his new sidekick, Colonel Burgevine. Gordon received them in the Tyson's small dining room, which had the most chairs. Gordon liked to sit at the end of the long table when he had foreign visitors so that he did not have to smell their whiskey breath. He knew Burgevine, a walking distillery.

Burgevine was well dressed for a change. His colonel's uniform was buttoned, his hair combed, and his whiskers trimmed. He saluted Gordon smartly and introduced Mr. Lindley of Liverpool, a respected international industrialist.

Gordon shook Lindley's limp hand and invited them to sit down. He was always cordial to first-time visitors, but he had no time for small talk and wanted to get down to business as quickly as possible. Since he knew what Lindley's business was, he waited for him to make an offer. If the offer was acceptable, he would simply shake hands on it and tell Lieutenant Mah to close the deal. Li Hung-chang would pay the bill.

Burgevine knew Gordon's temperament; he got down to business almost immediately. "Sir," he said, his voice loud and cheerful, "Mr. Lindley and I have come to propose a grand plan to conquer China."

Gordon was taken aback, looking stunned for a moment. He wondered if he had heard Burgevine right. "Will you say that again?" he asked with a deep frown.

"It's like this, sir," Burgevine went on. "The Manchus and the Taipings have been fighting like dogs and cats for God knows how long. Mr. Lindley here has dealt with the Manchus for years. Their army is so inept that even the London Fire Brigade could sweep them into the sea with fire hoses. The Taiping emperor is even worse off. Recently he begged me to organize an Ever-Victorious Army to do battle for him. I laughed it off. Mr. Lindley, you tell the general what the grand plan is."

Lindley cleared his voice. Chuckling pleasantly, he said, "I'm an old China hand. I know a Chinese fable: "A clam suns itself on the beach. A crane comes along and pecks the clam's flesh. The clam shuts its shell on the crane's beak and refuses to let go. Now a fisherman comes along.

He sees them and picks them both up. He takes them home and cooks himself a roasted crane dinner with a clam soup to go with it.

"What Colonel Burgevine and I see here is that you can easily be that fisherman."

Burgevine chimed in excitedly, "With your well-trained men and able officers, sir, you can seize the throne and become the Emperor of China!"

"If that happens, General," Lindley went on, "I don't mind being your prime minister. And the colonel here will make an excellent defense minister."

As Gordon listened, his face turned from red to purple. His breath short and eyes burning, he exploded. "Get out!! Get out of my sight, you bloody fools!"

Burgevine got up quickly and disappeared.

"Look here, General . . ." Lindley said, still trying to argue. Before he could finish, Gordon pulled him up from his chair, turned him around and booted him off the boat with a vicious kick on his behind.

More insulted than hurt, Lindley picked himself up from the gangplank. He turned to spit, but Gordon was no longer there. What he saw was Lieutenant Mah, grinning and cocking a musket at his face.

53

Hung was lonely for Su San-mei but since the last sexual encounter he felt sorry and ashamed. Her look of disappointment still made him feel chagrined. He did not know why; perhaps it was because of the fear of another failure that prevented him from sending for her again.

But with her, he could never separate sex from friendship. He still wanted her whole, sexually and spiritually. How he wished he were potent and robust, able to visit her freely, dine with her, chat with her and perform "cloud and rain" with her, reaching the top of *Wu Shan* together with total abandon. After that she would nestle against him, her cheeks pink and her heart thumping with excitement. He had read about such afterglow and gratification but had never experienced them, and it seemed that he would never be able to experience them now.

He had often avoided thinking of "cloud and rain," but it was so difficult whenever he thought of Su San-mei. It was almost impossible to shut her out of his mind entirely. Lately he often found himself talking about her, especially with The Faithful, who also seemed to like her a great deal. When they discussed the war, the subject invariably drifted to Su San-mei, then The Faithful, looking uncomfortable, changed the subject again and started talking about the war.

In Nanking, Gordon's fame grew. Hung was anxious to know more about this foreigner who conducted war with a magic wand. Since Run-kan had returned to Hong Kong to promote the Taipings' cause and gain sympathy from foreign powers, Hung consulted almost daily with David Brown about foreigners, their background, and their policies. He especially wanted to find out who this China Gordon was.

Brown knew little about him but offered Hung his opinion. "This China Gordon is only a ploy to draw more Western aid—meaning more Western weapons. To win this war you must buy more Western firearms to outgun the Manchus."

It was early morning. Hung had taken several spoonfuls of an herb medicine that was supposed to calm his nerves. There was a worried look on his gaunt face. He cracked his knuckles and sighed.

"Run-kan is in Hong Kong negotiating an arms deal, but it will take months for a shipment to reach Nanking. Besides, the foreign powers favor the Manchu government because of the favorable treaties they have signed. I don't blame them. A man always goes to the easy woman. I thought they would help fellow Christians, but I was wrong. All they can offer us is sympathy. Aid still goes to the easy woman who has a lot of flesh to offer. What about that gunner called Mr. Lindley? Is he still in Nanking?"

"He just returned," Brown said. "He took a trip with that rough-neck, Burgevine, and returned without him."

"Burgevine, hm," Hung said, cracking his knuckles again. "The name sounds familiar."

"He is that American who wants to be another China Gordon."

"Ah, I remember. He wants half a million taels of silver to organize an Ever-Victorious Army for me, plus a prince's title. I said no, though I don't mind granting him a title—Prince Greedy. But this Mr. Lindley, why did he come back?"

"This is what I want to talk to you about, Heavenly Emperor," Brown said with some difficulty. "I'm reluctant to recommend his services, but he wants me to tell you that he'll be happy to sell arms to you at half his usual price. He has also offered to train your gunners personally, for free."

"Hm," Hung grunted, pulling at his beard thoughtfully. "If he is a sympathizer, I'm afraid I have mistreated him."

"He is a man who is like a dogweed on top of a wall, to quote a Chinese old saying," Brown said with a short laugh. "He swings with the wind. He either believes that you will seize Peking, or he holds a grudge against China Gordon."

Hung raised his eyebrows inquisitively. "A grudge against China Gordon? Why do you say that?"

"He swears that he is going to aim his thirty-eight-pounder at

Gordon personally and pulverize him. And he said that when he wasn't drunk."

"Ah, interesting," Hung said with a faint smile. "Very interesting. Perhaps I should see him. At least it will be a pleasure to hear him talk like that."

The Heavenly Emperor bought a hundred tons of arms and ammunition from Mr. Lindley, who promised to smuggle the shipment to Nanking within one month. With the profit, he could have retired in Shanghai to enjoy women's bound lily feet for the rest of his life, but he volunteered to remain in Nanking to train Taiping gunners.

It was good news to Su San-mei. She had been trying to find an excuse to move out of Hung's palace. With her experience in Western weaponry, she offered to work for the armory, which was being expanded to accommodate the enormous new shipment. Prince Faithful knew that she was unhappy as a lady-in-waiting in Hung's palace. He pleaded with Hung to release her. Hung reluctantly let her go, but demanded that she be returned as soon as the war was over. Faithful agreed and appointed her as the head of the Taiping armory, a job for which nobody seemed qualified, as most of the Taiping leaders knew little about modern weapons. Many wars had been fought with swords, spears, bows and arrows. It was with the big guns that the British and the French had almost conquered China, even though they had been overwhelmingly outnumbered. Faithful was the first to acknowledge the Taipings' weakness, and insisted that the armory must be replenished with modern arms.

Training was equally important to him. He employed Mr. Lindley as a special consultant responsible for training gunners. Every time Lindley saw the prince, he offered to pulverize China Gordon personally with a thirty-eight-pounder.

The war went on with increased shelling. The news was not good. The Taipings had prayed that China Gordon would eventually lose his magic and die of the "trembling disease," but their prayers were not answered. In a week he was sighted again directing battles in the front line with his magic wand. After the fall of Suchow, Hangchow was threatened. Four-Eyed Dog desperately tried to defend Yulang on the outskirts of Hangchow, but Gordon stormed the small town and General Ching's troops quickly followed. They easily captured Hangchow, the Taipings' last stronghold in Chekiang Province.

The loss of all the cities and towns in Kiangsu and Chekiang left no room for maneuvering around the perimeter of the Heavenly Capital. Four-Eyed Dog had retreated to Anhui and joined forces with Shih Ta-kai, the Shield Prince. Hung held daily meetings with his princes and generals in Nanking, discussing Nanking's defense. The capital was practically encircled by enemies—the Hunan braves on the south, General Ching's troops on the west, the Ever-Victorious Army on the north. Only the east side was left open, the capital's lifeline.

The Heavenly Emperor sent repeated dispatches to Four-Eyed Dog and the Shield Prince to break the encirclement and lift the capital's siege; but rescue forces never arrived, except for some food and ammunition that was smuggled in through secret tunnels on the east side.

Faithful made several attempts to repulse General Ching's army on the west, but his troops were so outnumbered that it was almost like assaulting a human wall.

Su San-mei, having fought alongside Prince Faithful in many battles, believed that he was incapable of betraying Hung. Every word and deed from him had been proof of his character. He seemed to be attracted to her, but he never exhibited any affection other than words of encouragement and praise. Even though he sheltered her in his palace after she had moved out of Hung's palace, he had never entered her room. All their contact was official. How she missed the small talk, the laughter, the lively conversation that had nothing to do with war. Nanking seemed doomed, and she had a premonition that she would suffer the same fate. She knew that Faithful, too, would die with the city. She would die alongside someone she respected . . . perhaps loved.

She only wished there were some indication of love from Faithful; it would ignite hers. She knew her own passion, a wild horse that had been harnessed and tied. It wanted so much to be freed and to gallop to *Wu Shan*, the mysterious mountains of ultimate love. Then she would die happy. She did not want any next life. All she wanted now was the final moment of happiness only known to lovers . . . that complete gratification of "cloud and rain" she knew she could achieve; but the right man must ignite it and wholeheartedly share it.

She did not like to work with this foreigner, Mr. Lindley. But since
he had supplied the ammunition and was training the gunners, their
daily contact was a necessity. Always tipsy, he tried to flirt with her.
Luckily the armory was always full of busy people.

Somehow Mr. Lindley was giving some comfort to Nanking's defenders. Whenever people mentioned China Gordon's invulnerability
and his magic wand, Mr. Lindley said, "Fiddlesticks! When the time
comes, I'll man the big gun myself. I'll blast him to pieces! Just wait
and see."

Because of his exhibition of confidence, the Taipings treated him
well, saluting him, giving him the thumbs-up sign and saying, "*Ding hao,
ding hao!*"

The armory was a large brick building with many tunnels. Most of
the ammunition was stored underground, especially the gunpowder.
Nobody could take anything out without Su San-mei's personal seal.
Every time Lindley needed ammunition for training purposes, he would
come to the armory personally to obtain Su San-mei's seal. He even
suggested going underground with her to inspect the gunpowder. She
always declined. One afternoon, after he had obtained her seal and while
nobody was looking, he pinched her breast. She floored him with a flying
kick. When he picked himself up from the floor, he looked as though
he would shoot her. She dared him with such a glare that he backed
out of her office quietly. Not a word was exchanged.

That evening Su San-mei reported the incident to Faithful at the
dinner table. She expected Faithful to show anger. But to her disappointment he only sighed. "Maggots grow when meat rots," he said,
quoting an old saying. "This foreigner's promise is his 'magic wand.' He
will flourish as long as Nanking is in danger. Even the Heavenly Emperor
begins to depend on him for a miracle."

Su San-mei kept quiet. She chewed the old saying for a moment,
"Maggots grow when meat rots." Had Faithful lost faith in the Heavenly
Kingdom? The thought pained her. If a man as solid as Faithful had
openly expressed such pessimism about the kingdom's fate, the inevitable
must be near. Hiding a tear, she left the dining table.

| 54 |

Edging closer to Nanking in his flagship, Gordon made detailed plans for seizing the city. He had already suggested to Li Hung-chang that Shanghai would be safe if the waterways were cut. Then he could concentrate on Nanking's capture. He still firmly believed that the only way to shorten the war was to ignore the limbs and aim at the head. He had already reconnoitered the Taipings' strongholds in Nanking's vicinity. His goal was to encircle the capital with the Hunan braves on the south and the Imperial Army on the north. The Ever-Victorious Army, keeping a low profile, would mine the city's west gate with explosives. He would enter the city first and throw all the other gates open to let the invading armies in, but allow the civilians to escape through the east gate. He wanted to occupy Nanking with as little bloodshed as possible.

"Absolutely no massacre," he warned General Ching, who pulled his whiskers and nodded. Gordon did not trust him. He decided that next time there would be no resignation. Instead, he would simply put a bullet through General Ching's head and let fate take its course.

Meanwhile, Lieutenant Mah, through his government grapevine, reported that he had a piece of cheerful news. Li Hung-chang had approached the emperor in Peking, requesting His Majesty to bestow upon General Gordon the right to wear the Imperial Yellow Riding Jacket and the double-eyed peacock feather.

But Gordon could not be cheered up. He was preoccupied with the invasion of Nanking and it was not a cheerful matter.

"You want to control General Ching?" Mah suggested. "Get that double-eyed peacock feather. General Ching will be so impressed that he will lick your boots and do your bidding like an obedient little puppy. He will even shoot himself if you so order."

"First I'll order him to wipe that perpetual grin off his face, then stick a pin in his neck so that he can't nod his head anymore. By the

330

way, what can that bloody double-eyed peacock feather do besides tame General Ching?"

"It's a symbol of high rank . . . high enough to be worth a hundred kowtows. You can sell it to a rich American for a lot of money. Too bad you hurt Mr. Lindley's pride by giving him such a kick on his behind. He might have bought it and paid you enough to retire to London. And you could hire me as your number-one boy."

Gordon had no time for small talk, but he thought the peacock idea was rather funny. He didn't mind taking it home as his only souvenir of his adventures in China. For a long time he had not laughed. Now his own laughter cheered him up. Yes, he would accept the royal gift this time. He would ride around London in his Imperial Yellow Riding Jacket, sporting that bloody double-eyed peacock feather in his felt hat.

About a mile away from Nanking, Gordon landed with his troops and set up camp just out of range of the Taipings' cannonballs. The west gate was reinforced with sandbags, and the massive gray walls, fifty feet high and reputedly ten feet thick, were full of bullet marks. The Imperial Army had made several assaults on the west side in the past —made a lot of noise and wasted a great deal of ammunition. As soon as they withdrew, the Taipings had suddenly appeared from nowhere and swept up all the shells, which they reloaded and used in their own arsenal.

Gordon preferred to take the city at night. Working closely with General Ching, he obtained a thorough knowledge of Nanking's defenses and the Taiping troops' movements elsewhere, especially those of Four-Eyed Dog, who might sneak back from Anhui and try to break the encirclement. After he had positioned his men at various strategic points, he reiterated his insistence that there be no massacre or looting after the fall of Nanking. Then he and a handful of his personal guards— some of them ex-Taipings—set out to mine the western gate with explosives. Meanwhile, in coordination with the mining, the Imperial Army and the Hunan braves poised for assault on the south and north gates. Both General Tzen and General Ching had agreed to order their troops to make noise by shouting, firing muskets, and waving flags, to lure the defenders away from the west gate.

It was a dark summer night, with thick dark clouds floating overhead.

Occasionally a crack opened to show a few distant stars gleaming faintly in the stormy sky. Gordon had prayed for a night of thunder and rain to cover his activities, but the storm never came, except for an occasional lightning bolt that brightened up the city momentarily. Working in the darkness, Gordon, still waving his cane, directed the mining with all his engineering knowledge and expertise. But language difficulty slowed him down. Lieutenant Mah was a good interpreter, but technical terms made him wince in frustration. With the help of sign language, the two dozen trusted men worked slowly but steadily, making as little noise as possible. Luckily, all the Chinese were good diggers. They dug all the holes exactly according to plan. The night flew by quickly. Soon roosters in the city began to herald the dawn. Gordon and his men, fighting drowsiness and fatigue, frantically planted the mines as the rising sun flamed in the eastern sky.

The noise made by the Manchu army rose and fell; sometimes there were lulls and silence. "Opium time," Gordon grumbled sarcastically as he wiped sweat off his brow. The Hunan braves had kept their bargain; Gordon could still hear their faint battle cries amid occasional cannon fire, which became less frequent as the day wore on. He knew very little about the Hunan braves, but he had heard about this rich Hunan Province, China's rice bowl in the South, famous for hot peppers, soldiering, and passionate women. Gordon was sure that the Hunan braves were not as inept as the Manchu troops. The infrequent firing of their guns was probably due to frugality. When the mining of the wall had still not been completed long after daybreak, he decided to leave their fate in God's hands. He mumbled his favorite prayer, "Be not afraid, only believe."

55

Prince Faithful knew that the siege had reached a life-and-death crisis. The food situation had worsened and the entire city was starving. Only the Heavenly Emperor's palace had enough food to last another two weeks. But he had heard that Hung had stopped eating his meals, pretending that he was not hungry. Every time he saw him, he looked more gaunt and pale. He had begun to walk like an old man, dragging his feet as if he had lost all his spirit, even though he was only forty-nine years old.

When Faithful inquired about his health, Hung always seemed angry to hear such a frivolous question. "Health!" he retorted. "What's so important about my health? The nation's health is in your hands. Think only of the kingdom's health!"

Faithful believed that the Heavenly Emperor's health was the kingdom's health. He went to see the empress. She looked pale and thin, her face covered with new lines and her hair turning prematurely gray. But she was still able to smile, and her voice was still sweet and calm.

"Every morning he stays in his study," she said, hiding her pain. "He reads the Bible and prays. In the afternoon he goes to the garden to harvest lentils to eat."

"Why?" Faithful asked, shocked.

"He says lentils have medicinal value. Good for stomach ailments. He is only trying to save food for us ..." She stopped and began to choke.

The next day Hung issued an edict ordering Nanking's population to eat lentils and weeds that were growing wild all over the city. Faithful and Su San-mei both tried, but they became violently ill. Faithful threw up what he had eaten. He went to see Hung immediately.

Hung was sick in his bed, but he struggled up and walked to his chair. He would never think of conducting an audience lying down.

Faithful implored him to flee the city while there was still time. He told Hung that Nanking was encircled tightly and China Gordon was ready to mount an assault on the west gate, but the secret route to the outside was still open on the eastern side of the city.

Hung seemed angry again at such a plea. "No," he said firmly. "I will live or die with Nanking. So will all the people, including the army. Anyone who tries to escape will be charged with treason. But it will be up to you to decide what to do about such a crime."

Faithful knew it was futile to argue with him. He also knew that Hung had left a wide-open door for anyone to escape, for he had given Faithful the authority to deal with the so-called treason.

He asked all the concubines and ladies-in-waiting to keep a vigil and report to him immediately any change in Hung's health and mind.

Mr. Lindley became extremely busy during the turmoil. The moment he learned that China Gordon had been sighted outside the west gate, he immediately aimed his biggest gun at the west, and kept looking for Gordon through a pair of field glasses, interrupting his vigilance only with an occasional swig from his bottle. Su San-mei volunteered her services as his gunner. Mr. Lindley was surprised but happily gave her the assignment. He never held grudges against attractive women, believing that problems caused by them were only ploys to play hard to get. Su San-mei was an efficient gunner. She loaded the thirty-two-pounder and told Lindley it was ready to fire.

Lindley finally spotted China Gordon. He personally aimed the cannon at Gordon and fired. But the gun did not go off. With a curse he ordered it loaded again. Su San-mei obeyed readily, filling it with gunpowder and a cannonball. Again it did not fire. The maddened Lindley jumped up and down in fury, cursing and yelling orders. But he did not lose sight of Gordon. Before the cannon was loaded and fired a third time, there were several earth-shaking explosions and the west city gate blew up, shooting bricks and debris sky high. Clouds of dust and smoke rose to cover the entire area, blocking out sight of the Taipings who were ready to fight.

Thousands of Gordon's men poured in, with Gordon leading the invasion on horseback, waving his cane. Lieutenant Mah rode closely behind. The streets were quiet and deserted; most of the doors were closed. Many wild dogs, all skin and bones, were searching for food, some snarling at each other over a corpse or a bit of inedible trash. A few barked, too weak to chase the passing horses. Gunfire was still heard in the distance.

"Mah," Gordon called, "take us to the emperor's palace. I want to get there before the Imperial troops or the Hunan braves."

"Righto," shouted one of the British officers who was riding beside Gordon. "Let's be the first ones to seize the palace!"

"Not to seize the palace, you bastard!" Gordon retorted angrily. "I want to prevent another massacre!"

"Say, let's save the Heavenly Emperor's life," another European officer shouted. "There might be money on his head."

Gordon ignored his European officers. They were still a bunch of riffraff in uniform, desperadoes beyond redemption. As long as they did not loot, he would tolerate them, especially now. This was probably the end of their tour. Any one of them could put a bullet in him behind his back.

Entering the palace, he was surprised to see hundreds of men and women kneeling in the audience hall, wailing and tearing their hair. All were formally dressed in court costumes of the kimonolike Ming style. Gordon looked at Lieutenant Mah, who had just finished talking to a weeping court attendant. Most of the men were wiping their eyes; some even howled unashamedly.

"They are mourning the death of the Heavenly Emperor," Mah said. "He has committed suicide by swallowing pieces of gold."

Gordon stared at the tear-washed faces of the wailing women, utterly stunned. Some of them were even bashing their heads on the ground in agony. It was obvious that all his people, from serving maids and guards to the concubines and the empress, were devoted to him. Gordon had never known a man who was loved so much by so many. He was astounded. He would never have believed it had he not witnessed the mournful scene.

Gordon wanted to see the emperor's body. The attendant took them to Hung's bedroom. Candles were lit. The room was heavy with incense smoke. Hung's emaciated body, lying on his enormous bed in his dragon gown, looked pathetic. His face was paper white, his teeth protruding from his dry, colorless thin lips, his large nose a bare bone, and his cheeks two large hollows. Gordon knew that he had starved himself for days and that the swallowing of gold had only hastened his death.

When he left the palace, he ordered a detachment of his troops to stand guard, with strict orders to protect the palace, Hung's body, and all his women.

Back on the street, fire and smoke had begun to rise everywhere. People were crying and running. Gordon had thrown the eastern gate open. With Lieutenant Mah's help, he personally guided many refugees to the eastern gate. Thousands refused to flee; some set fire to their homes and died in them.

"They are obeying the Heavenly Emperor's orders," Lieutenant Mah explained. "Everybody must live or die with the city."

Prince Faithful returned to his palace late, his face bloodied and his clothes torn. He discharged all his personal guards and his servants, and told them to flee Nanking while there was still time. He found Su San-mei in his mother's room, trying to comfort the distraught old lady, who insisted that she must die with the city. The prince had tried to persuade Su San-mei and his mother to escape but his mother had refused unless he accompanied her.

Faithful had vowed to burn his own house and die in it. Now that he saw his mother weeping in Su San-mei's arms, he wavered.

"The emperor is dead," Su San-mei said, looking at him pleadingly. "Someone must live to carry out his will. If you decide not to carry on, I shall die with you."

Faithful looked between Su San-mei and his old mother, who said nothing, but her eyes seemed to be pleading—begging him to change his mind. Faithful paced restlessly, rubbing his face with a hand. Suddenly he stopped. He told his mother and Su San-mei to change into peasant clothes.

The maidservants had all escaped. Su San-mei went to their quarters and picked out some clothes that the servants had left behind. Faithful also changed into civilian clothes. He packed some food and all the money he had saved through the years, making it into a bundle to carry on his shoulder like a peasant. The three of them sneaked out of the palace and joined the refugees who were streaming toward the eastern gate.

Faithful was surprised that no Imperial troops were chasing them. Many houses were on fire. The stench of burning flesh was overpowering. He gave his bundle to Su San-mei and picked up his frail mother, who could hardly keep up with the fleeing refugees.

Outside the eastern gate the refugees, carrying as much as they could, moved in several directions. Some of them pulled loaded carts like animals, since mules, donkeys, and horses had long since been eaten. Half-naked children toddled and cried alongside their starving parents, who trudged like ghosts.

When he reached some brush, Faithful went behind it, put his mother down and made her comfortable. He sat down to catch his breath. Su San-mei lay down her bundles and sat down beside him.

Faithful could not forget the Heavenly Emperor. He still agonized over his death. "Without that China Gordon," he said quietly, his voice devoid of anger but full of sorrow, "Hung Shiu-ch'uan would have been sitting on the dragon throne in the Forbidden City by now." He shook his head sadly. "That foreigner must be invulnerable to firearms. Even a cannon would not fire."

Su San-mei was quiet for a moment. She had a secret that she had wanted to tell; now was the right time. "Prince Faithful," she said deliberately, trying to sound calm and hoping not to anger him, "he is just like you and me. If I had not wetted the gunpowder, Mr. Lindley could have pulverized him, like he promised."

Faithful looked shocked. "You wetted the gunpowder! Why?"

"We have been fighting a long war. Millions have perished. Why prolong it?" She cast him a longing glance, lowered her head and added, "Besides, a woman cannot serve two men."

Faithful thought for a moment, then grasped what she meant by "two men." He was touched, and felt his pent emotions ready to burst. His throat tight, he asked, "The Heavenly Emperor hinted many times that you were his true love. Is that right?"

Without answering, she turned away. For the first time he saw her beautiful hard eyes soften, full of tears.

| 56 |

The sporadic volleys of musketry stopped soon after Gordon rode back to the Tyson with Lieutenant Mah. He had left his army in Nanking to keep order, praying that they would be orderly themselves until General Ching could take over. The Hunan braves had lived up to their name, brave and disciplined, agreeing that the massacring of enemies only alienated the people. General Ching seemed to have changed. Gordon had seen him say, "No" without smiling or nodding.

Nanking was burning fiercely. Gordon sat in the Tyson's dining room and watched billows of smoke and long tongues of flame licking the darkened sky. For the first time, there was no massacre following a victory, but the fire was wiping out everything. It was worse than looting and killing. He refused to feel sad. He convinced himself that since God was omnipotent, whatever happened must be for the best.

"A cup of coffee?" Lieutenant Mah asked.

"No," he said.

He dismissed Mah; he wanted to be alone for a while to sort out his thoughts. Nanking was captured. The Ever-Victorious Army had done its work, but it was still a horde of dangerous ruffians and it must be disbanded as soon as possible. As for money, he remained as poor as when he had arrived, although the knowledge that he had shortened the war and perhaps spared thousands of lives comforted him.

The next morning he had a brief meeting with General Ching in his cabin. They readily agreed on the terms of Nanking's security and the Ever-Victorious Army's immediate fate. To his pleasant surprise, General Ching had indeed changed his habits. A smile meant a smile and a nod meant a nod.

Gordon decided to return to Shanghai. His army would meet him in the old Shanghai barracks and wait for orders to disband. Having settled a few disputes among the European officers, he ordered the

Tyson to sail. Shut in his cabin, he started a long overdue letter to his sister Augusta:

> The job is finally done. I am on my way back to good old England. I may reach home before this letter reaches you, but as things stand, nobody can predict that I'll be home for Christmas, or be home at all. If that's the case, at least you will have heard from me.

As he scribbled, he heard a hullabaloo outside. He rose to look through his cabin window and found, to his surprise, that the riverbanks were lined with soldiers cheering and waving flags and lanterns. Firecrackers exploded amid the roar of gongs, drums, and horns.

He called Lieutenant Mah to his cabin. "What is going on out there?" he asked.

"A send-off celebration for General Gordon," Mah said with a smile.

Gordon was touched. Undoubtedly General Ching was responsible; he had hinted that China would show her gratitude by making his triumphant return a memorable event. Gordon had not expected it to be such a carnival.

As the Tyson steamed past the people shouting farewell to him on the banks, he stepped out and waved back. It was indeed a glorious return. While he was called general he was in reality still a lieutenant colonel. He was going to receive an Imperial Yellow Riding Jacket and a double-eyed peacock feather, one of the highest awards ever bestowed by the Emperor of China. He would probably see more carnival-like send-offs in Shanghai. Yet he was leaving China with regret.

Back in his cabin, he resumed his letter to Augusta:

> During the long civil war between the Christians and the Manchus, tens of thousands of Chinese have been killed, and the Western powers have been partially responsible. I wish I really had a magic wand and had shortened the conflict by at least ten years.
>
> After I saw this Taiping emperor on his deathbed, his room and his well-thumbed Bible, I began to think that he was probably a devoted Christian, somewhat misguided. I have known

evangelists who have enriched themselves in the name of God. I have witnessed Western spies stealing and cheating in the name of God. There is no reason to crucify a man who wanted to overthrow a tyranny in the name of God.

Now, as I am sitting here alone in my cabin, returning to Shanghai in triumph, I am still wondering if I have fought on the wrong side, a regret I shall probably bear forever.